Further Praise for Dusk

"I read *Dusk* in a couple of days, unable to put it down. I *like* this guy—he's made himself an utterly convincing world which is wholly his own. There are echoes of folk such as Erikson—that hard-edged, unflinching way with a story—but he's a unique voice. There are so many things to pick out—the Machines, the Red Monks, the Shantasi. His towns and cities—Pavisse, Noreela City—are places where I can imagine a hundred other stories waiting to be told, and I was almost disappointed when they were left behind—but then began the trek across a blasted land which is committing suicide. Lebbon has a way of throwing staggering images at you which you almost have to pause and think about before you can fully grasp. This is fantasy for grown-ups—and the ending made my jaw drop. This is an excellent book, and I would not say that unless I meant it." —Paul Kearney

"*Dusk* is a deliciously dark and daring fantasy novel, proof of a startling imagination at work. Lebbon's writing is a twisted spiral of cunning, compassion, and cruelty." —Christopher Golden

"An exquisitely written, unique world is revealed in this novel, a world inhabited by flesh and blood people rendered with often brutal honesty and clarity of vision. It's rare indeed to witness the conventions of fantasy so thoroughly grabbed by the throat and shaken awake the way Tim Lebbon has done with *Dusk*. Even more enticing, this first novel in the series concludes with a jaw-dropping finale, and for what it's worth, such a reaction from me is not a common occurrence." —Steven Erikson

"A gripping and visceral dark fantasy of five fugitives in flight from terrifying pursuers through a decaying world brutalized by the Cataclysmic War. In *Dusk*, Tim Lebbon has etched a powerful new version/telling of the traditional magical quest, whose tortured twists and turns will (alternately) disturb and electrify its readers." —Sarah Ash

"*Dusk* is dark, twisted and visceral, with a *very* shocking sting in the tail—the perfect jolt for anyone jaded by the creaking shelves of cuddly, rent-an-elf fantasy. [...] voice in the fantasy field. Bring on [...]

"Tim Lebbon writes with a pen dipped in the dark stuff of nightmare. The world he creates is eerie, brutal and complex, and the story abounds with action and menace." —K. J. Bishop

"Totally original. I've never read anything like it . . . New wonders at every turn . . . One might subtitle it 'A Riveting Work of Staggering Imagination.'" —F. Paul Wilson

Further Praise for Tim Lebbon

"Tim Lebbon is a master of fantasy and horror, and his visions make for disturbing and compelling reading." —Douglas Clegg

"Tim Lebbon is an immense talent and he's become a new favourite. He has a style and approach unique to the genre." —Joe R. Lansdale

"A firm and confident style, with elements of early Clive Barker." —Phil Rickman

"Tim Lebbon is an apocalyptic visionary—a prophet of blood and fear." —Mark Chadbourn

"One of the most powerful new voices to come along in the genre . . . Lebbon's work is infused with the contemporary realism of Stephen King and the lyricism of Ray Bradbury." —*Fangoria*

"Beautifully written and mysterious . . . a real winner!" —Richard Laymon

"Lebbon will reward the careful reader with insights as well as gooseflesh." —*Publishers Weekly*

"Lebbon is among the most inventive and original contemporary writers of the dark fantastic." —Ramsey Campbell

"Lebbon is quite simply the most exciting new name in horror for years." —*SFX*

"Tim Lebbon is one of the most exciting and original talents on the horror scene." —Graham Joyce

ALSO BY TIM LEBBON

NOVELS

Mesmer
The Nature of Balance
Hush (with Gavin Williams)
Face
Until She Sleeps
Desolation
Berserk

NOVELLAS

White
Naming of Parts
Changing of Faces
Exorcising Angels (with Simon Clark)
Dead Man's Hand
Pieces of Hate

COLLECTIONS

Faith in the Flesh
As the Sun Goes Down
White and Other Tales of Ruin
Fears Unnamed

DUSK
TIM LEBBON

BANTAM • SPECTRA

DUSK

A Bantam Spectra Book / February 2006

Published by
Bantam Dell
A Division of Random House, Inc.
New York, New York

Book design by Glen Edelstein

Bantam Books, the rooster colophon, Spectra, and the portrayal of a boxed "s"
are trademarks of Random House, Inc.

Library of Congress Cataloging-in-Publication Data is on file with the publisher.

Printed in the United States of America
Published simultaneously in Canada

www.bantamdell.com

BVG 10 9 8 7 6 5 4

For Tracey, Ellie and Dan, with love

Acknowledgments

Thanks to Jason and Jeremy at Night Shade Books for giving me the chance, Katherine Roberts for her support whilst writing this novel, Chris Golden for a sympathetic ear, Rich SanFilippo for first contact, my long-suffering agent Steve Calcutt

and

a huge thanks to my wonderful editor, Anne Groell, for her sharp eye and unending wit, and her refreshing interest in Welsh place names. I can't help living in Goytre.

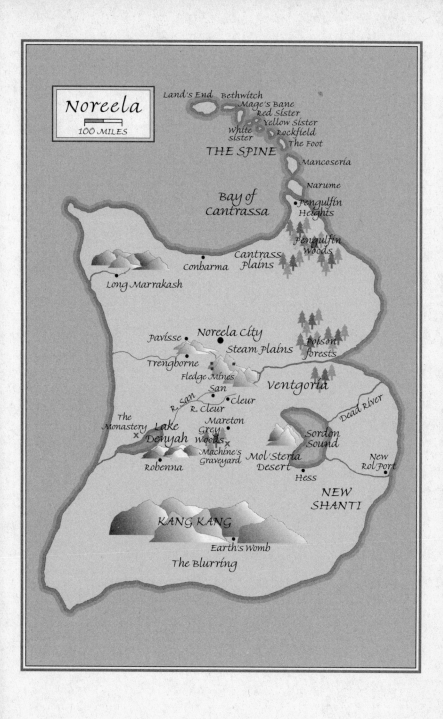

PART ONE
First Signs of Night

Chapter 1

WHEN KOSAR SAW the horseman, the world began to end again.

The horse walked toward the village, the rider shifting in fluid time to his mount's steps. The man's body was wrapped in a deep red cloak, pulled up so that it formed a hood over his head, shadowing his face. His hands rested on his thighs. The horse made its own way along the road. Loose reins hung to either side of its head, its mane was clotted with dirt, and its unshod hooves clacked and clicked puffs of dust from the dry trail. Only one man on a horse, and he did not appear to be armed.

How, then, could Kosar know that death followed him in?

With a grimace he stopped work and squatted. A warm breeze kissed the raw flesh of his fingertips—the marks of a thief—and took away the pain for a few precious moments. Blood had dripped and dried into a dust-caked mess across his hands and between his fingers, and they crackled when he flexed them. The unhealing wounds were a permanent reminder of the mistakes of his past.

Kosar decided that the irrigation trenches could wait a few minutes more. It had taken two years for the village to decide to commission

them; another moment would make no difference to the crops wither-
ing and dying in the fields. Besides, they needed much more than water, though most would refuse to believe that was so. And now there was
something more interesting to grab his attention, something that might
bring excitement to this measly little collection of huts, hovels and run-
down dwellings that dared call itself a village.

He stared along the road at the figure in the distance. Yes, only
one man, but a threatening pall hung about him, like shadowy
echoes of evil deeds. Kosar looked the other way, past the old stone
bridge and into the village itself. There were children playing by the
stream, diving and resurfacing in triumph if they caught a fish between their teeth. Elsewhere, drinkers sat silently stoned outside the
tavern, mugs of rotwine festering half-finished in the sun, the other
half coursing through veins and inducing a few cherished hours of
catatonia. It was a false escape that he, Kosar the thief, would never
be permitted again. At least not where any form of law still applied.

The market was small today, but a few traders plied their wares
and squeezed tellan coins and barter from the village folk. Skinned
furbats hung from hooks along one stall, their livers intact and ripe
with rhellim, the drug of sexual abandonment. He had already seen
three people skulking away, a furbat beneath their shirt and their
eyes downcast. Their children may not eat tonight, but at least
the parents would be assured of a good screw. Another trader sold
charms supposedly from Kang Kang, banking on the fear and awe in
which that place was held to make the buyers see past the trinkets'
obvious falseness. There were food sellers too, offering fruits from
the Cantrass Plains. But the journey from that place was long, the
route difficult and most of the fruits had lost their lively hue.

Kosar turned once again to the stranger. He was much closer
now, and the sound of his progress had become audible in the heavy
air. The figure raised his head almost imperceptibly. The cloak
shifted to allow a sliver of the falling sun inside, and Kosar squinted
as he tried to make out what it revealed. His eyesight was not as good
as it had once been, scorched by decades in the sun and weakened
by lack of nourishment, but it had never misled him.

The stranger's face was as red as his cloak.

Kosar stood and shielded his eyes. His first impulse was to grab
the pick he'd been using, so he could swing it up in a killing arc if
necessary. His second urge was to turn and run, and this surprised
him. He'd always been a thief but never a coward. It was why he was

still alive now, and it was the reason he could live among people, even with the terrible unhealing brands on his fingers.

He also listened to his hunches. Instinct was for survival, and Kosar followed his as much as possible.

But not this time. Instead, he crept back along the trench toward the bridge. Every step felt heavy, each movement against good sense. Something inside shouted at him to turn and run, abandon the village to whatever fate this red man brought with him. The place had never *really* done anything for Kosar. Acceptance it had given grudgingly, but never affection, never any true sense of belonging. They'd put up with him because he worked for them, nothing more. He'd spent the last mid-summer festival skulking past the stone bridge while the town cabal handed out ale and food. The revelry had jibed at him as he watched the setting sun alone, even though the jibing was mostly his own.

Turn and run.

But he could not.

Turn and run, Kosar, you bloody fool!

Even though instinct urged him to flee, and good sense told him that death's shadow was already closing over the village, there were children here, playing in the stream. There were a few women in the village that he liked, or would like to like, given the chance. And more than anything, Kosar was a good man. A thief, a criminal, branded forever as untrustworthy and devious, but a good man.

The horseman was no more than two minutes away from the village. Kosar had almost reached the end of the trench where it joined the stream, the bridge a hundred steps away. The children had finished their fishing and playing and climbed the bank, and now they sat on the bridge parapet, swinging their legs over the edge, laughing and joking and watching the stranger approach. Such trust, in a world where hunger and fear made trust so precious.

He was about to call out to the children, when the horse broke into a gallop.

He could have warned them. He should have shouted at them to turn and run, go to their homes, tell their parents to lock their doors. Kosar had seen enough trouble in his life to recognize its flowering, and he had known from the instant he'd laid eyes on the horseman that he was not here for a drink, a meal, a bed for the night. He could have warned them, but shouting would have drawn attention to himself. And in this case, instinct won out.

The man in red dismounted on the bridge and approached the children. His horse remained where it had stopped, head bowed as if smelling the water through thick stone. The children stood, jumped around, giggled. Kosar glanced across into the village and saw several people looking his way, a couple of them striding quickly toward the bridge, one woman darting into the brothel where the three village militia spent most of their time.

For a moment all was still. Kosar paused, unmoving. The breeze died down as if the land itself was holding its breath. Even the stream seemed to slow.

The man in red spoke. His voice was water running uphill, birds falling into the sky, sand eroding into rock. *Where is Rafe Baburn?* he asked. The children glanced at one another. One of the girls offered a nervous smile.

Later, Kosar would swear that the man never even gave them time to reply.

He grabbed the smiling girl by her long hair, pulled his hand from within the red robes and sliced her throat. His knife seemed to lengthen into a sword, as if gorging on the fresh blood smearing its blade, and he swung it through the air. Three other children clutched at fatal wounds, shrieking as they disappeared from Kosar's view below the parapet. The two remaining boys turned to run and the hooded man caught them, seemingly without moving. He beheaded them both with a flick of his wrist.

Kosar fell to his knees, the breath sucked from him, and rolled sideways into the irrigation ditch. He cringed at the splash, but the hooded man strode across the bridge and into the village without pause. Kosar peered above the edge of the trench and watched through brown reeds as the man approached the first building.

The village was in turmoil. A woman screamed when she saw the devastation on the bridge, and others soon took up her cry. Men emerged from doorways clutching crossbows and swords. Children ran along the street, their eyes widening with a terrible curiosity when they saw their dead friends. Goats and sheebok scampered through the dust, startled to the ends of their tethers, crying and choking as leather leads jerked them to a standstill. The man in red walked on, the robe still tight around his body, hood over his head. From this angle Kosar could see only his back, and for that he was glad. From the glimpse he had caught of the red face, he had no desire to see beneath that hood again.

A woman, mad with grief, tried to run past the man to hug her dead child. His arm snaked out and buried the sword in her stomach. He jerked it free without breaking his step, the woman's blood splashing his robe. Her scream wound down like an echo in a cave. There was another shout from the village, and the whistle of a crossbow bolt boring the air.

It struck the man in the shoulder. He paused momentarily—

This is when he goes down, Kosar thought, *and then they'll fall on him and he'll be torn to shreds.*

—and then continued on his way. The bolt protruded from his shoulder, pinning the cloak tighter to his body. The shooter reprimed his crossbow, loaded another bolt and fired again, his eyes blinded with grief but his aim still true. This one struck the man in the face. Again he paused, his head snapping back with the impact. And again he went on his way once more. His pace increased, dust kicking up from beneath his red robe, clotted black with his own spilled blood.

Someone stumbled from the door of the brothel farther along the street. It was one of the three militia, naked, flushed and erect from his regular afternoon dose of rhellim, yet still of sound enough mind to bring his longbow with him. A whore staggered out after him, frenzied from rhellim overdose, grabbing at the soldier's crotch even as he strung an arrow and sighted on the red-robed man. He nudged the whore aside with his knee. She sprawled in the dust and shouted her rage up at him. The soldier let loose his arrow.

It thudded into the man and burst from his back. He stood for a moment like a red butterfly pinned to the air. The first man with the crossbow ran at him, raising his weapon to strike the murderer around the face, but the aggressor moved so quickly that Kosar barely saw the sword shimmer through the air. The crossbow spun across the road and into the stream, closely followed by its owner's head, mouth still wide in a silent scream.

Another bolt struck home, fired from somewhere beyond Kosar's field of view. Another, then another. The man barely paused this time, as if becoming used to the impact of wood and iron, his body adjusting itself around the alien objects puncturing and shredding it. He reached the tavern where the regular drinkers were stirring from thoughtless slumber and slaughtered all six of them. He did so slowly, seeming to relish every thrust and slice of his sword, oblivious to the bolts and arrows pounding into his red-robed body.

The other two militia had emerged from the brothel and all three now stood in the street, ridiculously naked and sweat-soaked and hard on rhellim. The whores huddled back against the brothel wall and watched as their men plucked arrows from their quivers, strung, fired, strung and fired again. Each arrow found its mark, and the nearer the man in red came to the militia, the more damage they did.

One shaft struck his throat and exited the back of his neck, carrying a stringy mess of gristle and veins with it. The air was thick with blood. Kosar could not believe what he was seeing; the man should be dead. He resembled a cactus—there were two dozen arrows and bolts peppering his body, and more hitting home every few seconds—and yet he walked. He swung his sword, hacked at the villagers, and their bodies spilled blood into the dust. Kosar watched aghast as the man in red reached the militia. They stood their ground as they were trained, wide-eyed and terrified. They took up their swords, engaged the arrowed-peppered figure together and died together. One was split from throat to sternum by a twitch of the blade, another lost his rampant genitals before his guts followed them to the ground. The third, mad and brainwashed to the last, ran at the enemy with the intention of wrestling him into the dust. The robed figure spun at the last instant, and the soldier was impaled on his own arrows.

With the militia dead, the massacre of the villagers began in earnest.

The man in red still wore the hood over his face. His hands barely seemed to move before another body fell to the ground. And arrows and bolts still thrummed into him.

Time to leave, Kosar knew. He glanced at the bridge, queasy because he had not gone to help those children. But at least this way he still had the stomach to feel sick.

He turned and made his way along the trench on his hands and knees. Each splash in the shallow water was accompanied by a scream from the village, or a groan, or the thud of another useless arrow finding its mark. He'd seen some things in his time, some strange, some unpleasant, some weird and wonderful. But he had never seen a man fighting with thirty arrows letting his blood and twisting up his insides.

He started to pant, and realized only then that he was panicking. The sounds from the village were receding as he lay distance down behind him. They were worse than before—the screams of children once more — but they were quieter now. Certainly not easier to hear, but less of a threat.

Kosar paused for a moment and lifted his hands from the muddy water. The ground was clay here, hardly ideal for planting crops but perfect for coating unwary crawlers with a bloodred deposit. He hung his head until his long hair dipped in as well, perhaps willing himself to be bloodied. He had done nothing. Those children on the bridge, innocent, ignorant only because their parents were ignorant, so alive, so trusting . . .

He had done nothing.

"Oh Mage shit," he whispered wretchedly.

The noise from the village stopped. No more screams. No more shouts. No more crossbows twanging, arrows whistling through the air or swords met in sparkling fury. Nothing but the slow, methodical footsteps of one man.

Kosar held his breath and raised his head slightly, looking back over his shoulder, the only sound now the thick water dripping from his hair. His hands were slowly sinking into the mud at the bottom of the ditch, his wounded fingertips stinging under the cold caress. It felt as if they were pressing into spilled guts, and the image horrified him. He was a thief, not a murderer.

How would he know what spilled guts felt like?

And then he realized. As his eyes drew level with the dried grass and he saw the man in red strolling among the dead, he knew. He knew the feel of guts because he had seen them spilled, smelled their tangy scent, heard the screams of their owners as they tried to catch them. He knew because he had stood by and watched those children die, when he could at least have warned them that this man was danger, this man was *death*. And because a sick realization suddenly dawned and he knew this man, who he was and where he was from. He'd heard whispers of legends, listened to outlandish stories by campfire light or the smoke-hazed atmospheres of taverns a lifetime from here.

The stranger was a Red Monk.

Which meant that somewhere in the land, magic was living again.

———

FROM THE HEIGHTS above Trengborne, Kosar watched the Red Monk wandering the silent village. From this distance, the Monk resembled a huge spider, body bristling with arrow spines, his web a trail of blood in the dust. Sometimes he went inside the buildings, and occasionally there was a distant scream as he found someone hiding and silenced them at last. By the time his bloody route crossed and recrossed itself, he was barely moving.

Kosar hid in the shadow of an overhanging rock on the valley slope, fascinated and terrified by what he was seeing. And seconds before he saw the Monk keel over and lie still at last, he caught sight of another shape beyond the village. It was on the facing hillside, so distant as to be little more than a speck moving on the gray rock face. Someone climbing quickly, fear urging them on. Another survivor.

Kosar wondered who it was. There were plenty down there he would never mourn, but there were also those that had shown him some measure of kindness. Looking at the sun bleeding down into the horizon, he knew that he had to find out. He would follow the survivor and perhaps they would share their stories.

Kosar was a branded thief who had lost the only place he had ever even thought of calling home. There was nothing better for him to do.

Chapter 2

RAFE BABURN SAT huddled on the hillside and stared down at the ruin of his life.

He was shivering, though it was still warm. Sweat beaded his skin, and the setting sun was still strong enough to bake his scalp, yet he shook and shuddered like a sheebok pulled from a mountain stream. He tried to cry out but his voice had gone, eaten away by shock. His memory too, slaughtered as surely as those children on the bridge, the militia outside the whorehouse. And his parents.

His father, probably still clasping the rusty old crossbow he'd not had the chance to fire.

His mother . . .

But no, he would not think of that. He *could* not. He must think of something else, turn from the village and stare at a rock, wonder what it had seen in its long life, explore underneath to see if there were any secrets hidden—

She had run to his father where he lay bleeding on the stilted platform in front of their home. He was dead already, Rafe knew, but still his mother went to him, perhaps thinking that her love could mend all wounds. The sword whispered through the air and sang a song of violence as it buried itself in her chest. She fell with the sword still in her, and the killer, the murdering *bastard*, placed his red-booted foot on her breasts to lever the blade from bone and flesh.

Rafe had wanted to close his eyes. Hiding beneath the platform, dust showered down over his face. His father's blood had already pattered onto his forehead and dripped into one eye, and now his mother's blood was adding to it, urging him to drift away, forget what he had seen and never dream of it again. The blood was as warm as his parents' hands on his forehead when he was having nightmares as a child. Or his father's fingertips, massaging Rafe's tense scalp when he had so recently woken from strange dreams, unknown voices still muttering inside his head.

But he had not been able to look away. He was afraid that if he closed his eyes, then the man in red—*clicking* and *clacking* as the arrows piercing his body knocked together—would find him. The murderer paused, standing with a foot at either side of Rafe's dead mother, staring into the house. Rafe heard a sniff as he tested the air. He seemed undecided, unsure of whether or not to venture into the house or move on to the next. His decision was made for him when two screaming men charged onto the platform, attacking him with rusty swords.

The man had swatted them aside and opened them up as they fell to the ground. Several arrows whispered through the air and thudded into his chest and arms, and he left the platform to pursue the shooters.

Rafe had waited for a little while, terrified to move, listening to the sound of death around him. It shifted across the village, tagged onto the red-robed man like his own shadow and, when Rafe judged it to be sufficiently distant, he ran.

He had tried not to look at his parents. He could smell them as he scrambled from beneath the wooden platform and he could hear the *drip*, *drip* of blood as it ran between the boards. He did not want to see them lying there dead. He wanted to remember them as they had been, not as they now were.

But of course, he had looked anyway. Unable to help himself, he saw what was left of the man and woman who had taken him in and brought him up from childhood, and who had died so obviously trying to protect him. And as his eyes alighted on the bloody ruins, flies already finding the wounds, another of the strange voices twisted into his head. He squeezed his eyes shut and fisted his hands, desperate to drive it back whence it had come. But he did not know where this was or why it was, so he was all but powerless against the ripple of weird words echoing through his consciousness.

Then a scream had cut through the sound and banished it for a while. Another cry followed, closer this time, so Rafe turned and ran. Guilt pricked at his neck like the gaze of the dead. His parents lay there unburied, open to the world, offering themselves to the scavengers and carrion that would come wandering in from the fields and hillsides soon enough. But there was also something urging him on: the sight of his parents' deaths seen between rough boards; the sound of the man's sword as he twisted it from his mother's cleft ribs; the knowledge that, by returning and offering himself up for the same fate, he would be betraying them in the worst possible way.

A dead thing is just that, his father had once told him. *A dead thing is less than a rock in the fields. A rock has seen the past and will see the future; a dead thing will rot to nothing, go back to the earth and perhaps care for the next circle of planting and harvesting. It's what the dead thing was that matters, not what it is now.*

His parents were no longer there. They had gone to wherever the ideas of living things go when they die. Into memory, perhaps, or an afterlife, or simply into the Black to add themselves to history.

So he sat on the open hillside and shivered and shook as he viewed the village lying dead in the valley. Ten minutes ago the man in red had dragged himself across the bloodied ground, leaving a smear in the dust behind him. He looked like a porcupine slowly winding down, or a cactus given brief life. His robe was pinned even tighter by the arrows, soaked a darker red by his copious blood. Then he had stilled. He had not moved since.

Rafe wanted so much to go back and make sure the killer was dead. That he had been alive when he killed Rafe's parents was impossible, of course, with so many arrows venting his blood. But now that the man in red was silent and still, Rafe wanted to make sure. And, perhaps, he wanted to exact some sort of useless revenge. Take a sword to the corpse. Spread him across the village to accompany the death he himself had meted out.

The teenager—barely a man, though he liked to think of himself as such, his parents' blood drying to a crust on his cheeks and forehead—did the hardest thing he had ever done. He turned his back on his village and started climbing. Through the mountain passes and into the next valley lay Pavisse. His uncle Vance lived there, he would help. He would know what to do. And he was all that Rafe had left.

Almost blind with grief, Rafe stumbled upward. He was sobbing and crying, hearing the dying shriek of his mother with every step.

High above, skull ravens rode the thermals and stared down.

———

IT WAS WAY past midnight by the time Rafe crested the mountain pass and started to make his way down into the next valley. Pavisse sat like a glinting gem in the distance, spread across the valley floor and creeping up its slopes where mines sank wounds deep into the land of Noreela's skin. Fires flickered in the night, street lamps scored lines of light into the landscape, the bustling noise of the town reached him even this far up. He guessed it was still a few hours' walk, but at least the lights would guide his way.

He had heard many stories about Pavisse but had never actually been there. They ranged from the gentle-but-firm advice of his mother to stay away (*It's a hole, Rafe, a pit full of everything that isn't good in the land*), to excited babbling amongst his friends about how there were naked women in the streets, warriors in the bars and an ancient wizard who had forgotten his own name living on the edge of town. But any past misgivings had been thrust aside by the deaths of his parents. Dangerous and unseemly Pavisse might be, but tonight it was safety, a light in the dark, a balm to Rafe's grief. Something to aim for now that murder had made him aimless.

Already he could smell the town. A giddying mix of stenches wafted up from the valley, helped on its way by a steady breeze coming down from the north. Some he recognized: the warm smell of just-cooked bread, rich and comforting; horse crap sweating in the heat; freshly turned earth, either from the fledge and coal mines that honeycombed the hills, or the fields on the flood plains. Stale beer too, reaching him even this far out. How much spilled ale, he wondered, to make such a stink? He'd heard the tales of bar fights and muggings in gloomy byways, but Rafe had faced a greater danger today and survived. Drunken miners did little to scare him.

But there were other smells he could not identify, however hard he tried. A rich, acidic sting, vaguely earthy, that may be something to do with the mines. A perfume that reminded him of rot. And an odor that was undoubtedly food, but no food he had ever tasted. Spice-rich, hot, even the smell promised a tortured stomach.

This high up in the mountains the land was completely untamed, and Rafe had to move cautiously to avoid stepping in a hole and breaking his ankle. Rocks hid among the sparse, low heathers, ready to trip him and send him stumbling. Melt trace as well, low ridges of loose stones left here after the last Age of Ice, virtually untouched since then except by the seasonal caresses of nature itself. Some of them were obvious, dark lines of shadow twisting along the hillside. Others were hidden by shrubs or long grasses, like snakes awaiting a catch. These were more dangerous.

The life moon was out, lending a three-quarter light to his trek, affording him a silvery touch reserved only for the innocent and pure. But there were many definitions of pure, and Rafe suspected it was simply another legend left over from the time when magic was still alive. The sheen of moonlight on his skin gave him a sense of calm, because being good and pure was something his parents had so often told him was important. *Wish for whatever you will*, his father had said, *but yearning is different from having. To have impurely is worse than never having at all.*

Well, he still lived in Trengborne, or he had until hours ago. A nothing village, a poor farmers' settlement inhabited by simple folk out to make their living day to day, hour to hour. A place where his future promised little more than scratching a living in the dirt, celebrating when a new calf was born, getting drunk on the autumn windfalls, marrying a village girl and raising children to run through the same ageless scenario . . .

Except that things had changed.

Not only now, when a change was thrust cruelly and bloodily upon him. But before, days and weeks ago, a hint that something was occurring in his mind over which he held no real control. Something involving words he could not understand, themes and ideas that should be painting a picture for him but which, in reality, were merely keeping him awake. Yet they formed a concerto of change in his mind, unleashing his hobbled imagination. However terrible things now were, this journey seemed right. Meant to be. His parents were dead and there was a black pit of mourning opening up inside of him, but things were going the way that was intended. He was certain of it. From the day he had first heard those voices, he had known that he was destined for more than a life of farming.

There was a noise behind him.

Rafe crouched down low, spun on his heels and rested a hand on the hilt of his knife. He caught his breath, wished he could still his heart to hear better.

The noise again, a scattering of tiny pebbles and loose stones slipping down the incline as someone or something made their way down from above. He concentrated in the dark, sweeping his head left and right in the hope that he would pick out something from the corner of his eye. The life moon revealed nothing. Whatever was up there knew he was looking and had hunkered down into another shadow.

But Rafe knew what it was. A demon, bleeding and moaning and coming for him on legs pierced by arrows and bolts. A man eager to complete the work he had so recently begun. The man in red, somehow still alive, colorless in the moonlight.

Rafe turned and slipped and went sliding down a patch of slick grass. He cried out, and there was another rattle of stones from above. He struggled to find his feet and slid down the hillside, digging his hands into the loamy ground and feeling his fingers slice through. He struck a rock. It opened a gash on his cheek and spilled warm blood across his face, but Rafe was glad. It made him feel alive. The pain invigorated him and drove him to his feet. Soon he was scampering down the hill, dodging rocks looming darkly from the night, hands held out to either side to afford him some balance and break his fall should he slip again.

He did not look back. To look back would be to invite the wrath of the thing pursuing him, give it an opportunity to hack and slice its way through his defense of pain and panic, cleave him in two from head to foot and let his insides cool here in the hills until the scavengers came. Instead he concentrated on the glittering spread of Pavisse, tinted silver by the life moon. And before long he was running like a mountain goat, leaping from hump to hump, missing the gullies in between that would bend and snap his legs, avoiding the rocks, their sharp edges promising to finish what the man in red had begun.

If there were noises of pursuit he did not hear them. There was no need to be silent now, and breath was punched from his lungs with every slap of his feet on the ground, every impact as he landed and sprang onward. Rafe's mind seemed to retreat as he ran, revealing nothing of the passage of time, the shifting of night, nor the exhaustion he was forcing himself into. His body protected itself by driving him out of his mind.

By the time he reached the stone walls—the first touches of humanity since leaving his dead village—dawn had broken and spilled its glow along the valley. Rafe paused, hardly able to breathe, his heart hammering, his legs ready to fold beneath him. For the first time in hours he looked back, became aware once again. Shadows still hid beneath rocky overhangs higher up on the hillsides. He wondered what hid within them.

———

ON THE WAY into Pavisse he passed by an old mine. Its throat was open to the air like a badly healed wound, the land around it scarred blank by dust, horses' hooves, and the feet of the workmen who had lived and died hauling coal and fledge from the ground. To one side of the opening, overgrown and decayed down over the centuries since it had died, stood a machine. Its gray flanks of stone were supported by rusted veins of worked metal, and there were empty spaces where pieces of it had once been.

A machine! Rafe had only ever seen small ones, as big as his head or torso, their forgotten purposes only guessed at. But this one was huge, almost as large as the house he and his parents had lived in. Birds nested in its upper portions, and a soft breeze whistled through its long-petrified guts. Rafe wondered what its function had been, but the very idea of this massive, mysterious thing moving shocked and astounded him. His parents had told him that these things had not worked since the War, but that they had been here forever.

He passed the mine and approached Pavisse, and as he neared other people—and, he hoped, safety—the effects of the night truly began to weigh him down.

His parents' blood was a crisp across his face. His own, still dripping from the cut, had dried over it.

Sometime during the night he had also soiled himself.

Crying, trying to shout but far too tired to do so, mumbling about his dead village and inviting curious stares from the waking population of Pavisse, Rafe entered the town to find his uncle.

Chapter 3

ALISHIA HAD NEVER heard a dead man sing. She had read accounts of many wonders: shades calling from the depths of a bottomless cave in the mountains of Kang Kang; holes in the ground, swallowing rock and soil and anyone foolish enough to venture too close; a woman stumbling into a cloud of mimics and breathing them in, watching in terrified wonder as they fluttered from her mouth in the shape of a golden butterfly. She had read of skull ravens feasting on living cattle, two rivers flowing in different directions in the same valley, and a place where ancient machines had once gone to die. Indeed, for a librarian she had imagined a very colorful life, and dreamed of much that was wrong in the land. But Alishia had always thought that imagination was better than experience, because it was so pure.

Still, she had never heard a dead man sing.

He stood in one of the aisles far, far back in the library, a place barely frequented, rich with the dust of ages. Some of the books there were so old that Alishia did not know of anyone who could read them. This man had been browsing beyond her sight for hours.

His song echoed mournfully in the still air. His voice was low and weak—what more could be expected of a dead man?—but filled with emotion. Alishia did not recognize the language, though that was not unusual in Noreela's capital city. But she sensed something of what the song was about nonetheless, and heard the undertones of longing, the cadences of sorrow hidden in the folds and twists of his throaty warbles.

When he had come to the desk hours before, Alishia stepped back in shock. He was the oldest man she had ever seen, certainly the most frail-looking, and she could not conceive how someone in such a state could still be alive. But alive he was, a breathing fossil, his organs barely contained within skin so thin it was almost translucent. He said a few words in a tongue Alishia had never heard before and then wandered off, shaking his head and mumbling quietly under his breath.

Ever since then the singing, and the echoing sound of pages being turned. Alishia knew he was in the farthest, oldest corner of the library because she had looked everywhere else for him, using the arranging of shelves as an excuse to wander the tall aisles, brushing aside cobwebs and lifting dust that had slowly spread to fill the air with a haze of dead skin.

What was a man so old looking for in books so ancient? These tomes were from a time before her grandfather's grandfather's father was born, and they were retained now only because if they were removed, it was likely that the building would collapse. They had almost fossilized into place, their leaves bound together with damp, stiff covers strengthening the racks of shelves they stood upon. Alishia had looked at some of them, but most were written in languages she had never seen. The diagrams and pictures told stories, and sometimes these were enough. There was enough strife and heartache contained within the books she *could* read. So she browsed these old tomes only occasionally, and every time she opened one she felt as though she was intruding into histories that should never be remembered.

Sometimes, on those rare occasions when they were written in words she *did* know, Alishia found truths that she wished she had not.

She felt at home here with her books. Some days she would be all alone, all day long. There were things in the world that demanded people's time more than books—failing crops, fading health, a reversion to harsher times—and the people of Noreela City would often forgo the luxury of leisure time to cater to the expanding flaws in their own lives. Many of these problems were self-inflicted, but there was also the seed of regression that had been planted in the land after the Cataclysmic War. As time went on, Noreela City and all its satellite communities were being drawn back from the level of civilization they had reached almost three centuries before to an older, more savage time. People viewed rapes and murders in the street in broad daylight, and swords remained sheathed, as did the pangs of guilt. In many ways time had started again after the Mages, and instead of recognizing this year as Year of the Black 2208, people regarded the War as the beginning of the current age instead. Even Alishia was not certain of the exact year; she had read books, used charts, referred to ancient texts, but somehow the Year of the Black had found itself overshadowed by the Cataclysmic War.

As far as Alishia was concerned, the old magic could stay dead and buried, whatever effect its absence was having on the land. Her own small, unimportant opinion was that civilization advanced in waves and cycles, and they were on something of a downward path right now. Soon there would be a discovery that would draw enthusiasm and goodwill back into the people, infuse them with a new zest for life, and therefore more respect for it. Besides, Alishia saw magic every day. Her imagination was fed and nurtured every time she read a word, or a paragraph, reminding her of some years-old dream. The beautiful poems of Ro Sargossa brought to mind the dream of making love with two of the Duke's champions; a treasury of foodstuffs made her think of the differing meals she had considered, their separate tastes, their curious blends of exotic spices and juices and herbs from faraway lands. Everything she read invoked a rush of dream memories, so an afternoon on her own in the library was like living parts of her life again, however unreal that life may seem. Sometimes she was made hungry by the scents of old, untested foods. Occasionally she was stirred by the recalled cradling of well-muscled arms, though in reality she had yet to be cradled. But every time, every day, she was glad to be alive.

Let them talk about ruin and degradation and death. She would not let it happen to her.

He was still singing. The old man had been here for several hours now, hidden away behind those ancient shelves, humming words that Alishia could not quite grasp from the cool air. She tried, leaning forward on her chair with her head to one side, but her heartbeat smothered the echoes. It was as if being alive prevented her true understanding of the old man's song.

So she tidied, cataloged, skimmed a few pages from a map book charting the progress of Noreela City's ever-shifting river over the centuries, read a love poem by Ro Sargossa. But she could not ignore the singing, however hard she tried. Sometimes it felt as though it was inside her head; she could not hear it, but still it was there. Other times it came strong and loud, filling the library and sending many-legged things scuttling into the dark spaces beneath book towers.

At last, she decided that she had to find him.

Alishia rarely left her desk when there was no one to watch over it, but today was quieter than most—the old man was the only person she'd seen so far, and she guessed ten minutes away would do little harm. Besides, who would steal? Few in Noreela City had any inclination to even come in here and read a book, let alone await the opportunity to slink in and steal one when her back was turned. Sometimes she wondered whether there was any intellect left in a world where famine also starved the mind, and dust and fading gods ate away at the tenacity of the people.

She slipped from behind her desk, crossed the uneven wooden floor scattered with comfortable reading chairs—moth-eaten and rotting through lack of use—and passed between two tall towers of books.

She was in Geography. The books reached to the ceiling on both sides, those at the top hardly touched since the day she had started working here ten years ago. It was not that there was nothing of interest up there—Alishia suspected there were accounts of paths long since faded into time, trade routes discovered and discarded—it was simply that people seemed so lethargic that it was far easier to pluck a book from one of the lower shelves. There were six ladders scattered around, but three of these invariably leaned against the stacks of children's books. These were soft and comfortable, cloth-covered pages, bendy and pliable for young hands to twist and young mouths to gnaw upon. When Alishia was not working, this was where Byran and Magella huddled away to screw and sleep and eat. Their thoughts rarely stretched any further.

Her footsteps, naturally soft anyway, were completely muffled by the stocked shelves. She breathed in the must of their pages, the musk of decades of damp and heat and damp again. Mold painted great swaths across the spines, interrupted here and there where a book had been removed and replaced in a different place. History nestled around Alishia, slowly moldering away just as the land was fading back into history. There was a certain poetic justice to that.

She paused, swept her long hair back over her shoulders to free her ears. The singing was still there, though even more muffled now that she had entered the maze of books. That was another thing she loved about the library: whoever had built it had given no consideration to order, arrangement or the need for browsers to be able to find their way out in less than a day. It was more than a maze; it was a conundrum of words.

Often when she ventured into the heart of the library she was sure she traveled a route she had never known before, a byway between alleys, ankle-deep in paper dust and redolent with the musings of yesteryear. This time a path between stacks led her not only left and right, but up and down as well. There were places where the floor dipped and raised, but she had never seen steps. She glanced at the books to see what strange subject could be stored in such an ambiguous place: needlecraft. Ten thousand books on sewing, knitting, tapestry, darning, skin-melding, hair-braiding and web-weaving.

On she went. And turning a sudden corner, she found him. She stopped and backtracked slowly, not sure whether he had seen her. His song did not falter, his voice unwavering, his mouth moving in rhythm with his hands. He sat amid a pile of books, manuscripts, torn pages and shredded sheets. He was a lump of flesh at the heart of a mountain of paper, a weak and yet terrible-looking man picking through remnants of history. Obviously he had yet to find whatever he sought.

He was in the far corner of the library building, perhaps aboveground, maybe below. The ceiling was low here and adorned with mineral stalactites, water stains mottling the stacked books and promising little but rot within their pages. This section, Alishia knew, was old magic. Hidden magic. Lost magic. Many people had forgotten about that, and so the area was only visited rarely. Those who did still study it often wished they did not.

The man rustled his way through another sheaf of pages, discarding them at random. They fluttered down around him like dying butterflies. He spent very little time on each page, certainly not long enough to read even a tenth of what was written. He must, Alishia knew, have a very definite idea of what he sought.

Lost magic.

But why here? Seeking a truth about his childhood, or that of his parents? Trying to find the route to the missing history of his clan? Or simply curious?

Dust. That was one of the curses of the library. Scraps of paper and the shed skin of those who had written or read the books over the centuries, all existing in an enclosed, still atmosphere. Alishia breathed in and felt the first tickling signs in her nose. At the same time she saw the old man pause in his search, his eyes widen, his hands grip tightly around the book in his lap. Alishia's nose twitched and itched, pressure built behind her face, her eyes began to water with the strain of withholding the sneeze.

The man stood. Torn papers fell from his lap, the book held out at arm's length like a carrier of some horrible contagion.

Alishia turned and ran. The sneeze exploded. She tried to keep it muffled behind her hands, she had turned several corners already, the book stacks should have absorbed the sound . . .

. . . still, he may have heard.

Alishia wondered why she even cared, but at the same time she knew: her instinct told her that the man brought danger. She hurried back through the maze of books and dust and age, turning corners, desperately relieved when she found a familiar row that led back out to the open area around her desk. Once there she rooted around beneath her desk, closed her hand around the hilt of the old knife wedged in between two piles of books beneath the scored wooden top. And she gasped as the man walked around the corner.

He was sweating. He must have been running to have arrived so quickly behind her, but what she found more worrying was that he tried to hide this fact. For a second she was undecided—stand with the knife, or let it go and face whatever threat he may pose?

He decided for her. "Nothing," he growled without even glancing at her, the language obviously alien to his lips. He walked past, so close that she could smell his sweat and fear. He was *scared*. She wondered whether she smelled the same to him.

Alishia said nothing, even though she could plainly see the book slung under his arm like a recent kill. She watched with a mixture of relief and embarrassment as he paused at the door, picked his blood-red robe from a hook on the wall, shrugged it over his shoulders and left. As he exited into the sun he turned the hood up over his head.

A *Red Monk?* Alishia thought. She had read passing reference to them in several books, but little was known about them other than they were mad. And deadly. But the man had gone, and Alishia breathed a sigh of relief and thought: *Thank my heart. Thank my lucky heart.*

─────

ALISHIA CLOSED THE library early that afternoon. The strange experience with the old book-thief had shaken her more than she cared to admit. Besides, nobody would notice, and if they did they would not say anything. And even if they did it would not matter.

The entrance to the library was below the road, and as she climbed the worn stone staircase, Noreela City revealed itself. Many years ago—centuries before her birth—she would have seen spires and arches and domes from the first step, but over the years since the Cataclysmic War they had crumbled into disrepair, or been pulled down when they became unsafe. Now the first she saw of the surrounding buildings was as she mounted the fifth step and the Tumbling Window of the courthouse stared down at her. In her time she had seen many criminals—murderers, rapists, pseudo-magicians—pushed from this high window. Some of them died on impact. Others, the unlucky ones, clung to life for days, bleeding across the stones, untouched and unaided. The *really* unlucky ones were taken by dogs in the night.

Great place to work, Alishia thought for the thousandth time. *Opposite a slaughterhouse.* Because that's all it really was. She had once seen a man shoved from the Tumbling Window for stealing coins from a street trader to buy rotwine. His wife stood and watched as he fell, his knees popping, ankles breaking, ribs cracking inward and spearing his lungs. She squatted by his side as he gasped bloody bubbles into the heat of the noonday sun. Then she smiled and left him to die alone.

These were bad days indeed, and Alishia knew how lucky she was to be the librarian, in charge of one of the least-visited buildings in the city, unknown by most, usually ignored even if someone did recognize her. Perhaps people believed she would have them arrested for talking in her hallowed hall of books.

As she started down the street she realized how pleased she was to be out of the building. It was an alien feeling because she loved it in there, but today had been tainted by the activities of the weird old man, and she felt lighter of step and heart now that she was away. Even Noreela City—dark, dilapidated and sad—was welcoming in its own strange way. Perhaps she really had escaped some awful danger. Whatever the reason, she felt an unaccountable high, unhindered by the constraints of worry and stress.

A woman passed by, trailing a snake of children behind her, all of them painfully thin and pocked with weeping sores. The woman was a barrel of a person, rolling along with great strides. Her jowls almost touched her chest, which itself could have easily harbored a herd of tumblers beneath its mammoth overhang.

"Spare some tellans," the woman croaked, "we've not eaten for a week."

Alishia could see the truth of the statement in the children's eyes, and the lie in the woman's.

"I'll give the kids tellans," she said, reaching into her backpack.

"They're my kids."

"All of them?"

The woman refused to look away. No shame. "Some of them."

"I'll give the kids tellans," Alishia said again, and the woman nudged her aside with one fleshy elbow and continued on her way. As the line passed her by, Alishia rustled in her bag. She gave the last child—a pale-faced, sad-eyed boy—a sprinkle of silver tellan pieces. He smiled his thanks but it did not reach his eyes.

Alishia stood in the shadow of an abandoned shop and watched the straggly line disappear around the corner. There were other people on the streets now, sleepwalking from buildings at the end of a day's work, little to look forward to at home, even less in the bars, where all the talk would be of failing crops and how the tumblers in the hills were taking more children and elderly each month. There would be arguments between those who believed it was due to the carnivorous plants being more confident, and those who blamed the Cataclysmic War. That old war, ended long before anyone alive now had been born, had replaced the gods as the ultimate scapegoat.

Alishia believed both were true. One fed the other.

Bad days indeed.

———

ALISHIA SLEPT ABOVE a stable on the outskirts of the city. It was cheap for two reasons: first, the stink of horses was rank and the noises unpleasant; second, the nearer the edge of Noreela City, the more dangerous a place could be. There were stories of Noreelans being dragged from their beds by mountain bandits, raped and eaten, only their heads and feet remaining when they were discovered days later (the heads because they were full of impure thoughts; the feet because they had walked in shit). There were all manner of unpleasant stories abroad these days, but that did not necessarily make this one a lie. Alishia slept with a knife beneath her pillow.

Most mornings she was woken by the horses stirring and shitting and being fed by Erv, the stable lad who had more than once tried to force his way into her room. She would stir slowly, listening to Noreela City waking up around her, smelling breakfasts cooking on iron skillets in the streets, tasting the rankness of the stale food she'd eaten the night before. Erv would talk louder than he had to and exercise the horses below her window when she was dressing. She always kept her knife close at hand. Erv was a nice lad on the surface, but his eyes shone with lawlessness.

This morning, however, something else brought Alishia from dreams of a field sprouting rotten corpses. She was glad to be awake, but for an instant she thought she was still in her dream. She could smell the acidic scent of burning. There was shouting coming from an unknown distance, the meaning of words stolen by street corners. But panic in the voices could not be disguised.

Instinct told Alishia that it was still the early hours and yet she could see around her room. Her clothes were in a careless heap on her chair, like a figure collapsed from exhaustion. She stared at them and they moved.

Her hand slid under the pillow so quickly that she pricked her finger on her knife. She yelped and fell from the bed, never taking her eyes from the shape on the chair, pulling the blade from beneath the covers and cursing when they entangled her hand, panicking and twisting the blankets more, expecting at any second—

But they were only her clothes, and the illusion of movement was given by the flickering light outside. The shifting, wavering light of a fire. A very big fire.

Alishia rushed to the window, completely forgetting her nakedness and the possibility of Erv already being in the yard below. The city glowed in the night, lit from the center by a huge conflagration. It was not the location that convinced Alishia that it was the library. It was not even the disturbing events of yesterday. Ash revealed the unbearable truth. That, and the thousands of burning pages fluttering in the air like incandescent birds.

"No!" she said, instantly thinking of the man in red with the broken book beneath his arm. "Oh *no!*"

Outside, fire turned the nighttime streets to dusk. People bustled and hurried and there was a surreal, almost carnival atmosphere as Alishia pushed her way through the dawdlers and curious. Food vendors were hurrying toward the fire, pushing their carts before them, obviously anticipating a profitable day. Families were trailing along the streets, moving aside whenever a horse-drawn cart came by, babbling excitedly the nearer they came to the conflagration. Alishia tried not to cry, but the smoke stung her eyes, so at least she had an excuse. Her rough cloth dress itched and scratched where she sweated, perspiration dripping with her tears to the old stone streets of a city that had been neither kind nor cruel to her, merely indifferent.

It seemed that this night, that state of affairs had changed.

As she entered one of the east squares and fought her way through traders setting their market stalls for the day, a cry went up. "Fire!" someone shouted, others echoed it, and Alishia almost laughed out loud. The column of smoke already reached the heavens, flames licked and danced at its base and the stench of burning overrode even the warm tang of oiled spices and freshly squeezed rhellim. How could they only now acknowledge its existence? But then she saw the flaming stall in the corner of the square, and she understood. Before, the fire had little to do with them. A distraction, a novelty, something to chat about while they awaited their first customers of the day. Now it had touched one of them by sending down a flaming page from a book, kissing a stall-covering alight, seeding itself away from the library. The threat of it engulfing all of their lives became immediately apparent. A couple of the traders rushed to help the frantic owner haul what she could away from the voracious flames, but most merely tried to protect their own stalls. They threw buckets of water across the canopies, packed away stock, calming their mules as best they could.

More flaming confetti floated down from the sky. Some of the little fires had burnt themselves out before they hit the ground, but a few—those feasting on a particularly rich history text, perhaps, or those with several pages stuck together by time—blazed into whatever they touched.

A man bashed at his own head to put out the flames in his hair. A woman squatted and pissed on her burning furbat. Novelty mutated into panic as the whole city seemed to speed up. Where people had been walking they now ran, where they'd been running they were now sprinting, whether toward or away from the fire. Water carts careered through the streets. Barrels bumped and spilled their precious cargo back into the gutter, and by the time Alishia had run to the fire, there were already several wagons parked around the old, misshapen library building. Groups of sweating men and women swung buckets back and forth, fire glinting on their strained faces, skin seeming to stretch and redden even as they worked.

Hopeless, Alishia knew. All hopeless. There were a billion places for the flames to hide, and even if they did manage to douse the conflagration and drown it from the fabric of the building, the books would smolder and simmer inside, the fire biding its time, ready to leap out and finish the destruction as soon as their backs were turned.

Why she personified the blaze she could not guess. It scared her at first, giving it a soul, an aim, a cruelty that she could barely comprehend. But then she thought of the man in red as he had left her library, the broken book beneath his arm, the torn and tattered pages he had been sitting amongst when she crept between the stacks to spy upon him. *Nothing*, he had said, but he had been lying. He had found something. And once that something left the library with him, perhaps there was no reason to leave anything else behind.

"You bastard," she said as she watched the building burn. What right did he have to destroy history like this? "Oh you bastard!"

———

THE MILITIA CAME, more to clear the streets than investigate the burning. Alishia told them who she was and they asked a few perfunctory questions. When she mentioned the man in red they seemed not to hear. They ushered the crowds away and left.

She stayed by the library for three days, watching as the building folded in upon itself, giant roof members exposed to the air like blackened ribs, only walking back to her room at night. Life went on around her, ignoring her grief. A man was sent from the Tumbling Window, but she barely registered the sound as he hit the ground.

On the third day a thunderstorm—mockingly late—extinguished the last of the smoldering ruin.

At last the librarian could pick her way into the rubble. There was very little left. Some of the book stacks still stood, but their contents were charred into one hard mass, knowledge petrified by fire. In there perhaps pages still read correctly, but Alishia could not find the will to go through every blackened lump, searching for whatever dregs of history may have survived. Instead she pushed them over and watched them crumble into black paste.

Crowds passed by the ruin with nary a second glance. The library was no longer interesting now that the fires had burnt down. Really, Alishia knew, no one had ever found it interesting.

Except for one man. An old man, so old that he should have been dead. The first dead man that Alishia had ever heard sing.

Chapter 4

RAFE'S ONLY SENSE was touch. He could feel the hands holding him down, the water sluicing his body, the rough scouring of something scraping across his stomach, his chest, then down between his legs. He struggled, but to no avail. He tried to open his eyes, thought he'd succeeded, but he saw only black. Either he was in total darkness or he was blind. He could not smell anything, and although the water trickled into his open mouth, there was no taste.

He was panicking, but it seemed at a distance, a remote fear for the well-being of someone he knew only vaguely. It was a sensation he had felt before. When he was young he stole a bottle of rotwine from Trengborne's shop and sloped out into the fields with his friends. He felt big and brave, but within an hour of the first gulp he wished he had never even heard of the drink. He had often wondered why those men and women sitting inside and outside the tavern looked so lifeless, so devoid of emotion, and now he had found out. Everything receded until there was only fire in his veins, blurring the edges of his senses.

His father had found him and dragged him back to the house,

sat up with him all night until Rafe came to and vomited across the floor. His parents did not tell him off. They said he had scolded himself, and that they hoped he had learned a lesson.

His parents. They were kind and thoughtful, not impulsive and cruel like so many people he knew. They were also open and honest, and he loved them for that. Most people would have chosen never to tell their son that he was not truly their flesh and blood; that they had found him out on the hillside, a babe abandoned by rovers or a family too poor to care for another child; that though both as barren as some of the village fields, they had been so desperate to have a child that they had taken him and called him their own. Such honesty had troubled him at first, but in time it had made him love them even more. The trust implicit in their telling of the truth revealed the depth of their feelings for him.

And now they were dead.

"Dead!" he shouted, but hands pushed him back down as he tried to sit up, and he realized they were trying to help. The washing had stopped and now he was being dried with a rough towel, the cuts on his legs and arms stinging as clumsy but caring hands scoured them.

Rafe sat up again, pushing at whomever held him down. He touched his face to see if his eyes were open—they were—and the confirmation helped his vision creep back. With it came sound, and smell. He looked around, sniffed and began to wish he was still unconscious.

The room could have been a slaughterhouse, or a refuse tip, or perhaps it had been used to house corpses during the Great Plagues and someone had forgotten to take them away. The stink of rotting meat was tremendous: a heavy, warm, sweet smell that twisted Rafe's guts into agonized knots and brought saliva to his mouth. He hated himself for feeling hungry. He looked around to try to find the cause of the stink, but he saw only the huge man who had been tending him. Perhaps, he thought, this person was the source of the smell. It seemed all too likely, judging by his appearance. Over six feet tall, all of it scruffy and filthy, a beard that housed tiny crawling things and arms so hairy that they looked like furbats attached to his shoulders. The man's face was scarred down one side, old whip-wounds black as death. Rafe recognized the signs of a tumbler attack from the stories he had heard back in Trengborne.

"Boy?" the man said, and it was as if the ground had spoken. His voice sounded like rocks grating together.

Rafe raised his eyebrows, too shocked to answer.

"Boy," the man said again, smiling slightly. The smile tempered the voice and made it kind.

And then Rafe looked into his eyes for the first time, and he saw a cool, calm intelligence there, something belying his appearance. Rafe knew those eyes, recognized that intellect.

"Uncle Vance?"

"Rafe," the huge man grumbled, "my boy, I haven't seen you for so long. What in Black's been happening? Why're you all bloody and cut up?"

"Uncle, they're dead," he said. Actually saying it seemed to make it all final and real, and the dregs of unconsciousness flitted away to the corners of the stinking room. "All of them. Mother . . . Father . . . everyone."

"Royston? Dead?"

"Dead," Rafe said again, and began to cry. He tried not to blink because every time he shut his eyes, images of his slaughtered parents came to him. But keeping his eyes open made him cry more.

Vance, his expression one of stunned shock, came to him and held out his arms, touching Rafe's lips with something cool and rank. "Best sleep, then," he said, and before Rafe could reply, sight, taste and sound faded out once more. The final sensation was his uncle's hand on his brow, shaking slightly as the big man shed his own shameless tears.

———

"HE RODE INTO the village," Rafe said. "Then he killed everyone. And there was nothing anyone could do. The militia fought him, but he killed them. He had arrows in him and bolts and everything, but still he walked and killed. I watched him from the hills when I escaped . . . I watched him die, I think . . . but then I was followed. I think he's following me."

"A madman. There are many of them nowadays."

"But why kill Mother and Father? There's no rhyme, no reason."

"People don't need reasons," Vance said. "They just need the urge." He stared off into the corners of the room for a time, though Rafe was sure he was seeing much farther. "Royston," he muttered, and shook his head.

"How did I get here?" Rafe asked through their shared pain. "I don't remember. I know I came down from the hills, there was something following me, but I don't know how I found my way here."

Vance looked up. "There was someone following you, but it was no madman. He brought you here after you collapsed in the street."

"Who?"

"Some thief."

Rafe shook his head, frowning.

Vance grunted. "He knew where I was, somehow. Said he'd been here before. Said he'd been most places." He hawked, and spat a huge gob of mucus onto the floor. "All the damn trouble there is in the world, and you get mixed up with a thief."

"I wasn't mixed up—"

"I know, I know. That's not really what I meant."

Rafe watched his uncle move across the room and open a cupboard. He brought out a bottle and uncorked it, slurping noisily as he downed half of its contents in one swallow.

"Aren't you going to tell anyone?" Rafe asked.

"Huh?" Vance's eyes were glazing.

"We have to tell someone."

"Who?"

"I don't know. I have to go back, bury Mother and Father, do something . . . do something for—"

"They'd have been taken by now, by *things*. Night things. And Rafe, there's no one to tell. I could ride five days to Noreela City, and if the wraiths or tumblers or bandits didn't get me first, and if they even let me through the city gates, they'd ask me why I'd come. Then they'd laugh and send me away again. Trengborne is an unknown little village in a big bad world. Nobody would give a Mage shit about what's happened."

"But *everyone's* dead!"

Vance stared, and Rafe felt himself shriveling beneath that gaze. It held knowledge of all manner of things, and most of them must surely be bad. "Two moons ago, so it's said, a village two days to the east—two days nearer Noreela City, mind you—was swallowed up. Sucked into the ground by a sinkhole. Everything mixed and blended into a soup. A thousand people. And you know what they sent from the city? Nothing. No help, no militia, not even a Mourner." He looked at the ceiling, took another swig from the bottle and belched. "Everyone dies. It's just that these days, people are doing it more often." He drained the bottle and smashed it into a corner. "Nobody cares anymore."

Vance found a fresh drink and virtually dismissed the terrified boy. In minutes he was drunk and dribbling, and a long hour later he was asleep.

Grief threatened to overwhelm Rafe, but anger held it at bay, or at least kept it contained. Perhaps shock was still shielding him from the reality of the moment, deadening what had happened. He shed more tears, held his head in his hands and tried to remember all the good times.

———

LATER, RAFE LEFT the room and found his way out from the maze-like building. People were lying in hallways, asleep or dead. Rats rooted around and under them, crocodile beetles sought moist holes, and the slew of protection charms drawn on the walls in faded blood displayed a desperate, superstitious hope in a magic faded into myth. Rafe was not used to seeing such signs and they stirred something unknown within him, a memory that had never happened. He traced one sigil with his finger, and the dried, crusted blood scratched his skin.

The stink of his uncle's room seemed to have percolated throughout the whole building. Either that, or every room stank.

Rafe wondered who the thief could be. There was Kosar, the worker in Trengborne, but they had never even spoken to each other. And surely he would have been killed along with everyone else.

He found his way out of the building. Weak sunlight greeted him and, though they were frightening and strange, he introduced himself to the afternoon streets of Pavisse.

———

HE HAD HEARD much about the town. Some of it was hearsay, rumor passed through the young community of Trengborne and propagated by their desires of what the big town could offer. Some was from his parents, usually accompanied by warnings never to go there. It was a useless place, they had said, marked only by crime and badness, in dire need of rescue. Rescue from what, they had never expanded upon, and neither had they explained their stern words of caution.

Rafe felt as if he was betraying his parents by even wandering the streets, but venting his grief in the presence of his drunken, frightening uncle felt worse. And it was such a strange and shocking place that curiosity got the better of him. Somewhere, perhaps that vague idea of help still existed . . . but it was a nebulous concept now, as distant as he felt.

Pavisse was a mining town first and foremost, and most of its inhabitants had something to do with working the ground. Groups of miners strode along the street, proudly wearing the unavoidable badges of their trade. Coal miners had leathery black skin and broad shoulders. They also bore scars and injuries from the many accidents and cave-ins underground: missing limbs; empty eye sockets; faces cleansed of anything approaching joy. Those who dug fledge had eyes yellowed from their constant proximity to the drug, and bald scalps, a side-effect of its use. They were tall and thin, willowy men and women who twisted and turned their way through the many fledge arteries that networked the underground. They stared at something far away—memories of better lives, perhaps—and to Rafe they looked like ghosts seeking somewhere to lie down in peace.

The miners had something else that set them apart, and it did not take long for Rafe to realize what it was. Three fledgers shoved him aside, walked on without giving him a second glance, and he knew then what he was seeing: total disregard for anyone other than fellow miners. Not just ignorance or aloofness; they could have been a different species.

Before long, Rafe became completely overawed by what he was seeing. In Trengborne, a simple farming village where the folks worked to live, and lived simply, there was little out of the ordinary. Rafe had seen a raid by tumblers when he was very young—he remembered them congregating around a fallen child, playing with him, toying with their prey before one of them rolled forward and pierced him with its barbs—and sometimes, in dreams, he thought he remembered a wraith. But other than that, nothing *extreme*. Here, the sights saturated his senses very quickly. Rafe's simple perception of things was soon drowned out by the excesses of Pavisse.

A man was lying in the road being kicked by three coal miners, their boots impacting with his head and stomach and groin, and yet all who passed averted their eyes. The victim looked like fodder— dregs of an ancient race once bred for food in Long Marrakash—and although Rafe had never before seen one of these sad creatures, he hid his fascination and walked on. Elsewhere, a naked woman sat in a rocking chair in a doorway with her legs wide open, beckoning men to sample her wares. One fledger stopped, did his business there and then, paid her and walked away. The woman put on her stock alluring smile once more, scanning the street, eyes glazed with bad wine and skin grayed by years of rhellim use. The display was horrific and sickening, and Rafe thought of the many rumors he'd heard from the young men in Trengborne. Naked women in the streets, they had said. It had sounded dreamlike. In reality, it was a nightmare.

He passed through a narrow byway and emerged into a huge square bounded on all sides by buildings four stories tall, all of them seemingly overflowing with people waving long scraps of colored cloth. They were relatively silent, although the strange sounds of grunting, feet scraping on stone and heavy breathing seemed to give a secretive whisper to the crowd. Every now and then the impact of wood upon stone or something softer inspired a groan. Rafe stood back for some time, unable to see past the knot of people standing before him. He stared up at the windows and balconies, trying to make out from their expressions what these people were watching. On a few faces he saw vague disinterest; on a few others, outright fascination; but generally they seemed excited and enraged at the same time. He'd seen similar expressions on the faces of the rhellim-fueled whores back in Trengborne, desperate for business but sometimes, when the militia were away, ignored and looked down upon.

He pushed his way through the crowd.

They had a tumbler in there. It was a big one, obviously well fed in this gladiatorial ring. The wooden pen had walls twice the height of a fledger, curved inward at the top, spiked with barbed metal prongs to prevent the tumbler from rolling out. Rafe had once heard that they reacted to sound, zoning in on playing children or couples courting in the long mountain grass. That explained the silent spectators.

There was a man in the enclosure with the tumbler. He was not really there to fight, but to stay alive. How long he could do so, and the inevitability of his eventual demise, was obviously the entertainment for this crowd.

The tumbler left an intermittent bloody track across the cleaned stone square as it rolled. Crushed into its plantlike hide was a second man, dead, pierced by the thing's many natural spikes and hooks. One arm flipped free as the tumbler rolled, thumping the stone in a rhythm that gave that silent place a grotesque heartbeat.

Rafe turned and pushed his way back through the crowd, ignoring the hostile stares and vague threats of violence. He tried to find his way back to his uncle's home, but the streets conspired to keep him to themselves, confusing him with corners where he was sure there had been none before, new buildings, strange views, hidden courtyards. The farther he went the more lost he became, and each way felt wrong. He looked for Uncle Vance just in case the big man had come out to search for him, but every face he saw was a stranger, and none of these strangers had any interest in him. In the end he curled up in a shadowy doorway and closed his eyes, shaking with fear, preferring to sink down into sleep peopled with calming memories of his parents than subject himself to more of what this place had to offer.

His poor, dead parents. How right they had been: Pavisse was fit only for madmen and wraiths. Eyes closed, Rafe tried to remember his way back to Trengborne, back to before things had gone so insanely wrong. But even though in his mind's eye he was there, everything was dark. He felt as though he were in a warm cave where the air was heavy and wet, and safety thrummed like his mother's heartbeat.

Someone touched his arm. Rafe opened his eyes. He groaned out loud.

The woman was short and stocky, and of some indefinable age. She had wild hair that formed a filthy halo around her head, strands twisted and pointing away from her skull in all directions as if seeking escape. Her eyes were a dark green, their whites speckled with the flush of broken veins. Her face was scored with swirling tattoos that started at the corners of her eyes, spiraled and multiplied across her cheeks—there were patterns there that he thought he should know—until their branches conjoined again to enter her mouth at both corners. Rafe was sure they continued inside, just as he was certain that those eyes saw everything.

It was the first time he had ever seen a witch.

"So what's a nice boy like you doing in Pavisse?" she asked.

"You should know."

"Me? Why me?" She shrugged and looked almost offended, but her green eyes were glinting with humor.

"I know a witch when I see one," Rafe said, "and witches know everything." He was trying to appear brave and knowledgeable, but he sounded like a child. Tears threatened and he swallowed them back. They burned.

The woman looked him up and down, licking her lips.

They eat people, Rafe remembered one of his friends saying, fear and fascination distorting his voice.

"Actually, I'm a lady," the woman said, "and I don't quite know everything. Almost, but not quite." She smiled, reached out quickly and grabbed Rafe's cock through his thick trousers, squeezing and twisting it slightly. "Never been dipped, that one. I can tell."

Rafe pushed her away and drew his legs up, trying to force himself back into the solid wooden door behind him. "Leave me alone!" he cried, sounding more frightened than ever.

The woman leaned back and laughed, stopped suddenly, then looked back down at Rafe. She staggered back two steps, her eyes so wide open that Rafe was sure they would tumble onto her cheeks. "Oh my sweet old heart!" she gasped.

This frightened Rafe more than having the old woman grab him. At least then he'd known what she was doing—touting for trade—whereas now, her sudden fearful reaction was even more disturbing. He scared her, that much was plain. Her mouth had dropped and the tattoos elongated across her cheeks, like extra screams to complement the one that seemed to be building within her.

"What?" Rafe asked, feeling a confidence building from nowhere. A group of fledgers passed by, their dull yellow eyes skitting across the scene as if he and this woman had always been here. From elsewhere a roar suddenly rose from the maze of buildings, alleys and courtyards, and he wondered whether the man had killed the tumbler, after all.

"Come with me!" the witch said, her voice shaking. She stepped forward as if to grab him again, but paused with her hand hovering inches from his shoulder. Her voice lowered. "Please. Come with me. I can hide you. I can *help* you."

"I don't need your help! Leave me alone, witch. Got a prong in your palm? I know that's how you do it, stick me and poison me—"

"That's for charlatans and those that betray the name," she hissed. "I fear you, but don't put me down for what I have to do. I am what I say, and I do what I do to survive. We all know there's no magic in anything now, don't we?" She stared at him for a few seconds, unmoving, seeming not to breathe as she awaited whatever answer he would give.

"So why help me? I have nothing. You can't screw me for tellans."

"Such language!" the old witch said, and for a brief instant Rafe heard his mother in her tone.

"Fuck," he said, and started to cry.

"Come with me," the witch said again, on the verge of panic now. She looked over her shoulder at a pair of coal miners who were loitering across the street. Rafe followed her gaze, wondering what they wanted, sure that they had not even noticed him and the witch. A horse clipped up the dusty road, slow and tired, and the man sitting astride it was hooded and slumped in the saddle.

Him, *him*! Rafe thought, but this man's robe was black, not red, and Rafe could see his face, the heavy gray beard that hung down over his chest and stomach.

The witch froze, seeming to sense Rafe's brief flush of fear.

"You've already seen a Red Monk?" she asked.

Rafe frowned, wincing at the sudden sharp memory. "The man wore red . . ."

"With me," she said. "Quickly now!"

"I have to find my uncle."

"We can do that later; right now you have to get off the street. Now! If you've seen one Monk and survived, there'll be more yet. Though *how* you survived . . . ?"

She was suddenly not threatening at all. Rafe had been scared of her at first—those tattoos, her grabbing his cock, the simple fact that someone in this sprawling, ugly town had noticed him—but now he heard his mother's tone in her worried words, sensed a level of concern outweighing any intent to hurt or abuse.

In a way, it felt as if she knew him.

"How do you know me?"

"I don't. But I know what you'll know and what you'll seek. I'm honored, boy, and amazed, and I think perhaps I'm only dreaming here. But for now no more, eh? Let's keep our lips sealed and our minds our own. Get off the street, get hidden, that's the priority for you right now. Follow me, keep quiet, and in a few minutes we'll be safe and we can talk. And listen. Only I guess *I'll* be doing the listening. I have been for all these years, watching and listening . . ."

"I don't—"

"Understand. Yes. Boy, what's your name?"

"Rafe Baburn."

"Pleased to meet you, Rafe. I'm a witch, as you rightly said, and a whore in with it too. My name's Hope. There's irony in that, because it's the name I took for myself years before I knew that's what I'd spend my life doing: hoping. Praying to the Black and the sleeping gods and the bloody shitting Mages if I had to that . . . well, we should go."

Rafe did not understand the witch's ramblings and he thought that perhaps she'd lost her mind. She showed no signs of rhellim usage, none of the side effects of fledge, and her breath smelled of old cabbage and bad meat, not alcohol. But she talked nonsense. A strange nonsense. A nonsense directed at him and *about* him. He missed his mother. He missed his father. And now this woman, this witch-whore called Hope, wanted to take him home.

"I'm very hungry," he said. "I haven't eaten since . . . since I saw my parents killed."

The sympathy that filled her eyes could not be faked. "Oh Rafe," she said. "Come with me. Then we can talk."

Hope grabbed Rafe's hand and pulled him quickly into the mouth of a narrow alley. And they entered another world.

———

IT WAS A city within the city. Rafe smelled it before seeing anything, wafts and hints of what was about to be revealed drawing them through the alley; the strong, mysterious tang he had sensed up on the hillside, and the vague aroma of old alcohol that he knew from Trengborne. But there were other smells here too, rich aromas that seemed to emanate from the moss-covered walls of the alleyway, strong and weak, sickly and dry, inviting and disgusting. He breathed in deeply and gagged on the stink of shit, and his next breath caused a stirring in his loins as rhellim fumes stroked his mind. Contradictions and confusions accompanied him as he followed Hope away from the bustle of the Pavisse he could just understand and into the hidden city he could not.

They turned the final corner of the alley. He should have expected something like this, he supposed. No varied raft of smells like that would come from a few vagrants sleeping rough beneath the skins of stolen furbats. But it still came as a shock when he saw the hundreds of people, the alley widening into a street, the chaos of a town that seemed so different from the one he had just left. Back there Pavisse was a rough place built well, a once-proud town turned sour after the Cataclysmic War had robbed it of magic. Here . . . it was newer, Rafe knew, but a place such as this did not thrive on hope. It lived off bitterness and crime, desperation and hate. It had been formed after the Cataclysmic War and was a product of it.

The street curved into the distance, passing beyond view maybe five hundred steps away. Some of the buildings may have been the rear facades of those he had just passed in Pavisse's main street, but back here they were deformed, half-collapsed, mutated by the additions and changes wrought by their strange inhabitants. A heavy machine formed part of one building, its use long since forgotten but its exposed innards curving up toward the sun, making room for a few tall, thin fledgers to lie back and chew their drug. The machine was rusted where it was metal, smoothed by time where it was stone, and there were bones too, the flesh of its biological parts long since rotted away and added back to the ground. The building had seemingly grown around it, and Rafe wondered what had been here first: machine or construction. Perhaps one had been to support the other, although Rafe could not now guess at which way this could have worked.

There were more machines, small and large, a few with obvious uses—those that had moved as transport, others that had probably once ploughed and planted in the fields—but most with purposes lost in the turbulent mists of time. They were all incorporated in some way, chopped and changed and altered as if those that had used them were frustrated at their lack of animation. The channels were there within these machines, the empty reservoirs and sacs and current routes that had given them the strange life they once lived, but they were dead. Dead as the sand beneath the dwellers' feet, dead as the air they exhaled, dead as the corpses Rafe saw in the gutter in one or two places. There was a fledger, his or her body twisted and ripped from whatever had killed it. There was also something else, something that must once have been fodder because of its size, exposed ribs torn back and knotted by the accelerated growth, slabs of flesh and muscle ripped from its wet corpse. As he watched, disgusted and terrified, a small lizard darted from a rent beneath one of the larger machines, buried its nose in the fodder and darted away again, dinner in its mouth.

The fodder shifted, turning its misshapen head and uttering a low, wretched groan.

"Mage shit!" Rafe exclaimed.

"Leave it be," Hope said, walking by without giving the pitiful thing a second glance.

Help, it hissed. Rafe looked down, but the fodder was not looking at him. Perhaps the sound of its plea had simply been air escaping its slashed neck.

"Leave it be!" Hope said again. She'd turned back to him now, conveying the same message within her stare. Rafe glanced around. A few people were watching him. A female fledger, bald, eyes yellow as a rancid wound, beckoned him over with one impossibly long finger. She was naked, and hung from a twist of metal and stone with one hand. Her body was speckled with soft black spots. It looked as if she were rotting from the inside.

"Fun, stranger?" she said. Her voice was strangely quiet, high, musical. Almost hypnotic. "Fun with me, stranger?"

"Not with you, no!" Hope said.

The fledger hissed and dropped from her perch, landing on the street wide-legged and crouched into a fighting stance.

"Paid you already, has he?" she hissed.

"He's with me, yes," Hope said. Rafe glanced sideways and saw that she had one hand inside her jacket. Furbat, he noticed, picking out a crazy detail in this loaded moment. Furbat jacket, so old that the leather was denuded of all fur, shiny with age, darkened with sweat and rain and who knew what else. This jacket had seen its fair share of years and places. How much of this had been upon Hope's shoulders, and how much on other peoples'?

The fledger hopped a few steps closer like a jumping spider. Rafe could smell her. Rank, rotten and sad.

"Fledge, young one, stranger, a bit of fledge with my legs around your face, you've never eaten so well!" She thrust her groin forward and displayed the hairless crack there, like a jagged slit in the earth.

Rafe could not help looking down. There were speckles of fledge across her pale yellow thighs, a mustardy trace that hinted at more drug within.

"I won't warn you again," Hope said. Something in her voice brought a moment of silence, a period of nervous calm. But there were others watching now—fledgers, coal miners, people who simply had nothing else to do—and the fledger did not wish to lose face.

"Screw you, witch!" she said.

Hope brought her hand out from her pocket. Even before she opened her fist Rafe saw the fledger's eyes widen with fear. The others backed away as well, suddenly having more urgent things to attend to. There was real terror here, Rafe saw, a rich reverence the fledger must have held for Hope from the first moment. But the confrontation was all about face and respect, and once begun, her pitch had to be carried through, one way or another.

Hope held a handful of spiders. One was green, another bright orange, the third black. All of them were fat and fast. She lobbed them at the fledger and muttered something under her breath, and then she walked quickly away.

The fledger leapt onto the uneven wall and pulled herself up, grasping at uncertain handholds and rusted projections before she disappeared up and over onto the rooftop, moving like the spiders she fled. The orange arachnid followed her up, while the other two went in opposite directions along the base of the building as if to outflank her.

The fledger screamed all the way.

"What was that?" Rafe asked quietly. They were walking quickly now, the screams of the fleeing fledger echoing from above. A small smile perked the corners of Hope's mouth. "Those spiders, Hope. What were they? They were following her."

"Of course they weren't," Hope said. "They were only wood spiders. I colored them myself. I always carry a couple in a skin-sac in my pocket, just in case. Often come in handy."

"But why . . . ? What do they know? The fledgers, the people?"

"They know that I'm a witch. That's enough. I'm a witch, I throw spiders at them, they're going to run."

"No spells? No magic?"

Hope paused and glanced back along the street. Like a stone thrown into a pond, the ripples of their passing had already settled back to nothing. The street's life had returned to normal, and if she was still screaming, the fledger was now far too distant to hear.

"No spells," Hope said. "No magic. Because magic has gone. You know that as much as anyone." She stared into his eyes. "Maybe more."

"But . . . I thought witches . . ."

Hope smiled sadly and shook her head. "Not even witches, farmer boy." The tattoos on her skin seemed to stretch to make her smile more solid. And even though her comment sounded dismissive, Rafe heard more respect in her voice than he'd heard for a long, long time. Respect, and perhaps fear.

They continued through the streets, the warrenlike maze of alleys and roads and courtyards, all of them that much wilder than the greater part of Pavisse, that much more downtrodden. Yet the life here seemed faster and more intense, as if this part of the city was reveling in the fact that it was hidden within the greater whole. There was drinking and fighting and fucking in the streets. Bodies too, victims of drunken brawls or robbery or dark, seedy revenge. A couple of the dead were covered with ragged blankets as if to hide their wounds from sight, but each corpse was being slowly eaten. Rats, lizards, wild dogs, carrion snakes as wide as Rafe's arm and four times as long, all of them emerging from beneath the buildings or out of the ground, snatching their fill and then disappearing again. Rafe wondered what must exist beneath the streets to give birth to such a variety of wildlife, all of it fattened on carrion. He paused, kicked away sand and stones from around his feet until he found solid ground beneath.

Words stared back up at him, a language far away in time or place. Symbols and letters combined, all of them mysterious, and none of them for him. He imagined these words spoken as the strange whispers he had heard in his head, and the idea seemed to fit.

"Hope," he said. She paused and turned. "What's this?"

She glanced down at his feet and kicked sand back across the carved stone. "History," she said, turning away again.

More to ask later, Rafe thought. There were more things to life than he could have imagined, more than his parents had ever told him, and he felt small and alone in this place. All eyes seemed to be staring at him, and back here in the streets behind streets they mostly belonged to people he had no desire to mix with. Fledgers stared with yellow eyes, coal miners shoved him aside without even noticing, other people mingled and argued and occasionally fought. And the buildings themselves were equally as threatening. One tall stone block, drilled with toothed windows, was spiked with long obsidian prongs, thrusting out into the street and up at the sliver of sky. Parts of an unknown machine maybe, or more likely adornments, a few of the spikes held sticky remnants. Black birds darted down and alighted on the spikes, picking at the mess, screeching as they took off again and flew straight back up. Even they seemed afraid to land for too long.

Hope turned right into a narrow, uneven doorway, and glanced back at Rafe. "We have to go in here," she said, nodding with her head. "I've been through here before. It's safe."

Rafe looked into the doorway. The entire inside of this building was a machine, vast and old. Hope was hunching down and entering a veined hole that looked like a giant's intestine, hollowed out by time, contents gone away to dust. Rafe stepped forward and watched her worm her way in, and he caught a brief but potent whiff of old dry rot. He stepped back again and bumped into someone, receiving an elbow in the ribs for his trouble. The face of the building bulged out above him. The machine—whatever it was, whatever strange task it had been built to perform—hung over him as if ready to tumble at any moment. Its outside was ridged and bumped with projections weathered smooth over the decades, metal edges rusted, stone creases worn.

"Come on," Hope said. "It's not far." And then she crawled into shadow.

Rafe followed. It was that or remain where he was, lost, so far from his uncle Vance that he would surely never find his way back.

They passed through the machine. It was dark and heavy. Rafe felt the thing pressing down at him, like a huge presence paused with its foot held ready to stomp.

On the other side there was another, narrower street, the faces of buildings so close that Rafe could almost stretch out both arms and touch them. People shoved by to and fro, some of them eyeing him suspiciously, others ignoring him. He could see addiction in their eyes: alcohol; fledge; rhellim. And there were other forms of abuse going on here of which Rafe had no knowledge. One man held a fleshy bag in front of his mouth, breathing in and out quickly as his eyes rolled up in his skull and his face seemed to darken. A woman sat cross-legged in a window above the street, sighing as a swarm of insects drew blood from self-inflicted gashes across her shoulders and neck. He had never imagined any of this. He was a farm boy, just like Hope had said, and the more he saw the more nervous he became.

"Hope," he said, and the witch turned to look at him. She must have seen the panic in his eyes because she put a hand on his shoulder and smiled. Her tattoos smiled with her, and Rafe felt calmer.

"We're nearly there," Hope said. "My place. We can sit and eat and talk. I want to know what happened to you, and I think . . . I think I may have some things to tell you."

"About what?"

"About why you're here."

"My parents were killed," he said. He expected to see the flash of a red robe at any moment. But they were ignored, just another couple of unknowns in this refuge for the unknown. "That's why I'm here."

"No," Hope whispered, "I think you know they weren't your real parents. And you being here is fate." She smiled, held his hand and led the way.

Chapter 5

THE MINES WERE rich on the day Trey Barossa left. The seam of fledge was wide, the mood among the miners high, the song at the end of the dig vibrant. On his food break Trey had sat back, chewed a fistful of fledge and drifted, penetrated the earth, moved through a mile of rock to flit against Sonda Susard's mind, and there he had sensed an interest. He was a part of her thoughts, and he liked that. He hoped that given time she would cast her mind back and see what he thought of her.

Wending their way through the shafts toward home, songs echoing back in carefully judged harmonies, it could have always been like this. There had never been machines to help them mine. There had never been machines to take fledge up to the surface. Things, Trey could have believed, had been like this forever.

Trey followed along near the rear of the line. The song echoed back to him, each echo intricately timed with allowance for tunnel travel and multiple reverberation from the mine walls, so that every miner heard a slightly different song. In the pitch black he could feel the sound waves impacting his skin, stirring the fine hairs on his face and around his ears. He added his own few words where appropriate and heard them blending with the whole, being swallowed and modified and expanded by echoes already living along the tunnel tonight. The song left the group and found its own routes back to the fledge face they had recently left. Sometimes it would remain there and fade into the earth itself, enriching it. Other times it would escape into a crack or vent too fine for any of the miners to work their way through, and on occasion a song would be heard ages away in another part of the mine, hours or days after its original singing. It was not magic, this strange transference, though irresponsible parents often told children that lie. It was simply one of the strange ways of the mine. It was easy to get lost down here.

Trey held out his arms as he walked, trailing his fingers along the rock walls when he came close enough. There would be some subdued light back in their homes, but mostly they worked and lived in total darkness. They had been excavating the current fledge vein for a thousand shifts now, and any one of them could have found his or her way back to the home-cave with nothing to guide their way. Every day after their shift there were signs: the scents of cooking, strength and direction drawing them on; the gentle hum of occupation, a background noise made of the bleat of goats, the muttering of people, the pounding feet of larking children. And the home-cave itself exuded a gravity, something apart from the senses that also gave out its own strong signal. Down here in the mines, death was always close by. Safety, and family, were strong draws.

So he touched the walls of the old tunnel, marveling that everyone who had worked on this particular stretch was now long dead and gone. He felt individual pick marks in the rock, and made out signature impacts: here, a left-handed miner had made his mark; there, someone right-handed; here, someone who had used their pick sideways instead of straight up and down. There were more definite signatures too, and Trey recognized one or two carved names from the countless other times he had run his fingers along these walls. He wondered at the history behind them, who they had been, whether any of them had ever gone topside. These tunnels held history in their rocky embrace, more ancient the nearer they came to the home-cave.

As usual, when they came to the suddenly smoothed seam in the rock that marked the time when machines had been at work, Trey took his hands away.

The songs died down as the miners walked through these machine-excavated tunnels. The routes had been made more than three hundred years before, when many things had been different. The echoes of their footfalls told Trey that there were occasional hollow pockets in the tunnel walls; evidence that fledge had been taken out. He wondered what dreams that fledge had given, and to whom. One of the men up ahead stumbled to his knees. Others helped him up, and they completed the journey in silence.

As ever, they were glad to reach the home-cave. Lights guided their way for the last thousand steps, a weak glow to begin with, brightening as home came closer. It gave their eyes time to become accustomed to the illumination, although they would still squint for a while yet, so used were they to complete darkness. None of the miners or their families really needed the light, but it was tradition to light the home-cave. They were human, after all. Fire gave them safety.

Trey looked around for Sonda, but she was nowhere to be seen.

Machines and magic had carved out this huge cavern. Miners had remained living and working here since the Cataclysmic War, and so over time they had made the place totally their own. Walls were hidden or remodeled by hand, the cavern expanded or altered to suit new homes, fresh caves dug into the extremities, walkways and ladders added to connect one area with another. There were even those parents who told their children that their ancestors had made this place, giving no mention at all to machines. Trey felt uncomfortable with this; however terrible the past was, it was set in stone and should be remembered. Altering history for a child's sake was establishing life on a lie. Where would it go from there? When he found a partner and had a child, he fully intended on taking it to view the Beast. This old, dead machine, monstrous and haunting in its continuing state of decay, sat at the base of a deep pit two days' travel through the mines. It had been sinking a new shaft at the time of the Cataclysmic War—it was still rumored that it had found the richest vein of fledge ever—and when magic withdrew it had died and remained there ever since. Almost everyone knew where it was, but nowadays few had any desire to view it.

He remembered his father taking him to see the Beast, through old tunnels and workings where people had not labored for generations. The silence down there, the loneliness. The awe he had felt upon first seeing the dead machine, then fear, and then after a time, the pity.

Eyes stinging from firelight, Trey set off down the main street. He knew virtually everyone here by smell and sight, and he nodded to those who he sometimes conversed with, relishing the fact that they could see him. After a long shift, most miners were silent for a time after returning home. The power of sight gave them a rest from talking.

He was looking forward to a long dust bath. He had a fist of fresh fledge in his rucksack, and he would lie back and gnaw on that, letting the drug settle him and open his mind. As usual he would seek Sonda, try to make out what she was thinking and doing at that moment. And perhaps yet again he would try to communicate what he would like to be doing with her in his dust bath. He saw her sometimes, they talked, and if she had touched on his guilty thoughts she did not show it.

Trey made a quick visit to a water bar, where the first drink was always free for a returning miner. He gulped down the cup of fresh water, closing his eyes as its coolness washed dust from his throat and brought his insides alive. There were others there whom he had spent the long shift working alongside, but they had little to say to one another now, so he gave a nod and left. Some of them would remain there for a while yet, moving on from the water to some of the insipid rotwine that was brought down from the surface. His father had died from this stuff—it had eaten his insides, his mother told him, and twisted his mind—so Trey hated the very thought of it. And yet, talking to some of the older miners, he sensed something vastly alluring in its murky depths. They told him that it gave an escape that fledge never could. Fledge enhanced, it did not stultify. Maybe he was too young to realize just why this was an attractive proposition.

Back on the main street a puppet master was performing for a group of children. Trey knew Lufero, an old miner who had lost both legs in a cave-in decades ago, as did all of the children in the home-cave. His puppet shows were a constant on the main street when the fires were lit, and his clumsy magic tricks—wide sleeves and deep pockets shouting the truth—made him a popular entertainment. And later, when children grew up, they saw fresh truths in his shows, serious statements hidden away behind childish displays. His metal puppets, most of them made from parts of small machines he had cannibalized from the mines, always played themselves, great thundering things that ruled over his long bony finger puppets. Through the slapstick and humor and laughs for the children, every play ended on a melancholic note with the machines grinding to a halt. Lufero would sit still for a while, his finger puppets staring at the dead machines as if willing them to move again, and the children would leave, thinking that the play was over. But Lufero would remain there, his face sad, his eyes confused. And sometimes it took a long time for this part of his play to end.

"Lufero," Trey said. The old man looked up and nodded, smiled. Then he returned quickly to the show, not wishing to disappoint the group of children sitting on the dust floor of the street. No machine-puppets today. That was unusual for Lufero. Instead he held one hand of long finger puppets, and his other hand was hidden down below the cloth-covered table.

"They dug and they dug," the puppet master said, each of his long fingers taking on a life of their own. His yellow eyes glanced up at the children, and his smile touched them. "They brought out the fledge in great bundles, rolling them up and setting them aside for the riser to take them topside for trade. And Petra, the young miner who thought he knew so much more than his more-experienced friends, kept digging and digging and digging, even after the others had stopped and sat down for their food break." Lufero's fingers laid down and relaxed, but his thumb kept on working at the rock he'd lifted onto the table. "He scraped and he picked and he prised, and soon he found a narrow crevasse, just wide enough to take his small body. He willowed in, as all miners do, using his long feet and big hands to steer the way, and all the while he was thinking, 'I'll get the best, I'll get the biggest, I'll find what the Beast was looking for the day it died.'"

"I'm frightened!" a little girl said.

Lufero glanced up. "Good," he said. "You should be. Because Petra should have been frightened too, instead of stupid. He didn't listen to what he was told, you see, by those who knew better. He didn't realize that behind every comment given by his elders was a whole host of knowledge, a history of reasons and a wealth of caution. 'Don't dig past your time,' he'd been told, and the miners who told him that knew only too well of the dangers."

Trey knew what was coming because he'd seen this play several times before. First when he was a child, and it had given him nightmares. Again when he was a teenager, when it had made him ask questions. And a couple of years ago, as a young miner back from his first shift. After the stories he had heard during that long first day, nothing could have scared him more.

The puppet master started working his puppets again, keeping the other hand ready behind his back.

"But Petra didn't listen. He thought he knew better. He wasn't a bad boy, and there's the tragedy. But he did think that he could change things, when we all know that change is something gradual that none of us can steer. We miners change—we grow taller, our limbs longer—but it's something that the land controls and gives us, even after magic has been taken away. We're all part of the language of the land. Petra did not believe this." Lufero grew quiet for a few moments, his thumb still working at the rock, the other fingers on his hand stirring now as the puppet-miners rose from their food break.

"What happened?" said one of the children.

Lufero glanced up at his young audience, looking over their heads and along the main street to where it ended against a rock wall. "Petra woke the Nax," he said.

Even though he knew what was about to happen, Trey still jumped when the old miner brought his hand out from behind his back. His pale fingers were painted bloodred. He clawed his hand at the pitiful finger puppets, clasping, letting go, clasping again like a spider hugging its prey. His long nails slashed, tracing red lines across the puppets' intricately painted faces and chests. In the flurry of movement, blood splashed onto the cloth-covered table. Trey had never been able to tell whether it was real or not.

Some of the children screamed. Two of them stood and ran away, their parents casting scolding glares Lufero's way when they emerged from shops or food caves. A few of the braver children watched wide-eyed as Lufero's bloody play drew to a close. The finger puppets lay down one by one as the ravenous Nax continued to whirl and slash at them like a tornado of disc-swords. And finally, a few quiet moments after the Nax had slunk away behind Lufero's back, Petra emerged once again from behind the rock to survey what he had done.

The children left, some of them clapping as they walked away. Trey stood back, watching Lufero. The old man seemed to be asleep, but then his thumb moved again slightly, Petra casting his gaze across the destruction he had unwittingly brought down upon his folk.

"I always thought Petra should have died," Trey said.

Lufero looked up, startled. "He did," the old man said. "Nothing escapes a fledge demon once it's woken."

"We've not heard of one for years. Maybe they've gone. Maybe they're used to us now and they've gone deeper, down into veins we'll never mine. Down past the Beast."

"The Nax sleep," Lufero said. "They don't run. No, they're still there. Hibernating in the fledge, dreaming whatever it is they dream for years and years on end. It's just that mining's such a slow process now. And if a band of miners working in the Pavisse range or the Widow's Peaks ever did encounter one, you think we'd hear about it? Not anymore. People don't talk anymore."

Trey dug into his rucksack and brought out a lump of bright yellow fledge. "Here," he said. "It's fresh."

Lufero smiled and accepted the drug. He closed his eyes and rolled it beneath his nose, and in his smile Trey saw a thousand precious memories.

He walked on, left the main street and climbed a series of rock terraces and steps to his cave. His mother had lit a small fire at the entrance, and she was cooking a stew of cave rat and blind spider. A pinch of Trey's fresh fledge would make it exquisite.

———

AFTER DINNER HE went to the back of the cave and slid into the dust bath. The dust was so fine and light that it slipped around his body like oil, its inherent warmth soothing Trey's tired muscles. A little firelight found its way back here, and Trey enjoyed watching it flit across the walls like lost insects. He imagined that it was performing its own play for him, and as he drifted away he made up stories to follow the dim light's movements.

His mouth was sweet and sensitive from the fist of fledge he had chewed as part of the meal. His mother had taken some too, and she had fallen asleep soon after. She was old now, and she rarely made any effort with the fledge. It must haunt her dreams, but there was nowhere specific she wanted it to take her. Trey pitied her sometimes, and other times he was jealous. His own life seemed so meaningful that he wondered what it would be like to not care anymore.

The fresh fledge was so much purer and more powerful than anything sold or used topside; it faded as it rose, and sunlight drove it stale. Some young fledgers did try to make it on the surface, offering to sell their talents to the highest bidder, but their sight would soon fade away. And as fledge lost its effect, so the fledgers' talent to use it dwindled. It was as if the sun was so alien to them that it treated them the same as their drug, and they all became just another top-sider waiting for death.

Trey had never been tempted to the surface by false dreams of power or status. His home was the underground. And he loved his fledge fresh. It passed from his stomach straight into his bloodstream, thinned the blood and drove it faster, speeding his heart, finding his organs and massaging them with its benevolent touch. Plunging into his heart and out again, the drug surrounded the goodness in his blood and made itself a part of it, riding directly into Trey's brain, where, like something almost sentient, it settled itself onto and into everything that made Trey what he was. It played with his memories, aggravated his desires, stirred his emotions, and with a slight effort of control Trey reined in the power of his mind and rode it like a horse. Trey's mind—young and energetic, yet old enough to know some of itself—was the perfect age to lord over the fledge's influence. A fledge journey was more than memory and less than experience, a realm hanging somewhere between dream and recollection, knowledge and foresight. And because of that, it was precious.

His mind floated. It remained with his body for a while, reveling in the intimate touch of the dust bath, imagining Sonda there with him, having her wrap her naked legs around him and clasp him secretly beneath the dust. Soon tiring of the pretence, Trey went in search of the true Sonda. His mind was lighter than memory and richer than fantasy as it drifted from his home-cave. It took effort—concentration, will, his physical self tensing and straining in the stone enclosure of the dust bath—but it brought results that were more than worth the effort. Out of the cave, into the space of the home-cave, Trey could look down and see the place that had always been his home. The main street was cut into the floor of the cavern, caves leading off from either side, a wide public area built up with decorated stalagmites which could be made to glow if just the right heat was applied. They used this area for their celebrations and rituals, weddings and funerals, and it was known to everyone as the Church. Either side of the main street were the dwellings, built around and into the five giant pillars that had been left in place to support the cavern roof. Higher up these great pillars were platforms and small caves, homes to the five mayors who took joint control of the home-cave. Trey soared and circled one of the pillars, glancing through the entrance at one of these homes. He could not probe inside, which meant that this mayor was shielding his dwelling from prying minds. He turned away and drifted toward the opposite side of the cave, taking long moments to do so. The cavern was huge. It took three thousand steps to traverse it, and even a mind wandering on fledge took time.

He briefly touched on the mind of a blind spider that had its home in a crack in the cavern ceiling, a chilling, alien encounter that bore no words or explanation. For that instant his sense changed, his perception altered so radically that it denied translation, and back in his dust bath Trey cried out. He withdrew quickly, disturbed but equally thrilled by this surreal experience.

Past another pillar, past the expanse of cave moss and fungi that gave food, dipping down to where the river rushed by way below the home-cave and carried its detritus and waste away, Trey drifted aimlessly by the many homes carved into the rock extremes of the cavern. A few of these caves were natural, but most had been excavated over the several generations since the Cataclysmic War. Many were ongoing efforts, expanding all the time as families grew and caves were passed down from father to son, mother to daughter. He dove into the misted spray that rose from the river below, trying to clear his memory of the spider mind, and back in the dust bath his body prickled with cold.

Trey knew exactly where to find Sonda.

Her family cave was dark, but that did not mean that she was absent. Her father was a miner and her mother worked in one of the food caves along the main street. Sonda herself was training to become a topside runner, the small group of mining folk who spent their lives traveling back and forth from the home-cave to the surface to trade fledge for essential supplies. Runners were those most likely to try to make their way topside, and few grew old in the caves. Sometimes Trey mourned Sonda's leaving already.

For a moment images blurred and fought in his mind. He drew back slightly, becoming more aware of his own body back in the dust bath, the sound of his mother's snoring, and as he opened his eyes he saw the weak firelight still prancing across the rock ceiling. He could even taste fledge in his mouth, instead of the cavern's fresh open air. Or perhaps it was guilt.

He closed his eyes again and concentrated, moving himself back to Sonda's cave, hearing her soft song from within, smelling the rich tang of the river sweeping past way below his feet. He remained there for a while, a strong consciousness cast across the space of the cavern, the tinge of guilt he felt at spying more than counteracted by what he was beginning to feel for Sonda. This journey was innocent, the pure necessity of a burgeoning first love. He was not trying to see the future, he was not spying on the girl as she changed or bathed or slept. He hardly even probed inside the house.

And then her singing stopped, and Trey knew that she was dreaming a fledge dream. If only she would ride the dream and come to meet him out here.

He moved away and slipped down one of the many shafts that led to the river. Like the tunnel he traveled every day to the fledge face, this river held history and the future in its grasp. The miners buried their dead here, dropping them into the water and letting them ride the river forever. And they drew water from here as well, catching the future before it hurtled past and lost itself deep beneath the mountains. The future was upriver, the past downriver, and this one moment beneath Trey was the most important of all. The river was all noise, a mind-shattering roar which, broken down, could be saying anything. He cast his consciousness down, tempted to plunge in and see where the waters would take him. Many had done so, and some came back mad.

Trey returned up the black shaft and burst out into the light of the cavern again, veering away and entering one of the old fledge tunnels. This shaft was not worked anymore, not because the fledge had all been mined, but because it had become too dangerous. It was here that Lufero the puppet master had lost his legs many years before, and others had lost more than that here more recently. Cave-ins, a flash flood and a plague of stingers had caused them to abandon this tunnel, leaving it to the dark and whatever eventually crawled in there, out of sight and mind.

Trey liked to travel through here on occasion, his body safe at home while his imagination sought whatever had driven his elders away. He was not the only one; he occasionally brushed past other minds steering this way, but like them he kept to himself. It was not exactly forbidden, what they were doing. But it would be frowned upon by the mayors. This was not a safe place. It had been abandoned for a reason. Many reasons, in fact; most of them told, some of them still held on to by the old miners that had worked this seam. Secrets. Trey knew that the whole truth had never been revealed, and like most people his age, the mystery intrigued him.

Like Petra in Lufero's puppet play, Trey pushed on.

The shaft was long, winding, and soon it dipped and ran deep. There were several vertical shafts in the floor where machines had once toiled, and newer steps and staircases carved into the tunnels by hand since the Cataclysmic War. Trey had once started down one of these pits, trying to push his consciousness deep, smelling and sensing his way down, way past the river level and into a darkness so thick that it seemed to have weight. He had gone too far, he'd known that even as he pushed, and his body had stiffened and cooled in his cave as his mind plummeted. That shaft had no bottom, and its depth had a gravity. The air held hints of strange things far below, and the turning point had been the touching of an alien mind on his. Only briefly, barely a kiss of consciousness, like something turning its head and its hair swinging out to touch his face.

That had been enough. Trey had somehow hauled himself back, and he'd been sick for the three shifts following.

So now he kept to the tunnels and the mine workings themselves, leaving the old shafts to whatever it was that haunted them. He had asked his mother whether the machines could have become ghosts, but she had scoffed and stormed away, cursing his foolishness.

He traveled until he found the old fledge seam. Even after so long he could sense the toil of the miners that had carved their way this far. It was a wide seam, rich, and Trey guessed that it continued on and on beneath the mountains. Its surface smelled rancid after such a long exposure, but he pushed inside just a little and it was fresh and fruitful, good fledge, free of impurities. A pity that this seam had been left alone. A pity that stingers had come and scared them away, and cave-ins, and . . .

What else? He pushed farther, because there was something in there. Something denser than fledge. Trey stilled, his body tense and tight in the dust bath, his consciousness holding a moment five thousand steps away. He waited because it seemed the right thing to do, to hold back and make himself quiet and unseen, because something was about to happen. He had stumbled across a held breath.

Trey felt his heartbeat rippling the surface of the dust bath. His mind was submerged in fledge, and borne of it. And he was suddenly very, very afraid.

A heartbeat amongst his, deeper, slower, harder, trying to hide between his own but failing because he had been listening for it.

A heartbeat . . . something alive in the fledge . . . alive but sleeping, hibernating, because his heart beat a hundred times before he heard another strange pulse.

Nax?

He tried to pull back. He wanted more than anything to wake in the bath, his mind his own, and to tell his mother about the fledge nightmare he'd had. But this was no nightmare, and Trey could not pull back. Because he had already brushed against this Nax's mind, and his frantic thought of escape was merely a vain attempt to avoid what was coming.

It came in quickly:

Threat from above, safety being slaughtered, magic returned to shift the balance of things, death and war and change that would seep down even this far, through the cracks in riverbeds and past the roots of the oldest trees down through the earth the danger given an easy route via the holes gutted into the world by those who still plundered . . .

And more, much more, none of it in words, all of it in hateful alien expressions of such contempt that Trey, physically ensconced in his dust bath as if that could possibly keep him safe, began to cry.

Eventually he pulled free, or was let go. Flailing, horrified, venting psychic screams that echoed before him and gave many home-cave sleepers instant nightmares, Trey fled back to his own body. As he did so he sensed other minds waking through the earth, some near, some farther away. Minds angry not at him, but at what the future promised.

He flipped from the dust bath and hit the stone floor hard, bruising his limbs and shoulders, running through his cave naked, tripping over his sleeping mother and gashing his elbows open on the ground, giving premature blood to the land. He rose again and tore aside the leather curtain at the cave's entrance.

"They're awake!" he screamed. "The Nax are awake!" He could see shadows of people moving to and fro on the main street, and he imagined the puppet master's red-painted hand clenching and cutting, taking them all down.

There was an outburst of screaming from all across the cavern. Other fledge dreamers were traveling too far this night.

———

THE FIRST NAX came from the same tunnel Trey had fled in his fugue.

The Nax were also known as fledge demons. No one had ever seen one and lived. Most had an idea of what they were — myths, stories, legends handed down from generation to generation, drawings in books, ancient cave paintings that smeared some of the rock walls of the home-cave Church — but as well as sometimes being exaggerated with time, the truth can also be diluted. Most people had no idea what they were about to face.

Heads turned as the shadow burst from darkness into weak firelight. It flew across the cavern and landed at the base of one of the five giant pillars. And then it started to kill.

Trey fell to his knees and screamed. His mother shouted in her sleep, sounding as if she was being choked. Other cries rose up across the cavern, high-pitched and androgynous with terror. Because as well as the sight it presented its victims — wings spread, various limbs tipped with spinning bone-clawed appendages, openings that may have been mouths steaming and spitting gobs of flaming gas — the Nax gave them so much more. Its mind reached out as well, probing with alien fingers, seeming to touch everyone in the cavern. And it was like eating shit.

Trey pressed his hands to his ears, screamed, shook his head, trying to drown out the feeling that he was being invaded, his senses turned in on themselves, twisted and forced and split apart. He saw the slaughter that had begun below, people spinning and coming apart as the Nax danced across the uneven ground, limbs slapping at the air just as Lufero had shown in his play. Coughs of fire leapt from its mouths and wrapped around heads, stomachs, bounced along the ground until they found something to burn. People ran but few escaped; the Nax was too fast. It could run, it could fly, it could whip out its long tail and haul the escapees back into range of its killing limbs. They saw all this, but there were also images that could only have been seen through the Nax's eyes. And with those images came outlandish glee. There was the smell too, the burning of flesh and spilled blood as Trey's friends died before him. He retched, and his stomach rumbled with hateful hunger. Screams of pain and terror drove him mad. He tried to cry out again but he seemed to roar instead, a fledge-filled scream of fury and pent-up hunger that was echoed around the cavern by a thousand other voices, each once unwilling and yet reveling in its new freedom. The Nax was sharing itself with its victims before it killed them. A creature of the drug, its casting of its own consciousness was part of its makeup, a facet of the hunt.

Trey fell back and crawled into the cave on his hands and knees. "We have to go!" he said to his mother.

"We can't leave," she said, shaking her head, trying to shed the alien images. "We'll fight, there are plenty of us, we'll have to—"

"Mother, I sensed it, I felt it waking. There were more than one. Something woke them. I think something's happening topside, and it angered them and drew them out of hibernation. Mother, we have to leave! We'll go topside, somehow. Whatever, we have to get out of the cavern."

"The mayors will know what to do," Trey's mother said with blind, humbling faith. But then she glanced over his shoulder, and he knew what she was seeing without turning around, because the image was shared between them all. A second Nax burst from another tunnel and powered straight into one of the pillar dwellings. Trey felt the walls and balconies of that place splintering, and he knew the weak flesh of the mayor was parting beneath the onslaught of the spinning and ripping limbs.

"Come with me," he said. "Ignore everything you sense, just keep one thing in your mind: escape."

"I have to get some things," she said, and she turned slowly, dazed, confused. Trey grabbed her arm and squeezed hard.

"Mother. *Please*. These are Nax! We can't waste any time, if there's a slightest chance of escape we have to take it *now!*"

His mother winced and glanced down at where he was squeezing her arm. He had never hurt her before, not physically, not emotionally. She was strong. When she looked up there was a tear in her eye. "Oh Trey, I'm so scared."

Trey hugged his mother, but only briefly. He could not be close to her with these images, these smells riding the psychic waves from outside. He felt corrupted.

He dressed quickly, then nudged aside the curtain and looked out. Many of the smaller cave fires had already been extinguished—the miners' natural state was darkness, and that was where they found most safety—but new conflagrations were being seeded across the home-cave by the Nax. The hateful images and sensations were confused now, and Trey could not tell if there were still only two Nax down there, or more. People were running, screaming, whispering and trying to steal away. Some passed his cave and headed down the steps. Trey called after them, but they did not hear. He ducked back inside, breathing hard, not knowing what to do.

"Can we get out?" his mother asked. "Is there a way?"

Plenty of ways, Trey knew, but none of them sure. None of them safe. And what about Sonda? He'd looked across to her side of the cavern but there had been only darkness. That could be a good sign, because it may mean the Nax had not visited there yet. Or perhaps it meant that they had been, and finished.

"We'll have to get through the tunnels to the rising," Trey said. "There's an old seam, one that was mined way before the Cataclysmic War, that gives a route between the face we're working on now and a tunnel leading straight there. It's never used, it's too narrow, too awkward. Barely a crawl space at times. If we can get there, get through, maybe we can make it up. If the Nax haven't been there as well."

Trey's mother looked sad. "I can't do all that, Trey. Look at me."

Trey looked. His mother was big around the waist, even though their mining caste erred toward tall and thin. Her hands, on the coldest parts of the year when fires merely drew in colder air from deeper caves, were crippled into twisted claws. And she was old. She had been down here forever, with only a few visits topside to break up her underground existence. These visits, legendary in her eyes and related whenever she had the opportunity, had all been made safely, and via the proper routes.

But he loved her. He took her for granted and sometimes she annoyed him, *always* here for him. "I will not leave you behind. I don't know much about the Nax—I don't think anyone does, only what's told in legend—but I do know that this is the most dangerous place to be. We can't stay. Maybe if we can just get into the tunnels and hide, it'll all be over soon."

He knew that was a lie. And he thought his mother did too as she nodded, stepped past him and peered out into the cave. There were more screams out there from farther away, closer to the dark holes that plummeted to the underground river. There was also the occasional twang of a crossbow being fired, and here and there Trey saw the glint of steel as disc-swords were unsheathed. He turned quickly and ran to the rear of the cave, grabbing his own disc-sword from beneath his bed. If he came close enough to a Nax to use it he would probably be dead already, but there were other things out there. If they made it into the tunnels there may be stingers in the old fledge seam, hiding away from the miners. Past them, if Chartise and his mules were still alive, perhaps there was topside, the world of sunlight and moonlight and starlight, the world of no darkness. And there probably dwelled countless dangers of which he had never dreamed.

Trey was a miner no longer.

If he lived past the next few hours, he would be a survivor.

———

THEY WORKED THEIR way down the series of steps and balconies carved into the walls of the cavern. They hid behind huge pots on the landings, breathing in the meaty fumes of moss and trying to figure, from the ghastly psychic twinges they felt in sight or sound or taste, just where the Nax were unleashing their slaughter. Trey touched the ball of moss before him and squeezed, reveling as ever in the feel of this cold growing thing, pleased that his own sensation was covering those exuded by the murderous Nax.

He sensed a held breath, a diversion of frenzied attention away from one place to another, and he remembered that he still had fresh fledge in his system. He cursed himself silently and removed his hand, thinking *Fuck you* as he grasped his mother's hand and led her down another uneven flight of steps. He'd tried to sling the disc-sword across his shoulders, but he was unused to carrying the weapon and the knot kept slipping. Unsheathing it gave him an unreasonable sense of power as the metal sang against the old dried leather.

"What is it?" his mother whispered. Trey turned and placed his finger across his mouth. *Shhh.*

When they reached the cavern floor they met a group of people milling around the mayors' militia cave. The militiamen were nowhere to be seen—Trey suspected that the crossbow shots he'd heard earlier marked their fate—but still these people seemed to think that safety existed here.

"We have to get out!" Trey said. He recognized a couple of fellow miners from his shift and smiled at them in the poor light. He touched them as he spoke, pleaded, cajoled, his touch a familiar form of communication that made up for facial expression whenever the miners talked in the pitch black. "This place is finished, we can never beat the Nax, we have to leave and go topside until it's safe again."

"Why topside?" one of the miners, Grant, asked. He did not use touch as he spoke, a sign that he was angry or terrified, or perhaps both. "Why can't we go into the tunnels and hide this out?" A few of the others mumbled in confused agreement.

"The militiamen are dead by now," Trey said. "The Nax may not have fed for centuries. And they know this underground even better than us." He looked around nervously, expecting at any second to feel the surge of displaced air tickle the hairs on his neck as a Nax swept in through the cave air.

"I doubt that." Grant turned his back on Trey and his mother and spoke to the others. "We can go into the current working and wait in there. I know it like the touch of my own hand; there are tunnels and crevasses where we can hide. These fledge demons will be sated soon enough. As Trey said, the militiamen will be dead by now. The Nax can feed on them."

"They'll continue their slaughter," Trey said. "It's not only food they woke for, it's something else as well. Something that's driven them to fury."

"What makes you an expert on the fledge demons?" a woman asked.

Trey looked at the group for a few seconds, wondering whether they would apportion blame. He realized that he barely cared. Wanting to remain down here was foolish, and if they blamed him for what was happening that made them even more so.

"I sensed them waking," Trey said. "I was on a fledge trip. I went farther than I should have, found a Nax and withdrew quickly, but I knew that it wasn't the only one waking. They never hunt in groups. They exist alone. That's why I know there's something wrong. I think there's something going on topside that has enraged them and—"

"And you want to go there?" Grant said, spinning around.

"Trey . . ." his mother whispered, afraid.

There was a series of screams from across the cavern, accompanied by several loud thuds. They did not last for long.

"I'm saving my mother," Trey said. "Anyone who wants to come with us, you're welcome."

Trey and his mother left on their own.

"They're just afraid, Trey," she said as they hurried past deserted caves and skirted the Church. "This is all they're used to. It isn't Grant's way to be like that, he didn't mean it."

"He's going to get them all killed."

They continued in silence, passing by one of the mayors' pillars, glancing up but seeing no sign of life on the balconies overhead. Each time they met someone Trey said, *To the caves.* Sometimes the miners would follow for a while before doubt took them and they slowed, trailing off, perhaps waiting for someone in authority to tell them what to do and where to go, not this lad wielding a disc-sword like a boy playing at war.

Trey tried to close off his mind to those sensations thrown off the Nax like sweat flicking from a fighting man's skin. But at the same time he listened for the sense of pursuit, a hint of the chase as a Nax zeroed on them. It never came. Whatever had noticed him as he squeezed the moss had obviously found something else to warrant its attentions.

As they reached the opposite side of the cavern—the place where the entrance to the current working sat like an open throat a few steps up the cavern wall—there was very little light by which to see. Trey moved from memory, holding his mother's hand and guiding her along. His ears were perfectly attuned to echo, distance and proximity, so each footfall told him just where he was. He grumbled in his throat here and there to launch a low, deep sound to echo back, and when he found a space in that echo he knew that the cave entrance was before them.

He leaned back and brushed his hand across his mother's cheek, stroking his fingertips across her lips in a sightless smile. "We're here," he whispered.

They were alone. A dull red glow lit the center of the cavern, throwing two of the huge pillars into silhouette. Trey could hear another volley of crossbow bolts being fired, then another. It seemed that the militia were alive after all, and putting up a sustained fight. Again he wondered about Sonda and looked across toward her cave, but there lay only impenetrable blackness. He closed his eyes and went into a crouch, trying to cast himself across this disturbed space, but the mixed input from the Nax—which he had quickly been able to filter and block so that he received only a hint of the terrible sensations they were reveling in—prevented him from casting himself at all. Besides, the fresh fledge was wearing off. Perhaps when they were farther into the mines they would pause, Trey could take some fledge from his shoulder bag and try to discern Sonda's whereabouts.

A brief flush of guilt burned his cheeks in the cool darkness. There were two thousand others down here.

"Come on," he said to his mother, leaning close and pressing his cheek to hers. "I'll look after you." He hefted the disc-sword, turned and entered the mouth of the mine.

They soon left behind the noise, the slaughter, the fighting and screaming. And within five hundred paces, gone too were the dregs of the Naxes' psychic emanations, swallowed into the rock and fledge seams that had been their home for so long, miners and Nax both. Whether they would ever coexist here again . . . that was a concern for the future.

Right now, Trey had to get them topside. He wondered what awaited them up there, and just why the Nax had risen in such a fury.

———

TWO THOUSAND STEPS into the new working, Trey and his mother paused for a rest. Trey had listened to her labored breathing, her grunts and groans as the landscape of the tunnel floor surprised her, twisting ankles, jarring her old bones. She tried to keep the pain to herself. He had passed this way thousands of times now and he knew the tunnel, how to navigate in the dark, the heavy sense of the tunnel walls repelling him and showing him the way. It was best they traveled as fast as him, not as slow as his mother.

He had sheathed the disc-sword and succeeded in slinging it around his shoulders. In this enclosed space he would sense danger long before it reached them.

They sat and took a drink from the leather gourd in Trey's shoulder bag. There was very little water, he had not refilled it since his shift.

"How far?" his mother asked at last. Trey had been dreading that. He had known that this question would come, and he had felt the silence between them thickening with its weight.

Trey reached out and touched his mother's face, not conveying anything in particular, just touching.

"Maybe two days," he said.

"Two days," she echoed. "I'm exhausted already."

Trey sighed and sat back against the tunnel wall. They would reach the old fledge seam soon, and then they would have to start working their way through that hollowness, that place once filled with fledge that had been mined by machines generations ago, taken topside by machines, transported across Noreela by machines. Try as he might, Trey could never imagine what these things had looked like working and moving. Although he'd seen images of them in books and on wall depictions back in the Church, they imparted nothing of what they had looked like *alive*.

"Did I ever tell you how they time the days topside?" his mother asked.

Trey smiled to himself in the dark.

"By the movement of the sun and moons. The sun rises and falls, that's the day. The moons appear and disappear, that's the night. The moons are sent away when the sun rises again. Two halves of each day are so *different* up there, one so bright and warm, the other so dark. And short? They're so *short!*"

"Three days to one of ours," Trey said. She had told him many times.

"Yes. Everything is over so quickly topside. You just get used to the heat of the sun on your face, and then it's time to sleep, and then suddenly it's time to rise again."

Trey had never been up. He'd never felt the urge. He was terrified.

"We should go," he said. "The old seam starts just along here. We can walk for some of it, Mother, but I think we'll be doing some crawling too." He did not repeat what he had suggested earlier—that they would simply hide in the caves—and neither did his mother. They had both known that there was no returning to the cavern, not for a long, long time. Trey felt tears threatening, at his mother's bravery and his own fears, but he held them back. He did not want her to sense him crying. He needed to be brave.

They started into the old, mined fledge seam. At first it was little different from the tunnel they had just traveled, other than the floor being more uneven and the walls unsmoothed; the machines had never been afraid of sharp edges. Trey went first, uttering the little grumbles and clicks that echoed back and gave him an idea of the topography of the seam ahead. His mother followed on behind, one hand holding on to the loose belt on Trey's jacket, the other held out to her side for balance. They made good progress. There was no hint of pursuit, and the sense of danger seemed to recede as they left the cavern farther behind.

If I knew to come this way, Trey thought, *others will as well. So why no sound? Why no signs that no one has come this way already, or are behind us working their way through?*

They moved on. The seam dipped and turned, and for the next thousand steps their route snaked through the rock of the world as if in an effort to throw off pursuers. Trey's miner senses led the way unerringly, and his mother followed, sighing, grunting, breathing heavily but never once complaining or asking him to stop.

Once or twice Trey mused that they really could linger here. But then he remembered that brief touch with the mind of the hibernating Nax—the fury, the rage, the hunger—and he knew that they had to go on. They may be out of immediate danger, but the Nax were unlikely to be sated with only one cavern. There were mines throughout the Widow's Peaks, and probably long, arduous routes between them, untraveled and impassable to humans but known to the creatures who truly owned this underworld.

And so they moved on, resting now and then, licking mineral-rich moisture from the walls. And every step they took frightened Trey more.

They were leaving behind danger, but they were also moving away from the only life he had ever known. The people in the home-cave were his people, the pale fires and the moss pots and the stingers and the blind spiders and the cave rats and the mayors, the Church and the constant, comforting distant roar of the underground river . . . all his, all part of the memories that made his life. He always worked hard at the fledge face, but once back in the cavern he was contented, happy in the knowledge that he did his bit for their underground community. Sometimes there were thoughts of going topside, but it was curiosity more than desire. He was interested in why people would choose to live up there when there was obviously so much more to living down here. Certainly there were dangers in the dark—stingers took one or two people each year, and cave-ins, though infrequent, were often deadly. But he had heard about the inimical inhabitants of topside as well: the tumblers that roamed the surface of the hills, sweeping up children and unwary travelers; the bandits on the plains; raids along the coastal towns by savages from the sea. And fighting in the towns, a malaise in the villages. People topside, it was said, had no care anymore.

Trey felt comfortable history staring at his back and mourning his leaving. Before him, with every step he took into the darkness, lay his future.

———

THEY ENCOUNTERED A nest of stingers. There were only a few and they were small, no bigger than a man's fist. And because they surprised the creatures, Trey was able to unsheathe his disc-sword and slice most of them down before they even had a chance to attack. The surviving stinger came clicking at them, aiming for Trey's mother, but Trey kicked out at where he felt the thing passing through the air, knocked it into the stone wall and struck it down with the disc-sword. Sparks flashed, and in their brief light he saw the creature dying in a splash of its own blood.

They moved on. Trey was pleased that he had seen them through this danger, but it only went to remind him that there would be more challenges ahead. And not all of them would be stingers.

─────────

TIME TURNED THEIR escape into a long, painful haul instead of a panicked flight. They were both still conscious of the danger behind them, but the effort of navigating the seam occupied most of their thoughts. They had already made their way through one narrow passage—at least three hundred steps long—in which Trey's mother had almost ground to a halt, too exhausted to pull herself through. He had tied his belt beneath her arms, hauling her after him like a mule pulling a fledge-laden cart.

Five hundred steps after this narrow stretch, Trey began to notice something in the air. A smell. The smell of people.

And beneath it, so distant as to be almost imaginary, the tang of blood.

"How long have we been moving?" his mother asked.

"A shift," Trey said.

"A topside day," she muttered. "I need to sleep, Trey. Very soon, I'll need to sit and sleep. Are the Nax following? Do you think they have our trail?"

Trey sniffed and knew that there was a menstruating woman in the group that had come this way before. For a hopeful moment he thought that could be the blood he sensed, but there was something else. He kept up the pretense, though he knew it was false.

He had chewed a finger of fledge a few hours before. He had cast his mind back several times since then, searching, watching the way they had come, to see if anything was following. Clumsy though this casting was—he was doing it on the move, trying not to let his mother know what he was doing—he was certain that the psychic picture he drew of the empty seam behind them was true.

"Nothing's following us," he said, and his mother breathed a heavy, heartbreaking sigh of relief and exhaustion. "But, Mother, someone has come this way before us."

She sniffed at the air for a few seconds, an old person's heavy, unsubtle inhalation. "I smell nothing," she said. "I used to have a nose like a cave rat, though I know I'm old now. Are you sure?"

"I'm sure," Trey said. *Because there is blood here. Human blood.* He wished he had cast forward too, but now that he smelled the blood he was afraid. If there were still minds to meet, he would meet them soon enough.

"How far away could they be? Surely not that far. Nobody had a chance to get into these caves much before us."

"We had to get across the cavern from our side," Trey said. "Then we stood talking with Grant for a while. We've rested a good few times, and when the seam narrowed . . ."

"I slowed us down, I know. But still, they can't be more than a couple of hours ahead."

"Probably not."

"We should try to reach them, Trey. I'll do everything I can, I'll breathe harder, I'll push harder. Let's go and meet up with them. The more of us there are, the better the chances of reaching the rising in one piece."

"I guess so." The pause stretched into an uncomfortable silence. "Trey?"

"There's blood, Mother!" he blurted. "I can smell blood. It's one of the women's time, but it's not only that. I'm afraid of what we'll find." He started to cry silently, and his mother knew. Not because of the smell or the way it changed his voice, but simply because she was his mother.

"Oh Trey, we won't know until we get closer. Maybe one of them was injured. Perhaps one of them fell and cut themselves, or ran into some stingers. With our own people ahead of us and the Nax behind, I know which I choose."

Trey tried to stifle his sobs but failed. The shock of what had happened hit hard at last. Beneath it, always there but so easily shut away, was the idea that it was all his fault. He had touched on the mind of the Nax and sensed the strange happenings topside that had woken it, but still, if he had not disturbed the fledge demon, perhaps it would not have come at them. It was a crazy idea, but right now he felt crazy.

"I'm proud of you, son. Your father would be too."

"I'm useless!"

"No, I don't think so. Let's go. Trey, I can't lead the way. Next to you I'm blind in these caves."

THEY MOVED ON. The smell grew in strength, and Trey could make out now that its source was stationary. They passed through another narrow seam, this one sloping steeply, and they had to slide down feet-first. His mother managed on her own, though Trey could sense the effort draining her final reserves of strength.

For an hour before they found the bodies the stench was strong and sickening. Blood, insides, shit, everything that went to make up people laid bare to the air. It went a little way to prepare Trey and his mother for what they found.

The bodies were scattered across the floor in a wide part of the seam, ground into the walls, their clothes ripped and soaked with blood. The smell was bad enough, but the feel of the human wreckage beneath their shoes was enough to make them retch.

"Anyone alive?" Trey asked, already certain of the answer. For some reason talking to the darkness made him shiver. He felt as if he were conversing with wraiths.

"Let's move on, Trey," his mother said.

"The Nax may be ahead."

"Well, they're behind us for sure. I think whatever did this came at them from up ahead. There must be ten dead folk here, and most of them are in one huddle. One or two back here, nearer to us, as if they were caught trying to run away."

Trey turned his head left to right, sniffing. She was right.

"The Nax probably found another way through. Whatever Grant may have said, those things have been down here thousands of years longer than us. They know their way around. The one that did this is probably back in the cavern right now . . ."

Sonda was here. Trey stopped breathing, terrified of the scent he had just caught. It was the dusky, slightly spiced hint of Sonda's skin, the warm herby smell of her breath . . . and drowning it all, her blood.

"Oh no!" he said, leaning forward until he slumped down onto the ground. He pleaded with the dark, asking its wraiths to prove him wrong, but there was no answer. Sweet Sonda, barely aware of his existence, yet at times throwing him a coy smile that set him alight and fueled many guilty fledge dreams, and many castings to seek her mind. He had always drawn back, guilty and respectful, but how he wished he had been more brash. He had thought he'd seen love in her eyes once, but he had so little confidence that he believed it must have been for someone else, left over from a previous thought as Sonda chatted to him in a food cave, smiled, ran a hand through her braided hair. Love in her eyes, warm and bright and so often hidden in the pitch darkness of the caves.

His mother held him and tried to give comfort, but for a while Trey was far away.

————

LATER, TREY PUSHED them on. They had to move quickly, although deep down where he barely even knew himself, he no longer believed they could escape. They had been given this subterranean world for a short-term loan, allowed to plunder its wealth, wound it, pull fledge from its ancient seams as if drawing blood from the veins of the world. Foolish, smug in their pride, thinking they now ruled this place. Even after the Cataclysmic War the fledge miners had considered themselves insulated from the rot setting in topside. They had heard of the strange things happening to the land, as if the ties that bound it together safely were slowly snapping and unraveling. And stories had filtered down with topside runners of the world slowing down, tales that the retraction of magic had murdered the peoples' confidence. Three centuries after the withdrawing of magic, humankind topside was like an old person waiting to die. Still eating, still drinking, still dreaming, looking to the rich past more than the short, doomed future.

Down here, smug and foolish, the fledgers had believed themselves safe. Now they were being shown just how unimportant they were.

Any petty plans Trey had once entertained for his future were slaughtered as surely as Sonda and those others, ground into the rocks and spilled across cold stone by the Nax, who truly knew and possessed this place. Fledge demons, the humans had called them, unconsciously classing them as monsters. People know so little.

So he pushed on, and his mother never once complained. They stopped now and then, licked moisture from the rocks, ate a handful of moss even though they knew it could make them sick. They needed the energy right now, the input of sustenance to carry them the distance to the rising. They hoped that Chartise was still there with the mules, ready to raise them up to the surface. All the while, unuttered, not even hinted at, the certainty in Trey's mind that they were both destined to die down here. And he did not care. Grief and exhaustion had hobbled his mind and distanced him from the truth.

Eventually they halted to sleep. They were both cut and bruised from the last thousand steps, all of which had been uphill through a narrow, twisting seam. It had taken them four times as long as it should have, because Trey's mother was exhausted beyond tears. Still she did not complain. Trey pulled her, she pushed, and they made it. But time was running out.

Once, halfway through this narrow and dangerous seam, they had heard a loud noise from far, far behind them. A scream or a cry. Pain, or anger. It had not been repeated.

Trey chewed on a fist of fledge as he drifted into a sleep bordering on unconsciousness. His mother sat beside him and whispered in his ear, motherly things that he would only remember much, much later. She stroked his cheek, ran her fingertips across his closed eyelids with the subtlety of a breath of air, and when she was sure he slept, she stood and walked away.

———

TREY WANDERED THE nearby caves in his sleep, his mind distanced from his body through the influence of fledge. He took some control—he knew what was happening—but he did not steer where he went. There was nobody to touch upon, nothing to find, so he drifted into one large cave, passed down into a deep, dark lake filled with unknown things, forced through a hundred steps of solid rock, found himself in a smaller cave . . . and suddenly there was someone there he knew.

His mother.

She had not taken fledge before sleep, he was sure, though he had hardly been in a state to know. This was really her, her bodily self, not just her wandering mind. She noticed him suddenly, spinning around and smiling as his presence made itself felt.

Son, she said, and invisibly he smiled back.

What are you doing here, Mother? How did you get here? It's dangerous; you should be back with me.

I thought I should let you sleep. And I want to set you free.

What do you mean?

There's a long way to go yet. Trey. Distances to travel, days to work through. And already I'm a hindrance.

Mother . . .

I've been topside, son. It's a wonderful place. And hateful. Wide-open spaces, and terribly confined outlooks. The people up there are so different, remember that. Some will love you for who you are, and some will cut your throat for a fistful of fledge. There's no finer sight than seeing the sun sink behind the hills, but as it leaves, danger arrives in its wake. It's backward up there, Trey. They live in the light and find safety in it; it's the darkness they fear.

Why?

Because they never know what's in it. We thought we did once son. That's what pride does. It blinds you better than the dark.

Come back now, Mother. I'll wake. We should go.

I am going, Trey. I love you. I'm proud of you, so proud. But I'm old and weak, and . . . and I don't want to be the cause of your death. She was crying now, really crying, and in his sleep Trey could almost hear her sobs echoing through the caves.

Mother, I don't know what—

Don't follow me, son. Follow yourself. Always.

Trey's disembodied mind watched his mother tip sideways into a black maw, a hole with sharp edges that seemed to go down, down . . . She fell, and although he obeyed her last wish and did not send his mind to follow her, he sensed in her last moments an immense peace and conviction that she had done the right thing.

Seconds later, suddenly, she was gone.

Trey screamed himself awake. The sound terrified him—they had been almost silent for the entirety of their journey—and so he screamed some more. He thought he heard something answering from far away with a scream of its own making, but perhaps it was an echo already lost.

———

TREY WENT ON. He remembered only brief flashes of the remainder of his journey. He continued to lick moisture from walls or drink from underground streams. He ate moss and it started making him sick. He had to defecate every few hundred steps, feverish, dislocated, driven now by instinct alone. Images flashed in and out, places and smells and distant sounds, but he did not know whether they were true memories or imagined by his fledge-fueled mind. He saw an underground waterfall venting itself into a bottomless pothole, but its sound could have been the roar of a victorious Nax. He swiped with his disc-sword at something in the dark as it flapped in and bit him, slapped at his ears with leathery wings. He cried himself to sleep as the minds of the dead touched his own. He dreamed of Sonda.

Trey remembered reaching the rising. It was a great cavern carved out of the bowels of the world centuries ago by machines as large as the entombed Beast. Traces of them remained, littering the cavern's perimeter, metallic ribs exposed and rotted with rust, old byways and hollows where something once existed now sad and vacant. In a pit in the center of the cave flickered the Eternal Flame of the underground, ever-lit to guide in miners with their cargos of fledge. It illuminated the whole cavern and blinded Trey, showing just how deserted that place was.

He had expected to find people here, but there was no one. Even Chartise, the Chief of the Rising, had vanished. But the rising still turned. A great construct of wood and steel, it was pushed by a team of fifty mules, each of them tethered in its own enclosure, each of them forever stepping forward to bite at the food that hung from a huge cogged wheel just above and ahead of them. And this wheel was slowly spun on its axis by the constant motion of the mules. If they stopped in unison they might never start again, but once the rising was begun they only halted when forced to do so. The construct kept turning, and the cogged wheels and giant oiled pulleys continued to lift the timber platforms up, up, topside. The rising was the closest thing there was in the mines to a living, working machine. The mules were its living part; the rising, adapted by Trey's ancestors soon after the Cataclysmic War, the machine.

Trey should have been awed. This was beyond belief. But he was way past any outside influence, immersed as he was in a miasma of grief, sadness and terror. Every creak from the rising was the sound of the Nax bearing down on him, saving him as their final sacrificial victim because he had woken them, he had cast himself too far and disturbed them from their endless sleep . . .

Trey fell onto one of the moving platforms and was carried higher than he had ever been.

Time passed. He slept. He raved and raged. And even when he felt sunlight on his skin, helping hands shading his eyes and giving him water, hands that touched him and communicated along with the gentle voice as if their owner knew the language of the mines . . . even then, he did not believe that he had escaped.

The heat on his face married with the cool certainty that he never would.

Chapter 6

KOSAR THE THIEF had not been to Pavisse for a long time.

He had been in Trengborne for most of the three years since he had been caught and punished, and that slowing down of life had suited him. He had been a traveler for most of his fifty years. He had seen many things, and stolen more than a few of them. That little, unassuming farming village had quickly become a sort of home, and he had barely strayed beyond its borders in all that time. There had been those there that shunned him because of his scars, but a greater number accepted him, though grudgingly. And it was the first place where he had felt accepted since he was a child.

His long career as a thief had come to an end far to the north in Long Marrakash, stealing furbats from a caravan of rovers. It had been a foolish, clumsy endeavor, and pointless. There were a glut of the unfortunate creatures for sale in stalls and shops all across Long Marrakash, and any of them would have been easier to rob than the rovers. But he had followed the caravan for two days, staying up in the hills as they traced the Long River along the valley bottom. There were maybe fifty rovers with two dozen wagons, horses, a herd of sheebok and a hundred furbats flapping in their cages. As each hour passed, Kosar became more and more certain that it was folly to steal from these people. Rovers were not renowned for their charity at the best of times—they had a law and a religion of their own, both actively excluding outsiders—and to steal from them was madness.

Perhaps he had *wanted* to be caught. He had thought about this long and hard since it happened, trying to recapture his mind on that day, in that place, just to look inside and see exactly how it was working at the time. He'd had tellans in his pocket, having robbed a group of rich traders just a death moon before. He rarely used rhellim, because his drive in that matter had always been strong and balanced. And furbats themselves were not easy to transport in relation to what they would be worth. Perhaps he could have made away with a dozen at most, each of them worth six tellans, and he already had three hundred tellans in his backpack. There was no sane reason why he ever should have tried to rob those rovers. Trade with them, maybe. Sit around their campfire, talking of dark days and drinking bad wine, perhaps, if they had let him.

To rob them was suicide.

They had caught him as he slipped a furbat cage from the fifth wagon. The wagon was rocking as he stepped onto it, and he heard the guttural grunts of a couple fucking inside. They must have noticed the change in rhythm beneath them, however, because he was suddenly face-to-face with the two rovers: an ugly, tattooed man, and a young long-haired woman, both of them flushed and panting from rhellim.

The next few minutes would have been comic, were they not so painful and destructive.

The man had pushed him from the wagon and proceeded to beat and kick. Kosar had been in more than a few fights and he could look after himself, but this rover's rage had been beyond anything he had ever encountered. Kosar fended off the first few blows, but then his rhellim-flooded attacker knocked him to the ground and, erection waving and glistening in the moonlight, started kicking his head. The naked woman jumped down to join in, and even through the pain Kosar noted her beauty. Others added to the beating, almost all of them naked and drugged. Kosar was beaten into unconsciousness by a group of naked men sporting erections and women glistening wet.

After the beating they strapped him down in the open and left him there for three days, remaining encamped nearby to observe his slow death. They watched with mild interest as wild animals took bites from his arms and legs. One of the women stripped him and forced a dribble of rhellim down his throat, laughing as he grew hard in the blazing sun, not following through on her implied offer. And then, feigning benevolence, the rovers had freed him.

They made him an offer: they would kill him quickly and painlessly, or he could brand himself a thief.

Kosar had done the cutting himself, sprinkling dried powdered Wilmott's root into the wounds to prevent them from ever healing properly.

It had been harder for him to travel since then, more difficult to make friends. Even though he wore gloves, they grew bloody. Everyone knew what he was. Honest folk shunned him because he was a thief, and thieves shunned him because he had been caught. So he had traveled down the western side of Noreela, looking for a place to settle, realizing the farther he went that his life must now change.

He had stayed in Pavisse for several moons. His wounds had betrayed him there as well, yet in Pavisse that had seemed not to matter so much. The mining town had more than its fair share of criminals, and they formed something of an underclass, a society within a society. It was the last town he visited before finding and settling in Trengborne.

And now he was back, seeking to renew an old acquaintance.

——————

SINCE LEAVING THE boy Rafe with his uncle, Kosar had wandered the bustling streets of Pavisse. Trengborne had sometimes numbed his senses with its blandness—the smell of dirt, the taste of cooked sheebok, the sounds of farming and families going about their mundane lives—but here they were opened up once again. The odors, the sounds, the sights of the streets amazed him for a while, worn traveler though he was, and he realized that his history had been gradually smothered by the constant glare of the Trengborne sun, and the idea that he had found his niche. The realization did not please him. He had been *enjoying* the life he had made for himself. There had even been a sense of reparation there, the idea that in a way he was making up for the damaged life he had been living. Not redemption, *never* redemption. Simply repair.

Now he was back in the world. He mourned Trengborne and its people, he was terrified and shocked by what he had witnessed and he needed to talk to someone friendly. This very fact proved just how far he had drifted from the life of a wandering thief.

He had spent only a few moons here but he had made friends, fellow rogues and vagrants who were happy spending their lives in taverns and food halls, exaggerating their exploits and commanding respect from like-minded exaggerators. Kosar had never embellished his past, nor glamorized it. Sometimes he had done his best to downplay what he had been, what he had done. Already, back then, he had been changing.

One of the friends he had made had been very special. He sought her now. He thought that she might know something about what he had seen back in Trengborne, the Red Monk that had slaughtered the village, what it all meant. She was a true traveler, a descendant of the Shantasi race that had been brought to Noreela in slavery thousands of years before. Their original home was long forgotten; some said it was an island to the east of Noreela, thousands of miles away across an uncrossable ocean. Others believed that the Shantasi had actually been brought into being by errant shades in the mountains of Kang Kang, their pale skins camouflage against the snow, their purpose to provide those incorporeal souls with premature flesh and blood homes. The Shantasi themselves were perpetually silent about their origins, but they could not hide one of their greatest gifts: knowledge.

A'Meer Pott had also been Kosar's last lover.

The Broken Arm looked exactly the same as when he had last been there. The sign above the door showed a massive machine, its use or purpose clouded by the passage of time, its metal-and-flesh arm ripped and bent at one of its elbows. Bloodred wine flowed from the arm, or wine-red blood, it was not quite clear which. It continued to amaze Kosar that such an establishment had paid an artist a good amount for this piece of work. Inside, the absence of wealth was almost a theme.

Kosar nudged the door shut behind him and smiled slightly as the noise lessened, commotion slowed. He held his arms by his sides so that the patrons would not see his bloodied gloves, glanced around with feigned disinterest as if looking for the bar. He had hoped that A'Meer would call out from the darkness, but perhaps it was unreasonable to expect her to still be here.

As he took his first step the atmosphere in the tavern quickly returned to normal. He leaned on the bar and ordered a beer. The barman did not seem to recognize him from all those moons ago; there was a generous flow of travelers and criminals passing through all the time, and Kosar's was just another face.

"Which one?" the barman asked gruffly.

Kosar raised his eyebrows. "You have more than one brew? You *have* gone up in the world."

"Sarcasm will get you a face full of fist, thief. We have Port Brew, or Old Bastard."

Kosar smiled and was pleased to see a brief response on the barman's face. "Then a pint of Old Bastard, please." As he poured, the barman—Kosar had never asked his name—launched into the endless stream of chat that Kosar remembered from his previous time here.

"So you been here before, then? I don't remember your face, but then I wouldn't, I've long since stopped seeing faces. I see tellans passed across the bar and that keeps me happy, that's what I'm here for. I see the faces of pretty women, sometimes, but by the time they leave here they're usually ugly. Always ugly inside, they have to be to come here, that's what I'm told anyway. I don't listen to a word. I like my customers, always have. No pretense amongst the downtrodden, no play at being civilized or rightful or law-abiding. Honest, that's what these folks are. They know the way the world's going and they don't mind admitting it. And they get what they can out of it while they can, enjoy what they will. Like this." He thumped down the jug of Old Bastard and stepped back, sighed, as if viewing a recently completed work of art. "That's half a tellan for that. A lot, I'll grant you, but wait till you taste it."

Kosar handed over a coin. "One for yourself," he said, and he enjoyed the flash of gratitude in the barman's eyes.

There was a sudden burst of laughter from a corner of the tavern, and Kosar spun around. *How can they laugh,* he thought, *when Trengborne lies dead, massacred? How can they laugh like that?* But of course they did not know, nobody knew other than himself and the boy Rafe Baburn. Kosar looked at the group with envy. Three men, three women, comfortable in one another's company, casual with their affections, their conversation easy and light. If only he had so few concerns, and so many friends.

"I don't suppose you know A'Meer Pott?" he asked the barman. "She's a Shantasi, used to come here three years ago."

"Still does," the barman said. "In fact, she works for me now and then."

Kosar frowned, trying not to imagine what that work entailed.

"Don't worry, thief," the big man said. "Not that sort of work. I leave that side of things to the Twitching Twat down the road. The Broken Arm is a place to rest the mind, not exercise the body. No, she collects glasses, works the bar, makes food sometimes if there're those here who'll buy it."

"Will she be in today?"

"She should be, come sunfall. Nice one, A'Meer. Very knowledgeable. A real traveler, so she keeps telling us. Though the fact that she's stayed here so long seems to mar that image a little."

"She *is* a real traveler," Kosar said, smiling at the memory of her telling those stories, the disbelief of people when she openly proved them as true. "But for a Shantasi, a few years is nothing. They live a long time."

The barman leaned over the bar and motioned Kosar closer. "She once told me," he whispered conspiratorially, "that she's been right to the end of The Spine."

Kosar nodded. "She told me that too."

The barman frowned and stood back up, picking a jug from a hook to serve another customer. "The Spine *has* no end," he said.

"That's what we're supposed to believe," Kosar hefted his jug in a toast and then left the bar, searching for a free table, finding one beneath the wooden staircase that led up to another level of tables above. He sat there alone, looking around, blending in with little effort. He caught a few patrons' eyes, but there was neither threat nor any real interest in their gaze. Most of them were here to forget old trouble, not make new.

The wood of the tabletop was scored with graffiti, some of it recent, much of it old, all of it telling a story. There were many names mentioned, most of them with some reference to the impressive or pitiable size or function of their sexual organs. Places were named too, often in childish bravado, like *I went to Kang Kang and it stank of shit.* And here and there were messages. *Xel—meet me at Friar's Bridge, sunfall, noonday—Yel.* Kosar wondered if Xel and Yel had made the meeting, and why, and what had come of it. He wondered whether they were both still alive, and if not whether they had died happy. Death was free nowadays, handed out on a whim by militia and murderers alike. And Red Monks too. A Red Monk slaughtering a whole village . . .

He looked around the tavern and shivered. He had heard what

the Red Monk asked the children on the bridge before he killed them: *Where is Rafe Baburn?* The only villager that madman had not killed was the one he was seeking. There was a message in that, more hidden than those carved into the oak of this tavern table, and yet far more important. For a Red Monk to be abroad, it meant only one thing: that magic was back in the land. And for the Monk to be seeking the boy Rafe . . .

He shook his head and took a huge swig of his ale. It truly was an Old Bastard, coursing into his stomach and blurring his vision within minutes. It had been a long time since he'd taken a drink like this—back in Trengborne he was lucky to be given a bottle of rancid rotwine—so he would have to be careful. He had no wish to greet A'Meer by sicking all over her.

Yet strong ale would not purge the fear that had been seeded in his mind. Kosar had never felt a terror like this. He had been afraid many times in his life—fearful for himself, and those he sometimes had cause to call his friends—but never *terrified*. Even when the rovers had tied him down and watched as a weasel nibbled at his thigh, he had been certain that he would survive. Perhaps it *had* been the cocky conviction of a younger man, someone who almost always got what he wanted by stealing it, but it had seen him through. This was different. Earlier fears had been based on know-able threats, the knife in this man's hand, the whip in another, a herd of tumblers chasing him for a day and a night across the foothills of Kang Kang. Those threats were tactile, understandable. What he felt now was a terror of something transmuted into myth and legend. Secondhand, yes, but no less heartfelt for that.

During his travels Kosar had come to learn a little about magic, how it had once fused with the land, and the fact that it had stopped working when the two Mages misused it to their own ends. They had been expelled from Noreela at the end of the Cataclysmic War, driven north out of the land and into the unknown. Watching stations had been set up along The Spine—the series of islands extending into the seas north of Noreela—to warn of their approach, should they survive and seek revenge. But here rumor truly took control, because there were even more legends about The Spine than the deadly mountains of Kang Kang. The Spine is endless, and the Mages are still traveling its length. The Spine moves, shifting over centuries like Noreela's giant tail, and should its tip ever touch wherever the Mages ended up, they and their armies will swarm back into Noreela, sporting fury nurtured over three centuries of banishment.

A'Meer truly had been along The Spine, and she had told Kosar the truth: it was far from endless. And the warning stations and islands, though most were still inhabited and functioning to some degree, were all but worthless.

Therein lay Kosar's terror. Magic was back in the land. It had once served humanity well, maintaining the balance of nature and making known the language of the land. But the Mages, were they still alive, would have their ways and means to hear of it. The Red Monk—part of an order sworn to keep magic from the Mages, should it arise again—had been looking for Rafe Baburn.

Kosar the thief, whether he liked it or not, was involved.

———

A'MEER POTT HELD her age well. She had told Kosar that she was almost one hundred Noreelan years old, yet she still looked younger than him. She was short, her body lithe instead of thin, her long black hair locked into twin braids that fell to either side of her snow-white face. Such paleness emphasized everything about her features, from the deep, dark eyes to her pale red lips. As usual, she was dressed in black. He had heard the Shantasi described variously as walking corpses, living shades and angel messengers to the land, but Kosar had formed the opinion that they were a mixture of all three. Like Noreelans, the Shantasi trod a narrow path between jubilation and damnation.

He watched her enter the Broken Arm and smile at some of the patrons, exchange greetings with one or two. She drifted to the bar, and Kosar was pleased to see that she and the barman were friends. They seemed to talk trivialities for a few minutes as A'Meer slipped off her cloak and took a drink. The barman glanced across the tavern into Kosar's shaded nook beneath the stairs once or twice, but Kosar shook his head, held a finger to his lip. Eventually A'Meer went about her business, and as he watched her move between tables collecting mugs, wiping down spilled beer and nattering with the customers, Kosar felt a deepening nostalgia for their time together.

Their relationship had been short, and ruled more by lust than anything else. He had met her in this very place, and their mutual delight at each other's tales of travel drew them close very quickly. Of course, Kosar's tales were pale and lackluster compared to the accounts she told him over the following moons. That first night had ended with them falling drunk into each other's arms, and before they knew it they were back in Kosar's rooms screwing like old lovers. The sight of those cherry-red nipples against her pure white skin, the black hair between her legs like a hole in virgin snow, her long dark hair loosened so that it drifted across the landscape of her shoulders and breasts had driven Kosar mad. They eventually left his room two days later, but only to eat and drink.

The sex had been central to their relationship, but they had also developed a deep and lasting trust which both admitted felt new and fresh. Kosar was a marked thief, and few people trusted him now or ever would again. A'Meer was a Shantasi, a race that even after all this time was held at a distance by Noreelans, their distinct features and ambiguous history setting them too much apart. Both loners, they reveled in the companionship. He had told her much about himself, some of which he was surprised at even remembering. She had told him of her travels, the things she had seen, dreams of places yet to see.

Leaving A'Meer and Pavisse had been the final penitent act of this wandering thief looking for a home.

Kosar had finished three mugs of Old Bastard waiting for A'Meer's arrival, and he felt more than a little light-headed. He needed some food, he needed sleep, he needed escape from the horrors he had witnessed the previous day. He watched her as she approached, moving from table to table, collecting mugs, sometimes chatting with the drinkers and sometimes not. She wiped at his table where he had purposely spilled some ale. He leaned back on his chair, his face in shadow beneath the staircase.

"Another mug of Old Bastard, please," he said in a low voice.

"I'll wipe up your mess, but I'll not serve for you. Get your ale at the bar, friend, and try not to spill it next time. Old Bastard is too expensive and too good to waste."

Kosar grabbed his mug before she could reach for it, lifted it and offered it to her.

"Thief," A'Meer said mildly upon seeing his bandaged hands. She bent down then, peered beneath the staircase, and her face broke into a delighted smile. "Kosar! You treacherous old bastard, what in the name of the Mages brings you back to this stinking shit pit?"

"You," he said, pleased by her smile. He had left her rather quickly after all, and with little real explanation.

"Liar! It's the ale, isn't it? And the bustling center of art and culture that is Pavisse." She pulled up a chair, hesitated, leaned forward and hugged him warmly, then sat down.

"A'Meer, it's great to see you." He meant it. He felt panic pressing in, a potent combination of terror and alcohol driving him to distraction, and her familiar face was welcome.

"You too! I haven't had a fuck as good as you for years."

Kosar laughed despite himself. "I haven't at all since you," he said.

Her eyes widened fractionally, but she did not comment. It had been a long time, and although they both seemed pleased to see each other, there was an awkwardness here. He hoped it would dissipate soon.

"So what urges you to leave your little village, eh? Wanderer's life bleeding back into your system now that you're used to the brands?" She held his hands gently and unwrapped the bandages, grimacing at the bloody wounds on his fingertips. "Fuck, Kosar, all for a few furbats. I remember what used to soothe the hurt. You remember?" She arched her eyebrows mischievously, and yes, he remembered.

"A'Meer, it's something bad," he said quietly, his tone killing the moment. Suddenly it was as if they had never parted and here they were in the Broken Arm, swapping stories, drinking, sinking into solemn discussions about how things might be turned around, how the long-ago loss of magic might just be weathered and survived. Everything was falling apart, they would say, and A'Meer would tell him about the plains south of Kang Kang where things fell into the sky and the air was turned to glass.

"How bad?" A'Meer asked. When Kosar did not answer she let go of his hands and sat back in her chair. "Bad enough that we need a bottle of rotwine to talk about it?"

"Get two," Kosar said without smiling.

"Oh Mage shit." A'Meer rose and went to the bar. She exchanged a few words with the barman, slapped him on the back and then returned to the table with two bottles filled with black rotwine. "I've got the evening off," she said.

Kosar nodded, popped the lid on one of the bottles and filled the glasses A'Meer had brought. "A'Meer," he said, lifting his glass and seeing how the fluid seemed to swallow the light, "I think things are about to change."

Chapter 7

IT DID NOT feel the cold. It had only a vague sense of things, a concept of shape and size and direction that was barely enough to guide it on its way, abstract ideas of how things were supposed to be as opposed to observations of how they actually were. Its whole world was its own, contained within its potential mind, where a slew of instincts were all that existed; no experience, no history, nothing to shape this shade any more than nature had already done. The faults were already there, not planted by outside intervention. There are mistakes even in nature.

It did not know that it was a mistake. It was perfect. It had been told so by its god, and that god had sent it on its way, launched it from endless waiting out into the world with an aim in mind. It could find itself a home, the god said, somewhere to settle and spread, let its potential filter down into flesh and bone, heart and desire, mind and body. And then—the hardest part—it would leave this home and return.

It was all instinct, and the instinct was to never go back. But one of the knots in its makeup made it, so its god said, better than perfect.

It made it *exquisite*. It gave this shade, this empty space of potential mind, soul, spirit, experience and existence, something of a life already.

It was loyal to its god.

It traveled quickly, seeking out whispers echoing through the spaces surrounding it. Ideas, words, visions it had been told to watch for. The whispers had silenced already, but the shade knew the direction, even if distance was something as yet vague. It traveled beneath the surface of the world, behind the plane where true life existed, and though the temptation was to immerse itself in this reality—the draw was huge, the power great, the shade's potential aching to be let in—it knew to wait. It had its instructions. So it traversed spaces where there had never been anything, passing by others similar to itself as they waited patiently for life. They did not notice its passing, though in its wake they were scrutinized one more time for any imperfections. There were none; their creation was thorough. This shifting shade was an oddity, an echo of something not there, and something not noticed cannot be forgotten.

Its imperfections dipped it into the world on occasion, and the sudden shock of life flung it out instantly:

a brief instant of cold as it hits a field of white, things darting away in terror, the white solidifying and becoming clear in its path;

more cold, subsumed in fluid, life swarming and seeding and ending around it, life as small as a piece of nothing or large as the mind of its god, and all of it shocked at the shade's brief arrival;

something more solid, rich in the history of life though holding little, only sleeping things, even older than its god and so much more unknowable.

The shade withdrew with something akin to fear. It was its first true emotion, and it was quite apt.

Time passed, though the shade did not know time. The places it skirted became warmer, the oceans more full of life, the sky lighter and more loaded with living things. Nothing saw it—there was nothing to sense—but the mood of wrongness at its passing sent a pod of blade whales on course for a distant beach, a giant hawk into seabound freefall, and the crew of a fishing boat into a murderous madness.

It moved on, listening for more whispers to carry back to its god.

Chapter 8

HOPE'S TATTOOS SEEMED to reflect her mood. They emphasized the set of her face and now, as she spoke sadly of what was past, they drew down the corners of her mouth, painted themselves as deep creases around her eyes. They made her look very old.

The boy had not yet given her a satisfactory answer. Hers was the only one that made any sort of sense, crazy and terrifying though it may be. There were other ways she could check, but she was too terrified. If she looked and saw and it was true . . . then everything was ending. Ending, and beginning again.

This was the moment she had been living for.

———

"BUT I'M ONLY a farm boy," Rafe said yet again, as if his insistence would make it so.

Hope shook her head in frustration, her spiked hair snapping at the air. "You're impossible, that's what you are!" She stood and went to pour them both some more water. Rafe was not sure quite what she meant.

He wanted to curl up and sleep. He may be in this strange place with this strange woman, but he was exhausted, physically and mentally, and sleep lured him as a welcome retreat. He might dream of his parents, but then he might not. And he hoped that if he did dream, then for a while they would still be alive. A million good memories awaited him in sleep.

"How do you explain what you're hearing?" Hope asked yet again.

"I don't know what I'm hearing! Just . . . things. Whispers. Words I don't know. Other things."

"What other things?" She gave him a glass of water. She'd asked him already, but she looked determined.

"Hope, I don't know, I've *told* you. It's like . . . have you ever tried to explain a dream? A really strange dream, one that makes perfect sense to you when you're in it but once it's over and you're awake you can't put it into words, can't make sense of it, even to yourself?"

Hope stared at him, nodding.

"That's what I hear. Stuff I can't explain. But I don't even understand it when I'm hearing it."

"What you're hearing," Hope said, "is an ages-old language. Few alive now have spoken it, or if they have, then only to themselves. It's the language of the land, Rafe. It's the language of magic."

"But what does that *mean*?" She had told him that several times now, old languages and words no longer spoken. But it made no sense. It did nothing to distract his mind from his parents' deaths, nor explain them. He needed sleep.

Hope sighed, looked down at her hands. They twisted around each other as if trying to wring something out. She was a whore, she had told him. Those hands had done a lot.

"I'm older than I look, Rafe," she said. "I'm a witch. I have ways and means to keep myself young." She waved around at her room, adorned as it was with plants and roots and dead things hanging from the walls, shelves lined with old books, opaque containers scattered across every available surface, their contents hidden away. "And all my life I've been waiting for you.

"You must know of the magic, the old ways Noreela used to live before the Cataclysmic War? Better times. The world was at peace with itself, and as we took from nature, so it gave. All that was stolen away by the bastard Mages because of their greed and avarice, their pride in thinking they could usurp nature and make the world their own. And now, because of them, there's no peace in the world, and the more we take the more the land dies."

"My parents always told me there was more myth than truth in those stories."

"Lots of myth, to be sure!" Hope agreed, laughing with little humor. "But lots of truth as well. Stories that big have plenty of both. You've not traveled the land, you've not seen how much it's changing."

"You've been waiting for *me*?" Rafe asked, his voice weak and vulnerable.

"My family have always been witches, Rafe, even before the Cataclysmic War. Back then, my grandmother's grandmother's mother used magic to help her heal, help her look after people. And since nature has taken magic back, my ancestors and I have used herbs and spices and potions, those things nature has left us with. And I've always, *always* believed that nature would forgive us one day. There's a prophecy, uttered by a few, believed by fewer; it says that magic will come back, and it'll be reborn in a child."

"I'm not a child."

"You're an innocent. And your origins . . . ?"

Rafe sipped the water and thought about the voices and sounds he sometimes heard, the way they seemed to know him so well, even though he could not understand them. And he thought of the day his parents had told him about when they found him, abandoned and alone on the hillside. "I know what you're saying," he said. "At least, I think so. I'm not sure. I'm so confused. I'm just a farm boy!"

"There are ways to know for sure," Hope said, suddenly standing from her chair and reaching for Rafe.

He sat up and shuffled back on the bed. "What do you mean?"

"Your parents weren't your blood parents, were they?" Hope stood with her arms outstretched, as if ready to catch him from a fall. *How does she know that?* "How do you know?"

"Because they *can't* have been."

"Why?"

Hope came to him, smiling, but there was something behind the smile he did not like. Something old, and desperate.

"I can show you," she said. "We can look together. You're tired, Rafe. Look . . . watch . . . haven't you ever wondered?" Hope reached for his shirt and he did not have the energy to draw back. He felt her sharp nails scratch at his stomach as she lifted his shirt, higher, and then she gasped and stared down at his stomach. "Haven't you ever *wondered?*"

"What?" His voice came from a distance. He felt so sleepy.

"You have no navel," Hope whispered. "It's true. It's you." She looked at Rafe, and then smiled.

Something whispered to him, and Hope's lips were not moving. He smelled grass in a wide, sun-kissed meadow, even though outside this room he could hear the sounds of hidden Pavisse going about its bleak business.

"You tired, farm boy?"

Rafe nodded, vision blurring as the room rocked him from side to side, and he could taste fresh mountain air taking the sting of Pavisse from his tongue.

Hope was whispering, but he no longer understood. He was listening to something else, something that welcomed him down into deep sleep with words beyond understanding. Behind it, comforting memories awaited him.

———

HOPE TOOK THE glass of water from the sleeping boy's hand and emptied it into the drain. She was careful to wash the glass several times before replacing it on a shelf. *A few sewer rats will be giddied this afternoon,* she thought.

She sat for a while and watched the boy sleeping, staring at his bared stomach. Poor soul, he had been through so much, seeing his parents and friends slaughtered like that. He deserved a rest. Already his eyelids were twitching as he took brief respite from the ills of the world.

Hope was afraid. She had spent her life waiting for magic's return. She called herself a witch, but one thing she had always craved was to actually live the life. She wanted to heal with magic, not herbs. She wanted to treat madness with a touch of her fingers and a few cooed words, not a mug of GG's honey, which invariably would not work. And over the years, she had been searching.

Now she had found Rafe.

There had been hundreds of men in her bed, but few of them had she ever let sleep. They'd come in here drunk or lonely, had sex with her and then paid with talk: where they had been on their travels; who they had met; what they had seen. She had asked them whether they ever heard rumors from Kang Kang, and all but a few refused to even talk of that place. *You think I'd ever go there?* they would say. *You think I'm mad? I don't even listen to talk of the place, let alone think on it.* Other things too. She would extract her payment through idle rumor, travelers' gossip, whispers beneath the wind. It suited most of her customers fine, and many of them returned day after day, year after year. Sometimes, they had new tales to divulge. She was always searching for knowledge, picking through the lives of those sex-sated men for hidden truths and realities that would make no sense singly, yet considered as a whole might one day tell her what she had wanted to hear for so long: that magic was back in the land.

The boy mumbled in his sleep and Hope strained to listen, but he was talking Noreelan, nothing more.

She was breathing heavily, trying not to build her hopes on this lost lad's fate. The world was getting harsher, and a slaughter in an insignificant little farming village was hardly news. But here she was now, staring at the living proof.

And now she knew: the whispers her mother and grandmother had carried down from their own ancestors, magicians and charlatans both, were all true. They were words she had never heard again, not all the times she had questioned those men, and she had begun to suspect that they were ideas open only to the women of the land. It was a female concept, after all. No man had an inkling of what the birth of a miracle could mean.

He's heard the language of the land. He hears the whispers, he feels the movement of rivers through the soles of his feet, the breath of the world brushing against his skin. Don't tease yourself, Hope! It isn't so hard to believe.

She stood and turned away from Rafe, hearing him mumble again in his sleep. This time she could not make out the words.

Facing the walls of her little room, she took in everything that made her what she was today: a pretender; a charlatan; a profaner of magic. She had no magic yet she called herself "witch," and some foolish people even went in fear of her. Old fears must run as deep as blood, she thought, and deeper than history. Here were a hundred spices and herbs and drugs known to anyone, and a few others unknown. Tumblespit, hedgehock, rutard, Duke's Folly, stale fledge from several distinct regions, grass dew, hedge dew, rock dew, Willmott's Nemesis, GG's honey. A small earthpoison tree grew in the corner of her room, fed with the blood of rats. A selection of jars contained bodies and body parts from many creatures of Noreela, most known, some very rare, one or two little more than myth. There were lotions and potions whose uses even Hope had little concept of, handed down as they were from her mother, unopened all these years. Some of these jars had become opaque with time, and Hope had no idea what grew within.

And yet . . . no magic. Only tricks and turns, deceptions and delight in ruse. She could mix and match well after all these years, curing with products of the land and, if required, creating ills as well. She did a fair trade in her medicines, and earned even more from the occasional, more unpleasant commission. The sex, though, the whoring, that was where her true pay originated. The gathering of knowledge, the search for a hint that magic had returned and things were about to change.

And now here was a boy asleep in her room, a boy who had apparently escaped the endless wrath of a Red Monk. A boy who heard unknown voices, felt unknowable sensations deep in his naïve farmer's mind. He could explain none of it, yet his exposed stomach explained it all.

Breathing heavily, Hope knelt before Rafe and started to undo his belt. He grumbled a little in his sleep and whispered something she did not understand. Her excitement grew. *Words of old!* she thought. She slipped his trousers down slowly, glancing at his pale limp cock.

He has no navel.

There could be other explanations. She had missed it, perhaps, or a trick was being played, a complex deception for the amusement of some of her regular customers, those of whom she always asked her questions, again and again as if they would suddenly remember.

But she looked again.

He has no navel!

"Mage shit, it's really here." The tattoos on Hope's face were in flux, shifting and moving as her emotions swayed from fear to elation, delight to terror. Here was the living future, and the dead past. This boy was more myth than reality, a story so rare that she had never heard it told other than by her own mother and grandmother. *Magic is destined to return,* they had said, *and it will be in a child unbirthed, offspring of the womb of the land in darkest Kang Kang.* She had never truly understood what that meant, but now she was faced with the myth in the flesh.

For a few seconds Hope held her breath, terrified that Rafe would simply disappear. She had realized the impossibility of his being here; perhaps that knowledge would drive him away. But he remained, squirming on the bed and frowning as he tried to make sense of some deeply hidden dream, a recurring voice in his head that must be trying so hard to make itself known.

Hope held his cock and squeezed slightly, feeling it grow hard in her hand, the incredible heat as his blood coursed through his body, driven by the turmoil of his dreams and drawn to this point. When it was fully hard she stood and raised her skirts. She could take him inside her, have his seed, and what would that make her? A part of things? More than just a witch without magic, a fool mixing herbs and chanting mock hope back at herself? She waited for long seconds, poised, staring down at the boy's face and seeing conflict etched there in his skin. Her own tattoos itched as she fought her own private battle.

She did not know what would happen, what she would gain, if she took him now. But she knew what she would lose: his trust.

She covered him up with a smooth furbat-skin blanket.

"Sleep easy," she said. "Get what rest you can. Listen to the voices, but don't let them frighten you."

She looked at the paraphernalia of her life once again—all suddenly redundant, like so much medicine pumped into a dead person's veins—and then sat back to watch Rafe sleep.

Chapter 9

IT DID NOT take long for Alishia to decide to leave Noreela City.

With the library gone, she no longer had a job. She had saved a good hoard of tellans over the past few years, but in a city like Noreela she could not live on them forever. And besides, there was little for her there now. Her books were gone, burned to ash by the old madman, and it was as if their destruction had brought her back to the present. She began to see just how bad things were. Before, she had seen the city on her walks to and from the library, and that was all. Now, aimless and wandering, she had more of a chance to register what she saw, to actually be a part of things instead of being lost in the histories of her books. She felt vulnerable and alone. She felt unprotected. Erv, the stable lad, had become even more threatening, sensing her vulnerability and perhaps intending to prey upon it given the first opportunity.

Alishia had started carrying her knife in a sheath on her thigh, hidden by her dress. That single act of insecurity and fear had in itself persuaded her that her time in the city was at an end.

Besides, she was alone. Her parents had passed away when she was a teenager, leaving her a pile of books and living memories, but little else. These memories had kept her going while she made new ones of her own, and eventually she had found employ with the library. She had few friends, and certainly no one close. She had never been beyond the city walls, and only rarely even ventured outside her own district. Alishia lived in her head, exploring the realms of fantasy revealed by the books she read, the accounts of things near and far that were sometimes truth, sometimes fiction, and more often one disguised as the other. Her own private world was a rich one, yet she had hardly seen the real world at all.

There was little for her to leave behind and even less to take. She bought a horse and saddle, spending a sizeable proportion of her savings, and stabled it with Erv the night before she left. It would carry her and her few clothes and books out of the city and into the unknown.

Alishia did not sleep that night. She lay awake and listened to the sounds of the nighttime city—the laughter, the whispering, the shouting, the screams and calling, the dogs barking in shadowy alleys, the grunting of fights, the smashing of glass, the rumble of carts and the lethargic clatter of clumsily shod horses passing by—and she felt less a part of it than ever. Somewhere deep inside she had something that this place eschewed: hope. Not purely for herself, but a wider belief that things *could* get better. And that set her apart from many of the inhabitants of Noreela City. They seemed content to exist in a world running down, where fields yielded less each year and murder grew more common, where the Tumbling Window was busier month by month with executions for more petty crimes, where children died in the streets because parents would no longer give them a home. If there were others like her who wished for good rather than accepted bad, they were a silent minority.

The following morning, when she left, Erv tried to give her a kiss. Nervous, she allowed him to brush her cheek with his lips. He blushed and muttered an inept apology.

"Good-bye, Erv," Alishia said. She felt ridiculously grateful, and surprised. She had grown to fear the boy and the potential violence she had sensed in him, yet now he seemed more pathetic than dangerous. She wondered whether her suspicions had been a product of her underlying mistrust of Noreela City.

"Where you going, Ally?"

"I don't know yet." Erv did not respond. Alishia and he stood facing each other for a few awkward moments, and then he made a cradle with his hands so that she could mount her horse. Her ride was well watered and groomed, and the saddle had been polished, the harnesses tightened and shined where brass fittings clanked together. Alishia smiled at Erv as she settled herself atop the horse. It was years since she had last ridden, and already it was uncomfortable.

"Take care, Erv," she said, and she kneed the horse from the cobbled courtyard.

She had expected to feel sad as she left the city, but she did not. Instead, she was instilled with a vivid excitement, a tingling belief that she was leaving behind all that was stale and familiar and unpleasant, and that past the plains surrounding the city were fresh experiences to be had. She knew that the rot had spread right across Noreela, but quitting Noreela City felt like ridding herself of the most concentrated source of failing, a heavy, black influence that would drag her down in the end. Perhaps she had survived because she had never truly lived there; in her mind, in her books, she was an inhabitant of Noreela as a whole, not just a city.

Bored militia watched her ride out through the main gates. They were more interested in who came in, not who left. And therein lay one of the Duke's greatest failings, Alishia often thought. He should be gathering good people to him, not letting them leave. Giving them a chance. Allowing hope and enthusiasm to root. Instead, in people like Alishia, it was being diluted across the land.

She had never been this far out, and it felt wonderful. Ahead of her, twenty miles distant, were the lower slopes of the Widow's Peaks, their heads obscured by distance and wispy clouds, the veiled faces of true mourners. There were at least three distinct fledge mines in there, as well as scattered villages nestled between mountains like children in loving mothers' arms. The sky above the mountains seemed larger and wilder than here above the city, its clouds richer, the colors deeper and more luxuriant. There were huge hawks above those mountains, so high up that they could never be seen, living out their lives on the wing and floating on air currents even when they were dead, drying out, going to dust and painting summer sunsets red. She had read about the hawks, though few people in the city believed in them anymore. She had read about so much: the Breakers who roamed the land dismantling ancient machines, still hoping to find dregs of old magic hidden in sumps or forgotten veins; the Violet Dogs, a race of walking dead that had supposedly invaded Noreela before any true records began, leaving their mark in forgotten caves and lost temples to the night; the Sleeping Gods, powerful beings that had taken to hibernation millennia ago and whom magic, should it ever return, was supposedly destined to wake. She had read about all of these wonders and myths and terrors, and now she had a chance to find out some of them for herself.

She had no idea where she was going, or what she would do when she arrived. But for the first time in as long as she could remember, Alishia felt alive.

———

THAT FIRST NIGHT she camped out on the plains.

The Widow's Peaks were farther away than she had thought, and the route from the gates of Noreela City more circuitous and problematic than she had imagined. She had passed through several small hamlets populated by a mixture of farm folk and those that had obviously fled the city for shady reasons. The first settlement she passed through was quiet, a few faces peering from behind half-closed doors. At the second she was stopped and forced down from her horse, questioned by a pair of bogus militia, hassled until she gave them a tellan each to let her go. She had feared that this would become a road tax, a way of stealing without any true threat, and that she, a woman traveler on her own, would fall victim every time. But at the next collection of dilapidated homes peopled by a few disheveled occupants, she surprised herself.

The first man pulled her down from the horse. The second started to rifle through the bags hanging from her mount's saddle hooks, but by that time Alishia already had her knife drawn and pressed into the helper's throat.

What in Kang Kang am I doing?

"Hey now, lady, no harm done!" the second man said, backing away from the horse, hands outstretched. Alishia was disgusted but thrilled at the power she felt. He was genuinely *scared*. The other man slipped away from her and ran around the back of an old log-and-mud dwelling, closely followed by his mate. Alishia leapt onto her horse and galloped inexpertly away, afraid that she would tumble from the saddle, equally terrified that a crossbow bolt would find the back of her neck at any second.

A few minutes later she slowed the horse to a trot, invigorated with success. Later still, she decided that the men had not really been afraid of her. They were afraid of the type of people who usually traveled these roads, those that were used to actually using knives once they were drawn.

Alishia was far more cautious after that, leaving the rough road to skirt around the hamlets, even though it slowed her progress. She comforted herself with the thought that a journey with no end cannot be delayed. This was all a part of what she had set out to do. She had read about the dangers of travel in this degenerating world, and now she was living with them.

She set up camp way off the road, sheltered from the cool northerly breeze by a shelf of rock that marked where a river had flowed before real time began. There were several small firepots in her saddlebags and she set these around the camp, lighting them to ward off any predators that might be roaming the dusky landscape. There were bandits in the mountains, and sometimes they came down this far to slip into Noreela City via sewers and tunnels. If they passed her way, there was nothing to stop them from having their fun with her as a prelude to their incursion. And there were skull ravens that buzzed the plains at night, looking for weak cattle or lonely travelers. She could fight them off well enough if she was awake when they arrived, but not if she slept. Not if they could nudge her sleep into unconsciousness before pecking their way through her temple and into her skull.

And tumblers. Even they came down onto the plains on occasion. The fact that there had been no sightings for a long time was of little comfort.

So Alishia sat behind the rocks and cooked a jug of sheebok and herb stew she had brought with her. Her dinner spat and sizzled, covering any noises from farther away. Her horse stood quietly nearby, tied loosely to a lightning tree growing from the sparse earth between the rocks. She thought of her little room above the stables; of Erv panting in dark shadows as he watched her shadow dance on the ceiling as she undressed; of the old man in red who had burned down the library and changed her life, intentionally or not. And although she was afraid, she was also glad. The knife strapped against her thigh had helped her once already today. There were dangers out here, yes, but probably no more than she would find spending her life day to day in Noreela City, risking the wrath of the increasingly lawless population and belligerent militia. Even though she had never been out here, she knew of the dangers. She had read about them.

Eventually, Alishia slept.

———

SHE FOUND THE stranger just before noon of the next day. She had left the plains behind, heading up into the foothills of the Widow's Peaks and wondering just where to go next. Fifty miles west was Pavisse, the old mining town that was known to be a haunt for criminals and undesirables. East lay the steam plains of Ventgoria. These were usually passable with care if the traveler kept to the marked routes, but Alishia had heard of markers being moved—although it was never clear who was to gain from leading travelers into steam pits—and the steam vents themselves were becoming more and more unpredictable. She had read a book not a dozen moons ago, a travelogue published on cheap paper with a print run of less than a hundred, which told of ventings the size of the largest buildings in Noreela City, great explosions of toxic steam from deep within the land as if it were sighing at the way things were going.

So Alishia had chosen the Widow's Peaks themselves, and upon making that decision she had almost been overcome with a sudden, delicious realization: she was an explorer! She had always wanted to see a fledge mine. Perhaps if she was daring enough, she would even try some of the freshly harvested drug.

Still, finding a fledge miner dying out in the open air was not the introduction to mining she had expected.

She saw him from a distance, a pale yellow form slumped on a hillside. She paused, looking around for danger, aware that trickery like this was a bandit's favored lure. The landscape was quiet but for the lonesome cry of a bird of prey, circling high overhead as it called to some distant mate. Birds hopped from rock to rock on her left, seemingly undisturbed. A group of sheebok grazed farther up the hillside, too far away to see her but near enough to the body to be startled away should it stir. She kept her eyes on the sheebok and birds, and edged the horse slowly forward.

Twenty steps from the fledger, she knew that this was no trick. His pale yellow skin was stretched from the sun, displaying how

strange daylight was to him. Even unconscious he had one arm resting across his face, shielding his eyes. *Yellow eyes*, thought Alishia,
yellowed from the drug. I can't wait to see them.

She dismounted and knelt beside the miner. He was tall and
thin, like all fledgers, and he still wore the sheebok leathers that kept
him warm beneath ground. Alishia slowly peeled the clothes away
from his body. He was soaked with sweat and he stank, but she finished removing the coat so that his underclothes could dry in the
sun. A strange circular weapon lay unsheathed nearby, the blade
smeared with dried blood. Alishia froze, looking around, trying to
make out whether there had been a struggle here, but there were no
signs. So she closed her eyes and tried to picture where she was, re-
calling the maps of the region she had pored over many times before. The nearest fledge mine was only a couple of miles from here,
deeper into the mountains. The fledger stank of the drug, his sweat
a curious mixture of sour odor and sweet fledge. She dabbed her fingers to her tongue, tasting the salt of his sweat and the undertones of
something more taboo.

He was battered and bruised, his neck bleeding from several
deep scratches, his nose caked with dried blood, his hands, fingers
and fingernails black with gore, apparently not his own. She glanced
again at the strange sword. Whoever or whatever he had stood
against had come off worse.

"Hey," she said, not expecting an answer. The fledger did not
stir.

Alishia returned to her horse and pulled a water gourd from the
saddlebag. She would need to find a stream to replenish it soon, but
for now there was enough to give the fledger a drink and take some
herself. He seemed in a bad way. She was no nurse, but at least she
could bathe and clean his wounds. As she knelt down next to the
wounded man, he grabbed her wrists.

"They're out!" he hissed. "They're awake!"

Alishia started, but his grip prevented her from backing away.
His eyes were squeezed tightly shut, teeth bared, pain clear on his
face and evident in his voice. He let go of her at last and started
moaning.

"It's all right," she said, leaning forward again, tipping a splash of
water into her palm. She had read many books about the fledge
mines and those that mined them, and she had great respect for the

way they had continued following the Cataclysmic War, machine-less. In the dark, miles down, they used touch as well as sound to communicate.

She dripped water into his mouth, shaded his eyes, touched his forehead and cheek and the underside of his nose as she tried to calm him down. With each utterance she would gently stroke the skin of his face. She knew the method, not the language, and for all she knew she could be abusing the memory of his ancestors while trying to soothe him. But eventually it seemed to work, and the suffering man did not object when she draped one of her spare dresses across his face to shield it from the sun.

"The sun's very high, it's midday," she said. "I know your eyes will be sensitive. Keep that there. I need to clean your wounds. I'll keep talking as I move around so you know where I am. You're safe, though, fledger. Whatever you were fleeing, it's gone now."

"They'll never be gone," he said, but Alishia did not reply. Serious discussion would be for later. Right now she simply needed to keep him awake.

While she worked, pulling back his shirt and bathing the cuts and scrapes across his skin, trying to ease the sunburn where his flesh lay exposed and reddened, she talked about things she knew. She started with fledge mining and how it had changed through history. Sometimes he snorted, other times he seemed entranced. She moved onto other things, random facts hauled from her memory, until the legend of the Violet Dogs seemed to grab his interest. There were songs, she said, although she could not sing. Ro Sargossa had written poems about the myth, but she could never do them justice.

"Where were they from?" the fledger asked.

"Beyond Noreela."

"What's beyond Noreela?"

"Sea. More sea. Whirlpools. Ice. Islands, some say, even big islands, with wild people and savage animals living on them. We're the center of things, and beyond Noreela is the rough edge. That's where the two Mages and their army fled to after the Cataclysmic War."

"Something's happening up here," the miner said, wincing as Alishia caught a flap of loose skin over one deep cut.

"What do you mean?"

"Something bad, something threatening. The Nax know it. They're awake! They killed Sonda, they took the whole cavern. They're awake and angry!"

"You're safe now," she said, distracted. She glanced at his bloodied sword again. "Is that what you killed with your weapon?"

The fledger laughed and it was a sickly sound, like someone gargling with vomit. "The Nax! With a disc-sword? You have no idea, topsider."

They remained silent for a while, Alishia tending his wounds and the miner letting out the occasional grunt or grateful sigh.

"I'm Trey," he said at last. "Trey Barossa. This is my first time topside. My mother died in there. So did everyone else."

"I'm Alishia. I'm sorry about your mother."

"I have to tell someone, have to reach someone who can help."

"Like who? The Duke? No one's seen him for years."

Trey frowned. "I don't know," he said. "Are there militia? Authorities who should know, those who protect Noreela?" He opened his eyes slightly, and Alishia saw the tears. They were not only from the pain of sunlight hitting his yellowed eyes for the first time.

"You have very beautiful eyes," she said, unable to help herself.

"I'm sorry," Trey said, shaking his head. "I didn't realize you were a little girl."

"I'm not! I just—"

"Sorry," the miner said again, sitting up, holding his head in his hands and letting tears darken the ground between his knees. "But is there no one we can go to? There are hundreds of dead people down there, and the Nax will spread beneath the mountains. We have to tell the other mines. There are thousands of people living beneath these mountains alone. You know there's a whole world down there, Alishia. The Nax can destroy it. We've known that forever, but forever they've kept quiet. Now they've been woken."

"Woken by what?"

Trey grasped his knees and squeezed, as if trying to wring out the truth. "By whatever's happening up here. Anything that wakes them up means bad times falling on us, always. Just never *this* bad. In the past, there was only ever one at a time . . ." He trailed off, tracing the pattern of his tears on the dry grass, as if communicating through the language of the mines as he spoke. "Sonda," he whispered. "Mother."

Alishia rigged a sun screen with her blanket and some broken branches from a nearby tree, and went about preparing some food. Trey remained awake and silent. Occasionally she heard a sob from him, but she left him to his mourning, traveling some way along the slope as she searched for wild potatoes.

What she had read about the Nax had always been written as myth, grand and great stories with which to frighten children or startle susceptible adults. She had never read a serious book where there was anything more than a passing reference, supposition dressed as fact, and she had always assumed that the Nax were mostly make-believe. But then, many people believed that the Violet Dogs were imaginary as well, a dread tale of invasion and slaughter dreamed up generations ago to fulfill some political or religious agenda.

"I thought the Nax were a legend," she said quietly as she approached Trey. She dropped an armful of wild potatoes and began chopping them into a bowl with a pinch of herbs.

"They are," he said. "They were. Everyone down there believes in them, but there's little proof, little to tell the truth. Moments in history, but history is easily distorted. They're our gods and our demons."

"All gods and demons make themselves heard or felt from time to time," Alishia said. She cursed inwardly, stunned at her clumsiness in conversation. This poor man was mourning his mother's death, and the deaths of those he knew and loved, and here she was spouting her naïve librarian's philosophy. "I'm sorry," she said, "I didn't mean—"

"No," he said. He was looking at her properly for the first time now, holding the blanket above his eyes to shield them from the sun. "That's all right. I'm sorry I said you were a little girl. I can see that I was wrong."

Alishia turned away, blushing. She felt so inept. She was not used to talking to people, especially strangers.

Especially fledge miners!

Trey Barossa ate little, and after food he thanked Alishia and said that he needed to sleep, to travel, to warn . . .

She watched confused and fascinated as the miner took a chunk of fledge from his shoulder bag and chewed it as his eyes closed, his breathing slowed and his body seemed to relax, molding itself to the ground. She sat nearby and looked back across the plains at Noreela

City. It was still visible in the distance, a bruise on the land with a brown haze of smoke marking the sky above it. The city was less than a day distant, and yet it already felt a lifetime away.

Later she wandered over to the sleeping miner and gathered his things. His shoulder bag fell open. She caught sight of a lump of yellow fledge within.

Alishia looked back at the city again. More than a world away.

———

IT DID NOT take long for Trey to drift away. He felt the heat of sunlight on his skin, even through the blanket the girl had erected above him, and he smelled a hundred smells he did not know, heard wind brushing through nearby trees, felt the cool smoothness of grass beneath him, a thousand experiences he had never known living underground where the air was cool, the cavern filled with man-made smells and the breeze came from deeper within the caves, bringing only rumor. He should be reveling in this place. There was so much to see, yet he had barely opened his eyes.

But sleep was welcoming for him, and the travel that came with it. He had to move his mind across mountains, try to touch the awareness of miners farther away, deeper down. He had to *warn* them.

The sounds and smells faded as sleep took him, and Trey rode the power of the fledge. He moved away quickly, shifting straight up into the air like a cave bat gone wild, flailing invisible limbs to try to regain a sense of balance. His mind spun, and with it his perceptions. Up and down ceased to exist. There was simply around: an all-encompassing awareness of being surrounded by space, unhindered by rock, a million different routes open to him from where he hung, unplanned, unrestricted. Trey's mind exulted and rose higher, touching clouds that tingled his skin and made him shiver where he slept on the hillside far below. Shapes circled him for a while, black birds with cruel curved beaks, and he was aware that they had something of the talent he possessed. They knew of his presence, though they could not see him. They circled some more and Trey shifted away, watching as the birds dipped and rose, trying to find him again. They called out and he heard them twice, up here in his mind and down below with his sleeping man's ears.

He felt more free and unimpeded than ever before in a fledge dream. The space around him was staggering, the potential overwhelming. He wished Sonda could have experienced this; he wished that they could have been here together. But Sonda was dead, slaughtered by the rampaging Nax.

Trey tried to rein in his mind and steer it across the mountains. He passed between peaks, dipped down to touch a tumbling stream that came from deep within the mountains, wondering whether it was connected with the underground river that had played the background to his life forever. He went farther from his body than he ever had before. The distance was frightening—he could feel the space between his conscious mind and his subconscious—but it also felt safe. It was no wonder, as his mother had once told him, that so many of the fledgers who visited topside decided to stay forever. Up here there was such *freedom*.

He passed the cave and shaft in the hillside where the rising had brought him to the surface, raging and mad with grief, sending him out blind into this new world. The rising had halted in its tracks. Way down below, the mules were dead.

Trey moved on, eager to put distance between himself and that evidence of his former life. He flew into the mountains, passing a small lake speckled with signs of thousands of fish breaking the surface. A scar on one hillside told of a recent landslide, and the ground revealed below glowed and glittered, as if the blood of the land was drying in the sun.

Onward, farther into the Widow's Peaks. On one steep slope he spied a herd of creatures rolling uphill. He moved closer and made out something of their makeup; they were like shifting plants, great balls of growth that hauled themselves effortlessly against the slope with barbs and hooks and sharps stems. Closer still, and then the whispering began. Deep down in his mind voices rose up, some in languages he could not understand, a few relating words he could. There were many whisperers, and although Trey was sure they were not actually directing their speech at him, he felt exposed and vulnerable floating high in the fresh mountain air. He went even closer and the voices grew louder. Their whispers were rhythmic and spellbinding, drawing him in. He tried to make out whether they were talking in pleasure or pain, glee or grief, and when he saw some of the shapes decorating the outsides of these tumbling things—the flash of bone, old cloth flapping as the things moved, the occasional damp darkness of rotting things—he realized whose voices they were.

He rose quickly, escaping this band of things as they tumbled inexorably uphill, and within minutes he was out of range of their muttering victims.

Trey flew on until he found what he was looking for; a wound in the land, a mine shaft, cauterized by time and continuous usage. There was no evidence of any sort of rising here. A huge machine sat dead and pointless way beyond the mouth of the shaft. Great chains, links as long as a man, lay rusted into the soil, mostly overgrown but visible here and there as a reminder of old times. They connected the redundant machine with whatever means had once been used to haul the mine's product to the surface.

He dipped down, hovered at the mouth of the mine and took a mental sniff. It was fledge, but old, little sign of any new batches of the drug having been brought to the surface in a while. He drifted inside, immediately finding the going harder now that he was confined once again in tunnels and shafts. He stopped suddenly, his incorporeal self standing at the black entrance to some unfathomably deep pit.

Out of the darkness came silent screams.

Trey reeled, spun back, passing into rock and out again, his movements slowing, and for a few rapid heartbeats he was terrified that he was becoming stuck down there, caught in the sickening outpouring of pain and agony, trapped in the knowledge that slaughter was happening at that exact moment. The mental anguish poured up and out like an eruption of pure torment, scalding him where he lay.

Somehow Trey withdrew from the mine. He fled into the sunlight, letting its heat bathe the screams from his floating mind.

———

ALISHIA DRANK WINE sometimes. Nothing else. She had certainly never tried fledge.

She knew of some who used it, and she was more than aware of its effects: nullifying, dulling, somnambulistic. In her readings about the fledge-mining communities that had existed for generations belowground, there were hints at its spiritualistic properties, the idea that its real use was as a perception-expanding compound more than as a mind-numbing drug. She had been drawn to the conclusion that its effect depended largely upon the user, what they desired from the drug and what drove them to sample it.

She was sure that she had nothing to fear.

The chunk was the size of her little fingernail, surely not enough for the sleeping miner to miss. She sniffed at it, enjoying the sweet aroma, and dabbed it to her tongue. The taste sat in her mouth and then seemed to spread, sinking through her cheeks and across her face in a warm, glowing sensation. It was nice. The sun did not change, the landscape around her remained unaltered; there were no adverse effects.

Trey had chewed a lump of fledge the size of his closed fist. Surely a negligible piece such as this would do her no harm. She was an explorer now after all, and as Ro Sargossa had written, *experience is the mother of knowledge.*

She glanced at the sleeping miner. He had shivered a few times, moaned in his sleep, groaned once or twice. He seemed calm now. She looked up again, across the plains at Noreela City. Even in the warmth of the afternoon sun that place seemed cold and distant, like a memory cast in heat haze instead of a real place.

Alishia lay down on the grass and chewed the fledge into dusty fragments.

———

SHE DID NOT travel, but she did dream.

Alishia dreamed of secrets. She knew many supposed secrets, gleaned from the books and maps and diaries and other ephemera she had read through her life, but she did not understand them. To her, they were simply knowledge. So much of what she had read was forgotten, lost in the mists of time and degradation since the Cataclysmic War. The words she had read changed now into pictures, the pictures into rich images, the images into dream memories: the Violet Dogs stormed ashore in a time gone by, screaming and whistling and eager to consume; a man passed a box beneath a table, inside the box a charm, inside the charm a spell of death, and the fate of a long-dead Duke was sealed; a soulless shade cried in the dark, a place without sun. There were many more, dreamed together into a miasma of experience that Alishia thought little of knowing. In her fledge-fueled dream these things simply *were.*

Erv was there in her dreams, so awkward and pathetic and far less frightening. He was the guide walking her from one image to the next, holding her hand like the Duke guiding the Duchess down a dangerous path. There was no real threat here; he was Alishia's idea of what he always should have been. There was no surprise when she told him she loved him, because maybe in a much different world—a world where safety was assured, not craved, and where people lived instead of merely existed, with time for leisure and pleasure instead of filling their hours with the fight for survival—maybe in that world, it could have been so. Alishia's dreamland made that world, speckled as it was with the precious yet deadly stones of arcane memory, her naïveté finding succor in the fact that perfection could still exist above and around all the things she knew. Terrible things, some of them. So terrible, so heinous, that their memories had been all but lost, locked away between dusty age-yellowed covers and buried in the deepest piles of books. History, befuddling itself with terrors of the present, had no real import for people fighting day to day to stay alive. The austerity of Alishia's existence made her a natural receptor for such knowledge.

She passed from one time to another, one place to the next, distance proving no barrier, though time was spelled out for her. Shifting from three centuries pre-Cataclysmic War to the first few years following that dreadful event was exhausting, as if for a few seconds she herself had lived those times. She toured the deserted battlefields of the Cantrass Plains and the islands of The Spine, seeing the giant war machines already rotting into the poisoned ground, sensing the skewed influence of the Mages as nature struggled to right its wronged self.

More time passed. Alishia's dreams continued, laying her knowledge out for her own inspection. She was aware of the astounding passage of time, and also the meager couple of hours she had spent sleeping on the foothills of the Widow's Peaks. She was content in the knowledge that she was safe.

But things were changing.

Because as dream-Erv loved and guided her around the labyrinthine landscape of her own understanding, Alishia sensed something impenetrable in the distance. Past the realms of her own mind and intelligence, way beyond knowledge, a black space had opened up in her mind. She understood its emptiness. She understood that it was a potential nothing, not even a nothing itself, less substantial than total darkness, which was merely an absence of light. And for the first time, she was afraid.

She turned her back on this inscrutable absence and tried to walk away, but Erv held her back. He had changed now. He was no longer the innocence she craved, the naïveté she admitted, even to herself. Now he was something else entirely.

Something came out of the dark.

———

ALISHIA SCREAMED HERSELF awake. She had not cried out like that since she was a little girl. It hurt her throat, terrified her. In the distance a rage of skull ravens took flight, and nearby the fledge miner rolled from his front onto his back and sat up, looking around in obvious distress.

Alishia immediately knew where she was, but she could still feel that impenetrable nothingness seeking her out, searching across mountains and through valleys for her vulnerable mind.

"All gone," Trey muttered through a slew of tears. "They've come and taken them all."

They've come . . . Alishia thought, and although she had stopped screaming, her fear was just as rich and bright.

The questing thing was a dream memory, fading as the hot sun sought to burn it away. But that did not soothe Alishia. In the comfortable, passive landscapes of her memory, something had actively opened its eye and seen her, something hiding away in a place she thought was safe.

And now it was searching her out.

Chapter 10

THE SHADE WAS building on instinct. Experience was not yet available to it, but knowledge and, more importantly, understanding increased with each successive moment. As a thing of prospect and latent existence it craved a fixed point of reference, something it could home in on and investigate, examine, with a view to making its own. Let loose by its god, the shade's potential was staggering, an all-enveloping pressure that required expending and exercising.

It knew whispers, but none of them hinted at the object of its search.

It dipped more frequently out of the planes bordering existence, and the shock became less intense each time.

Time and distance juggled with the shade, shifting it by esoteric travel until it sensed a true solidity around it, the material of reality, where the inanimate and the long-dead swarmed with teeming life. Here, the shade knew, it would find a home.

Twisted as it was, any home would suit. It was stronger than a shade should be, more capable in its potential madness, more able to drive out a previous life to make room for its own pending existence. And it could do that here, a tumbling mind in a valley, alone and free, seeking something enriching; or there, a great consciousness floating much as itself, old and wise but perhaps too removed. Because whatever actions the shade took were informed by its god. It could lose itself, find a permanent place and plant its seed of wrongness, but that would mean betrayal. And if it weren't for its god, it would not even exist as it did now; it would be less than nothing, a total absence of potential, memory and intent. At least now it knew of itself. Given success, the rewards from its god would be greater still.

So the shade passed by a multitude of hosts, dipping past some and causing a brief frisson of fear, ignoring many more. Searching. Seeking the perfect home. Hunting for a place where whispers were rich and rumor was rife. Here it would create itself at last. And when the time came, it would return to nothing.

The shade felt fear at that, a vague emotion filtered down like a whisper from the future.

And then suddenly it found what it sought. There were many minds displaced and it passed them all—most were tired and introverted and alone. But this one . . . this one soared. It traveled in memory and reveled in knowledge. It hunted new ideas, not content to make do with the old. It was a mind that knew the potency of the past and the promise of the future.

The shade noticed it, and the mind was aware of being noticed. It was rich and wide, and suddenly the shade knew emotion—real fear, real freedom—and it lurched. Its own would-be mind stumbled away through the darkness, and when it settled, the mind it sought had withdrawn, back down into the world of reality.

The shade was not concerned. It had dipped out to the world many times now, and it was no longer afraid. It would seek out this mind and find room in there for itself.

There it would sit, and listen, and wait.

Chapter 11

LUCIEN MALINI WAS less than a man and more than human. His single-minded drive, his reason for being, the one true aim that informed his waking hours and haunted him when he slept, had driven him mad long ago. Madness was no hardship for his kind; indeed, most of them welcomed its inevitable grasp. It focused the mind, excluded all outside considerations and drew everything down to a point. That point was as sharp as the tools of killing he carried, and just as deadly. And though insane, his mind was powerful and vibrant—and put to one task, it pursued it doggedly. He often spent days sitting and meditating on the purpose of his life. There were times when he shed his understanding of any language, any sight that did not in some way appertain to his cause. And this guided him unerringly to his end result.

Lucien could go without food and water for a full moon, such was his mind's manic grasp over his body. Its dedicated train of thought, consideration, philosophizing was so powerful that it could take control of his physical self, stretching the laws that governed its use and limits and, if damage was ever great, it could steer it ever onward until death overcame even madness. He knew that it would be a grand struggle.

This madness also bred hatred. The extremity of his dedication transformed any intellectual consideration of his cause into an all-encompassing loathing, a rich, blood-hot despising of the target. And that target was magic. His abhorrence of it was bred into him and handed down from those who had first committed themselves to its eradication. He had perpetuated and enriched that hate.

It applied also to those who purported to carry magic. They were equally sullied, equally *guilty*.

Lucien hugged his red robe around him and started down into the valley that harbored a subject of this hate, a carrier, the first true carrier for a generation. This was what he was made for. Today would be the culmination of his life.

Soon, when he knew that the others were ready, he would move. He would enter the sprawling, degraded town of Pavisse to find Rafe Baburn.

———

THE RED MONKS had no god. They worshipped no deity, ascribed to no doctrine, prostrated themselves at the feet of nothing. They feared magic, though that was no devil, and their dogma preached little save the expunging of this fear. They worked for the land, though the land had not asked that of them. The Monks knew that magic was the true way of things, yet still they sought its exclusion.

If they had true enemies, they were the Mages Angel and S'Hivez, who had taken magic to themselves and twisted it far past the flexing that the laws of nature were prepared to withstand. They had broken it over the rock of their own vanity. The Monks hated them fiercely, and they harbored no love for anyone to provide balance. Theirs was a philosophy of negativity, a religion—if it could be called such—where destruction was a high command. Seeking magic, courting its return, that was heresy, because should magic return, there would always be evil to take it again. And heresy deserved the ultimate vengeance.

During the Cataclysmic War, the Monks' predecessors had fought alongside those desperate to save and protect Noreela. The Mages' power had been strong, their perverted use of magic more powerful and deadly than anything the Noreelans could muster. The Monks' ancestors—pagan priests and academics who drove the war machines, combining and communing with the great constructs as they battled the Krote hordes of the Mages' armies—died quickly and painfully, as did their charges. For while the magic of the land drove the machines and gave them power, the Mages' twisting of this magic gave them an edge: more power; greater strength; the transgressing of life and death itself to expand their armies at an exponential rate. When one Krote fell, two would rise in his place: his revivified physical self and his soul, the wraith captured and tortured by the Mages.

Yet somehow, Noreela won out. The Mages were driven north, out along The Spine, until there was nowhere left to flee. The remnants of their armies commandeered ships and sailed them burning into the unknown. And then magic left the land.

Those pagan priests that survived the fighting had seen firsthand what magic could accomplish in the hands of the Mages. They had had their own close bonds with the machines cruelly broken, and now they were adrift. Nature had betrayed their trust and faith, and their beliefs mutated into an abiding hatred. Slowly, over a few years, the survivors drew together, knowing what had to be done. Magic was gone and it must never return, not while there was even the slightest chance that the Mages could reacquire what they had once ruled, start again where they had left off.

The priests went mad. The Red Monks rose from their madness, feeding upon it and dressing themselves in its color. They became ghosts of the Cataclysmic War, wandering the land, searching for hints of magic's return. Vowing, with every breath they took, to put it down.

The Monks became something of a myth, fading away into the past in the company of other truths. They hid away in their retreats, keeping watch, and if ever magic was hinted at in the land, they investigated.

These past days, the Red Monks had been sighted all across Noreela.

———

A FLASH FROM the opposite hillside told Lucien that the time had come.

He shifted his sword and signaled back, and then he saw movement as the other dozen Monks began their descent from the hills into Pavisse. They had encircled the mining town, remaining high up so they would not be spotted, keeping to old sheebok trails and finding concealed places to await the signal to move. This was a much more coordinated effort than their assault on the farming village over the hills. There, Carfallo had gone in on his own instead of awaiting the arrival of his brethren. He had obviously believed that he could take the village singly—and he had—but he had also allowed escapees. Lucien and the other Monks were not concerned at the number of people that had escaped Carfallo's fury. What they *were* concerned about was that one of them was Rafe Baburn. They had met at Trengborne as arranged, entered the village quickly when they saw what had happened, stepping past and through the destruction that held little surprise for them. There in the trading square of the village, surrounded by his stiffening victims, they had found Carfallo. Lucien had sworn that he was dead, such were the profusion of arrows and bolts and swords in his body. The dust around and beneath him was blackened, as if a huge bruise were slowly spreading across the ground, and his face was pierced and parted where the shafts had done their damage.

"No Baburn," he had whispered, and then his last bubbling gasp shook his body, rattling arrow shafts and scraping lines in the mucky dust. He had waited for their arrival before dying.

The Red Monks had remained in the village that evening, planning their next move, confident that no one would return. And if a few brave stragglers did come back to try to bury their dead, then that was simply more blood for the Monks' swords. For them, the colors of blood and madness were much the same.

The Monks knew many arcane things. Their divinations and interrogative techniques went far beyond torture and threat, extending past boundaries normally reserved for dead magic or living legend. The trails they followed were always cold and covert, and this one—although they still believed that Baburn was unaware of his legacy, his destiny—was no exception. It was that very ignorance that kept him from them. They had sensed the emergence of magic, their utter hatred of its promise lending it the characteristics of an unknown color, an impossible sound in their thoughts. But given that the boy knew nothing of the potential stirring in his head, to track it was nigh on impossible. They had to use techniques perfected by their ancestors as they spent lifetimes seeking magic. Sometimes dregs were found: a witch here, with a hint of enchantment about her; a girl there, finding her monthly cycle and with it a closeness to the land, a sight she could use to predict. The Red Monks tracked them down and destroyed them all, often annihilating those around them as well. There was always a risk that the magic had spread, like the disease they believed it to be. And even if that were not the case, death was meaningless to the Monks, and easy to mete out.

The skills they used were not magic, but rather forgotten talents, practices that had been mostly discarded long ago. The Monks knew the boundaries between where the laws of nature crossed and diverted, and where they were purposely bent out of shape. It was ironic that the greatest weapons they employed against the reemergence of magic could look so much like its use to any who bore witness.

Still, the Monks had their ways, and that night in the dead village of Trengborne they used them. It was a place rich in wraiths, the disturbed and confused souls of those so violently and recently killed, and the Monks had ways to question these. They sought them out where they hid, folded between moments and slipping madly from one moonbeam to the next, and while one Monk held them down with a mirific chant, another would seek out the mind—mad and confused, sad and raging—and question it with a Delving root. The Delving was a common plant near rivers and lakes, and its root, if picked at the exact moment between when it was sterile and when that sterility suddenly ended, became receptive to many hidden influences and energies. It planted itself not only under the surface of the land, but beneath the plane of the world, burrowing down from true reality to where the richest, purest sustenance was to be found. Only the Monks knew this, because over the decades they had wiped out anyone else with that knowledge.

Where is Rafe Baburn? they asked.

Dead, dead, we're all dead—

I don't know, help me, help me!—

Not you again, not you, not you!

Where is Rafe Baburn? they asked again. There was much madness in these new wraiths; anger and ire and bewilderment. But the Monks kept asking because they had all night.

Where is Rafe Baburn?

And eventually:

Rafe? My Rafe, my son? Is that you? Run Rafe, run! Flee! Go to Vance, find Uncle Vance in Pavisse!

Pavisse, the Monks said, and the root transmitted their smiles and made their emotions its own, a chemical message to spring into the ether where this wraith floated on uncertainty.

No! the stricken wraith said, but the Monks had withdrawn, and they left it to its raving.

They set out from Trengborne straightaway, traveling through the night, following their ancient maps and finding shortcuts through the mountains that even the most experienced shepherds did not know. As they walked, they planned. Their talk was spare, and in the space of a hundred words they had agreed that their incursion into Pavisse had to be carried out with more care. Trengborne had been only hundreds of people; Pavisse had a population of tens of thousands. The Monks would not be averse to killing them all if it meant that one of them was Baburn, but practicalities forced them to think logically. Not only would it be impossible to keep everyone in the town while the slaughter progressed, but that very act would take days. And as Carfallo had demonstrated, even a Red Monk could be worn down in the end. Madness had power, but only so much. Eventually a punctured heart needed more to run on than rage, and once its blood had drained and the routes for the fury had been slashed and cut, death was all that was left.

They needed stealth and speed. Their red robes would be seen, and some who saw might know what that meant. The word would spread. But the Monks still had surprise on their side. They were sure that the boy still did not know who he was.

They sought Vance Baburn. If they found him, they would find the boy.

Lucien headed down the hillside, aiming for the northern outskirts of the town, where a wide sprawl of shacks and tents indicated a growing influx of refugees. From his travels over the years he had come to realize that Noreelans, though fracturing into tribal elements once more, were still finding safety in numbers. The towns grew as the regions shrank, and the Duke found himself ruling over new kingdoms and independent states instead of simply Noreela. Perhaps that was why he barely ruled at all. Lucien viewed people as another part of nature, nothing special, distinct from it only because they had such a proclivity to destroy instead of nurture. They flocked, they feared, they were terrified at what they had sown, and yet they attempted little to right their wrongs.

He crossed a small wooden bridge spanning a stream. The water was barely a trickle, and as he passed over, it seemed to cloud. Bloodied from upstream, perhaps, or maybe he was seeing an echo of what was to come. He looked up but the stream disappeared between

buildings, like an artery drawing life through the dying town. Because
this place *was* dying. Lucien had been around enough death to recognize its stench, its sights. The refugees clung on to the town's outskirts
like premature mourners, here to take what they could and then flee
when the time came. The town stank of apathy: shit and rot left in the
open; a miasma of stale fledge and spilled ale in the air, drifting from
the many drink and drug establishments; food gone off, bodies un-
washed, and above it all the smell of burning. Lucien saw a pall of
smoke hanging above the center of Pavisse, evidence that even here
the Breakers were at work, paring down the old dead machines in the
hope of finding dregs of magic in their sumps, hidden away in petrified timber arteries, clasped in stone wombs never before seen, ossi-
fied by time but still potent. He would usually kill a Breaker as a
matter of course, simply because of what they sought, though none
that he knew of had ever found a scrap of magic. Right now his aims
were higher.

The look of Pavisse also marked it as a place waiting to die. These
encampments on the outskirts bled it out across the valley floor, but as
he approached the town proper it was difficult to tell where the shan-
tytown ended and Pavisse proper began. The buildings changed gradually, progressing from tents to wooden shacks, and then on to
dwellings with stone walls and reed roofs. But the degradation was
wholescale. Gardens lay dead and sterile, pools of dust where he saw
skull ravens bathing and plotting. Windows were mostly glassless, covered with swathes of sheebok fur to keep out the light and the stares of
prying eyes. Graffiti adorned many walls facing out onto the main
streets, sigils and codes marking the turf of one street gang or another.
But even that was old and worn down by the sun. The gangs were still
there, perhaps, but less zealous now, members more concerned with
their own personal survival than that of their mob.

Lucien passed a small street market where traders sold fruit and
vegetables on the verge of wrinkling into rot. There were craft stalls
and a furbat drainer milking his restrained creatures of rhellim,
stroking the fluid into individual vials that would sell for more than
most of the fruit in any neighboring stall. This trader looked well
fed, well traveled and relatively affluent. Lucien spotted a platinum
ring on his finger, a metal only mined and worked on the Cantrass
Plains three hundred miles to the northeast. A few of the sellers
called to Lucien as he passed by, inviting him to sample their wares,
but others fell silent at the sight of his weapons. He walked on with-

out glancing their way, but he felt their eyes on his back. Maybe they had heard stories. Perhaps one or two had even seen a Red Monk before, knew what he sought, why he was here. If so, they would do well to pack their stalls and leave.

His brethren would be infiltrating Pavisse now, pushing in from twelve different directions, opening their ears and eyes, trying to find any trace of Baburn or his uncle. He felt his sword hanging light at his belt, waiting to be fed and gorged again. He hoped that he would be the one to find the boy.

Lucien sniffed, but there was no magic in the air.

He passed by an old machine, a hollow oval the size of a man, whose use could only be guessed at. It had been incorporated into a building, framing the main doorway with its textured and ridged surface. There were stumps of hardened veins protruding from its top edge. As ever, Lucien was amazed at how casually people treated miracles. If this thing suddenly came to life it would scare most people to death. Perhaps it was a hole-maker, punching shafts into the ground a mile deep with energies gathered in its hollow center. Or maybe it was a break-healer, raising and lowering itself around a wounded body and knitting bones, patching torn flesh. Whatever, now it was a doorway into a whorehouse. Its ancient and inexplicable use granted it no favors. Lucien's hatred of magic was fed by what humankind had tried to achieve with it. The Mages had been the worst by far, yes, but all people were like that at heart. Those two had simply had the face to forcefully seek what they desired.

"That's a Red Monk!" he heard someone whisper behind him, and he did not turn around. It had been the grizzled old coal miner lounging in a chair outside the whorehouse; Lucien had heard him cough as he approached, and now he knew his voice as he whispered again. "Mean bastards, they are!" Whoever the old man was trying to impress did not reply.

He came to a tavern, peopled mainly with drunken militia being tattooed by a harem of Cantrass Angels. Approaching the bar, Lucien heard the scrape of metal on stone behind him. He turned slowly and peered out from within his robe's hood, spotting the militiaman who had moved. A Cantrass Angel was scoring a Ventgoria Dragon into his leg, substituting its customary steamy breath with a mythological burst of fire. The man's eyes were unfocused and bloodshot with alcohol, and he looked away immediately, slipping back into his chair.

Lucien turned to the barman, alert to any possible movement

behind him, and asked his question. "I'm looking for Vance Baburn to conclude a business deal."

"Never heard of him," the barman said, and he was telling the truth. Lucien could see the sparkle of fear in his eyes; perhaps he thought these drunken and stoned militia could help him, should the need arise.

Lucien turned away and left the tavern, hearing blustery mutterings behind him as the men revealed how they could have taken him, had they so wished.

The streets were becoming busier the farther into Pavisse he went. More impromptu street markets had sprung up, and their sellers seemed to be doing brisk trade, the produce richer and fresher than that sold on the outskirts. The traders nearer the river had their choice of the fresh wares, while those dealing on the outskirts probably brought their own produce in overland.

Every doorway could hide Baburn. Every alley, darkened as they were with wet clothes strung high up between buildings, could be the place where this could end. Maybe the boy had not even found his uncle and was hiding in the streets, sheltering in an empty house or trying to find work at the small docks. In a town of tens of thousands, finding him would not be an easy task, however aware or unaware he may be of his burgeoning powers. Time was not on the Red Monks' side, and Lucien knew this only too well. He would not sleep. He would not stop looking or questioning, and if needs must, he would move past questioning, start using some more direct methods of interrogation. Someone here knew of Vance Baburn.

He paused in front of another tavern, rested his hand on the hilt of his sword and went inside.

———

IN THE END, Vance Baburn came to Lucien.

"I've been looking for you!" a voice hissed behind the Monk.

Lucien had strayed from the main streets and found an area of holding pens for sheebok, goats and a couple of chained and spiked tumblers. The cages were heavy and thick, and he wondered just what else they had been designed to hold. The air stank of stale shit. There were a few people milling around—feeding the animals, clearing out stalls, nervously teasing the tumblers—but not many. Lucien had asked his question and was about to leave when he felt the point of a knife in his back, heard the whisper in his ear.

"You're not hard to find, you know. Dressed like you are. Like blood-colored shit."

"I've been looking for you too," Lucien said. The knife was pressed harder into his back and he felt the skin part, the cool metal sliding half a finger-length into his flesh. It did not hurt straightaway, but it stirred his blood. He felt his face flushing with rage, the sword twitching at his belt, and yet he did not turn around. He knew that he could use this movement to his advantage; he simply had to reign in his fury for a few heartbeats more.

"Where's the boy?" the voice hissed.

"I don't know, I'm looking for him myself."

"What have you done to him? Killed him like you killed my brother and his wife? Butcher! What possible reason—"

"That was one of my brethren," Lucien said, "and he did it—"

"I don't care for your reasons! If you're in with that murderer, I should kill you right here."

"You can try," Lucien said, and there was a pause. They stood there like that for a long moment, Vance Baburn holding the knife piercing the Red Monk, Lucien facing away from the man he sought, trying to control his rage, telling himself again and again that he needed this man alive, needed to question him, find out where the boy had gone. After a sufficient pause he made his move. "Or we can go to your home," he said, "and talk about this sensibly."

"I won't talk sense with a madman," Vance hissed.

"We're not all mad. Some of us are more obsessed than others. Like mad old Carfallo who found your nephew's village."

"He didn't find it, he slaughtered it."

"He killed some there, I admit, and for that I offer no apologies. But not all of them. A few militia, and some men who attacked him. Rafe—your nephew—escaped before Carfallo could kill him."

"You admit you want to kill him? Why? And what makes you think I can't push harder now, cut those words right out of your putrid body?"

"He's a danger to everything!" Lucian said, trying to rein in his anger.

"He's just a farm boy, what danger could that be? And he said the whole village was dead."

"A young farm boy's exaggeration. I'll not lie to you, Vance Baburn, I *do* seek to kill him. But I can make it easier on you, and your nephew. And easier on the people of Pavisse. Because we know he's here somewhere, and I'm not the only Monk searching these streets."

"Then we'll slaughter you all! I'll start with you right now, and the militia will clean up the rest of you like rats' bodies rotting in the streets!"

"Militia like those I just saw being tattooed by Cantrass Angels?"

"They're not all like that," Vance said, but the desperation in his voice was obvious. He pushed a little more. The knife sank deeper, and Lucien tensed, slipping the sword from his belt. The moment hung like that, ready to go either way. Lucien's instinctive rage could take full control, flushing him with the bloodlust and madness, spinning him around and slicing this man in two. Then he would slaughter those who watched; he sensed them hiding, terrified and fascinated. Or the men would part and go to Vance's home, and maybe Lucien would find what he sought.

"You can't kill me like that," Lucien said quietly, leaning back so that the knife penetrated even deeper. He heard Vance gasp as thick red blood gushed over his hand. "See? Nothing."

Vance stepped back, withdrawing the knife.

Lucien spun around, his sword in his hand, and faced the man. Vance was looking around, seeking help or an escape route.

"Don't make me run you down," the Monk said. "Where do you live? Is it far?"

Lucien knew that he had the upper hand. His heart was stuttering as it tried to keep pace with the rage coursing through his body, the madness that discarded pain like so much sweat. His face was flushed, the sword ready in his hand. *Not long*, he thought. *Not long and you can sate this bloodlust. This one first—slowly, painfully, punishment for his presumption—and then the boy. He'll sing his last on the point of my sword, and if any magic words escape him when he's dying, I'll stamp them down into the dust and shit on them.*

"Your house," Lucien urged. "We can talk there."

Vance nodded, glanced around uncertainly once more and then slipped his knife into his belt, resigned. He turned and led the way.

———

AS SOON AS they were through the door the Red Monk attacked Vance, kicking him to the floor, scattering empty wine bottles and smashing a wooden table into splinters. The big man tried hard to stand and protect himself, but Lucien's rage was up, his legs spasming with the kicks, stamping on one knee until it popped and crunched beneath his boot. The man screamed and the Monk jumped on his face, kicking down until teeth broke into his tongue and cheeks, blood gushing into his throat and bursting out in a shower as he coughed. The attack went on. When Vance tried to sit, Lucien kicked him in the hips and the base of his back, cracking vertebrae. Vance screamed, and this time the Red Monk let him.

"Where is Rafe?" Lucien hissed, holding the ruined man by his beard and lifting him so high that they were face-to-face.

Vance could not speak. He shook his head instead, grimacing as something ground in his neck like shattered glass.

"*Where?*" Lucien shouted again. The sight of blood spattered across his red robe, sprayed across his hands, kicked into weird shapes on the wooden floor by the man's thrashing legs . . . he wanted more. Every bloody splash took him closer to finding the boy.

Vance shook his head and Lucien let him drop. He hit the floor and writhed there, groaning, eyes half-closed, broken fingers splayed across his chest as he tried to hold his crushed ribs. He could not speak. That did not matter. Lucien knew he had to be quick.

He reached inside his robe and plucked a small box from a pocket, shaking it slightly to wake the thing inside. He heard the chitinous rattle of docked wings, the hiss as the insect tried in vain to fly out of the darkness that imprisoned it.

"You *will* tell me the truth," Lucien said. He dropped the insect onto the wounded man's chest, and used the tip of his sword to slash a finger-long entry hole in Vance's neck. The creature scuttled across blood-soaked clothing and the man's broken fingers. It smelled the copious blood, but the leakage from the fresh wound was different. Here the creature found what it desired most: thick, rich arterial blood whose flow would soon cease.

It burrowed inside. Skin and flesh parted, tearing around the cut Lucien had already made, and soon the lump that marked the creature's presence disappeared as it drove deeper, attaching itself to the man's spine with barbed claws, spreading its wing stumps so that other, finer limbs could extrude from its body. They delved through flesh and found what they sought.

Vance's throat began to rattle, his voice box agitated by the creature. "I'm going to die," he whispered hoarsely.

Lucien smiled, and nodded. "How true," he said. "Now . . . where is Rafe?"

"Don't know." The hiss was strange, inhuman, a caress of chitin on bone.

"Has he been here?"

"Yes."

"When did he leave?"

"Yesterday."

"Has he come back?"

"No."

"Where is he in the town?"

"I don't know."

"Does he know anyone else in the town?"

"I . . ." The hiss blurred, as if confusion had set in.

"Does anyone else here know him?"

"A thief."

"What's his name?"

"Don't know."

"How do you know he's a thief?" Lucien smiled at the man below him, because Vance's eyes were open again now. He was fighting, that was obvious, doing his utmost to keep silent. His eyes were filled with untempered hate. It did not frighten the Monk.

"Saw his hands, he has a thief's marks, he brought the boy to me, he . . . he . . ."

"So Rafe fled when he knew you wouldn't help him. He must have realized you were useless. I'm going to find the boy and kill him."

"No!"

Lucien stood and turned away from the dying man. The blood was running slower now, pooling on the floor and dripping down between boards, finding its way to the earth. With no sign of Rafe — not really any nearer at all — still he had someone else to look for. A thief. In a place like this, there would be hundreds.

"Kill you," Vance hissed. "Going to . . ."

Lucien turned around, but the man was already on his knees, knife in his unbroken hand, arm swinging around. He buried the blade in Lucien's stomach, slicing through, twisting it as the Red Monk stepped back, gasping. The men parted, Vance's eyes already drooping shut from blood loss.

"Untrue," Lucien said. And then he let his rage burst out.

Chapter 12

KOSAR AND A'MEER talked long into the evening. Their closeness had returned, along with a sense of attraction and comfort that set them fully at ease. There were a few jokes, some flirting, some out-right innuendos from A'Meer, but mostly the talk was serious. And mostly it concerned magic.

A'Meer had once fought a Red Monk. When Kosar started his story she mentioned it straightaway, trying to appear casual but knowing the reaction her revelation would invoke. Kosar, already drunk on Old Bastard and rotwine, leaned back in his chair and raised his eyebrows, waiting for A'Meer to continue. She had told him many stories during their time together, but never had she mentioned the Monks.

"I was traveling down through the stilted villages of Ventgoria. Everything is built high off the ground there, on wooden platforms set on the thick trunks of Bole trees. They try to make sure the villages—they call them villages, but usually there are no more than a couple of hundred people living in any one place—are built as far away from the steam vents as they can. The stilts keep them up away from the marshes and the gas floods that happen there sometimes, but really they're frightened of the steam vents as well. They emerge here and there sometimes, unexpected, as if they shift underground and break out wherever they desire. Some of the villagers believe the vents are caused by giant steam dragons, living beneath the ground and burrowing their way through the loamy soil. And each time they need to take a breath, they vent their steam out through the ground. Who am I to doubt their beliefs?"

"Everything amazes you, doesn't it?" Kosar said fondly.

"I'm Shantasi. We're more receptive to wonder than you fucking Noreelan wasters."

"I'll drink to that." Kosar drained his glass of rotwine and wondered whether he would wake up the next morning.

"I'd gone quite a way down through the marshes, doing a bit of hunting here and there, when I met him. He was riding a horse, but it seemed to know where to go without him having to guide it. I was on foot, so I stepped to the side of the trail when I saw him in the distance and started a fire. It's something of a tradition in Ventgoria that when you meet a traveler going in the opposite direction, you take food and a drink together. Not many people have cause to travel right across that place—there's not much there, especially for those who have no sense of wonder. So I was plucking a marsh goose I'd shot down a couple of hours before, gutting it, stuffing it with a handful of tumblespit I'd been drying in my rucksack. I had a bottle of wine too, from the village I'd just left. Kosar, you won't believe the wine those Ventgorians can brew! Their grapes grow in the open on string racks, no earth, only the sun to give them sustenance, and the long, loving care of the roots by the growers. Believe me, it's something to kill for."

"Naturally, you bought it," Kosar slurred.

A'Meer glanced up. "I traded." She looked back down at the table and continued, her glass of rotwine long forgotten. Her small hand traced the outline of somebody's carved name, and Kosar wondered if she had known them. "When he came nearer," she continued, "I'd already skewered the goose and it was spitting fat onto the fire. It smelled delicious. I knew of the Red Monks, of course. I'd been *made* to know their purpose. But this was the first one I'd ever met."

"Made to know how?" Kosar asked.

"I'll get to that, Kosar. Let me talk. You told me yourself what you think this all means—how relevant this boy Rafe could be, how his appearance might change everything—so now I have something to break to you. And this is my way. By telling you about the first time I met a Red Monk.

"So, on came the Monk. He had his hood up, as they always do, and he seemed to be asleep. Hands on his thighs, his head dipped, the horse's reins knotted on its back. The horse looked as though it had walked a long, long way. It sounded unshod, it was foaming at the mouth, and I could see its ribs rippling the skin with every step it took. My mouth was watering, but suddenly I wasn't hungry. Because I knew what was to come."

She paused, and Kosar stared wide-eyed, suddenly sober. A'Meer was revealing so much to him in so few words, telling him that there was something much more to her than met the eye. More than he had ever known before. They had been lovers for a few moons, and although they had talked incessantly, never had anything she revealed held as much import as this. The whole truth remained to be told, but already Kosar knew that things had changed.

A'Meer glanced up and for a few seconds Kosar was petrified. Her eyes . . . there was so much more pain there than he had ever thought possible. Pain, and secrecy. He could see that this revelation was hurting her. "What happened?" he asked.

"He came level with me, dismounted, drew his sword, and we began to fight."

Kosar was stunned. The first image that came to him was the Red Monk in Trengborne, marching through the village taking hits from arrows and crossbow bolts, every impact seeming to make him stronger, each splash of his blood on the ground empowering him more. And then he imagined A'Meer fighting one of those same creatures.

It took him a few dazed seconds to comprehend that she had won.

"I'm a warrior, Kosar," she said. "I grew up in New Shanti, as I told you, but not in New Rol Port. And my parents weren't fisher folk. When I was a girl they took me to Hess, the Shantasi mystic city. And there I learned a lot of things. A *lot*. Some of which I need to tell you now, most of which I can never tell you. However much I like you, Kosar—and believe me when I tell you I've never liked anyone more—my life and what I am has to remain my own."

Kosar stared at her white face framed by the beautiful black hair, those dark eyes that seemed to swallow even the reflection from oil lamps, giving out nothing. The raucous laughter in the Broken Arm seemed to fade away, little more than an echo, as if they had the place to themselves. He looked around and nobody was watching. In such a public place, he was about to learn secrets.

"What happened?" he asked again. He simply wanted to know, not discuss. Not yet.

"We fought for a long time. You've told me a little of what you saw in Trengborne, so you know the tenacity of these things. A Shantasi trained in the art of combat has few of the defenses a Red Monk has, because we're not mad. In fact, a Shantasi fights with pure logic, knowledge transposing instinct, certainty voiding chance. A Monk has madness as its ally. And true madness has twisted them into something other than human, something more like a machine. There's a bitter irony in that fact, but it's true. They suffer a cut, they feel no pain. They lose a limb, and balance becomes a product of their madness, just as strength comes to those enraged. Stick a sword into a Monk's gut and its muscles clench in rage, holding it, dragging it deeper in to bring its adversary closer. Slash an artery and insanity clots it, drives a fist of lunacy into the wound and stems the flow of blood."

"You sound like you speak from experience."

A'Meer nodded grimly. "I was armed with full Shantasi warrior weaponry at the time, as I was on all of my travels."

"You never said . . ."

"I told you where I went, what I saw, who I met. I never mentioned what I was wearing at the time."

Kosar nodded, waved his hand, as if the slight deception was unimportant. *And isn't it?* he thought. *I thought my story would surprise her, but she's spun the table.*

"I had to use it all," she said. "We went with swords to begin with—a Monk's sword is as mad as the Monk. It's made of a metal that reacts with blood, *craves* it, whines as its being sated. Spooked the fuck out of me. We fought for an hour, and I put in some good hits. It's strange, but a Monk is actually a very poor swordsman. They're untrained, and madness doesn't aid coordination. But madness is also their greatest weapon. The cuts and slashes did nothing to it, and when I eventually ducked, feinted, rolled and stuck my sword in its gut . . . as I said just now, it pulled me in. I didn't want to let go, I couldn't pull it out, and the sword was sinking deeper, the Monk's flushed red face staring at me, those eyes . . . so determined to finish me, and so confident that for a few heartbeats I thought I could never win. But then I let go and rolled back, and took up a slideshock. I slipped it onto my forearm as the Monk was pulling my sword from its gut, and I took my first swing bent almost double. The wire caught it under the chin and the slide hit my wrist. It should have taken its head off, but it was spinning, wrapping the wire around its neck and drawing me in again. I lost another weapon; the wire had slashed its throat and buried itself deep. It bled a lot, but that didn't seem to bother it. It came at me again and I fell, kicking it up and over my body and onto the cooking goose. The fire didn't get a good hold because its cloak was so soaked with its own blood."

She seemed to remember her rotwine and drained it in one gulp. Kosar leaned forward and refilled her glass, pouring some of the black wine for himself.

"We fought past dusk, and on into the night. The sky was clouded and the fire was out, but there are lights above the marshes in Ventgoria. Some say they are wraiths, but they sparkle and spit with energy, and a wraith has none. Whatever they are, they witnessed our fight. The Monk came at me with its hungry sword, and scored hits. You've seen the scars on my hip, the wound on my neck. I used weapon after weapon, getting in good hits but losing them all to the Monk in the end: throwing knives; my diamond ball; a handful of stinger eggs in its face; rotdust thrown into its wounds. I even ran for a time, circling as it stumbled after me, and I managed to score seven bolts from my wristbow before I tripped and lost the Mage-shitting thing in the marsh. And all the while it came at me, and all the while I was scoring hits. I was wounding it every time, Kosar. Every fucking time I went at it I'd take off a finger or push some rotdust into the wreck of its face.

"By dawn it no longer had any eyes, but it listened for me. And my only defense through all of this—the only reason I beat that damned thing, exhausted as I was, weaponless as I became—was that it was no real swordsman. Tenacity is a fine weapon, but I could dodge, sidestep, flip, shrink myself away from its sword. It was just a matter of stamina."

A'Meer fell silent, took another drink of wine and looked around the tavern. It was emptying now, drunken people tripping over chairs as they left, laughing at themselves and their friends. The barman had started to glance over, obviously suggesting that it was time for them to leave as well. Kosar waited for A'Meer to finish her story, but he could not wait for very long. He was drunk and tired, and she was teasing him, whether she knew it or not.

"And?" he said. "*And?*"

"And eventually the Monk fell down. I took its head off with its own sword. That Mage-shitting thing screamed as I did it, and it was still whining as I threw it out into the marshes. Then I dragged the body until I found a small gas vent and dropped it in. I stayed the whole morning to watch for the next venting. There were bits of the Monk in the steam storm, small bits. I had to make sure. I was utterly exhausted, hallucinating from the exertion, and maybe . . . maybe I thought there was even more to them than that. Maybe sometime in the night I'd come to believe it was immortal."

"Why did it fight you in the first place?"

A'Meer smiled then, leaned across the table and touched Kosar's cheek. "Gods, I've missed you Kosar," she said. "And it took you a while to ask that. Getting old, yeah? Losing it a bit up here?" She tapped his head and sat back in the chair.

"Drink-addled," he said. "And shocked. Imagine, my sweet A'Meer who likes it bent over a chair is a warrior, and probably the most dangerous person I know." There was no humor in what he said; he did not feel frivolous. If anything he was drained, and tired, and perhaps a little annoyed that she had made this evening all her own.

"The reason it fought me is why I have to ask for your help, Kosar. It fought me because I'm a Shantasi warrior, and it's our chosen cause to bring magic back into Noreela. And you have to help me because that boy you saved, the only other survivor from Trengborne, may be what I've been waiting for all my life."

———

THEY LEFT THE tavern arm in arm. Kosar had a hangover, his inebriation driven to ground by A'Meer's revelations. She felt light by his side, her arm thin, and he thought he could probably pick her up and fling her about his head with very little effort. Yet she was a warrior, and she had defeated a Red Monk in battle. Images mixed in his head; the Monk from Trengborne peppered with arrows, and the Monk in the Ventgoria marshes slashed and pierced by Shantasi weapons.

The streets were busy with drunks, prostitutes and drug dealers, yet Kosar felt removed. Here people continued their small existences, busy doing the same thing day in day out, busy doing nothing. He did not resent them that, nor did he look down upon them; they had to get by the best they could, and most of them were decent folk reduced by general decline. But although he was a thief, he was a traveler also. He thought he had seen many things.

Compared to A'Meer, he had barely left the place of his birth.

She had been born in New Shanti, a place where few non-Shantasi visited. She had been south of Kang Kang to The Blurring. She had traveled along The Spine to its very tip, a place that many believed did not even exist. And he suspected that she had been to other, even more obscure places she had yet to tell him about.

Kosar shook his head. "A'Meer, you amazed me so much when we were together, and you amaze me more now that we meet again."

"I'm sorry, Kosar. It's not something I wanted to keep from you—truth is, it's not something I did consciously. It's been a part of my life for so long that I really don't think I'm out of the ordinary. That was the first and last time I ever saw a Monk, and since then I've just been wandering. Never seen any sign of the magic I'm supposed to promote, and in all honesty I stopped looking long ago. It's not like this was an obsession. The Shantasi mystics gave us talents, and much more besides." She trailed off here, and Kosar thought, *Much more besides . . . That's what she can never tell me. It's that "much more" that makes her a stranger to me now.*

"But it was never an *obsession*." It sounded to Kosar as if she was trying to persuade herself.

"So now?" he asked, wincing as a gang of kids ran past carrying screeching bats. His headache had rooted itself firmly now, and the piercing screams seemed to thump inside his skull and become trapped there.

"Now we have to find the boy," she said. "But back to my place first. We can spend a while there, make plans. And catch up."

"I think I've done enough catching up for one night," Kosar said.

"I wasn't planning on talking." A'Meer's voice contained none of the flippancy he had come to know, none of the mischievous glee. It was low, urgent and very serious, as if she knew that tonight might be the last of its kind. She wanted one more fling with normalcy before things changed forever.

They walked through the busy streets until they reached A'Meer's home, a ground-floor flat in a block of three. A whore lived directly above her, A'Meer said, and the third flat appeared empty.

No one ever came, no one ever left. Windows were covered day and night. Another mystery in a town that cared little for them.

Inside the flat they heard A'Meer's neighbor going about her business. The floors were thin—only a layer of timber boards and whatever covering the whore chose to put down—and Kosar tried to ignore the sounds as A'Meer prepared him a warm drink. As he sat and drank, listening to the sated couple mumbling above them, A'Meer rooted beneath her bed and dragged out a big leather bag. She opened it up and began laying out weapons. Kosar knew some of them, and others he recognized from her description of the fight with the Red Monk. These were blades that had been slicked with a Monk's blood. Here was a slideshock that had been buried in its neck. Each weapon was wrapped in oilcloth, and they were all clean and greased. Beside them she laid a selection of sheathes and scabbards, equally well maintained. And beside them, other things that looked like nothing he had seen before.

A'Meer came to him suddenly. She straddled him on his chair and kissed him, fiercely and passionately, as if it were the last kiss either of them would ever know. Within a few seconds they were ripping at each other's clothes, revealing themselves to each other for the first time in several years. The familiarity was there, they both remembered what the other liked, and when A'Meer sank onto him Kosar saw the scar across her throat, put there by the Monk.

As they made love Kosar glanced across at the weapons and other fighting paraphernalia arrayed across her bed. The newfound knowledge added a chill and a thrill to the sex.

———

THEY LEFT A'MEER'S flat just before dawn. It had taken her a while to dress and strap on the web of leather and fur belts, straps and pockets she needed to carry all of her weapons. She looked even slighter when she had finished. And in her deep, soulful eyes, Kosar saw something akin to fear.

"I'm leaving," she said, staring around the room. "I've been here for years, and now I'm leaving. We first made love in this room, Kosar, many moons ago. I've been settled here longer than anywhere in my life, other than Hess. I have friends in this place. Pavisse is a shit heap, but some of the people aren't bad. Some of them, believe it or not, want to make things better. Though most of them have forgotten how."

"You'll be back," Kosar said, but as A'Meer offered a weak smile he knew how hollow that sounded.

"Curse it, I haven't worn this stuff for ages," she said, shrugging her shoulders to settle the gear better across her shoulders and hips. "I feel different already. Bastard things chafe and rub. And last night has worn me out. But there's always a time to move on. The Monks will have followed him here, you know."

"Yes, I know."

"We can't let them find him. There's a sick irony in the Monks' existence, because their reasons are so justified. Nobody wants magic back in the hands of the Mages, if they're even still alive. But madness informs the Monks' methods, and all they can do is destroy. There's no *reasoning* in them. This lad sounds more innocent than any of us."

"They won't know he has an uncle here. They won't know where he lives."

"Don't you believe it. They have their ways, their methods. Come on, show me where you took him."

A'Meer shut the door on her rooms without once looking back.

At this early hour the streets outside were quiet. A few drunks lay in the gutters or huddled in doorways, and there may have been more in other places hidden by darkness. The life moon was hidden by clouds, the death moon pale, and the only light in the streets came from weak oil lamps in windows and on hooks outside taverns and drug dens. There were a handful of people walking the streets, because in a town like Pavisse there is plenty of business carried out only at night. Some of them walked past Kosar and A'Meer without looking up, while others, perhaps catching sight of A'Meer in the ghostly light, hurried on or changed direction altogether.

Kosar saw shapes flitting through shadows without traversing the lit spaces in between. Wraiths. They were there in the daytime too, but sunlight negated them.

At the junction of two streets there was a band of militia smoking fledge pipes. They were muttering to one another, moving on the spot to keep warm. There were six of them, the dregs of law-keeping in Pavisse, many of them more criminal than some of those they sought to catch. Kosar knew that these men ran protection rackets, whoring houses and drug circles, and although they provided something of a ceiling above which crime was not allowed to stretch, it was a sad irony that they initiated much of it. They would have questions for the two of them, especially A'Meer. Fighters and mercenaries were not wholly uncommon, although their existence was grudgingly accepted rather than welcomed. But a fighter moving through the streets by night . . . yes, they would have questions.

Kosar and A'Meer backtracked and found an alternate route around the militia. It meant crossing the river, but they stole a small rowing boat and paddled over silently, the water tarry across the bow. The river smelled much fresher by night than it did in the day, as if darkness could bleed it of refuse, shit and the stink of animal corpses thrown in from sheebok farms up in the mountains. Unseen things made splashes but nothing troubled them, and they reached the far shore in a few minutes.

Within a hundred steps of leaving the river, with dawn bleeding across the mountaintops to the east, A'Meer paused and raised her hand. Kosar bumped into her and held her arms, his thief's scarring finding succor on her cool bare skin. He could hear nothing untoward, see nothing, smell nothing unusual. A'Meer did not move for a few long moments, but then she started backing up, forcing Kosar back as well. The two of them kept moving like that until they came to a house doorway, where A'Meer fumbled with the handle, drew something from her belt, knelt and popped open the lock in the matter of a dozen agitated heartbeats.

She opened the door and hustled Kosar into a stranger's house. It was only after she closed and locked the door behind her that she spoke, pressing her mouth to his ear so that it was more a breath than a word, unmistakable from a sleeper's sigh.

Monk.

Kosar backed away from the door but A'Meer held him fast. He saw her sense. They were in an unknown room, whose confines and layout were uncertain in the dark, and any movement could tip a table and send its contents tumbling to the floor.

He glanced down at A'Meer just as she looked up at him, and her eyes reflected weak lamplight from the street outside. They were wide and terrified. He put his arm around her shoulders and his hand on her chest. He could feel her heart racing as if trying to outdistance the moment. She shivered, her skin slicked with a cool sweat, and she pressed close.

They heard a noise outside. Footsteps, slow and methodical, but with no attempt at concealment. The Red Monk passed by the house, paused and carried on along the street, and then A'Meer began to shiver even more. She was shaking her head, breathing heavily, and two of her blades clanged together.

Kosar held her tight and buried his face in her neck, whispering inanities to calm her, warming her cold skin with his breath. She clasped his hands where they held her, pulled him tighter, and he realized with sudden shock that he had let her tale cloud his judgment. She was a Shantasi warrior, a trained fighter, but that did not mean that she was unafraid. In fact, he suspected it gave her more to fear. And those things she had not told him, could *never* tell him . . . perhaps they were even worse.

"It's gone," he whispered in her ear. "We should go too."

She turned and held him tight so that they did not need to talk above a whisper. "It came from the direction we're taking. They may have the boy already. He may be dead!"

"Only one way to find out."

A'Meer let go of Kosar, knelt and unlocked the door.

They were out in the dawn again, hurrying along streets, through alleys and across courtyards to put distance between themselves and the Red Monk. Kosar had come to know Pavisse well during his short stay here several years before, so now he navigated easily in dawn's early light, picking out landmarks and listening for familiar sounds. They followed the course of the river for a while before turning into the heart of the town, heading for the hidden districts. The name was a misnomer—everyone knew the places were there, just as most who knew of them stayed away—but they were much more than slums and home for criminals and outcasts. The hidden districts held hidden knowledge. In that respect at least their name held water.

That's where he'll be if anyone has him, Kosar thought. *That's where I'd take him to keep him safe.* The journey to Rafe's uncle's house had already taken on a doomed feel, perhaps initiated by the Monk's appearance. If the boy was indeed as important as A'Meer suggested, the idea that he may still be there with his relative seemed naïve. Rafe's very existence had brought Red Monks to Pavisse, and his potential had urged one of Kosar's best friends to revert to her warrior birthright. Rafe could hold the future of the land in his hands, or its eventual downfall. He had rapidly turned from a simple farm boy into someone both great and terrible.

Kosar steered around the outskirts of the hidden districts, and even here there were many old machines incorporated into buildings and street constructions, lending themselves as a skeleton around which Pavisse had grown and petrified since the Cataclysmic War. He saw one that he recalled from his previous time here, a great hollowed globe smashed in several places like a skull cleaved by an axe. It was buried deep in the rocky ground so that only half of its circumference protruded. It had once been used as a shelter by those who had no homes, and as he passed by Kosar smelled the familiar stenches of fledge, rotwine and waste.

Daylight was bringing the streets to life. A'Meer hurried along behind him, and when Kosar glanced back he saw that she was self-conscious of her new appearance. She looked utterly formidable, and the hint of mystery that had always surrounded the Shantasi added to the effect. And yet she was uncomfortable with her new apparel. He wondered just how intense her training in Hess had been, how long ago . . . and how much of it she would recall after so long.

They arrived at Rafe's uncle's house, a straw- and mud-walled building with an old iron fire pit in a lean-to on one side. It looked unused, and Kosar guessed that the boy's uncle had not shod a horse in many dozens of moons.

"It's quiet," A'Meer said.

They stood in the shadow of a building opposite, trying to make out whether there was anything to trouble them in or around Vance's house.

"It's early. Maybe they're still sleeping."

"No . . . the whole place is quiet. Pavisse is waking up, but not here. Listen."

Kosar listened. In the distance he made out an occasional shout, traders urging their mules to the best-selling pitches. Blackbirds and honey doves chattered across rooftops, vying for space much the same as the traders, and here and there a skull raven sat on its own, other birds too wary to settle nearby. A pack of dogs ran along the neighboring street, the subject of their pursuit letting out a solitary panicked squeal. Window blinds crashed open, people coughed and spat the night from their lungs. Wheels whispered along the dusty streets.

Vance's house was a dead zone in a place coming to life. No birds rested on his roof, no animals prowled the yard.

A'Meer drew a short sword from a leather scabbard on her belt and advanced across the street.

"Wait!" Kosar hissed. "There may be more Monks."

A'Meer glanced back briefly. "I think they've been already," she said softly. And then she ran.

Kosar stood in wide-eyed disbelief as A'Meer reached the front door of the house, swung it open and disappeared inside, all before he had time to draw breath for a reply. He had seen her run across the yard, kicking up silent clouds of dust, making no sound as she swung herself inside . . . he had seen every movement and moment, and yet it was impossible. She had moved as if the air itself parted before her.

Kosar had taken only several steps himself before A'Meer appeared at an upper window, leaning out.

"The house is safe. They've been." And then she withdrew again, closing the window softly behind her.

Kosar found her in one of the bedrooms upstairs. He had smelled the body immediately upon passing through the front door, and as he climbed the stairs the stench grew worse; blood that was almost fresh, the rich tang of butchery. A'Meer was standing in an open doorway, panting as if she had just run twenty miles, and then he glanced past her at what was left of Rafe's uncle.

A sudden, staggering possibility hit Kosar. "What if that's Rafe?" he said.

"Did the boy have a beard?"

"No."

"Then this can't be him. There's only one person here, and this belonged to them." A'Meer lifted her sword, and dangling from its point was a clot of fur, blood and skin. It looked like a slaughtered furbat stripped of its wings.

"A Monk did this?" he asked.

"I assume so. Although they're usually very calculating, very sparse in their murdering. This Vance must have annoyed or angered it somehow to warrant this."

Kosar was stunned. So much had changed in such a short time that he could feel himself trying hard to catch up, failing at many points. The boy: a magician, a Mage? A'Meer, sweet A'Meer: a warrior trained by Shantasi mystics to seek out and protect magic? And his own existence, a life of travel and thievery given over to a simple, quiet way of life . . . changed suddenly and irrevocably by what he had seen, and what he was still witnessing now.

"You moved so fast," he said. "I saw you, but you were so *fast*." He was still staring past A'Meer at the mess of blood and flesh across the bedroom, yet the scope of his amazement and confusion was far wider than this small place.

A'Meer looked back at him at last, and he saw that she was no longer so on edge. She must have been terrified that they would arrive here to find a Red Monk. She had defeated one before, but that offered no guarantees. And there was more to her fear, more than simply the prospect of confronting a Monk. Perhaps she too had expected to find Rafe's remains mixed in with those of his uncle.

"There's a lot I can't tell you, Kosar," she said. "I've already warned you about that. And it's not simply because I'm not allowed to tell, but because much of it I just don't understand myself. I don't *know* how I moved so quickly. I was trained to do it and it happens. The mystics called it Pace, but I know that explains nothing. Accept it. I have to."

"And that's it?"

A'Meer shrugged. "That's it."

Kosar nodded. "Just warn me next time, perhaps." But A'Meer had already turned away and started rooting through the meaty remains of Vance's uncle.

Kosar started taking a look around the house, seeing if he could find anything that identified Rafe. If the boy had left something here—his jacket, boots, belt—that would indicate that he had gone quickly or been taken by force. If there was nothing of his, perhaps he had taken his own leave. Or maybe Vance had sent him away before the Red Monks arrived, knowing that his nephew was in danger and giving him the name of someone who would help or hide him. He found many empty bottles, piles of old clothes slowly rotting down, a few books with their pages stuck together by time and disinterest. Nothing of Rafe. No sign that the boy had even been here, although Kosar had brought him here himself. Perhaps he had not stayed for long. It was even possible that Vance had not wanted the responsibility. Knowing that the Red Monks might be on the trail of his nephew may have negated any familial loyalty.

Considering the state of his uncle right now, that may have been a blessing for Rafe.

"He's not here," A'Meer said as she followed him downstairs. "If the uncle knew anything of where the boy has gone, the Red Monk will have had it from him."

"I don't think he did know," Kosar said. "If Vance wanted to help the boy he'd have known not to send him anywhere he knew. He probably wouldn't have sent him out at all. And if he didn't want to help, or was too afraid, Rafe may have left on his own. In which case, I think we should look in the hidden districts."

"That's a whole city in itself!" A'Meer said. "And why so sure he's there?"

"I'm not sure at all, it's just a hunch. Rafe's a farm boy. If he left this house the natural route to take is down to the river, and that leads him past the outskirts of the hidden districts. And once there, a boy like that on his own won't be left alone for long. There are whores, crooks, muggers and fledge dens. He'd have been taken there, I'm sure."

"Of course," said A'Meer. "Kosar."

He turned and met her gaze. She was still afraid, but now there was excitement in her poise as well, as if it had taken time for the implications of events to sink in.

"You don't have to come," she said. "This is nothing to do with you. You're an old thief who settled down on a farm, for Mage's sake. You don't want to get mixed up with Red Monks. Or me."

Kosar found himself ridiculously hurt by her comments. She was right, this was nothing to do with him, and given any real choice he would steer as far from a Red Monk as possible. But he *was* involved, not only through his knowledge of what had happened to Rafe, but through her as well. He cared about A'Meer.

"I'll tag along." Perhaps she sensed how her comments had disappointed him, because she said no more as the two of them left the house. "There's a quick way into the hidden districts from here," Kosar said. "As long as you don't mind the dark." Any surprise A'Meer felt at his knowledge she kept to herself. Kosar had been here for only a few moons, but his type had a knack of discovering secrets.

They set off quickly, ignoring curious glances from passersby. Kosar led them back toward the river, and then ducked through an open doorway into a small square building. Inside he uncovered a hole in the floor, the vent of an old buried machine. "It's not far," he said.

"I'll go first."

Before Kosar could protest, A'Meer had drawn a small dagger for each hand and dropped down into the hole. He followed close behind, wondering what they would face at the other end.

Chapter 13

LENORA, LIEUTENANT TO the Mages, scarred from countless battles and her burning need for revenge, resident of Dana'Man for three hundred years but originally a Noreelan, circled her hawk high above the port of Newland and watched the preparations for war. Excitement coursed through her, because she knew where she would soon be heading. Excitement, and a calm sense of destiny moving things on. This moment was when her life would change again, and though she had been preparing for centuries, the actual instant was as sweet and satisfying as she had always hoped.

Below her, Dana'Man was a wasteland of snow and ice. A few lonely rocks protruded from the white blanket here and there. The stains of the Krote encampments on the lower hillsides were the only splashes of color, and it was so obvious that they did not truly belong. Mountains loomed above them, their dormant volcanic tips pointing skyward as if striving forever to reach the sun. It would never happen. This land had been cursed long before the Mages and their surviving Krotes had arrived, and it would remain cursed long after they left.

She circled, her hawk spreading its webbed tentacles to catch the meager thermals rising up from the town below. She could make out several warships in the harbor, their edges blurred by the movement of hundreds of people loading more equipment and weapons. Smaller vessels bobbed alongside, and farther out in the bay, constantly dodging chunks of ice many times their size, dozens more warships awaited the signal to depart. Even this high up there was a thrill in the air, a hint of excitement that Lenora had not felt for three centuries. Through all their time here—their catastrophic arrival, the battles that followed, the eventual subduing of the people they had found already living in this forsaken land—there had never been anything to really offer hope. Now Lenora thought that everything they had lived for down the years may well come true, something that even she had sometimes doubted. Fully armed and ready to fly south, she felt her love for the Mages glowing as strong as ever.

Their summons had come just that morning, and she had flown a hawk up into the Mages' remote mountain keep. They had told her of the whispers from Noreela—the Nax awake, the Red Monks on the move—and she had not asked how they knew. They had their spies and ways. The implication of their words was huge; that magic was back in the land! She had seen the light of exhilaration in their ancient eyes, and Lenora left knowing that this was her last day on Dana'Man. She had packed her weapons and clothing without a moment's regret.

Every breath froze her lungs, every thought was informed by the cold. This high up, Lenora picked up layers of sparkling frost on her face and clothing as the hawk drifted through hazy clouds. Her bald head glittered with ice. Her furs and leathers were stiff and cracked from the cold, but her blood burned inside, filled with rage and anticipation of the weeks to come. Soon she would feel the warmth of the Noreelan sun on her skin again. And then, when the fighting was done and magic was back in the hands of the Mages, Lenora would be free to seek her own very personal revenge.

There was movement far below, a hundred specks passing across the snowfields and then drifting across the harbor, rising higher and coming up to meet her. Her Krote warriors on their hawks. They all knew their mission, and she sensed their eagerness, heard it in the shouts and laughter that accompanied their approach. Weapons glinted in the ice-cold sunlight, and Lenora could not recall the last time she had seen so many of her warriors smiling.

They circled their mighty hawks above the harbor for several minutes, shouting to one another, waving good-bye to the snow and ice, full of bravado yet doubtless harboring their own private thoughts: relief and trepidation; excitement and fear. Each Krote carried arrows and stars, shield and slingshot, pouches and bottles of various poisons. Singly they were fearsome; together, in a group so large, they looked like the end of the world.

"Let's go and find some sun!" Lenora shouted. She was the first to peel away from the formation and dip her hawk's nose, heading out to sea. Warships passed by below her, then a couple of small coastal patrols, and then within minutes the sea's surface was disturbed only by giant icebergs, and the occasional splash of something huge rising and submerging again.

Lenora had dreamed of this forever. As they flew south toward Noreela for the first time in three hundred years, she remembered the day she left . . .

———

SOMEHOW IT HAD all gone wrong. The Mages—the exiled Shantasi Mystic S'Hivez and his lover, Angel—had lived so many dreams, won so many rapid victories, drawn so much power to their sides in the magic they had twisted to their ways . . . and now they and the remnants of their army fought their final defense on the northernmost beaches of Noreela. Disbelief clouded Lenora's vision. It was a hazy red, the color of life, as if blood were teasing her eyes before leaking away forever. She had no doubt that she was going to die. Whatever strange powers the Mages once had, the ferocity of the Noreelan people's army had shattered her confidence, leaving it strewn across the Noreelan landscape and trodden down into battle-bloodied soil. They had been fighting for weeks, and the only end in sight was death.

The beaches here on this nameless island were wide, high dunes marking the dividing line between sand and the lush forests farther inland. Some of the dunes sprouted corpses, like sapling trees seeking the sun, and the hollows in between were quagmires of blood and guts. The dead outnumbered the living, and their majority was growing every minute. Several days earlier the two Mages had still been able to raise dead Krotes and throw them back at the enemy—shambling zombies that the Noreelans could only stop by hacking to pieces. And ten days before that—at the Battle of Lake Denyah—dead Krotes' wraiths had been forced into battle by the Mages, a nebulous army that could not be stabbed or killed. Now they could do neither, and each Krote killed merely reduced their army by one more.

The Krotes were trapped between land and sea, on a stretch of beach maybe half a mile in length. They were harried at both ends by Noreelans mounted or on foot, while from the forests beyond the sand dunes came frequent machine attacks. The Noreelan war machines were graceful things, long legs and scything arms that kicked or cut Krotes aside every time they attacked. Some of them had been brought down—their mounts slaughtered, the machines themselves hacked at until they came apart—but still metal limbs thrashed at the sand, and ruptured stone bodies leaked blood and other fluids as they thumped across the beach.

The Mages' final machines had failed two days ago. As the last one ground to a halt and tipped over, crushing its rider, it was already stinking of decay. Lenora had stood aside in stunned disbelief as the Mage S'Hivez shouted and raged at the dead machine, throwing pulses of sickly light at its clotted arteries and molten metal joints. It had done no good, of course, and the Krotes had fled on foot. The Mages had drifted overhead, directing the battle from atop their hawks and sweeping down now and then to pluck up a screaming Noreelan. Several times Lenora had seen these unfortunate victims thrown from the hawks' backs, shriveled and denuded from their brief time with the Mages. Loose-limbed and bloodless. Eyes sucked from their sockets. The viciousness of the Mages had encouraged her to keep fighting.

The sand beneath her feet was sticky with blood, clotting to her leather shoes and slowing her down. She tripped over hacked-off limbs and headless bodies. Someone grasped at her ankle and she kicked him away, spitting down at the wounded Krote's face. His fight was over, hers was still at its height. If she remembered, she would go back soon to put him out of his misery.

She fought at their left flank, hacking at advancing Noreelans with her heavy sword. She had run out of stars and discs and arrows long ago, and she had lost her slingshot when it became embedded in a Noreelan's spine. That had torn a swath of skin from her right forearm, and now sand was stinging the wound. The agony kept her awake and alive, maintained the rage that had driven her for days, ever since they had burst from the Mages' keep and forced the Noreelan army back into Lake Denyah.

Then something had happened. Her memory of it was vague, its taste rank in her mouth, but it had been bad; a change in the air, a shiver through the ground as the land took a breath. At the height of battle, victory had been snatched from them. The Mages' grasp on defiled magic had held for a dozen more days, but a purer magic had seemed to present a final defense, empowering the Noreelans to launch a counterattack in such huge numbers that the Krote army had been overwhelmed. For every ten thousand Noreelans they killed, twenty thousand took their place. Zombies of Krote dead waded into the throng, taking twenty with them before they were hacked to pieces. Wraiths spun and thrashed, whipping at the flesh of the enemy and opening them to steam into the night, before Noreelan priests managed to put them down. The untrained Noreelan army had gathered momentum, sucking power from the land and launching it at the Krote army with wave after wave of machine attacks. Surprised, overwhelmed, the flight north had begun.

It had been one long fight until they reached the sea. Days without rest. Nights lit by the flaming fat of burning bodies. Those who tired fell behind and were slaughtered. Those who fought gained wounds as their badges of honor, and a creeping madness borne of exhaustion and the inevitability of what was to come. Lenora—a simple warrior then—had looked again and again to the Mages, expecting them to throw down some mighty defense. Their magic simmered darkly around their forms, heaving as they danced across and above the battlefields. But if they did try to fight back, the effects were so small as to go unnoticed. Dead Krotes shivered on the ground instead of rising to their calling. Shadows flitted from the corner of her eye, but these wraiths were all but gone.

The Noreelans drove on, pecking at the tail of the fleeing Krote army with their loping machines, and a thick line of blood was painted across Noreela.

And then they reached The Spine, hopping from island to island in stolen boats, until they ended up at this place. At least before now they were on the move, and even falling to the enemy had felt positive because it gave fellow Krotes a chance to move on. Here, on this golden beach turned red, the battle was simply an ongoing slaughter.

Lenora screamed as she parried a sword blow from a big Noreelan, ducked down and hacked at his stomach. Coils of gray guts spilled out and he looked at her in surprise. "Help," he whispered. She buried her blade in his face and wrenched, hearing bone crack as he fell. Another took his place, a woman already bearing terrible wounds to her neck and chest. Lenora gave her some more, then stamped her face into the sand and smothered her while fighting off a young boy. The lad was vicious and determined, but even when he buried a knife in Lenora's side she merely shrugged him off and hacked him across the throat. It was just another wound, one more step nearer death, and the closer death came the more she was ready to welcome it in. The rage was good and pure. The fury at the unfairness of things—the Mages and their followers had gained and lost so much, in such a short time— drove her on, into the embrace of this new Noreelan attack. She hacked left and right, screaming, her bloody face terrifying her attackers. The day before an arrow had sliced off some of her scalp, and she had shaved her head so that the terrible gash would be on view. Several times her foes' eyes drifted up to her weeping wound, giving her the opportunity to gut them with a simple thrust of her blade. The more wounds she took, the closer death loomed, but it became easier to mete out death as well.

Behind her, farther along the beach, the Mages were hunkered down behind a protective cordon of Krotes. Again and again the Noreelan machines sprang from the forest, strode or slid across the dunes and down the beach. And again and again the Krote warriors drove them back, at terrible expense. Hundreds lay dead, their slippery wet bodies offering added protection against the machines. Those left alive all bore injuries, some with simple cuts and bruises, others missing limbs or holding in their insides. Several machines lay across the beach. Their former Noreelan riders were little more than smudges in the sand—when they did manage to bring a machine down, the Krotes expended their fury upon its rider—and all but one of the machines now lay still, shattered and burned and melted by dregs of the Mages' magic.

Because dregs were all they had left. Earlier that day Lenora had seen them rise from within the circle and direct a sustained attack of shadowy fire at an advancing machine. It had taken all their strength and concentration to bring it down, and even then their warriors had to advance to finish the job. A week earlier they had been blasting troop ships from Lake Denyah and scything down a hundred Noreelan attackers with a wave of their hand. Now the Mages could barely summon fire. Magic had given, and so it took away.

Still Lenora fought. Her faith in the Mages was as strong as ever; it was the devious magic she no longer trusted. Caught by the Mages, it had refused to stay caught. And though she still felt it thrumming through her bones, Lenora was certain that something was about to change.

The sun was growing weak. The air seemed lighter than usual, less refreshing. The trees behind the beach had started to shed brown wrinkled leaves, though they had only bloomed a few weeks before. Even when this battle was over, Lenora thought, its effect would have only just begun.

Her final memory of being on the beach was of a machine rearing up before her. Its legs were shimmering, fiery things, and its rider screeched, his face red not with blood, but with rage. The machine's legs swished this way and that, scorching Krotes into charcoal shells. The rider fired arrows and followed every one with a growl. When he glared at Lenora she was certain that she was going to die. His eyes burned so deep—

And then something struck her across the shoulder, and pain like she had never imagined took her away.

———

LENORA SOARED ABOVE and ahead of her Krote warriors. Far to the south lay Noreela, and that beach where she had fallen. Much farther south than that, nestled in the mountains east of Lake Denyah, the village of Robenna. This is where she had been born and raised so long ago—an unassuming sprawl of dwellings, shops and farms that had made its living trading fruit from natural mountain fields. She had called it home, and from there she had been driven—pelted with stones, whipped with poison-tipped sticks—for becoming pregnant out of wedlock. The child was a memory now, drawn from her sickening body and taken into the Black one night in the foothills of Kang Kang, but the anger she felt at that place still simmered. Every act she had performed since then had been in the name of her dead daughter. At first she had felt only bitterness at the destruction of a life that could have meant so much. Then the rage had driven her mad, and the only place she found succor and acceptance had been as a part of the Mages' army. The bitterness had matured gradually into an all-consuming hate, tinted by the voice of her unborn daughter; laughing, crying, telling her mother how much she would have liked to live.

Others told her it was madness, but Lenora was convinced that it was her daughter's shade—her homeless soul, shorn of potential—remaining with her mother. Lost and useless. Abandoned and alone. And the only way Lenora could quieten that voice was to seek vengeance in its name.

On the day she was driven from Noreela, the voice of her unborn daughter fell silent. But Lenora had always nurtured that hate, and she had made a silent promise that, should the chance arise, Robenna would burn at her hand.

As they drifted south she wondered whether her daughter would be waiting for her on the beach.

———

ALISHIA AND THE fledge miner came down from the mountain slopes and headed west. She was shocked at how long they had slept—the afternoon had faded into evening by the time she screamed herself awake—and she suddenly felt unsafe remaining in the foothills. There were things in the mountains that had stalked Trey, killed his friends and family, and now as night approached she feared that they would come aboveground, hunting through the dusk as they had slaughtered their way through the eternal darkness belowground. The miner had remained silent on the matter, sitting atop Alishia's horse, bent forward and hugging its mane as he sobbed through his grief. If this is what meeting a Nax did to someone, Alishia had no desire to stay close to where they might surface.

And there was something else moving her on. The thing that had reached out for her while she slept the fledge sleep. That utter darkness, a void, repulsing her and fascinating her in equal measures. Instinct tore her away and told her to flee, while her intellect demanded to know more. Her fear, remembered from the dream like a taste or a smell, had been the purest fear of her life. Knowledge from books did not impart that level of emotion. Erv had disconcerted her, and some of the things she had seen in Noreela City had sometimes made her scared to wander the streets, but she had never before been as truly frightened as in that dream.

Upon waking, the screaming still stinging her throat, she had already begun to deconstruct and analyze the fear.

As a child she had nightmares when she was ill. She could never explain them to herself, let alone to others, although thinking about them still disturbed her even now. There had been a sense of space so huge that it belittled her and her existence, made her less than a gasp in a storm. She stood on a hill and the space closed in around her. Nothingness itself took on a weight and a pressure, grinding her down even though she *was* nothing, taking her away from the center of things so that she regarded herself as meaningless, an insignificant pollutant in the purity of void. As she grew older she tried to ally this space, this endless, pressing void, with the experience she lacked. A whole world sat around her and she had seen nothing of it. But however much she suspected this, in truth she knew that it was not the case. Her knowledge may be secondhand, but that was no reason for her to fear the world.

The thing that had reached out in her fledge dream provoked the same sense of fear as those sickening childhood dreams, but now it was much more real. Because even now, awake, Alishia was terrified.

Something beyond her experience had intruded into her sleep. She was horribly certain that had she not screamed herself awake, it would have come closer, until it finally touched her for real.

Trey sat huddled on the horse, shielding his face from the fading daylight as if he could make his own cave, take himself back belowground. Alishia heard him crying from time to time, but after her first couple of attempts to comfort him she decided to leave him be. She had read that the best way to temper grief was by letting it run its course.

If he had noticed that a small amount of his fledge was missing, he said nothing. Neither did he mention her screams as she had come awake. Maybe he thought she always slept with nightmares.

Alishia held her horse's reins and led it down out of the foothills. She glanced back from time to time and saw shadows hiding on the slopes, huddled beneath rocky overhangs or sitting comfortably in cave entrances. But the setting sun was keeping them at bay, bathing the hillsides in its rich golden light, blurring the mountains' sharpness as it struck a cloud bank far to the west and turned slowly pink. She walked faster, conscious that night was coming and keen to find somewhere suitable to camp on the plains below.

Noreela City was out of sight now, hidden behind the hips of the first mountain, even its glow no longer marking its location as dusk settled comfortably across the land. For the first time in her life she could look around and not see something of the city. She did not miss its excesses, cruelties, corruption, carelessness, murders, the screams at night or the cries in the day as another dose of skewed justice was meted out. And yet she did miss the city itself. It had always been her home, however distasteful it had become. Memories both good and bad stood out sharply as she increased the distance between herself and the city.

Intruding into her recollections, shadows crept around her.

She dwelled a little on the library she had been charged with keeping and maintaining. There had been little added to it during her time there, save for the occasional traveler leaving roughly copied tomes for her to catalog and lose amidst the ancient stacks. A whole building filled with more knowledge than one person could ever hope to attain. That place had been wondrous, and its loss hit her more keenly now that she had left the city than when it had burned down. Even then the evidence of it had remained, carbonized stacks of old paper and dead knowledge leaning drunkenly in the smoke, soaked to mulch with water and awaiting their final demise. Now it was only memory. But at least it was a memory true to her, something she had experienced firsthand, reveled in, smelled and touched and tasted, the library air redolent of a million different stories.

Alishia thought of the broken book the old man had carried out, and as she approached a huge boulder light was stolen from beneath it, and a shadow watched her pass. She steered the horse to one side and slipped the knife from her thigh, feeling foolish with the petty weight of metal in her hand. The shadow remained in place, and if it had eyes they did not blink. She glanced back a few times, and as it receded behind her the rock seemed to merge with the shadow, being swallowed or swallowing the darkness itself. It remained in place, brooding, threatening to expand and follow her down.

The hillside was flattening out slowly onto the plains, punctured here and there by deep holes, old surface workings or perhaps the homes of some unknown creatures long since vanished. Each hole offered a new shadow to seep beneath the ferns, spreading dark fingers where light no longer fell.

Alishia glanced up at Trey. He was still in some sort of fugue, sitting up now but with his eyes closed, lolling in the saddle as if he would fall off at any moment. He had never ridden a horse, he had said, but his long legs made it easy for him to grip its sides and remain in the saddle. She wished he would talk to her. She felt even more alone than she had upon leaving the city.

She thought of the old man who she was sure had burned down her library, and the shadows closed in again. There had been something about him, a niggling memory deep in her mind, but she could not dig down to it. His manner, his age, his language, his attire . . . they all stirred a memory of something she had read, something she knew. Her eyes drooped and she strolled along the aisles of the library in memory, running her fingers along book spines and recognizing every one, the names and titles and obscure publishing houses all known to her. She pulled out one book entitled *The Quest for Retribution*, a hate-filled tome that had been written soon after the Cataclysmic War. It called for an expedition northward to ensure that the Mages were properly accounted for, tied down, killed. It had been popular in its day, but it was one of a slew of reactionary literature that had flooded Noreela at the exact time that it needed optimism, not vengeance. Yet that had been a rich time in the literature of the land, and the sudden slurring of conventions and ideals, edging even the most creative and intellectual of writers to more radical outlooks, had been the start of the fall. People should have seen it, Alishia had always thought. They should have noticed that society was in a decline by the way the arts strove to refocus direction, diverting away from the more philosophical and cerebral explorations to those ruled more by animal instinct: conflict; survival; vengeance.

Alishia stumbled on a rock and went to her knees, calling out in surprise. She looked around quickly, startled and shocked. The sun had fallen and darkness had come out of the ground, closing in all around her, giving shadows more depth and potential than ever. Something was watching her from out there; she could feel its attention upon her. A thought floated away, leaving only the stale taste of itself behind. Something about the library, and the Mages, and anger. She shook her head, wondering whether she was suffering from a fledge hangover.

"You fell," Trey said from his mount.

"You're awake!" Alishia was embarrassed at the delight in her voice, but relief soon smothered the embarrassment. It was dark, there was something out there in the night, and now she was no longer alone.

"I have been for a while. I've been thinking. I've lost so much, and I really don't know what to do now."

"We have to find a place to camp," Alishia said. "It's too dark to keep moving, there are holes and crevasses to trip us. And besides, I need to light a fire. There's something stalking me." *Not stalking us*, Alishia thought. *Me*. It was a strange way to state her fear, but it seemed entirely apt.

"What is it?" Trey asked. His eyes were wide open now that the sun had gone down, and Alishia saw him stare in wonder at clouds silvered and smudged by starlight.

"I don't know. Something. I had a crumb of your fledge. I hope you don't mind, but I was curious and . . . I wonder if it may be because of that. Maybe I'm imagining things."

"You had fledge?" Trey asked. Alishia found his tone disturbing, and she stepped away. Here was a stranger she had found on a mountainside, alone with her in the dark. Her knife felt even more ineffectual than ever.

"Only a little."

"What do you sense?"

"I don't know. Something in the shadows."

"Nax," Trey said, so softly that Alishia was not sure he had actually spoken at all. The horse whinnied as if in response. "It's the Nax," he said again. "Now that it's night they've come up! Nothing left for them down there. They've come up to put right what woke them in the first place!" He was raving now, fear given voice, and in the deepening darkness his shout was louder than ever.

"I haven't seen anything," Alishia said, not entirely sure if that was true.

Perhaps the fledge miner's fear translated to the horse. Or maybe the horse itself sensed something then, the watchful thing Alishia had known in her dreams and which she now sensed in the surrounding shadows. Whatever the cause, the result was inevitable. The horse bolted. Alishia ran after them, mindful of the uneven ground and the holes she had seen, but desperate not to lose her horse, and with it the saddlebags and all her belongings. Trey fell and rolled across the ground, and the horse ran on, galloping into the night until it was little more than a shadow itself.

Alishia shouted in frustration. And then she heard the sickening sound of breaking bones, something big hit the ground, and the horse cried out in agony.

She tripped and struck her head on a rock. She was sure, even as pain took sensation away into unconsciousness, that she had tripped over nothing but shadow.

———

THE SHADE REDISCOVERED the mind down in the real world, still possessed of dregs of the freedom that had attracted the shade so much. It hovered for a while, noticing the passing of time purely via the changing of the mind it focused upon. The mind soared and dreamed and traveled in a rich vein of knowledge, opening itself up more than any the shade had yet encountered. It had been drawn back here by that openness, and the fact that such simplicity would surely be receptive to any signs of magic, hints that things were not quite as they had been. And it was this that the shade's god sought.

Again and again, skimming beyond the world, dipping in on occasion to gain experience and feel the slick shock of existence, the shade tried to tap into the mind. It offered itself first, giving the mind something to focus on, but it must have frightened it away instead. It had no way to lure — it was essentially nothing but future memory, so what could it possibly offer a mind of such magnitude? — and so instead it had to inveigle its way inside. It would use its pure, untempered instinct for life, the one sense that its god had perpetuated and encouraged and which nature, by judging it as an imperfect example of its sort, had sought to take away. And this life had the god at its center. The shade put ideas of its god into the mind's way, letting it stumble and trip and absorb, drawing it up out of the real world until it began to soar again, questing knowledge. Still it veered away from the shade, afraid of its blankness, but the shade persisted, planting more ideas, steering the mind, hovering and struggling to find a crack through which it would penetrate to become corporeal at last.

That crack came unbeckoned.

The mind suddenly exploded up and out of the real world, a maelstrom of confused emotions blended with pain and surprise. The shade backed away and let the mind soar, expand, open itself out until it settled once again just beyond the boundaries of unreality. There it dreamed and reveled once again in its knowledge. But there was something ever-present — a worry, a fear, a dread — that the shade could work on.

It approached, dipped down and found itself sharing.

The mind recoiled. The shade rejoiced. It spread itself and was instantly dizzied by the sensations and emotions therein. There was pain and the taste of grass and mud, the sound of distant shouting and the sense of a heartbeat, fast and irregular, grasped in an icy fist of fear. It opened its mouth and shouted, felt the thing it had become shouting along with it, raising a voice that echoed back again and again. It could smell heather and blood, feel something sharp pressing into its face and something soft and cool next to that, tickling its mouth.

It was a person. Its name was Alishia.

The shade screamed again from sheer delight and Alishia jumped to her feet, laughing and spinning around, tripping and jarring her knees and palms on rough rock, hardly noticing the pain.

For a few seconds that she could not explain, Alishia reveled in the simple fact that she was alive. And that life was rich with potential.

Chapter 14

WHEN RAFE WOKE it was dark. Weak moonlight bled into the room from two wide vents high in the wall, giving enough light for him to recognize where he was. He tried to sit up but his head thudded, pain spearing into his eyes and down his neck. He groaned, held his temples and sat up slowly, trying to hold the pain so that it did not move around. He'd had headaches before, but nothing like this. Perhaps Hope had given him some bad rotwine without his noticing. He had seen plenty of people like this in Trengborne, suffering harsh hangovers each morning and feeding them again come afternoon and evening.

He looked around the room—the walls adorned with many shadows, the odors of the place more noticeable now that he could see less—and then he saw Hope. She was sitting in a chair by the far wall. Her hair was silhouetted against the stone by the weak moonlight, sticking up like a nest of sleek snakes, and though her face was in shadow Rafe was sure he could make out her tattoos, shifting slowly to mirror the effect of her hair. He held his breath for a moment and heard her slow, heavy breathing.

He realized suddenly that he was naked. It was cold, even though a few spluttering embers remained in the open fire, and Rafe wished that he could find his clothes without moving. His headache had come to terms with him sitting upright, but still it pounded at the backs of his eyes.

He ran his hand down over his stomach. Hope had given him a reason for his lack of a navel, and it was not a reason he liked. She had been right, he *had* begun to wonder, but somehow the idea of asking his parents had always seemed wrong.

Something was whispering in his ear. He turned his head quickly to look behind him, wincing at the pain but holding his breath, waiting to see, wanting not to. There were only shadows, deeper within his own. The whispering continued, words in a language he could not understand. The meaning was way beyond his grasp. The source of the whispers moved to his other ear and then inside his head, soothing the ache there, numbing the pain and planting fresh, potent ideas that he shied away from. He did not understand fully, but there was nothing hiding the power that these voices imparted. They breathed the smell of grass in rolling meadows and the tang of fresh snow on mountaintops, inspired the taste of rain on his tongue and the feel of a breeze across his skin. The hairs on the back of his neck stood on end. The voices paused as if awaiting an answer, and when none was given—he did not know how—they faded quickly away, leaving him sitting there in the dark with no headache, warm and, for the first time in two days, unafraid.

"You've been dreaming as well," a voice said from the dark. Hope was still awake. Rafe was hardly surprised. "I've been sitting here watching you. Trying to come to terms with things, with what I know. Trying to work out what to do next. You've been dreaming and talking in a language I haven't heard spoken in my lifetime, and you sit there awake and now you'll tell me you're just a farm boy, you don't know what I'm on about. I can understand your confusion. But I also sit here confident that I have a miracle sleeping in my bed. And that miracle is the future."

"You gave me something to make me sleep," Rafe said, the intended anger failing to come through.

"You needed to rest. You've been through a lot, farm boy. And there'll be more to come. You need your strength, your energy. You'll need your wits about you. There are people who would do their best to hurt you, some who may want what you have for their own. Many who'll believe they can use you."

"Like you?"

Hope was silent for a long while, motionless in the darkness with moonlight kissing the fringes of her face. Rafe could just make out the tattoos now, and they shifted as if she was smiling, frowning, smiling again.

"I've already told you that I've been waiting for a long time," she said. "But now you're here . . . I don't know what to do. I just don't know."

"Where are my clothes?"

"I've washed them for you. They'll be dry soon. Don't go!" Her voice changed instantly, from calm to pleading. "Rafe, don't leave me. I've waited so long, I want to help you, I want to be with you for as long as I can. To see it happen. To be nearby when it happens!"

"When what happens?" Those voices again, whispering at the fringes of his mind as if plotting amongst themselves. This time he smelled the bitter mineral breath of the underground. Or perhaps it was only a waft of smoke from the dying fire.

"When you finally realize who you are."

"I'm Rafe Baburn. I feel like I'm going mad sometimes, but I know who I am. I'm Rafe Baburn, and my parents are dead."

She did not reply for a long time, as if sitting there in the dark trying to decide just what to say. Rafe hugged a blanket around him and sat there too, comfortable even though he could see little. Hope—this witch, this whore—had drugged him and stripped him, but still he was sure that she meant him no harm. If she did, she'd had ample opportunity to hurt him while he was asleep.

"I've been sitting here thinking all night," she said at last. "I've led a long, hard life looking for signs of magic, seeking it the only way I knew. Few people tell me the truth when they see I'm a witch—people regard me as a disciple of lost magic—but plenty of men talk to a whore. I've heard so many things, boy, while I'm cleaning myself up and they're lying fat and sated in that bed. I've heard about wives who no longer love, children who flee home, men who hate, and some who find love in those few minutes after we've fucked. Love for themselves, maybe, or for the wives they've just betrayed. Guilt is a fickle thing, and there's been enough of it in this room to last me lifetimes. Though never my own. I've never felt bad about what I do, never at fault or used. It's me doing the using, Rafe, because I know more than most. There are plenty of whores in Pavisse, but few who want to talk afterward. What wisdom they ignore! All that knowledge they waste, shunning talk for a chew of stale fledge or a drag of dream-mites. I've had a soldier of the Duke's Inner Guard in that bed, a banished Shantasi mystic, a sailor from beyond the Western Shores, a merchant who travels south of Kang Kang to trade favors and dreams with the things that live there . . . I've had them all, and spoken to them all. And every time I'm being humped or screwed or hit, I'm thinking about what you represent. I'm thinking about the magic that one day will give me a real life."

Rafe hardly knew what to think of what she was saying. Much of it confused him, frightened him, and so he stayed silent, not wishing to interrupt. No voices spoke to him, no smells or tastes came, and he wondered whether they too were silently listening to this old witch.

"And you're here, Rafe. And now that I think I know what you are, I have no idea what to do. Do you think that's foolish? Do you think I'm mad? I've waited for you for so long, but now that you're here I can barely move."

"Not mad," Rafe whispered, although he had little confidence in that.

"After all that time asking, searching, listening for a sign or the smallest hint that things had swung around, changed . . . I never expected to find you myself. Curled up in a doorway, trying to escape the world I've lived in forever." She fell silent for a time, rocking slowly in her chair.

Light was creeping back into the room. Rafe had not noticed it happening, but he could make out form in the shapes on the wall now, and when he glanced across at Hope he could see her closed eyes, welling tears.

"I'm hungry," he said.

Hope's eyes snapped open. She wiped at the tears with her shirt-sleeves and stood. "Of course you are. So am I. Son, I'm going out for food. There's a trader down the street who will have opened by now. You stay here. Don't touch anything, and *don't* open the door! You cannot be seen by anyone. *Anyone.*"

"I don't know what to do," Rafe said, and he felt his own tears coming. "Everyone I know is dead. I have to get back to Uncle Vance, he'll know what to do. He'll look after me."

"Is that the same uncle that left you to wander to the outskirts of the hidden districts? Not a good place to be, son. It's a good job it was me who found you and not someone else." Hope shrugged on a cloak and picked up a couple of objects from a table against a wall.

"He's all I have left," Rafe said, heartbroken at the truth of things. "He'll help me."

"Well, whatever. Stay here for now. I'll be back before you notice I'm gone. Then we can eat and talk things over a little more." Hope smiled at him before leaving, but it was not an expression that made Rafe feel comfortable and safe.

———

HOPE EMERGED ONTO the street and leaned against a wall for a moment, gathering her thoughts. There was plenty she had not told Rafe, but he was a mass of mysteries himself. He mourned dead parents that she was certain were not his. He wished for an uncle who was no relation, someone who had been so keen to help that he had let his grief-stricken "nephew" out into the streets around the hidden districts. He was a young lad barely embracing manhood, and yet he could well hold the future in his palms.

Hope shook her head. She had heard so many stories, so much wild mythology twisted over time so that any spark of truth must be long malformed, that she had stopped truly believing years ago. And now magic was alive and well in her basement rooms. She had *thought* she still believed, had continued living as though she knew it would happen eventually, but in reality, she had given up hope.

He has no navel. But even that was now more myth than anything else. She was thrilled, excited and terrified, but it might take some time for her belief to catch up with her enthusiasm. And perhaps it would take proof.

If Rafe was truly a conduit for magic reborn, she must surely see it soon.

She walked past traders setting their stalls and dodged people slumped in the gutters, drunkenness having negated prejudice to collapse them all together. The streets were coming slowly to life, and most people walked slowly, like apathetic blood through the veins of the aging city. Hope stepped aside to let an old fodder pass by, the woman's flabby stomach and breasts almost reaching her thighs. She wondered whether a woman from a race once bred for food could ever truly hope for anything more. If magic returned, would it help? Nobody really knew. Nobody alive now had known magic. It was a mystery, and evidence of its previous existence had been melting away. Those dead machines she could see around her had merged into buildings, many of the machines put to disrespectful use: a toilet; a water trough for horses; the frame of a brothel doorway. These things that generations ago had performed miracles were now merely building blocks of today's degradation.

She arrived at her destination and stood by while Mogart opened his shop. He was an old man, a coal miner whose stockiness had long since gone to fat, and Hope was used to him being slow.

"Morning, Mogart."

"Eh? Oh, Hope, you damn witch! What brings you here so early? I thought you preferred the dark."

"I'm hungry, you old fool." She clapped him on the shoulder and grimaced at the puff of dust from his clothes. "Anything tasty this morning?"

"Help me with this and I'll tell you." Mogart was shoving a timber shutter from his shop doorway, and Hope added her strength and guided it into its housing. Mogart huffed and puffed, turned to his cart and began uncovering boxes. Hope saw vegetables, a few wrinkled fruits and some pale fish, probably caught from the river last night. He would claim they were from fisheries on the Western Shores, of course, but Hope knew the difference. Fish from the Shores did not taste of shit.

"Anything nice?" she asked again.

"What?"

"Anything *nice*?"

"It's all nice, whore!"

Hope laughed and shoved Mogart into the shop ahead of her. The place stank as if it had not been cleaned out for many moons — which was probably the case — and Mogart was not the most hygienic of people, but Hope liked him. He had traveled some in his youth, working from mine to mine in the Widow's Peaks and the mountains of Long Marrakash. He had stories, most of which she had heard many times before, but he was also adept at keeping his ear to the ground. His feigned deafness served him well, as did his age and unkempt appearance. People with secrets never seemed to consider him a threat, and they often talked freely before him, in his shop or huddled in corners of the Dead Sea Tavern, where he spent his evenings.

"Anything for me this morning?" Hope asked absently, picking out the least rancid fruits for Rafe's breakfast. Old habits die hard, and even though everything had changed since yesterday, Hope still sought knowledge.

"Oh Mage shit, I think you'll like this one," he said. "Red Monks in Pavisse! One passed right by the Dead Sea last night! I didn't see it myself, of course, but three of the others were just coming in and they watched it pass. Didn't know what it was, but from their description, I knew. *I* knew! And down at the river this morning, old Mad Jennson told me he saw a demon in red just before dawn. Red Monks, Hope, what in the name of Kang Kang do we get next? You know, there's talk that . . ."

But Hope was no longer listening.

She dashed from Mogart's store and headed up the street, dodging people, barely hearing the protestations behind her. She realized that she had left with a handful of yellow apples, so she threw them down behind her in the hope that the trader would see. They had to flee, and she did not want Mogart's last thoughts of her to be *Thief!*

She opened the front door and ran downstairs to her basement room. *He's gone,* she thought, *he'll be gone and there'll be no sign of where. He's only just got here in my life and now he'll be gone.* But Rafe was still there, dressed now, sitting on the bed and looking up with fear in his eyes.

"We're leaving!" she said.

"But Uncle Vance—"

"He's already dead. There are Red Monks in Pavisse, son. They'll be looking for you."

"Why me?"

"Because you're everything they want to eradicate!" she said, immediately sorry for her harsh words but too panicked to apologize. "Your things, get them."

"I have no things."

"Give me a moment," she said, dashing to a cupboard for her shoulder bag. She grabbed a few items from the table, barely thinking, certainly in no mind to decide what could be helpful and what would merely add weight.

"Where are they?" Rafe asked quietly, cool fear in his voice. She stopped, breathing heavily, realized that she was probably terrifying him even more.

"I don't know," she said. "Someone I know almost saw one near here last night. Hopefully it's gone now, but we have to get away. We have to, Rafe! You can trust me, son, I mean it. Whatever you think of me, what I am, what I do and have done, I swear on my ancestors' graves that I want to help you. I'll do anything within my power to stop you from coming to harm. I know you're confused and scared right now, but you're also very, very important."

Rafe stared at her. "I heard those voices again when you were out," he said.

He's admitted it! Hope thought, amazed, but now was not the time.

"They're urging you to leave," she said. "They can advise, but I'm *here*, and I can *help*. And I'll do my bloody best. Now come on, we have to go."

"Where?"

Hope shook her head, exasperated. She should in be awe of him, but his ignorance only made her impatient. "Son, I have no fucking idea. Away from here. We can think about a destination after that." *Where should I take him?* she thought. *Is there somewhere he needs to be? Or do I only have to keep him safe until . . .*

But until *what* she did not know.

"Quick!" She waved him out. He passed her and started up the stairs to the outside, and Hope looked around her room for one last time. She had spent so long here, wishing for this moment, and now that it had arrived all she felt was an awkward sadness. She could not pin the emotion down—it certainly was not sorrow at leaving—but still it bore into her. Perhaps it was merely a hint of what was to come.

Before she closed the door she knocked a handful of pots from a nearby shelf. They shattered and spewed glass shards, spiders and scorpions across the floor. Unlike the spiders she often kept in a sac in her pocket, these were deadly breeds, their eggs gathered from the four corners of Noreela, nurtured by Hope, maintained to provide her with this defense. She slammed the door quickly and listened at the wood, just able to make out the mutter of feet on the wooden floor inside. The sounds ceased quickly as the creatures found places to hide. They would be there waiting for the next person to go inside.

That was it. She had left. She would never venture inside again. She had once seen the dreadful results of a slayer spider's bite, and it would take much for her to risk one herself.

Rafe was waiting for her at the top of the steps. She pushed past him, opened the front door a crack and peered out. She glanced left and right, left again, and realized that she had never been this terrified before. Never.

"It looks safe," she said, but even as she spoke she wondered whether *safe* would ever ring true for her again. "Come on."

As they slipped through the door, Rafe held on to her hand and squeezed tight. Hope paused and felt a lump form in her throat. *Stupid old woman,* she thought, but she could not hold down the feeling of pride his trust inspired.

She led Rafe out into the busy streets of Pavisse.

Chapter 15

IT WAS NOT really a tunnel, not in the true sense, but rather a shortcut between streets. Kosar and A'Meer were never immersed in complete darkness. Most of their journey was in half-light, shady passageways barely illuminated through cracks in the ceiling from basement rooms, where even now people were stirring themselves from slumber. In some places the passageway had true design—steps cut into the bedrock, brackets rusted on the walls where lamps had once hung—but in other places it took on a random effect. Sometimes their route was little more than an unintentional void between building foundations, the rough walls showing where builders had cut corners, the floor piled with rubble and other refuse, crawling with rats. The tunnel was spanned here and there by huge spiderwebs, many of them carrying silk-spun packages as big as an adult furbat. A'Meer pushed through these without pause, and at these moments Kosar was glad that she was in the lead. He never saw a spider. He wondered where they had all gone.

Here and there they heard voices, and once they must have passed under a narrow road; above them, just visible through mud-clotted slats in the ceiling, shadows passed quickly by, and shoes cast dust down into their eyes. The scent of cooking followed it down; fresh bread, and meats frying on a street skillet, breakfast for those who could afford it. Kosar's mouth watered at the thought, but then he remembered the house they had just left and the mess coating the walls and floor of the upstairs room. His stomach rumbled and he felt sick.

Kosar tapped A'Meer on the shoulder. "Not far," he whispered. "I think we're under the outskirts of the hidden districts. If we look for a way out anywhere soon, we'll be where we want to be."

"Good," A'Meer said. "But we should be moving faster. The Monk that killed Rafe's uncle did so hours ago. It could be anywhere in the town by now. I wonder whether it knew where to look for Rafe, or whether it thought the same thing we did."

"We can't know," Kosar said. A'Meer looked paler than ever down here. He reached out and touched her face, and was pleased at her grateful smile. "But we have an advantage. We know people here, you more than me. Instead of just searching, we should ask around, see if anyone knows of a strange boy in the districts, someone who might be harboring him."

"The word will spread quickly, especially with me in full Shantasi armor. The regulars at the Broken Arm would be in for a shock."

"By the time word spreads, we'll either have found him or . . ."

"Or they will. They're very efficient, the Red Monks. No emotions cloud their vision, other than hate. And that's cleansing."

"Is it?" Kosar asked, but things instantly felt different, as if the two of them were talking about something forbidden.

A'Meer turned away and started down the passageway again. Kosar followed.

Within a few heartbeats they sensed a breeze of aromatic air coming from their left. They took a fork in the passage, ducking under the twisted spiral of a metal machine where it supported the ceiling, and ascended rough steps cut into the side of some gargantuan buried thing. To left and right ran a crevasse, bridged only here by the steps that led up. It was pitch black, but Kosar had the sense of something massive hiding down here, not dead but dreaming, its exhalations making the dark darker. He shook his head but could not vent the visions. A'Meer glanced back, wide-eyed. She had felt it too.

Kosar had never been so pleased to see the filthy streets of the hidden districts. They emerged through a rent in the side of a building, framed by twists of fossilized machine, and a few curious stares greeted them. A'Meer shook herself, as if to shed her black hair and white skin of the dust of underground, and her packed weapons whispered together.

Kosar looked away from each set of eyes he met, only to meet another.

"Come on," he said. "We don't want to cause a stir." They headed off quickly, running deeper into the districts.

It was usually held that those who lived here were criminals—thieves, murderers, rapists, bandits on the run—but it was also true that the districts offered shelter for those poets and prophets who still listened to their heart. It was a rough, dangerous place, but at least here life still sang through the air on occasion, and the future held possibilities.

Most people carried weapons, much more so than out in the normal streets, but few to the extent of A'Meer. And as the two of them progressed, they drew attention whichever way they turned. Chatter stopped, trading paused, and Kosar could hear whispers from those hunkered in doorways or pressing themselves back against walls to let the two of them pass. Most of them had never seen a Shantasi warrior, and the crowd's fear was palpable.

"This won't help us find Rafe," he whispered to A'Meer. "It'll more likely hide him from us more."

"There's someone I know," she said. "She's not far from here; we'll go to her. She's always listening out for news of strangers passing through. She'll know if Rafe has been seen."

"Who is she?"

"Shantasi spy."

Kosar allowed A'Meer to draw ahead so that he could follow. He tried not to catch anyone's eyes, but after staring at the Shantasi they would inevitably move on to him, their gaze questioning, eyebrows raised in query. A few glanced down at his hands and saw the bloodied strips around his fingertips, and their curiosity grew. *A mercenary and a thief,* one of them whispered. *I wonder what he's hired her for?* Kosar stared at the whisperer, not moving away until the man averted his eyes.

But everywhere the looks and mutters were the same, and it did not take long for Kosar to become paranoid, fearing that the whole of Pavisse knew their business. In reality, much as their appearance caused a brief commotion as they passed, he knew that in the hidden districts there was always something else to draw attention. They may well be talked about, but their presence would not alter anyone's day.

He followed A'Meer blindly. Every time he heard someone raise their voice he turned around, convinced that he would see a Red Monk, blood-hungry sword drawn and eager to bathe itself in Shantasi flesh.

. . . and now mercenaries, and this is a dark day dawning for sure.

Kosar stopped, turned, trying to make out who had spoken. A group of children stood huddled against a timber fence surrounding a scorpion-plant garden, eyes wide and afraid. To their left an elderly couple stood arm in arm, and when he met the woman's eyes she glanced away, looking for something in the dust.

"*What* and mercenaries?" he asked quietly.

She did not answer until her partner jerked her arm, nudged her in the side. His eyes had strayed over Kosar's right shoulder to A'Meer.

"Monk," the woman whispered. "Red Monk."

"Where? When? Alone?"

"Last night, passing by my house. I couldn't sleep. I was sitting at the window watching the stars, writing a poem." She glanced up, perhaps expecting ridicule, but seeing only stern interest on Kosar's face. "I saw it walk by below my window. Even in the dark I could see its color."

"You didn't tell me —" the man said, but the woman continued, ignoring him.

"It stopped just past my window and raised its head, sniffing at the air. I could *hear* it, sniffing! It knew I was there, and it must have heard my heart. But then it went on into the shadows."

"In which direction?"

"No. It went into the shadows. It did not move, it slipped away. No direction." She was crying now, an old woman's tears that looked like those of a child.

Kosar glanced back at A'Meer, whose attention remained focused on the woman. "We should go," he said. "Find whoever it is you think can help."

"Was it a good poem?" A'Meer said suddenly.

The woman's crying stopped, shocked into silence.

"The poem," A'Meer repeated. "Was it good?"

"I'm not sure," the old woman said. "I think I've forgotten."

"Never forget the poetry in your heart," A'Meer said. "It may yet have some use one day." And then she turned and marched away.

Kosar followed, wondering what had happened back there. The old woman was not crying anymore, and as he looked back one last time Kosar saw the old man questioning her, touching her, trying to tear her gaze from the morning sky. Yet another surprise from A'Meer.

"If they came here and found nothing, maybe they moved on?" Kosar said.

A'Meer stopped and guided him over to a building, its walls composed entirely of the outer shell of an old machine. Breakers had obviously been at work here—a slab of the machine lay discarded in the street, and people walked around it rather than touch it or move it aside.

"If the Monks came here they came for a reason," A'Meer said. "We know there's more than one or two—there may be many—and coming out in force means that they know Rafe is here. They'll not leave until he's dead."

"How do they even know of him?"

A'Meer shrugged. "Whispers on the wind. Rumors. Mostly I think they can sense it; magic is their madness, and they're well attuned to its cadences."

"So why not do what they did in Trengborne?" Kosar asked. "Kill everyone so that they're sure Rafe is one of them?"

"It may yet come to that," she said. "But for now, I guess they know that if they start wholescale slaughter, Rafe will disappear in the panic. Pavisse is a little bigger than Trengborne." She smiled, but it barely touched her eyes.

Too many memories resurfacing in there, Kosar thought. Memories of her training, perhaps, and what she had been charged with. And recollections of her battle with the Monk in Ventgoria. Perhaps she was scared that she could not repeat that victory after living so long as a normal person.

"A'Meer," he said. "I don't have a weapon other than my pathetic little knife."

She sighed and rested her head on his shoulder. "Just how prepared are we, huh?" She drew a long, thin blade from a scabbard at her hip and handed it to him. "Listen to me, Kosar. I know you can take care of yourself, but this is a Shantasi blade. It's not charmed or cursed, but it *is* hungry. And it's sharper than anything you've ever seen." She was unlacing the scabbard as she spoke, slipping the leather cord out through other knots that held her own weaponry. She removed it in seconds without disturbing anything else. "If you draw this, you draw blood." She reached out and touched her hand to the sword he held, wincing as a line of blood appeared across her palm.

"Don't!" Kosar said, shocked. He stepped back and held the sword to his side, looking around to see if anyone had noticed. There were several people watching, too interested to let their fear drive them away.

"It didn't hurt," she said, smiling. "Believe me, once drawn, the sword won't settle until it's wet."

He looked down at the weapon, expecting it to curl around his hand like a snake. He touched one fingertip to its flat surface and a drop of A'Meer's blood slicked across the metal, catching the morning sun.

"You speak as though it's alive."

"No." A'Meer shook her head. "Of course not. Not alive, not magical, just . . . hungry. The Monks' swords are the same, but fed by their owners' madness so that the effect is magnified. With me it's more tradition, I guess, something that was drummed into me by the Mystics in Hess. But every tradition like that has some root cause."

As Kosar strapped on the scabbard—it was uncomfortable, as if molded specially for A'Meer's hips and not his own—he asked where they would go now.

"The woman I mentioned," A'Meer said. "She's a madam. Works out of an old machine a little way from here. Five girls, a couple of them fledgers. She even has a fodder. Novelty value, I guess, although I wonder how she stops men from biting her."

"You know the most charming people."

"Hey, I work in a tavern full of criminals, wrongdoers and misfits."

"Where you met me."

"That's right, thief."

They smiled at each other, not knowing what to say next. Banter did not feel right given the circumstances. Things were winding up, like a sling spinning and ready to release its shot. The direction it fired in depended wholly upon what happened over the coming day. By evening they may be on the run from Red Monks, taking with them the boy from Trengborne. Or perhaps they would be burying his remains, A'Meer mourning the magic that might have been. Or maybe they would both be dead.

"How did this happen?" Kosar said, not sure exactly what he meant.

"These things do." A'Meer stretched on tiptoes and planted a kiss on Kosar's lips, and then she turned and walked on.

———

THE WOMAN WAS huge. Her name was Slight—a misnomer if ever there was one—and Kosar had no idea how she could move. Her arms rested on massive hips, her legs were all but hidden beneath rolling waves of fat, and her eyes were tiny beads in a face that looked like a ball of pasty dough.

"A'Meer!" she screeched upon seeing them. "You've decided to come to work for me after all, then! But what's with the blades, vixen? You know I don't cater for that side of things."

"Slight," A'Meer said. "It's good to see you. Been cutting down on the fried sheebok fat, I see."

"I weigh almost as much as all my girls combined," she said proudly. "Who's the cock? He want some? You want some, cock?"

Kosar shook his head, unfeasibly embarrassed in front of this mountain of a woman. The inside of the great machine was unrecognizable, hung as it was with drapes and curtains. It was an assault on the eyes, so much color and form stealing concepts of up or down, left or right. Someone passed by on the other side of a drape wall, but they were little more than a shadow. Someone else snored gently nearby. From elsewhere, he thought he heard the muted sounds of lovemaking.

"Slight, I'm looking for someone," A'Meer said.

"Someone other than him?" the madam said, nodding at Kosar. The movement sent her whole bulk shaking. Her loose breasts, each almost the size of a small sheebok, quivered as if possessing of a life of their own.

"A boy," A'Meer said. "Slight, it's important. This boy is precious to me, and his life is in danger."

"Precious to you, or precious to New Shanti?" A'Meer did not reply. Slight looked her up and down. "And you all tooled up."

Kosar did not like her. She seemed too casual, too ready with a witticism, and all the while he sensed a wily mind working behind her button eyes.

"There are a few things about me I've never told most people," A'Meer admitted.

"I've heard about Shantasi warriors," Slight said, shifting her weight to one side and moving, slowly, toward a wall of curtains.

A'Meer looked at Kosar and shrugged. He frowned, trying to communicate his distrust.

"Girls!" Slight called. "Slight wants a word!"

"I'm busy," a voice said, sounding as if it came from the next street.

"When you've finished, then, Honey. Don't rush the gentleman; he's paid his way."

Shadows came first, appearing on curtains and drapes from different directions, slowly manifesting as women. They pushed through into the central room where Slight, A'Meer and Kosar waited. One of them was beautiful. One was fodder, fat and scarred with bites. One was with child, another looked half dead from rotwine and bad fledge, and the last was a fledger, tall and yellow-eyed.

"The boy a stranger?" Slight asked, and A'Meer nodded.

"Girls, my friend here's looking for someone. A boy. You won't have seen him before. Maybe he was on his own; or if he's a stranger, someone in the districts may have picked him up. You seen anyone with a stranger? Anyone we know?"

"Hope," said the fledger. "That mad old fucking witch-whore threw a sac of poison spiders at me. She had a boy with her, filthy little bastard farmer boy, scared."

"When was this?" A'Meer asked, but the fledger stared through her.

"When was this?" Slight rumbled.

"Yesterday."

"Where does Hope live?" A'Meer asked Slight, and the fat woman asked the fledger, and she told them.

"Street down south, Fifthborn Circle. Not too far from here." The fledger addressed A'Meer directly for the first and last time. "When you find that old witch-whore, are you going to slit her throat?"

"No," said A'Meer.

The fledger raised her eyebrows at Slight. The big woman nodded and her girls disappeared back through the curtains, their movement sending a whisper in every direction.

"Thank you, Slight," A'Meer said.

The huge woman smiled. "And yet again, you owe me. You'll have to come and work for me soon, Shantasi." She eyed A'Meer's weaponry, and through the fat Kosar could not be sure of her expression. Perhaps being inscrutable served her well.

A'Meer nodded, performed a low bow and then nudged Kosar out of the old machine ahead of her.

———

THEY HEADED SOUTH, moving as fast as they could through the serpentine streets. Kosar kept one hand on the new sword at his belt. It banged his leg as he ran, uncomfortable and yet reassuring with its presence. He could not shake the feeling that they were rushing headlong into trouble.

When they reached Fifthborn Circle A'Meer strolled quickly along the street, looking at doors as if she would perceive a witch's abode by its appearance.

"We'll have to ask," Kosar said.

A'Meer had stopped in front of a building, the door closed tight, windows shaded and mostly still unbroken. She stood back slightly and looked up at the facade, down at ground level, back to the front door again. "This is it."

"How do you know?"

"A witch marks her ground," she said, offering no more.

Kosar followed her gaze but saw nothing.

"She's in the basement rooms," A'Meer said, kneeling to take a look at the narrow slits piercing the building just above ground level. "Her signature is Willmott's Nemesis root, I can smell it."

"Let's go, then."

A'Meer stood and nodded. "Quickly, but quietly. And I'll go first."

Kosar did not argue. A'Meer stood with her hand on the door handle, paused, looked around at him, frowning.

"What is it?" he asked.

"Something—"

The door burst open, smashed from its hinges. It crashed past the frame and splintered wood stung the air. Kosar stumbled back as A'Meer was thrown against him. A shape burst from the opening, a Red Monk, its decidedly feminine mouth wide open in a frozen grimace of agony and shock. Kosar kept stumbling backwards, certain that his own feet would trip him, and the Monk trampled over A'Meer to get him. Its hood was snagged back by a spear of wood, and Kosar could see its bald head, veins standing out like worm-trail, red, leaking where they split the skin. Its eyes were wide and surely sightless, such was the rate of their expansion and the scarlet pooling of blood in their whites. Its hands stretched out, one of them grasping a sword that seemed to twitch at Kosar, smelling his blood.

He fell, finally, still trying to draw the sword from his belt, and kicked up as the Red Monk came at him. His feet connected and the Monk staggered back, screaming at last. Kosar was momentarily pleased, but then the Monk stumbled quickly away, still screaming, the shriek high-pitched and ragged as if its throat was being boiled.

"A'Meer!" he shouted, but the Shantasi was already on her feet, one hand holding a sword, the other sporting a slideshock. Her eyes were wide and terrified, her mouth hanging open as if to gasp in air, and Kosar felt terrified for her.

The Red Monk was running along the street. People scattered out of its way. Its arms flailed, and blood misted the air as veins on its scalp began to burst. It fell suddenly and moved onward on hands and feet, jumping from one place to the next like a foxlion, still shrieking.

"A'Meer!" Kosar called again, running to her. She had splinters in her face, several of them drawing dribbles of blood. She looked at him and shook her head, unable to speak. "We have to go after it!" Kosar said.

She shook her head again and looked at the shattered door, stepping back as if expecting another Monk to come through.

Kosar drew his sword and stepped in front of A'Meer in a foolish act of bravery. Here he was, a lowly thief, offering to protect a Shantasi warrior. He would have laughed had he not been so petrified.

"Inside," she said at last. "We have to check, quickly, and then we'll follow. But be careful, there are things in there. I think it was bitten by a slayer spider."

"Mage shit," Kosar whispered. He had heard about these creatures. Right then, he was not sure which he would rather face: a Red Monk, or a slayer.

A'Meer darted around him and slipped through the door. Her arm twitched and the slideshock whipped out, hitting something in the dark.

Kosar ran in behind her and sidestepped the still-twitching spider on the floor, fat as an eyeball. "Is that it?" he asked.

"No, I've never seen one like that before. The slayer must still be around somewhere." She headed downstairs to the basement rooms, Kosar on her tail. They were checking for Rafe, but Kosar was certain that his body would not be here. The Monk—inflamed by pain as it was—had also been clean. There was no blood on its sword, none splashed on its face other than its own.

"A'Meer, that Monk is on Rafe's trail."

A'Meer nudged open the door at the bottom of the stairs and went in, flipping her arm out and slicing a scorpion in two as it dashed from behind a cupboard. Kosar followed more cautiously, looking around, checking the walls to either side and above the door for any telltale shadows.

"Well, he's not here, at least," A'Meer said. "Stay alert, there are at least five smashed jars on the floor."

Kosar checked around his feet amongst the smashed clay shards. Nothing there. He glanced at the shelves, lined with hundreds of other jars and leather containers, wondering just what else Hope kept in here. He had never known a witch, let alone been in the home of one. The hanging herbs, the jars, the charts, the paraphernalia disturbed him, perhaps because of how this place would be perceived by many: one step closer to magic.

"We have to go," A'Meer said. She turned around, her eyes went wide and her arm flipped up quickly, the slideshock's weighted wire lashing out and plucking something from Kosar's shoulder. He felt the splash of its insides pattering his bare arm as the dead slayer spider dropped to the floor. "We really *should* go," A'Meer insisted.

"I agree."

They left the room to whatever was left alive, shutting the downstairs door in an effort to keep the dangers within.

A crowd had gathered outside. Children ran back and forth, collecting handfuls of the smashed front door to show their friends later as they bragged of what they had seen. Adults hovered farther away, their caution born of experience telling them that, really, this was not their business. And striding down the street, three militia rattled their swords with self-importance.

"Oh Mage shit," Kosar said. "They'll keep us talking till dusk."

"Stay close to me, don't say a word and try not to listen too hard to what I have to say." A'Meer glanced back at Kosar. "Think of something else, how we can track the Red Monk. Just how do we do that?"

The militia stopped, standing side by side so that they blocked the street and the route Kosar and A'Meer had to take. What had she meant? They would track the Monk easily. There would be a trail of people in the streets, chattering about what they had just seen, how much blood there had been: *Did you see that thing, it was running like a dog, a woman, it was a woman you say, but where did all that* blood *come*—

"Urgh!" One of the militiamen was holding his ears, and the others, cowering back against a fence on the opposite side of the street, looked so terrified that A'Meer may as well have been the Red Monk itself.

"Kosar, come on!" she called. She ran past the militia, and Kosar heard her mutter a gentle apology.

"What was *that*?" he asked as he followed. She did not answer. They ran to the end of Fifthborn Circle and turned left, following knots of startled people that were still drifting in the street like sparrows bobbing in the wake of a passing hawk. People stepped quickly out of their way and Kosar tried to smile at them, to tell them that there was nothing to fear. But suddenly, in the distance, there was. A scream, high and loud and enraged, not from a human throat. From much farther came a similar response, winging across the rooftops and startling birds and giant moths into flight.

"What in the name—"

"Shit!" A'Meer cursed. "There are more. It's calling them." She paused, panting, slideshock hanging from one arm and dragging in the dust. "If we keep following we'll come up against other Red Monks. *Unless* we catch it in the next couple of minutes, take it on, take it down and then get away."

"So what are we waiting for?" Kosar said, expecting her to offer him another quick, easy way out. He was only a thief, after all.

"I'm scared."

Kosar reigned in his surprise. "So is Rafe, I suspect."

A'Meer lowered her eyes, examined the dust-caked mass still stuck to her slideshock. Then she nodded and set off again, running, expecting people to get out of her way. They did not disappoint her.

The trail was easy to follow. The dried road dust held splashes of black blood, but even had they not been there, the expressions on the faces of those around showed the way. The streets were lined with stunned people, some of them shocked at the sight of the bleeding, screaming woman, others—those few who perhaps knew the true nature of the Red Monks—even more terrified. Rumor of the Monks' presence must surely have spread throughout Pavisse by now, but seeing one agitated and in action drove home the mortal danger that the town was in.

A'Meer went first. Kosar watched her black braids bobbing as she ran, the weapons in their slings, belts and scabbard tied in tight to her body so that they did not rattle and shake.

What did she do back there to those militia? A few muttered words and she had them whimpering like babies. What power, what talents could do that?

The Monk screeched again ahead of them, closer than before.

"How long ago?" Kosar asked a startled sheebok herder. He stood with his herd pulled in tight around him, as if they would offer protection.

"A couple of minutes." He glanced down at Kosar's sword, still unsheathed and warm in the thief's hand. "You'll need more than that."

Kosar ran fast to catch up with A'Meer. "It's close!" he called, but she did not need telling. They skirted around a huge old machine, its tendrils long since fossilized into broken stone spurs that still reached in vain for the sky. On its far side a man was lying on the ground, holding a heap of slippery intestines in his lap. He too was looking to the sky. A small girl was hugging him and shouting. She had her face buried in his neck. People hovered around, not knowing what to do.

"Come on," A'Meer said quietly over her shoulder, as if afraid that Kosar would stop to help.

Kosar glanced at the man as he ran by and for a second their eyes locked. He looked away quickly. There was nothing that could comfort a man about to die with his daughter's tears wetting his skin.

The Monk screamed again and was answered by several separate cries. The complex warren of streets and alleys misled the echoes, confused direction, until Kosar was sure that they were surrounded by Red Monks, closing in quickly and ready for the fight. *We could die here,* he thought. *We probably will. A'Meer is terrified of one injured Monk, and now there are several closing in, almost as if they're herding us.*

A'Meer ran fast, and it was not long before Kosar began to feel his age. The summer heat sucked sweat from him, soaking his shirt and trousers and fusing them to his skin. A'Meer seemed not to tire. It was as if she were eighteen, not over a hundred. *Another Shantasi mystery,* he thought.

They came to a courtyard filled with milling people, and sensing the urgency, a few of them pointed the way. A'Meer ran into the mouth of a small alley, glancing down now and then at the blood spotting the ground, and Kosar followed. They passed a line of wash hung out to dry, and he saw spray patterns of blood across the lower edges. Either the Monk had caught someone here, or its veins were still bursting from slayer venom.

"Not far now," A'Meer said.

At the next corner Kosar caught sight of the Monk's red cloak flitting out of sight around a bend in the alley. A machine bridged the path, and several people stood high up, whooping and waving and urging them on. Kosar had been to tumbler fights once or twice, and this small crowd reminded him of that. How much more would they be entertained soon?

Around the bend, the Monk was revealed, loping along on feet and fists like a wild dog. Blood spattered every time it landed on its hands, dripping and spraying from ruptured veins. The toxin should have killed it long before now—it would be bleeding inside too, stomach filling with blood, arteries ripping and demanding more and more of its heart—but it seemed as strong as ever. The madness A'Meer had spoken of was serving the Monk well.

They ran through another square, people shying away from the blood-soaked demon, and into another small street.

"Here!" A'Meer called, and the Monk turned at the sound of her voice.

Kosar stopped. He almost turned around and ran, ready to find himself a hiding place from which he would hear the quick battle to come. Because it would surely be over in seconds. The Monk was an image from Kang Kang, every bad dream, every demonic legend ever told in Noreela; blood-soaked, insane, its skin red with rage where it was not already pasted with its own vital fluids. One eye had burst, yet still it saw, sensed, sent its fury their way through a long-fanged mouth. Its teeth dribbed with saliva, diluting the mess on its chin. Its arms waved, feet pounded at the ground, and it did not slow down for an instant.

The Monk still sought its quarry, and no threat from behind would tear it from its pursuit.

A'Meer plucked a small crossbow from a pocket on her shoulder, brought her arm down and fired in one swift movement. The bolt struck home in the thing's burst eye socket and it screeched, turning and running faster. The Shantasi reloaded without slowing, fired again, reloaded, fired. Each bolt found its mark—one in the back of the Monk's head, one at the base of its spine—but the impacts seemed only to pin its cloak tight to its body.

"I'll take it, you get the boy," she called.

Kosar wanted to argue, but he knew that she was right. She was the warrior here and he was the thief, used to stealing things and concealing them.

They turned another corner and emerged into a large square, the crowds already apparently disturbed by something . . . and then Kosar saw them. On the far side of the square, heading for a wide gateway leading into a park, Rafe was running with an old woman. The witch, Hope. Kosar hoped that she lived up to her name.

The Monk screamed then, too loud to be human, too enraged to be sane. The witch and the boy stopped and turned, wide-eyed and terrified of this frenzied thing closing in on them.

The witch reached into her shoulder bag and pulled something out.

A'Meer flicked out with her slideshock and caught the Monk's ankle, tripping it and pulling herself down into the dust.

"Take them away from here!" A'Meer shouted at Kosar. She was already on her feet, thrusting her arm at the Monk, slicing its cloak and flesh with the slideshock.

Kosar skirted the fight and went to the witch and Rafe, smiling at the boy, hoping that he could ease his own fear as well. The witch's eyes flickered down to Kosar's drawn sword and she raised her hand, ready to throw something at him, something green that squirmed and flexed in her palm with sickly, stagnant life.

"No!" Rafe said. "He's a friend."

Kosar reached the boy and hugged him tight, an unconscious gesture.

"Shantasi warrior," the witch said, and the tattoos on her face twitched in surprise.

The Monk was standing again, pure insane determination overcoming the ragged break in its ankle, and it was trying to make its way to Rafe. Between it and Rafe, however, stood A'Meer. She closed in, lashing out with her sword, ducking, parrying, thrusting again, sinking its tip into the Monk's exposed neck and spinning on her feet. Blood arced from the wound and splashed a sheebok tethered to a stall nearby, setting the creature screaming as secondhand slayer venom burned into its eyes.

The crowds had pulled back to the edges of the square, fascinated with the fight, some of them calling out and cheering as a blow was landed by either side. They had no loyalties, Kosar realized, and no real understanding of what was happening here. They were simply enjoying the spectacle.

"We have to get away from here!" Kosar said.

"That thing's come for me," Rafe said. "But who is she?"

"She's a friend. Rafe, we have to get you away."

"Aren't you going to help your friend?" the witch said.

Kosar glanced at the fighting couple. "No. She told me to take Rafe and find safety. She's trained in this. She's taken a Monk before."

The witch's strange tattooed face showed mocking disbelief. "She can't be much of a friend if she lies to you like that. And you can't be much of a friend leaving her alone to die."

"The boy's precious—"

"I know that! That's why he's coming with *me*!"

A'Meer shouted behind him and Kosar spun around, afraid of what he would see. The slideshock had wrapped around the Monk's thigh, and now the Monk was twisting on the spot, blood flying, hauling A'Meer in. She was struggling with the clasps on her wrist and forearm, trying to free herself, when the Monk stopped and lashed out with both swords. She ducked. A trimmed lock of her black air floated on the agitated air. And then she stood quickly, flinging a spiked ball into the Monk's face. She used the second's respite to cut the blade of the slideshock and step back out of the Monk's killing range.

"We have to go now!" Kosar said again. "The Monk called others, and if they converge here *everyone* will die."

"Then we should slow them down," the witch said. And cupping her hands around her mouth she shouted: "There are more of these things coming! Quickly, get out of here! Go! Find somewhere safe to hide! They'll kill you all!" The crowd started to stir, a few people hurrying away, but most remained.

At that moment the Monk landed a sword blow on A'Meer's arm. She screamed and fell, and a flap of skin fell back along her forearm, exposing the meat beneath.

"There! See?" Hope shouted. "These demons will slaughter every single one of you and eat your children!"

This time the reaction was more extreme. Most of the people poured out of the square, clogging narrow alleys and streets, pushing and falling and fighting as panic took over.

"You've sent them straight at the other Monks," Kosar said, but even as he spoke he realized the cool logic of what she had done.

"It may give us some time," Hope said. "Your friend needs help." She nodded past Kosar and he turned to see A'Meer on the ground, kicking out in an effort to put distance between her and the advancing Monk. It had raised both swords and was grinning through shattered teeth, spitting blood and enamel ahead of it. A'Meer rolled away from the shower of gore—with her open wounds, the slayer toxin would be the end of her—and the Monk bore down.

"A'Meer." He took a faltering step, paused, felt the sword in his hand send a hot pulse through his palm.

"I'll tell you where we are!" the witch called out. Kosar turned in time to see her and Rafe moving toward the park with a few other people.

"How?" he called.

"*I'll tell you.*" The witch's voice faded quickly amongst the shouts and screams of the others. Rafe glanced back once before he vanished, and the look on his face convinced Kosar of what he had to do. The boy was scared and bewildered, but he seemed to trust the witch.

A'Meer was in trouble. Her arm was bleeding badly, and as she scurried backwards across the ground the Monk gave her no chance to stand. It thrust down with its swords, A'Meer spun in the dust and dodged them, kicking out at its wrists and snapping one with an audible crack. The Monk screamed and stood back . . . and then, eyeless though it now was, it knew that Rafe had gone. It kicked A'Meer out of its way and advanced on Kosar.

He had to make a choice: step aside and let the Monk pass, pursue Rafe and the witch, make everything A'Meer had gone through pointless; or stand and fight.

The sword knew what it needed.

Breathing hard, tucking the sword under one arm, Kosar pulled down his sleeves and wrapped them around his hands, protecting the open wounds on his fingertips.

"*Don't let it pass!*" A'Meer screamed, standing, drawing more weapons from her belt and a slip around her stomach.

Kosar hefted the sword and parried two blows from the Monk, three, staring all the time at its ravaged face, the exploded mess of its eyes sliding down its cheeks, the gore that ran from its mouth. He tried to remember everything he knew about fighting—all self-taught and used frequently during his earlier years of travel and robbery—and as the Monk brought back both arms to stab at him he ducked inside its fighting circle, lashed out with the sword and felt it grind against bone.

The Monk screeched and sent a splutter of blood at Kosar. He ducked and rolled, keeping a tight grip on his sword, twisting it as it slipped out of the Red Monk.

"Hey, you're turning me on," A'Meer said weakly, and then she darted at the Monk's back, driving in a barbed fork.

The square was all but empty now, save for a few diehard fight fans who had weighed the risks and decided to remain. They kept to the edges, moving around so that they could get a better view of proceedings, still cheering each time a blow was landed . . . but now Kosar felt their allegiance polarize. As the Monk walked toward the park Kosar ran to its left side, ducked a backward sweep of its sword and hacked at its leg once, twice, three times. With each blow a cheer rose from the few spectators. Kosar smiled, hacked again.

The Monk fell toward him, its slashed cloak falling open to reveal sagging breasts. He backed away, losing his sword where it had become lodged in the thing's thigh bone, and leapt out of the way as it hit the dirt. It growled, crawled after him, and as a bloody hand closed around his boot Kosar knew that it had fallen on purpose.

"A'Meer!" he shouted.

She came at them, right hand and forearm tucked into her shirt to shelter the bleeding wound from the Monk's blood. She hefted a small axe in her left hand, leapt at the last moment and buried it in the Monk's wrist.

Kosar kept crawling, the Monk's severed hand still clasped tightly around his boot.

The crowd cheered again.

A'Meer went at the Monk with the axe, aiming for its other hand as it waved its sword at her. It parried her first few blows, then slid quickly across the ground and surprised her with a stab to the ankle. She grunted and stumbled away, dropping the axe, slipping to her knees as blood flowered over the lip of her boot.

The observers fell silent.

"Hey!" Kosar was running to A'Meer, kicking the still-flexing hand from his foot, and he glanced up. A man stood in the corner of the square, waving his hands. "Hey! There's a tumbler pit this way!"

"Tumbler," A'Meer moaned as Kosar reached her.

"Are you all right?"

She looked up at him, and he could see veins standing out on her temples, edging their cruel fingers under her scalp. Her eyes were already bloodshot. "No," she said.

"Oh Mage shit, A'Meer!"

"One chance," she said. "I'll keep it here, fend it off. You go for the tumbler. Follow the idiot who shouted, make him show you."

"What about you, what about—"

"One death at a time, Kosar. I'll make sure the Monk doesn't get me. We'll worry about what's in my blood later."

The Monk had gained its feet and was walking once again toward the gated entrance to the park. There were a thousand places to hide in there, but by now Kosar was sure the witch and Rafe would have reached its far side. The Monk screeched again, and from nearby something answered.

"They're close!"

"We don't have much time, Kosar. Go!"

He started toward the corner of the square, then glanced back at A'Meer. She was struggling to her feet. He ran back past her, ducked under the Monk's sword and rescued his own blade from its leg, thrusting hard and sticking it in between the thing's ribs. He pushed, toppling the Monk onto its front, and then ran. He mustered a smile for A'Meer as he passed her, and she smiled back. *We're both going to die*, he thought.

The man who had shouted about the tumbler headed off before Kosar could reach him, trotting along a street, turning left, right, bringing them quickly to a high-fenced compound, a fighting ring for a tumbler. Kosar had been to a contest once or twice but it had not entertained him. However willing the combatants, the sight of them impaled on the giant rolling thing, the thorns and barbs taking out their foolish eyes and hearts, had done nothing for him.

You red freak, he thought. *Escape from this!*

"Where's the gate?" he asked.

"Here!" The man pointed along the fence, and Kosar saw the look on his face for the first time. He was more than excited; he was turned on.

"How do I aim this thing?"

"You can't. Once it's out there's little you can do but run."

"Great."

Kosar shook his hands free of the stretched sleeves. He drew his knife and hacked at the gate's wooden hinges, breaking one, hearing the scream of the Red Monk from the square behind him, seeing movement as the tumbler shifted slightly in its bed of moss. It was taller than him, though certainly not the biggest he had ever seen;

they were twice this size on the foothills of Kang Kang. It wore evidence of many kills. Bones were hugged to its hide by barbed hooks, some of them still retaining fleshy scraps, the tatters of clothes, jewelry. As Kosar forced the second hinge the tumbler flexed, shifted and then rolled with startling speed at the gate. The gate smashed open and he ducked behind it, gasping as it swung wide and pinned him against the fence. The tumbler rolled straight down the street, bouncing from wall to wall, the sound almost musical; the rustle of vegetation on stone, bones on dust, barbs scraping walls and offering a rhythm to its escape.

Kosar heaved the gate away and ran after the tumbler. Something screeched up ahead. It was not A'Meer's voice, and it sounded too strong to belong to the injured Red Monk.

"A'Meer!" he screamed, trying to shout above the grind and rattle of the tumbler. "It's coming!"

He reached the square in time to see the tumbler roll across its first victim. A Red Monk, just emerging into the square from an alley a few buildings along, became instantly impaled on its hide. The Monk screamed, and the tumbler paused to roll back, forward, and back again, working barbs through its victim until they held it firm. The Monk shouted again, hacking at itself, determined to cut itself free even if that meant evisceration.

A'Meer was where Kosar had left her, hobbling in a circle around the other mad Monk, launching throwing knives at its face and chest. The thing was hardly moving now, though it still stood and roared and spat blood at her, perhaps its final effective weapon.

The tumbler rolled in a small circle, still crushing down the Monk it had trapped . . . and then it paused.

"A'Meer, run!"

The tumbler accelerated across the square. It hit the wounded Monk a heartbeat later, smashing it down into the dust in a rain of blood, continuing on until it struck the wall to one side of the park gates. It pulled back and rolled again, crushing into the wall, pressing its prey deeper onto and into itself.

A'Meer had hobbled to a doorway, and she glanced across at Kosar. He waved her over but she seemed to be waiting, holding back, watching the tumbler. It rolled away again, trundling across the square. She hopped down from the doorway and retrieved Kosar's sword from where it was ground into the bloody dust. Then she started backing away from the tumbler, moving from door to door, following a woman who had been watching the battle as she too tried to slip away.

Kosar met A'Meer at the corner of the square.

"A'Meer!" he said. "Mage shit, A'Meer, I thought you'd be dead."

"It was only a splash," she said. "Only a . . ." Her white skin had grown livid as blood pooled beneath its surface. Veins stood proud on her forehead and cheeks, her eyes were flowered with bursting vessels and her nose leaked blood, but still she held out the sword to him. "It was my father's."

"We have to get away from here," Kosar said. He took the sword and sheathed it. Blood-caked dust fell from the scabbard. "The other Monks are heading this way. Most of Pavisse must have heard." He quickly unwrapped the sodden strips of cloth from his fingers and discarded them, fearful that some of the Monk's blood may have splashed there. He felt fine so far. No burning in his veins. No hint of death approaching, at least not from within.

"Rafe?"

"The witch took him through the park. She said she'd tell us where to find them."

A'Meer's eyelids were fluttering, and when she coughed she brought up blood. "She may have slayer antidote," she whispered. "Hey, done two Monks now. Getting good at this."

The tumbler was roaming the square, rebounding from walls and the park gates, pausing every now and then when one of the Monks cried out. It would rest on them, shifting position like a dog making a comfortable place to lie, and then roll on. Its movements were slower and more ponderous, as if it was sated for now. It left bloody prints on the ground, and soon it looked as if a hundred battles had been fought there, not just one.

Kosar bent down and let A'Meer fall across his right shoulder. She was heavier than she looked—perhaps because she still carried much of her weaponry, even though she'd left a good portion of it in the Monk—but Kosar headed off quickly, fear driving him on, thumping his heart and pounding his legs as he ran. He bore right and they passed from street to alley to courtyard, heading across the hidden districts to the other side of the park. Many people watched them pass, and a few pointed and nudged their neighbors. *There they are, fighting a red demon, I tell you! Amazing that even one of them survived.*

Kosar knew that they had to leave Pavisse. There was no point in searching for Rafe Baburn now; the witch had taken him away, and for whatever reasons she coveted him, she wanted to keep him safe. She would take him out of town and head north or east, away from Pavisse and Trengborne. If Hope kept her promise she would get a message to them somehow, although Kosar had no notion of how she would achieve this. *If* they could escape Pavisse, *if* they were not caught by Monks or militia, *if* A'Meer did not die and leave him floundering through this on his own . . . they were still back at the beginning. Rafe was as distant now as he had been before they left A'Meer's home.

Everything depended on Hope.

———

RAFE RAN. IT felt as though they had been running forever. Out of the square and away from the thief and the warrior woman, through the streets with the panicking hordes, Hope pulling him into an open doorway when the crowds ahead of them parted around a rushing figure clad in red. It swung its sword from side to side as if hacking its way through a jungle. Most people moved aside in time; a few did not. Rafe thought of Trengborne again, and his parents, and Hope need not have placed her hand over his mouth to keep him silent.

Although the witch was old it was Rafe who tired first. The last couple of days had been exhausting, physically and mentally, and the voices were bringing him down. The incessant whispering in his mind, as if there were things scheming in there that were apart from him, presences that used him as a channel to their own ends. He knew that this was wrong—there was nothing inside but him, his own wounded soul—and yet that frightened him more. It frightened him because it meant that perhaps the witch was right.

The voices spoke in images, like a dream trying to make itself known, and although some of the smells and sounds and tastes they gave him were familiar, combined they were an enigma. Perhaps they marked him out and made him special. But as yet they were doing little to really help.

Upon reaching the outskirts of the town they slowed to a fast walk. Hope paused at a stall now and then—bought some food, bartered for some warm clothing—but they never stopped for long. Because there were more of those things after them, those things that kept coming when they were shot and stabbed and beaten and knocked down, and even after they'd been bitten by a slayer spider they kept coming . . .

At the edge of Pavisse, beyond the final rough human encampment at a place where nothing ahead of them was man-made, Hope stopped at last. She looked at Rafe and smiled, and her tattoos smiled as well.

"It's dangerous out there," she said, nodding the way they had to go. "People don't travel that much anymore, and mostly for good reason. Things are changing. I've heard lots of gossip and myth, son, but if even a small part of it is true . . . well, it's dangerous out there."

"Worse than back in the town?"

She looked at him for a long time, so long that he thought something had happened to her. Maybe she'd fallen into some witchy sleep. But she was merely looking, and in her eyes he saw wonder.

"You know those things were coming for you, don't you, Rafe?"

"I suppose I do."

"And you know why. I've told you why."

He did not want to answer that, but he found himself nodding. *The voices,* he thought. *Because the land talks to me. It talks, and the Red Monks think that the Mages will hear.*

"I have to keep you safe," she said.

"What about the thief?"

"The thief and his Shantasi? Well, I did give my word. And I suppose we could always do with someone who knows how to use a sword. Don't worry, I'll get word to them, if they're still alive. Which I doubt."

"How will you do that?"

The witch stared across the plains at the horizon shivering in heat haze. "First, you have to help me find a skull raven."

They set off away from Pavisse and into the wilds. A steady breeze brought cooler air from the north. It seemed to quieten the voices in Rafe's head, but they were not calm. They were waiting.

Chapter 16

THEY RODE WAY above the clouds, seeing nothing of the world below, and yet Lenora knew that they were moving in the right direction. It was growing steadily warmer, for a start. And the hate in her heart was swelling at the smell of Noreela.

The hawks mostly floated, needing only an occasional sweep of their webbed tentacles or a blast from their gas sacs to remain afloat. The Krotes sat in their saddles, ate, slept, called to one another, stared up at the dark blue sky or down at the tops of the cloud cover. Occasionally the clouds parted to reveal more of the same: sea, and more sea, but now without the white speckles of ice floes. That meant that with every second they flew, Noreela was closer.

Lenora listened for her almost-daughter. The thought of that voice sounding again scared her, because it had been three hundred years, and that was too long for a mother and daughter to stay apart. And yet it excited her too. While the voice of the shade could never be the same, it would only encourage her in the fighting that was to come. She would serve the Mages as well as she had for centuries, and when the time came, she would serve herself. Robenna may well not even be there anymore, but if it was then the descendants of those who had driven her out would be living there. She would enjoy her moment of revenge.

As her hawk drifted onward, Lenora caught a glimpse of the sea between the clouds far below, and she remembered the last time her foot had touched Noreelan soil.

———

THE MACHINE MOVED on to other Krotes, its rider reddened with pure rage and bloodlust. He had left Lenora for dead and she thought perhaps he was right. She fell back, batting at the fire that ate into her shoulder and neck, and the sea welcomed her in as she faded away from the world.

She kicked. Her feet touched the beach, pushing her back.

Mother, said the shade that would have been her daughter. And then it faded away.

She kicked again, but her feet touched nothing.

———

TIME PASSED, AND it could have been minutes or centuries.

Lenora awoke with a new awareness of the world. She could smell cooking flesh, but also the taint of time on the breeze. She could taste blood in her mouth, her own and others', but she could also taste the craving for retribution, a bitter tang like the infection from a rotting tooth. She saw the rigging of a huge ship above her, reaching for the sky with sails and ropes that even now were bursting into flame; and then a familiar face leaning in close, smiling, her utter beauty complemented by the blood spattered on her face and the gore hanging like ringlets in her tangled blond hair.

Angel.

Lenora gasped and tried to pull back, but she was lying flat on the deck. Angel looked away from her for a few seconds, her eyes darting here and there, fiercely intelligent and plainly mad. Lenora took several deep breaths before the Mage looked back down at her.

"You're hurting," the Mage said. Her voice was smooth, yet deep with darkest knowledge. Snakes of shadow twisted around her head, out of her eyes, into her mouth, tails of dark magic exuded from her mind and inhaled once again.

Lenora could not speak.

"You fought bravely, and your hate remains rich. I'll save you from death and make you better. And if we have a future, you will be a part of it."

Lenora tried to speak, but the pain from her burning shoulder seemed to have paralyzed her throat and mouth. She could do nothing as Angel leaned down and kissed her. She felt something sliding down her throat—truly alien, malformed and yet reveling in its existence—and her fresh awareness took a massive leap outward.

As she passed into unconsciousness Lenora saw Angel stand above her and move away. And for an instant, it felt as though she knew everything.

———

THE SHIP WAS still on fire when she next awoke. Someone had dragged her to the edge of the deck and leaned her unceremoniously against the gunwale, and burning timbers and sheets of flaming sails drifted down around her. Somebody screamed, someone else shouted and a snake of Krotes stood across the deck, passing buckets to and fro in an attempt to douse the flames.

Lenora went to help, but she could not even stand. Her shoulder was a knot of agony, but when she looked at it she was surprised to see that the wound was no longer open. The agony was a memory of pain. She could no longer feel whatever the Mage had given her, but she sensed that it was inside her still, a shred of Angel's dark magic coiled around her heart. She was glad, but petrified. She had no idea what the future would bring.

A mast collapsed, people screamed as they were trapped and burned beneath it, and then the world suddenly changed.

Those not affected by the fires cried out in unison.

Lenora screamed.

Angel, somewhere out of sight, let out a wail that cracked timber, ruptured ears and blasted seabirds from the sky, dead.

"Oh, in the name of the Black," Lenora whispered, falling to the deck and scratching at the cracked wood. If she could have opened one of those cracks with her nails she would have gladly fallen through.

The wind that had been edging them away from Noreela died, and the dozen Krote ships bobbed helplessly in the currents. Clouds broke apart, a huge water spout formed and shattered one of the vessels to pieces, dead fish bobbed to the sea's surface, some as small as a human's finger, several almost as large as one of the ships. Their bodies ruptured and burst from the sudden exposure to daylight, and their insides were already rotten and rank.

Lenora thought of her daughter, and every minute that had passed since that miscarriage in sight of the Kang Kang mountains was wasted, hopeless, a travesty of existence. She cried, and the tears were bitter and hot. For a while she could barely breathe. It was as if something that had once breathed for her had suddenly been taken away.

"What?" she cried, "What?" But she was only echoing what everyone else was asking, and for that simplest of questions there was no easy answer.

The whole world shrugged and shivered, and when it stilled it was a lesser place.

———

MAGIC HAD WITHDRAWN itself from Noreela, leaving behind a vacuum of hopelessness and despair.

Many Krotes threw themselves overboard, giving themselves to the sea and the creatures that lived below its surface. Others drank poisons or fell on their swords. Lenora crawled across the deck, but by the time she reached the burning sail she had intended wrapping herself in, the flames had withered.

The Mages vanished from view. The next time anyone saw them was ten days later, when strong winds had carried them to an icy shore far to the north.

———

LENORA, SITTING ASTRIDE her hawk's neck and remembering that distant past, still shivered at the memory of magic's retreat. It had taken a long time for them to shake off the hopelessness that had descended across the whole of the surviving Krote fleet. And it had taken three hundred years for magic to show its face again.

This time, the Mages would have it for their own.

———

TREY WAS UNABLE to sleep. He was traumatized by what had happened, stunned awake by the simple conviction that none of it was possible. His mother could not be dead, Sonda could not be dead, their underground community must surely still be there, going about its business and wondering, in bars and shops and the square where the puppeteer played his plays, just where Trey Barossa had gone.

But as he watched the sun rise in the east he knew that it was true. All the pain, the suffering, the anguish was as obvious to him now as the cool dawn. The redness bleeding out between the mountains hurt his eyes and he turned his back to the sunrise to watch Alishia.

Since falling and banging her head she had turned strange. He thought she may have fractured her skull. The bump was not huge and it had hardly bled, but from that moment, after passing out for just a few minutes and then waking shouting and dancing and laughing, she had been all but comatose. Her eyes were open and her lips moved, making no sound. She sat up straight, hands on her knees, fingers flexing every now and then as if to work stiffness from the joints. But she said nothing, and she seemed unaware of his presence.

Perhaps she was like this most of the time. He did not know her, and she was a topsider, after all. Maybe this was the way she made friends.

Trey had never seen the sky before yesterday. After Alishia's fall he had returned to her, calmed his own panic, and then he sat and watched the sky all night. Darkness was his age-old companion, but he had never known it so deep. He had stared for hours, awed by the stars, amazed that so many dead could still show themselves as points of brilliant light. There must have been millions up there, and he scanned the sky from horizon to horizon many times, searching for his mother.

The life moon bathed the south, silvered like a smudge of hope forever promised by the sky. The death moon appeared as Trey sat watching, emerging from behind the mountains to the east as if raising itself on the souls of all those dead miners. Its pale yellow glow spilled across the landscape. He had heard about the moons so often down in the dark, where they were talked about in the same hushed tones as wide-open meadows, sunlight on skin, birds making the sky seem so high. Now that he was up here and he could see them, it all seemed so unfair. Why should he be the one who survived?

But guilt could not crush down his sense of wonder. He watched the skies change color as dawn came, bitterly awed, and when the sunlight finally touched her face, Alishia woke up.

———

HER HEAD ACHED. Blood had run from her scalp, caked her hair and dried on her face, and now that whole side of her head felt stiff and heavy. She flexed her jaw and turned gently, testing her neck. The skin of blood crackled as it broke.

Dawn was here, and the sunlight hurt her eyes. There were no clouds, but it was already cold, a cool breeze breathing down from the north. Alishia was in pain, yet she felt like laughing out loud.

"You came back," she said. Trey was a silhouette against the rising sun, and she saw him nod. "Last thing I remember was the horse going mad."

"It stumbled in the dark," he said. "I saw the hole clear as light, but the horse either didn't have such good eyesight, or it was more panicked than me. I thought the Nax were coming. I don't know why the horse ran. Dumb creature."

"They're actually quite intelligent," she said, trying to hold back a smile. "Where is it now?"

"Back where it fell. It's leg is broken. The bone's sticking out."

"Oh damn," Alishia said, feeling sorry for the animal. It had carried her this far this quickly, only to be left lying lame in the dark. She felt suddenly guilty, imagining what Erv would have said.

His name inspired thought. Where he lived, what he did, how he looked. Whether he spoke any strange words, knew languages she did not. Whether he could do things other people could not do.

She tried to forget the stable boy, shaking her head as if that would loosen the thought.

"We'll have to put her down."

Trey stood, turning slightly so that she could see his face at last. "Kill her?"

"Of course," Alishia said. "She can't walk. We can't fix her leg. If we leave her where she is, she'll be picked off by scavengers. That's not fair. What happens in the mines if a pony is hurt?"

"We eat it," Trey said.

He's out of his environment, dislocated for some reason only he knows. He talks of Nax, but how do I know it's true? He may be fleeing something else, or running toward something. Using me. Does he know the language of wind? Can he feel the land breathing beneath him?

"Oh," Alishia said.

"They do taste *very* good with cave spice."

"Not that," Alishia said. "I must have banged my head harder than I thought. Feel a bit weird, that's all." *Feel a bit . . .*

She clasped one hand to her breast, squeezed tight, laughing inside.

Trey turned around, looking at the ground to prevent the sunlight touching his eyes. "I can't do it," he said.

"I will." Alishia stood and took the knife from her boot, judging its length, wondering just how she was supposed to kill a horse with a six-inch blade. Through the ear? Slash its throat? Neither way would be quick, but it was a new experience, and it interested her.

She left Trey and walked down the hillside. She heard the horse before she saw it, breathing heavily and grunting as it tried in vain to gain its feet. It glared at her as she approached, eyes wide and terrified. It had been frothing at the mouth but it had dried now, brittle in the sun.

"Poor thing," she said softly, hands held out, knife hidden along her wrist. "Poor thing, shhh." The horse took some comfort from her tone, becoming still, panting. Alishia could feel the vibration as its heart beat frantically. Its front leg was broken and torn open, already attracting flies and a moving carpet of ants and small insects.

It took a long time for the horse to die. Alishia prevaricated long enough for the sun to rise and lift a thin mist across the plains, and when she finally decided that she should cut its throat it took her longer to work up the courage. In the end she jabbed once, hard, eyes closed, and the horse bucked and flung her away.

It screamed. She turned her back and walked away once she saw that it was bleeding to death. And although she felt sick and sad, she was also fascinated as well, enjoying this new experience of meting out death. It was as if the blow to the head had woken a part of her with little sense of squeamishness or pity, which reveled in the pure experience of slaughter.

I wonder if pain has a different sound, she thought. *I wonder if death is a whole new language?*

By the time she reached the fledge miner where he sat shading his eyes, the horse was dead.

"Breakfast?" she asked.

Trey looked around, glancing at her hands, evidently expecting to see her carrying chunks of fresh horse meat. "What is there?" he asked.

"I'm sure we can find something." Alishia knew from her reading that there were grubs living beneath some of the layers of moss in these foothills, and the flesh of the pirate plant was sweet and full of nutrients, and that it was possible to lure in a flightless pheasant with a softly sung lullaby. She sent Trey to look for some grubs while she went in search of a copse of pirate plants, keeping her eyes open for pheasant all the time.

There was a cool breeze from the north, even though the sun was rising to warm her skin. Alishia kept glancing northward, not sure what she was expecting to see but conscious all the time that there was *something* there.

My master my queen my god.

She was still suffering from the bump to her head. Her scalp was a cool burn where the cut lay open to the air, and as she bent to slice the stem of a pirate plant she felt the cool trickle of fresh blood through her hair. And yet although it hurt, she enjoyed the pain. She had been hurt before but this time she analyzed the sensation dispassionately, relishing it, turning her head so that it ran across her scalp like water, prickling in and down to her neck where the bruising was already spreading.

So good to be alive!

"So good to be alive," she whispered, and then wondered whether she had already said it. She had *thought* it, that was for sure, but speaking it gave her a sense of déjà vu that refused to go away, even when she stood and turned and walked, looked down at a small beetle crossing her boot, glanced up at a circle of skull ravens drifting on thermals a mile high, went back to where she and Trey were planning on eating their breakfast . . .

Trey had found several fat grubs and was trying to stop them from crawling away. The sunlight had them agitated, as if they knew what was about to come. He glanced up as Alishia approached and offered her a smile. She had a sudden, shockingly intense image of kneeling on the ground, hands fisted around clumps of moss while he rutted at her from behind, pounding his pale yellow cock into her, feeding her fledge in tiny crumbs with one hand, and grasping her breasts, her hips with the other.

Alishia stopped, wide-eyed, sat down carefully and avoided Trey's eyes.

"Do we cook these?" he asked.

"Yes." *Where had that come from?*

"I've seen more appetizing food hanging off the arse of a mule."

"They're very tasty."

Very tasty, very *tasty, just try it to see* . . .

Alishia was a virgin. She was used to thinking about sex in the privacy of her own company, using her imagination, pleasuring only herself because the world she lived in was lacking the highlights she could imagine. Now suddenly it was a force, a powerful drive that had reared from nowhere and grasped her insides, sensitized her skin and tongue and her own secret parts to such a degree that she found it hard to sit still.

"Excuse me!" Alishia said, standing and rushing away. She shook her head to shift the thoughts and felt something loose in there. Perhaps the knock to the head really had damaged her.

Trey called but she ignored him, still trying to shake the image of their rutting from her mind. And yet, as she stepped from rock to moss to earth, the idea pleased her. And deep inside in that place where the experience sat waiting to happen, it burned to be set free.

She sat in the shadow of a huge boulder, out of sight of the fledge miner, and stared northward across the plains. As her hand stole between her thighs she could not shake the feeling that she was watching herself from afar.

———

"I THINK WE should go that way," Trey said, pointing west.

"Why?"

He shrugged, keeping his eyes downcast to avoid the sun. Yet he so wanted to look. "It just feels right," he said. "Behind us are the mountains, and beneath them are the Nax. I don't want to be near them—I *can't* be near them! To the north is the city you've just left. I don't think I could be in a city, not with so many people, and not . . . not north. That feels wrong."

"This is your first time ever aboveground. How can anywhere be right or wrong for you?"

"I'm only saying what I feel," Trey said, and in truth, deep down he was scared. Behind him was death and the destruction of everything he had ever known—*everything*—and before him, laid out like legend brought to life, the plains and mountains and a sky so huge that it must surely crush him down. The horizon to the west was wide and low and smothered with sky. How could there be so much light without scorching him, so many plants without choking the land? There was little opportunity for darkness to hide now that the sun was climbing high.

The ghost of the death moon was hanging in the north like an echo, pale now in daylight.

"I don't mind where we go," Alishia said, and once again Trey thought that she was teasing him. One minute she was quiet and concerned and vulnerable, the next confident, brash, eager to move on and meet whatever was coming next.

After eating the cooked grubs—which Trey had to admit were delicious—and the stripped and kneaded pirate plant flesh, the two of them divided Alishia's belongings between their shoulder bags and set out westward.

They walked in silence for several hours, Alishia darting on ahead now and then, looking around, splashing in streams, lifting rocks, tasting moss from upturned stones. Trey did not comment; he assumed that this was her way of traveling, navigating their position, keeping track of where they were. She had a map rolled up in her pack, and although it had looked detailed in part, there were still vast tracts left uncharted to the south, east and north, the far-flung places of Noreela that even in his dreams he could barely imagine.

She was poor company. Sometimes she displayed pity and sorrow, but mostly she fueled her own apparently bottomless desire for knowledge and sensation. She had told him that she was a librarian. Trey had seen books, although not many, and he could not comprehend someone spending their life in a building virtually made of them. She had tried to communicate to him how the worlds she knew were alive in books, but Trey did not understand. Here was the world, and they were in it. Reality was doing its best to blind him with its brashness, terrify him with its size and light and multitudinous variations.

He tried walking with his eyes closed for long periods, but after the first few falls he gave up. Besides, the sun still found its way through. He wondered if he would ever see total darkness again.

For most of the day they walked across the plains with no real destination in mind. Then late in the afternoon Alishia stopped and waited for Trey to catch up, glancing back at him, smiling, her eyes sparkling with exhilaration.

"Swallow hole," she said. "See there?" She pointed, although Trey had already seen. How could he not?

Sometimes in the rivers belowground, at places where they

slowed and pondered in wide caverns before moving on once again, there were whirlpools; spinning sinkholes opening beneath the river and sucking its waters deeper, deeper into the earth to places no man or fledger had ever been. He had never seen one but he had heard of them, sitting wide-eyed and fascinated as his father told him tales of how these whirlpools could swallow a man whole, and how sometimes they did. These men were still sinking, his father had said, still spinning, drowned now but their journey downward never-ending, the water keeping their corpses fresh for discovery by whatever waited at the bottom.

This swallow hole was like one of those whirlpools, except that it existed in rock.

"I've read about these," Alishia said. "They started happening after magic fled. There was only one recorded in the first hundred years, but in the past few decades they've been happening all over. Flushing away all the badness left behind, some say. Maybe they'll eventually join up to suck the whole of Noreela away."

It was a mile distant but easily visible. Even Trey, new to the surface and ignorant of many of its features, knew that it did not belong here. It looked unreal and incongruous. And it sounded like a long, endless growl.

The ground stirred slowly around the hole, traveling in a lazy, decreasing circle, clumps of grass and rock and the waving arms of shrubs and trees turning and tumbling as they were drawn in. The air above it shimmered. Trey tried to picture the caves and passageways in the ground below, the places where this hole vented, but like the whirlpools in the underground rivers and lakes, he could not imagine it having an end. Not in this world, at least.

"It must have just started," Alishia said.

"Will it spread? Should we run?"

Alishia shook her head. "They're always quite small. It's probably a hole the size of your fist. Nobody knows where they go, but you can find traces of old ones sometimes, like deep throats at the base of a crater. If we wait here long enough, perhaps we can go and take a look."

The sight dizzied Trey; so much landscape still and peaceable, and this patch of it moving slowly at the edges, faster farther in, blurred into nothing at the very center. A big bird flew quickly overhead, dipped down at the disturbed earth to look for worms and insects and was sucked in, leaving floating feathers in its wake.

"What was that?" Trey asked, aghast.

"Moor hawk," Alishia said wondrously. "I've never seen one before!"

"Well, you won't see that one again."

"I wonder if it's still whole," she said, and the idea disturbed Trey into silence.

They sat and watched the swallow hole slowly consume everything within its reach. Plants and soil spat themselves skyward with the pressure, only to be caught again by the hole's influence and pulled down into its maw. And then the clays and rocks below the soil, the noise of their demise echoing across and vibrating through the land, grinding and smashing together, crushing, throwing up dust and shards that were similarly caught and sucked down. A rainbow formed briefly overhead as the air itself started to move, moisture condensing and darkening the spinning ground, small clouds forming high above and spiraling downward. Air breezed past Alishia and Trey, insects and birds fluttering uselessly against their fate. It was as if the hole was trying to suck in the sky.

At the end, with the ground around it stripped to the bedrock and air still condensing in an endless spiral from above, the hole whistled itself into oblivion. It was a hiss of gushing air that Trey recognized from the mines—sometimes breezes would come from and go to nowhere, sources and destinations both mysteries—and it gave him a shiver to realize that these things may be the cause. The hole's final breath could even now be exploring the underworld, fingering through passageways and caverns untrodden by humanity, blowing dust against things ancient, unknown and unknowable, passing by sleeping or waking Nax, eventually even reaching the stiff body of his dead mother and querying her demise.

"Are we going to see?" he said eventually.

"No. It's too uncertain. We'll skirt around it." Alishia's initial excitement seemed to have faded to a mild interest, tempered by her realization of how dangerous this thing could be.

"It'll be dark soon."

She nodded. "We need to camp as far away from here as we can. Maybe it hasn't quite finished."

They headed south to pass by the swallow hole, finding evidence of its presence as they moved farther away: uprooted trees; shredded shrubs; areas of stripped ground where the bedrock peered through. Two hours later, with the sun setting ahead of them and the life moon a waning silver against its more sinister sister, they spied a fire in the distance.

"Someone else on the plains?" Trey asked nervously. Alishia was the only topsider he had met and strange as she was, at least she had grown familiar. And besides, he owed her for saving his life. But to face others?

"Yes," she said. "People. We should go to them. They'll have food and water, and I'm sure they'd trade some for a crumb of your fledge."

"How can we be sure that they're friendly?"

Alishia was silent for a long while, staring across the darkening plains at the winking light. "We can't be sure," she said. "But there's a part of me that craves company right now. That swallow hole . . . I've read about them, but actually seeing something like that, something that is proof of the land changing, winding down and giving out on us . . . I want to be with other people. I need to talk. And besides, they may know a lot more than we do."

"About what?"

"Magic." So saying, Alishia strode off, heading for the fire, shrugging her backpack higher.

Trey held back. Alishia's comments about the swallow hole and what it meant had made him think of the Nax mind he had touched on so briefly and terribly. Something had been wrong in there, an understanding that things were amiss and that it had to wake to take action.

And now Alishia was talking of magic.

He could only follow, but the nervousness that had informed Trey's thoughts since Alishia had found him on the hillside pressed in stronger than ever. Given a target, it flowered into something greater.

He shrugged off his shoulder bag, grabbed a thumb of fledge and began to chew as he followed Alishia toward the light.

Chapter 17

THEY STOPPED RUNNING several miles beyond Pavisse. The fear was still with Rafe—the image of that demon coming at him, spitting blood, empty eye sockets seeing far more than they should, smelling the taint of something that even Rafe was still barely admitting to— but his body was failing. He could not run forever, however terrified he was. His legs were cramping, he had a stitch in his side that almost bent him double and Hope the witch had finally stopped trying to drag him. Now even she was struggling.

"There," she said, pointing. At the foot of a gentle slope sat a huddle of buildings, smoke rising lazily from a fire before being caught and blown away by the northerly breeze. "We'll get some horses."

"A farm won't just give us horses," Rafe gasped. He was bent over, hands on his knees, legs shaking and threatening to spill him to the ground. For the hundredth time he looked behind them, fearing a flash of red in the distance.

"I'll buy them," she said. "Farm folk are always open to secrets."

The farm was small, suffering as much as any from poor yield by the land. Its outbuildings were in disrepair, one of them leaning over so much that its timber columns had snapped, little more than habit preventing it from tumbling to the ground. There were several other open sheds and barns, all of them bleached by the sun and none of them full. Produce must be rare, such were the denuded stocks. From inside one of the smaller buildings came screeches and screams, rats fighting over some unfortunate victim. The farmhouse itself, a long, low, single-story affair, was adorned with animal heads in varying states of decomposition. Most of them were old, little more than bare skulls hanging on to shreds of leathery skin. But one or two were relatively new, blood dried but still evident in trails down the wall, eyes glassy where they had not been pecked out by birds. It was an old practice, displaying the heads of slaughtered predators, but it showed that life on this farm was not easy. There were at least forty heads nailed to the wall beneath the eaves: giant rats; the slab-shaped head of a ground snake; a sabre-toothed dog, its teeth painted bright red; and other creatures, some of which Rafe did not even recognize.

A herd of cows lumbered around a field nearby, chewing at grass that would eventually poison them, udders hanging slack and dry. One of them was mothering a calf, but it was a weak, diseased-looking thing, its red coat faded almost to white from lack of sustenance. A few sheebok wandered across the farmyard, lapping water from a small pond. They bleated and butted one another with shorn horns.

The farm wolf watched them walk in across the fields, eyes glittering and pelt rich and full. Some were eating well, at least. It remained stationary until Rafe and Hope passed the first of the outbuildings, and then it let out a short, loud bark.

From their left came the sound of something heavy stamping and shifting in an enclosed barn. Hope glanced at Rafe and nodded. "Horses," she said.

Rafe felt strangely at home. Trengborne had been a whole farming community, a hundred times larger than this place and far more advanced, and yet the smells and sights and sounds were the same: sheebok dung; a rack of tools in the farmyard; the background grunts and grumble of farm animals eating and drinking and sleeping. On closer inspection he saw that the sheebok all had eye-rot, and he wanted to find a redspit plant to shred and put in their water. But he guessed that the farmer knew his work, however bad a state his herds were in. Rafe's interference would not be appreciated.

Rafe heard a harsh whisper from out of sight. Running footsteps echoed behind one of the buildings. From behind the house more frantic whispers, the metallic sound of weapons clinking together, a hissed curse.

"Stand still, boy," Hope said when they reached the center of the yard. The wolf stood by the door to the farmhouse, watching them, bushy tail high. "They'll likely challenge us, but let me do the talking."

"But I'm a farmer, I'll know—"

"You're from a village, not a farm like this. These people will be used to fighting off bandits and tumblers, not sitting around nursing furbats."

Rafe felt slighted but he did as Hope said, standing still, arms held out from his sides to show that he was hiding no weapons.

The call came from their left.

"Who are you? What do you want?" The woman stepped out from behind the farmhouse, and as she strode into the yard the wolf stepped along by her side.

"My name's Hope, and I want to buy two horses from you. This here is Rafe."

"You're a witch." The woman had stopped a few paces from them, staring mostly at Hope and the tattoos illustrating her skin.

"Yes, a witch. I've got some trades I'd like to offer, if you've a mind."

Rafe looked the woman over. She was quite young, not much older than him, but she had evidently had a hard life. Every second of it was etched into her face. There were scars across her chin and throat from some old accident or attack, and her eyes held no fear, only defiance.

"We have only three horses, so why should we give you two?"

"Because of what I can offer," Hope said. She went to slip the bag from her shoulder and a man stepped from behind a shed to their right, leveling an over-and-under crossbow at them. He could kill them both within a heartbeat.

"I want no fight with you," Hope said quietly.

"Looks like you've had enough of fighting for a while," the man said, but the aim of his crossbow never wavered. Rafe could not tell whether he was tired or scared or bored.

"We're running from a fight, if that's what you mean. Forgive my appearance; I usually make more of an effort if I'm to meet new people."

"Your hair's a mess," the woman said, and Rafe was sure he saw a blink of humor in her eyes.

"I lost my comb," Hope said. The woman smiled.

"Running from a fight, eh?" the man asked. "Maybe you're not much to fear, then."

"No, we're not," Hope said.

"Do you bring the fight to us?" another woman asked, appearing from inside the farmhouse. She held a longbow, arrow strung and ready to loose. She was much older than the first woman—her mother?—and even from this distance Rafe could see that something terrible had happened to her; her face was a mass of pale scar tissue, knotted and badly healed.

"Not if we can make a deal good and quick," the witch said. "Then we'll be on our way."

"What if we can't make a deal?" the younger woman said, glancing at Rafe for the first time. He realized that she was much more frightened than she was willing to show.

"Then we will still be on our way," Hope said. "Though we'd appreciate some food and water. We have a long way to go."

"Are you being pursued?" the man asked.

"I don't know."

He stared at them along the length of his crossbow, eyes flickering from Hope to Rafe, back again. "I believe you," he said. "So, this is how it happens. The boy comes to me. Witch, you deal with Josie. And when we're all finished, everything goes back to normal."

"That's fine," Hope said. Rafe stared at her—*they want me as their guarantee!*—but she merely looked at him and nodded. Rafe turned to the farmer, tried to meet his eyes and see the intent there, but he was inscrutable.

There was a sudden rush of sound in Rafe's head, so loud and clear that he looked around to see where it came from. He knew straightaway that it was personal to him—none of the others in that farmyard were aware of it—and he knew what it was. When he looked down at his feet the land spoke to him. The voices and smells and sensations calmed him, like his mother's bedtime soothing when he was having a nightmare or his father's hand on his shoulder as they harvested another diseased crop, telling him things were all right. And although he still did not know the language, he knew the tones well enough.

He looked up at the farmer and smiled, and as he walked toward the man who aimed a crossbow at his face, Rafe wondered if this was the first real dreg of magic. *I've been told that things are fine*, he thought. *I'm being looked after.*

"Stop there, turn around, kneel down," the farmer said, not unkindly. "Don't move, boy, and everything will be fine. I've no wish to hurt either of you. I do wonder what you're doing with a witch, though."

Rafe did as the farmer instructed. "She's looking after me," he said. "My parents are dead." He felt the cool kiss of metal on the back of his neck.

"Sorry to hear that, boy." The farmer fell quiet, watching the trade between Hope and Josie.

Hope opened her shoulder bag slowly and pulled out a jar, a wallet of some unidentifiable material and a small book. "I want two horses," she said. "I know how precious these animals are to you, but right now they're worth more to us. As such, not only will I pay you enough tellans for you to ride into Pavisse and buy two more horses as soon as the mood takes you, I'll also recompense you with a trade. One of these three could be yours, over and above the going rate, which is . . . ?"

"A thousand," Josie said quickly.

Hope smiled. "Seems fair." She pointed at the jar. "Heart of skull raven. It never corrupts. It drains bad dreams, sucks up nightmares, gives you easy sleep—"

"Don't taunt us with fake magic, witch!" Josie hissed. Rafe stiffened, felt the farmer stretch forward and press the sharp bolt into the base of his skull.

"I don't taunt you at all," Hope said. "I know there's no magic, and I don't pretend otherwise. Where's the use in that? The skull raven's heart isn't magic, it's a resource, just like your crops or your sheebok. And what it does is a process. Just as you plant your seeds and water them and watch them grow, so this incorruptible thing will shrink your nightmares. Application to your head while you sleep, that's all it takes. Don't ask me how, I simply know that it works. That's what the name *witch* implies: not magic, but knowledge. Few people alive know the things I know, and that makes me a good witch."

Josie stared at Hope, glanced down at the three items set on the ground between them. Though she was trying to exude distrust, Rafe could sense the hope within her. The hope that this trade would work, and that her struggling family would come out with something precious and worthwhile.

"What about this?"

Hope picked up the strange wallet, tattoos pulling her face into awe. "This is something I've never opened. I don't know what's in it. I'm scared to open it, because it once belonged to a Sleeping God. This wallet has not been unraveled since before magic fled this land, and its owner is still alive somewhere, awaiting magic's return. There could be anything in here. Anything."

Josie stared at the wallet for a few seconds, and then glanced quickly toward Rafe and the man standing behind him.

"Ah, but this," Hope said, pointing at the book. "This is surely what you need. In here—"

"This really belonged to a Sleeping God?" Josie asked, pointing at the wallet.

Hope paused, then nodded. "Yes. Although I'm sure they're not really gods. And for all I know it could be empty."

Josie stared in awe at the wallet as Hope picked up the book. Rafe already knew what the witch would be giving away, and he thought she did too. Nevertheless, she opened the book and flipped its thick pages.

"This is a Book of Ways. It was written by Rosen Am Tellington, one of the great mapmakers, long before the Cataclysmic War. It charts the land of Noreela from north to south, east to west, with only a few obvious areas left blank. Back then, there was more certainty in things: a path did not change from one year to the next; mountains remained in place; swamps did not dry out and deserts did not become lakes."

"So what's the point in that now?" Josie asked. "The world's changing, and magic's gone. And we're only farmers. Why do I need a map of New Shanti when I'll never be within five hundred miles of it?"

"Tellington was a visionary," Hope said. "She knew that things would change, and so she thought around things as well as through them. She mapped out hidden routes that have long vanished into myth, and which only now exist in her books. And there are few enough of them. In here you will learn of underground paths through the Widow's Peaks, for instance, not fifty miles from here.

You can read of how to get from Noreela City to Long Marrakash without passing across the ground in between."

"Magic!" Josie scoffed.

"Some, yes, and that's inevitable. But as I said, Tellington was a visionary, and she knew that even magic may not last forever. In here are hidden Ways. Who knows when you might need them?"

"We'll take that," Josie said, pointing at the Sleeping God's wallet.

Hope sat back on her heels and frowned. "Are you sure? Don't you have nightmares? Doesn't the skull raven's heart—"

"We'll take the wallet," Josie said. She looked up at the man behind Rafe. "We're taking the wallet," she said to him.

"Yes," the man agreed.

Hope looked around at the man, Rafe, the woman with the longbow. Rafe thought for a moment that she was going to snatch up the wallet and run. Her face creased and the tattoos twisted, doubt holding her tense.

"The horses are in there," Josie said, standing. "I'll give you two old saddles, as a gesture of good faith. And now, we're busy, so please leave."

She snapped up the wallet, held out her hand for the thousand tellans, pocketed everything and walked away.

The man came around from behind Rafe and clapped his shoulder as he passed by. "Life Moon be with you," he said quietly. "And take good care of those horses, they've served us well."

Rafe stood and went to Hope. She was putting the jar and book back into her shoulder bag, staring after Josie as if judging whether she would be able to reach her, tackle her, steal back the leather wallet before an arrow or bolt found its mark.

"Hope," Rafe said.

"Boy." She did not turn.

"Hope, we should leave. We have horses now, we can put a good distance between us and Pavisse by nightfall."

The witch looked at Rafe and smiled . . . and her tattoos twisted into a smirk. "True!" she said. "That's true! Come on, let's see how friendly our new mounts will be to a witch and a farm boy."

———

A FEW MINUTES later they were riding away from the farm, listening to the farm wolf howl defiantly as they left.

"You lost something valuable, didn't you?" Rafe said. "I'm sorry. It's all because of me, everything that is happening—"

"I lost an old wallet that one of my clients left behind," Hope said, and she smiled across at Rafe. He did not like that smile very much; it twisted her face so that she looked as if she were in pain. "I knew they would go for the mystery. The skull raven heart and the Book of Ways—now, they *are* valuable, and who knows when we may need them?"

"But when they open it?"

"They'll find just what they wanted: an enigma. Sheets of old parchment with scrawls in a language they cannot know, because it's of my own making. A pendant carved from a tumbler's claw. Things they will wonder about for a long time, but never solve."

Rafe rode silently, staring ahead.

"Boy, it's not as if I fooled them. If that really had belonged to a Sleeping God, do you think it would have contained something that made more sense?"

"I don't know much about them, other than people think they're gods."

"Foolish people."

"But it's their faith you're playing with!"

"Foolish people, Rafe," Hope repeated. "They'll never leave that farm, they'll never do any good. They're not important! You are, and I have to look after you. If it means I have to fool some fools, then I'll certainly not let that disturb my sleep."

She's right, Rafe thought. *She's right and I know it.* He rode on in silence, following Hope, letting her steer him because, in truth, he had no idea what else he could do.

————

THEY RODE HARD for an hour, realizing only too quickly that the horses were weak, tired and malnourished. They slowed then, letting the mounts maintain their own pace. Rafe only hoped that the Red Monks had lost their scent.

His scent. It was him they sought.

The whole land whispered behind his eyes, and he felt protected.

As the sun dipped to the west and the life and death moons appeared from the blue, Hope spotted a rage of skull ravens. She dismounted and handed Rafe her horse's reins.

"I'll send your friends a message," she said. "Stay here. Stay still. And don't be scared."

The witch headed off across the grassland toward where the skull ravens roosted in a dead lightning-tree. She was making a noise deep in her throat, a series of clicks and snicks: a bag of stones being shaken, sticks being rattled. It set Rafe's nerves on edge and made the horses uneasy. The skull ravens jumped down from branch to blackened branch, making their way closer to the ground. There were ten of them in total, each with a wingspan as wide as Rafe was tall, their heads large, beaks long and thin.

They were waiting for Hope to arrive.

As she neared, still clicking and making that strange sound, the birds took flight as one and flew straight at the witch. She held out her arms and lowered her head, giving them room to roost. One on each foot, three on each arm, two on her head, Hope was almost lost beneath the beating wings and ruffled feathers of the skull ravens, though she stood fast. And the birds were making a noise now, calling out in clicks and clacks similar to those that Hope had been uttering.

Rafe gasped, wanting to help yet desperate to turn and ride away as fast as he could. *Don't be scared*, Hope had said. He could only assume that she knew what she was doing.

Hope stood that way for some time, the noisy communication continuing. The horses stood still and silent, perhaps asleep. The death moon revealed itself fully, becoming the brightest object in the sky, and Rafe stared at it for some time. The life moon was on the fade. Their combined glows did not fight, but merged peacefully, yellow bleeding to white, white tinting to yellow. And their light struck the ground in different ways. On a distant hillside a clump of trees sucked in the glow from the life moon, green leaves hued white at dusk. Nearer the summit of that same hill, an ancient burial mound reflected yellow, the dark rocks lightening at night. As Rafe stared at the death moon he thought of his parents.

The skull ravens called out loud, and for an instant he was sure that they were attacking Hope, piercing her with beaks and claws as retribution for some terrible tactlessness. The horses stirred and stamped their feet, and it was all Rafe could do to bring his mount under control while holding tightly to Hope's horse's reins.

The birds were taking flight. They rose as one, flying in a tight spiral above Hope. She stood with arms outstretched as if still inviting them back. It had grown too dark for Rafe to see her expression when she turned around, but the fact that she was moving, coming toward him, showed that she was unhurt.

The skull ravens cried out until they were high in the air, almost too high to hear. They were one of the few species that flew almost entirely by night.

"What was that?" Rafe asked as Hope approached.

She seemed exhausted. She rubbed at her shoulders and sides, sighing, hair hanging lank. Even her tattoos seemed tired, dragging her face down. "I gave them a message for the thief and his Shantasi," Hope said. "Rafe, we need to make camp and sleep. It's been a long time since I communed outside my species."

He thought there was humor in her voice, but because she had her head dipped he could not see her eyes. And he did not understand.

Yet somewhere at the back of his mind, there was a new comprehension dawning. Rafe had no concept of what Hope had done, but this new expansion of his mind, the fresh revelations seemingly being laid out again and again for his perusal, seemed to offer understanding. He had only to realize how to read it.

They found a place sheltered from the north by a jagged slope of rock. Hope set about making a fire, silent and slow.

"Won't the Monks see the fire?" Rafe asked.

"It's a risk if they're following us this way. But there are other things out there in the night, just as dangerous, that the fire will keep away."

"Must we camp? Can't we keep moving?"

Hope shook her head, and Rafe realized for the first time just how old and tired she looked. Perhaps up until now excitement had kept her young, the childlike gleam in her eyes whenever she looked at him emphasized by the eager shapes the tattoos seemed to etch across her face. But now, with darkness blanking the tattoos and the gleam in her eyes a pale reflection of the death moon, she looked so worn.

She said nothing more, and Rafe entrusted himself to her wisdom. She had yet to let him down.

With the fire built, Hope quickly fell into a deep sleep. Rafe sat up, huddled under a blanket the farmers had given them along with the saddles, staring up at the moons and stars. Wondering, as he had as a boy in Trengborne, just who or what else in Noreela was looking at this sight right now.

WHEN THEY WERE near enough to see what the firelight revealed, Trey and Alishia stopped.

Alishia could make out two people, one asleep, the other awake. Two horses as well, hidden back in the shadows of the rock slope, snorting in disturbed sleep. She drew Trey close, catching the hint of fledge on his breath. "Two people," she whispered into his ear.

He nodded. "I know. One is asleep and dreaming dreams I don't wish to visit again. The other is . . . strange. There's much more than a mind there, and I can't touch it."

"Are they safe?"

Trey shrugged. "How should I know how you topsiders are supposed to think? The one sleeping, she's frightened and excited at the same time. And I think she's mad. I'll not look again."

"And that one sitting there?"

"I told you, I don't know," Trey whispered. "Give me a moment." He sat back and closed his eyes, and Alishia's gaze went from him back to the figure sitting by the fire. After a few heartbeats the figure raised its head, startled, looking around as if hearing something in the night. The fire spat sparks that danced in the night air, pockets of sap bursting within the logs. The sparks stayed alive until they were high up, mixing with the stars, aiming at the weak life moon.

Trey gasped and slumped, shaking his head, spitting, rubbing his temples as if trying to rid himself of some vile invader.

"Trey?" Alishia touched his shoulder and squeezed lightly.

"More than a mind," he muttered. "There's much more than a mind."

More than a mind? What's more than a mind? "We should go to talk to them."

"No!" Trey said, louder than he should have. Alishia ducked down and watched the figure by the fire. It stood, shedding its blanket, and she saw that it was barely more than a boy. He looked in their direction but she could see nothing of his expression, read nothing in his stance. He seemed to carry no weapons. He glanced to the sleeping form, but that person remained asleep, dreaming whatever dreams had so disturbed Trey.

Alishia stood and walked toward the fire.

"Wait!" Trey hissed behind her, but she kept moving. The boy did not look dangerous. If anything he seemed afraid and alone, so surely he would welcome the company of other travelers to keep the dark at bay? Besides, he was someone new to meet, see, talk to. *To question!*

"Hello by the fire!" she said as she approached.

"Who's there?" The boy edged quickly behind the flames, stooping to pluck a burning branch and hold it before him. "Hope!"

Alishia frowned, wondering whether it was some foreign greeting, but then the sleeping figure sat up quickly and she knew it was a name.

A witch! Alishia had read of witches, much good and much bad, but she had only ever seen one from a distance on the streets of Noreela City. She had heard of the tattoos they seemed to favor, used to amplify the expression of their emotions and frighten and coerce people into seeing things their way. This witch showed fear immediately . . . but it was soon stamped out by anger.

"Stay away!" she said. "Keep in the shadows where you belong."

"I'm not here to harm," Alishia said. "I'm cold and hungry and my horse died. I only wish to share your fire."

"Get away and make your own," the boy said, waving the burning branch as if offering the flame.

"Please!" Alishia said. *He's the one that the fledger could not see. The one with more than a mind. What's more than a mind?*

"Are you alone?" the witch asked.

"No, there's a fledge miner with me, Trey Barossa. He's hiding back there. He doesn't think you're safe."

The witch stood and shook herself, untangling her clothes, running her fingers through knotted hair. "He's right," she said.

"You look as afraid as I feel," Alishia said to Rafe, and his eyes widened, the flaming stick lowered toward the ground.

Wider. Let me see inside.

She felt unaccountably excited, intrigued by this boy and whatever secrets he held restrained.

So soon? Have I found it so soon?

But she did not know what "it" was, and the strange thoughts confused and troubled her. Only a while ago she had pleasured herself to the song of these strange thoughts. She had considered that it was the fledge miner prying into her mind, traveling using fledge to view her innermost secrets and pique her desires, but he seemed too frightened to be plotting and scheming. And the thoughts . . . they were further removed from him. They were almost alien.

Alishia had begun to wonder whether she had made a mistake leaving the city.

"He's not scared," the witch said. "I'm looking after him, so he's got nothing to be scared about."

"Why are you looking after him?" Alishia said. "He can't be your son."

"Know a little about witches, do you?"

"A little." Alishia had read a lot. She knew that they were mostly made sterile by the poisons and plants they made their work. And she knew that the witch could be carrying poisonous creatures to throw, or blinding powders, or chemicala. The very tincture of her tattoos could kill.

The witch stared at her, edging slowly around the fire until she stood between Alishia and the boy.

What's so precious? Alishia thought. And then that other part of her mind again, the one that did not feel like her own: *Could he be so precious?*

"Tell the fledger to show himself," the witch said.

"Trey! Come out of the dark." Alishia heard the footsteps behind her, slow and troubled.

"It hurts my eyes," he said.

"Not been aboveground for long?" the witch asked, but Trey did not answer.

"Any more of you?" Rafe said.

His voice sent a thrill down Alishia's spine. She did not know why. "No," she said. "This is us."

"We have no food," the boy said. "Nothing to offer you."

"We have a little fledge," Alishia said, but the witch cursed and spat into the fire. It sizzled, as if just as mad.

"We don't want your drug!" she hissed at Trey.

The four of them sized one another up, and all the time Alishia's gaze was on Rafe. He was an attractive boy, maybe three or four years younger than her, but he looked tired and worn, as if time had suddenly caught up to show him what the world was all about. His eyes reflected the fire, but only reluctantly. It was the death moon that cast its color into his hair. *Maybe if I can take some fledge I can look inside, see what is more than a mind.* The idea was frightening—her

last experience with fledge had made her sense something awful—
but it thrilled that shaded part of her as well.

"I don't mind if you want to join us," Rafe said at last. He threw
the branch back into the fire, raising a splash of sparks. His eyes
never once left Alishia's. He backed away from the flames and sat
down, and Alishia followed suit. They smiled at each other as the
witch cursed and spat again.

"Rafe, we have no idea who they are! They might be after . . .
something. Anything. You know what I mean."

A *secret!* Alishia thought, and she almost laughed. Something
tickled at her consciousness like a name on the tip of her tongue, a
fact locked deep down in her mind and willing itself to be shown.

"They don't look like Monks to me," the boy said.

"Monks?" Trey had sat with his back to the fire, and he mumbled something else into the dark.

Monks, Alishia thought. *What sort of Monks did he mean?* There
were the bands of moon worshippers—life or death—that still practiced their religions, long gone though the magic of the land was.
And there were . . .

There were Red Monks. Red Monks like the bastard that had
burned down her library, stolen something away, charred her
dreams and memories to cover whatever he may have left. Red
Monks. Sworn destroyers of magic.

Magic! The shout was so loud in her head that she thought they
must have all heard, but the boy's eyes did not falter, the cursing
witch did not let up in her litany. And Alishia, staring steadily into
the flame, felt the darkened place in her mind open up.

Chapter 18

KOSAR'S FINGERS HURT like the Black. Yet now more than ever he needed his delicate touch, the gentle manipulation that years as a thief had bestowed on him, even after his self-inflicted branding. His fingertips were raw and bleeding, but the fresh blood was all his own. He did not appear to be infected with the slayer venom.

He breathed quietly and slowly through his mouth. His bare feet followed the contours of the ground, flexing and settling comfortably around stony protrusions, a patch of hay, a clump of horseshit. His hands were held out from his side so that his clothing did not rub and whisper. Each step took many heartbeats, so his weight had time to settle on its own.

He had not stolen anything for years. His heart was beating hard and fast—he knew the man could not hear, yet still he willed it to quieten—and the mere act of metaphorically tracing his own steps was thrilling. However near A'Meer was to death, however much danger they were in from Red Monks and whatever else might be on their trail, he was actually *enjoying* exercising the talents of a thief. He could not make himself calm, composed and collected, but he was still pleased to find that his skills were not as rusty as he had believed. He had already passed two horses without so much as making them move. The stable was dark—only a little of the dusky light found its way through the holed roof—and the ground underfoot was uneven. There was a whole range of sounds ready to alert the guard to Kosar's presence.

He came to within an arm's reach of success before he gave himself away. It was his sword, its unfamiliar length finally swinging and tapping against a wooden stall as he shifted.

The man stood and spun around, eyes wide and glassy with rotwine, hand reaching instinctively for his own sword.

So much for silent theft. Kosar leapt forward and punched him in the throat, silencing any shout he might have made, and as the man sank to his knees Kosar kicked the back of his neck three times in quick succession. The guard went limp and collapsed to the floor.

The horses stamped in their stalls and snorted, and Kosar did the only thing he could to quieten them down: he stood and waited. It did not take long. They were all but asleep anyway, and the flurry of noise had been brief enough.

Kosar bent to the shape on the ground, felt his wrist to make sure he was still alive, then slipped the ring of keys from his belt. He opened the first stall and saddled the horse quickly, soothing it and whispering into its ear as he moved. The horse in the second stall stood still and let him saddle up, and then he led them both out into the moonlight.

He looked up at the big house. No lights had come on, no windows were opened, no raging owner had come running from the doors. Even if they had heard they would more than likely leave the trouble to the stable hand, not wanting to face any potential problems themselves. They were rich enough to buy new horses. Kosar had no qualms about stealing their best two. The only fact that troubled him was how much he may have hurt the lad, but it had been necessary. He was not dead. At worst he would wake up to a headache and a screaming match with his employer.

Kosar opened the yard gates and led the horses outside, wincing at the din their shod hooves made on the cobbled road. Once out in the street he did his best to blend in. A few people gave the two horses appraising glances and that was good, that kept attention away from Kosar, with his bloodied hands and blood-spattered clothing camouflaged in the failing light.

He made his way quickly through the park gates that Hope and Rafe must have exited while he and A'Meer were still battling the Red Monk. There were few people using the park now; night must bring new dangers, people and things drawn from below the ground at dusk's first touch.

A'Meer was where he had left her, propped against a tree with her sword clasped in one hand. She was unconscious now, blood painting her beautiful pale face from eyes and nose and mouth. The veins on her temples and forehead stood out in stark relief, but Kosar was reasonably sure that they had not swelled any more. Perhaps the poison had slowed, its effect come to a head, but it might yet kill her. He bent closer, trying to make out her face in the weak moonlight. Where blood did not touch her skin, it was pale and sickly as the death moon.

"Come on," Kosar said, holding A'Meer beneath her armpits and lifting. His fingertips stung, but she seemed to help herself up, pushing weakly at the ground until she stood propped against him. He held her there for a while, gathering his strength to hoist her into the saddle. He knew that he would have to lay her across the horse's back, tie her there, and he had no idea what damage the pressure on her stomach might do. For all he knew it would aid the slayer's poison in bursting her innards, but there was no alternative.

That was his problem: he knew so little.

Something rustled the leaves in the tree above their heads and Kosar glanced up. He was badly on edge, and exhaustion was only just around the corner. He stared through the branches and leaves at the glow of the life moon, and the rustling stopped.

"A'Meer," he whispered into the unconscious woman's ear, "I have to lift you onto a horse. Go limp, let me help you up, then I'll tie you there to stop you spilling off." He wrapped an arm around her waist, held her uninjured arm across his shoulders and half carried, half dragged her to the horses. The animals stood still as he bent and let A'Meer fall across his shoulder. "Going to lift you up now." He stood, placed both arms under A'Meer's small waist and pushed. "Maybe I'll take advantage of you," he said. She slid onto the saddle and he paused, both arms locked straight to stop her from falling. "Come on, A'Meer, don't give me this shit, you're doing this on purpose." He pushed at her arm and shoulder, slipping her sideways across the saddle so that her arms dropped down the other side.

She was totally limp. There was no help from her, no attempt to aid him at all, and for the first time Kosar seriously thought that she might be dead. He dashed around the front of the horse and knelt by A'Meer's head, listening hard to hear her breathing, sighing with relief when she expelled a hot breath against his neck.

"A chair," she whispered, "I like it over a chair."

Kosar laughed quietly. "I'll get you out of here," he said, "then we'll see if the witch keeps her promise."

"Northeast," A'Meer said. "Away from Trengborne."

"And toward Noreela City?"

A'Meer moved her shoulders in what must have been a shrug.

Kosar jumped onto the other horse and led them from the park. The darkness was waking behind them—more rustling in the bushes and shrubs, splashes in the large pond as something rose from the depths, hoarse giggles from a gang of shadows flitting around the park's perimeter—and he was glad to leave.

Once back on the streets he rode fast, conscious that night was here at last and that the darkness turned the town into a whole new place. He saw shadows darting through deeper shadows, and they may have been wraiths. A huddle of fodder wound their way along the street, their inbred insecurity making the dark their preferred home. Metal scraped along stone, and wet slapping sounds came from the dark infinity between two large buildings. Machines were silhouetted against the moonlight here and there—not as many as in the hidden districts, but there were always some—and Kosar tried not to see their sharp spears, curved shells, blocked facades. On his travels he had heard rumors of machine graveyards, and dusk gave Pavisse that appearance. They disturbed him more at night; it was then that their purpose seemed so close to the surface.

More so tonight of all nights. Tonight, magic was on the run.

They left Pavisse quickly and without incident. He saw no Red Monks. That was a good thing for him now, but a bad thing for the future. It meant that the Monks had probably left Pavisse ahead of them, moving out from the town in pursuit of Rafe and the witch. And that meant that, whether Hope delivered a message to him and A'Meer or not, the Red Monks stood between them.

THE MESSAGE CAME soon after they had left Pavisse.

If Kosar had had his wits about him, the messenger would have been killed. If he had been paying attention, the witch's words would have never found their way to him and A'Meer. Many things changed in the land of Noreela that night, and many destinies were entwined. If Kosar had not fallen asleep on his horse, the future may have been a very different place.

He was on a boat, bobbing in the network of drainage ditches he had been digging around Trengborne for thirty years. They had expanded into canals, taking up most of the land and negating their original purpose, but their digging had become a purpose in itself. The boat was of his own making. He rode it alone, pulled along by a horse on the bank, and the people of Trengborne had gathered in the distance to welcome him back from another digging expedition. They had furbats and flowers and bottles of their best wine, and one of them, a boy called Rafe, held two tankards of Old Bastard for both of them to enjoy.

In the distance, past the crowds, the village of Trengborne had changed. When he had left sometime in the past it had been a dead place, filled with people waiting to die, the crops failing and the animals showing ribs through their weak hides. Now . . .

Now there were *things* in the village, large and small, fast and slow, moving and still, colorful and bland. Most were solid with pulsing sacs at various points around their constructs, stone mantels bearing dull yellow masses of fleshy parts, shimmering and steaming in the heat. Appendages shifted in the sunlight, turning on multijoints, digging or scraping or building, forming solid curved limbs that propeled them over the ground like carts, except that these steered themselves. Many had long, tapering tendrils sprouting from their bodies, dipping down to touch or pierce the ground, drawing energy, drawing *magic*. Because these were machines.

"Machines!" Kosar said, but then the people waiting for him along the banks of the canal drew suddenly nearer, and he saw that all but Rafe wore red.

And madness colored their faces.

———

"MACHINES!" KOSAR SCREAMED, and as his eyes sprang open he tumbled from his horse in shock.

"Kosar," A'Meer said, "I know where Rafe is."

The impact had winded him, his foot was tangled in the stirrup, his bare bloody fingers grated with dust, and now A'Meer—half-dead, infected with a poison that may yet kill her—was talking to him. He twisted his foot free and kicked at the horse's side as it trotted away. Then he glanced back at A'Meer's horse . . . and froze.

In the death moonlight he saw a skull raven perched on her back.

"Kosar!" she said. "Don't tell me you're still asleep after that fall. Did you hear me? I know where Rafe and the witch are. Help me sit up, and then we have to ride. Ride *fast.*"

"Keep still," Kosar said. "Very still." He stood slowly, painfully, and started drawing his sword.

"No!" she said. "This is the witch's message."

Kosar kept his hand on the hilt of his sword, moving closer to A'Meer's mount. The raven fluttered its huge wings and he felt the breeze lift his hair. It stared at him with black pearl eyes, reflecting a moon in each. "I don't understand."

"It spoke to me when I was unconscious, gave me the witch's words. They're camped a few miles north of here."

"That's a skull raven."

"Yes, she gave it the message. She's a *witch*, Kosar, she has her ways. Now, please, let me sit on my own. What blood I have left inside me is collecting in my head, and I can't think straight. At least let me die sitting up."

"You're not going to die," he said.

"I hope not. I don't know how much worse it is. I feel . . . strange inside. I think I might be bleeding in there."

Kosar helped A'Meer down from her horse, the skull raven flapping off to a nearby tree to watch their efforts. It cawed quietly, and Kosar kept glancing its way. He had never been this close to a skull raven, but all the tales he had heard were bad. He did not trust it one bit.

"How did it tell you?"

"In my sleep. In my dream."

"I had a dream," he said. "I saw machines in a village filled with Red Monks."

"We should get there as fast as we can," she said weakly, leaning against him, smelling like death. "If there is an antidote for this and the witch has it, the sooner I take it the better."

"And then what?"

"And then we run with Rafe." She said it simply, matter-of-factly, as if Kosar should have known that all along. Run with Rafe. *So that was it? His future was running from murderous Red Monks?*

The bird called out again, louder this time, and it was answered from somewhere far away.

A'Meer sat in her saddle, leaning forward so that she almost breathed in the horse's mane. Kosar found his own horse and remounted, and this time he and A'Meer rode side by side. The skull raven fluttered on ahead, waiting for them, flying on again, never quite losing itself to the dark. It circled overhead once or twice as if catching moonlight.

After hours spent traveling through the night, the bird still hovering but joined now by more shapes, all of them calling quietly, they mounted a small hill and saw the flicker of a campfire at its base.

RAFE WAS THE first to hear the horses.

He and Alishia had been watching each other through the dancing flames of the campfire, smiling, glancing away, looking again. Something about her eyes drew him in, but there was a disturbing factor there repulsing him as well, a sense that beneath her outside beauty lay something rotten. If he closed his eyes as she watched him he could smell bad things, feel the breath of the world stuttering against the walls of his heart, hear worried whispers passing through blades of grass, apprehensive heartbeats pulsing from the depths of the land. So he kept his eyes open, and while he knew that she was *wrong*, the young lad in him reveled in her smile.

The horses came quietly, but not so quiet as to be secretive. He knew who rode them. Hope panicked and Rafe spoke soothingly, reminded her of the skull ravens she had sent out, and soon Kosar and A'Meer rode into the circle of light cast by the fire.

A'Meer was dying.

Kosar took her gently from the horse and asked Hope about cures, antidotes, all the while refusing to see the witch shaking her head. Alishia watched, and Trey sat back in the shadows, keeping away from these new topsiders.

Rafe was told of a deep dread in the fledge miner's mind. The whispers told him. The echoes of sunlight filled his mind with news.

Something huge was growing inside. It was a potential already fat with possible futures, all of them far wider and deeper than any he had ever dreamed possible. He looked down between his feet at the pale green grass, the dust, the corpse of the land that had been rotting for three centuries since the Cataclysmic War, when the

Mages had taken nature's trust and torn it asunder, corrupting themselves and that trust in the process. And the growing knowledge
promised him a second chance. It was still hidden away, developing
in safety, but already its tentative tendrils were exploring outward,
experiencing Rafe's own senses instead of feeding sensations to him.
He knew the whole world—a million facts and the truth of a million
rumors—and it would have driven him mad, had not the world itself
been protecting him right then.

He went to A'Meer and she smiled at him, even though she
could surely not see him through eyes so bloodshot that they looked
black in the firelight. Her face and scalp were networks of raised
veins, some of them burst and hemorrhaging beneath her skin, filling her insides with life-giving blood that would soon kill her.

"All because of me," Rafe said, but A'Meer kept smiling because
she knew who and what he was.

And then he touched her.

———

THE SHADE SAW, and rose to the fore. Alishia stood and screamed,
an exhalation of pure rhapsody, because the shade knew that it saw
the future: its life, long and everlasting; its potential, realized again
and again; its reward from its god, all of it earned, given and taken
freely and with love.

It saw *magic.*

Behind it, repressed beneath the sudden exultation, Alishia's
true mind recoiled in terror, letting out a scream far beyond the
physical. The shade reveled in the feelings that evoked, rolled its
soul around the other and pulled away quickly, tearing scraps from
Alishia and watching them spin away into infinity. The time it had
spent in here was a time without end compared to the eternity it had
been less than nothing. And yet, alive though the shade was, it knew
that it had to leave.

*Magic! It had seen magic! The woman lay whole unbloodied and
afresh, and the people watching had stood back or fallen down in terror . . . all but the boy who had laid his hands on the dying woman,
dying no more.*

The shade had something to tell its god. One more brief period
of nothingness, back into the void, back into the blankness it so
hated, and then as promised its god would reward it fully. Reward it
with forever.

The shade's scream belittled Alishia's continuing psychic tumult, shattering her mind as it tore itself away, ripping her up as its immeasurable shadow tendrils withdrew, screaming again as it left the body and plunged back into less than nothing.

All the way back the shade screamed. But deep within the new thing that was its mind, where memories now dwelled and sensations vied to be recalled, it knew that its god would be pleased.

————

AFTER ALMOST TWO days flying day and night, Lenora had lost several hawks and their riders. None of her Krotes had shouted or pleaded for help as their mounts slowly drifted seaward, and she respected them for that. They died with honor, having not even sighted their target. They were as much victims of the coming battle at those that would die on Noreelan soil.

They had fallen below the cloud cover now, and the sighting of their first boat caused much excitement. Lenora sent three down to kill the fishermen, and when they came back up they carried the heads of five people with them. They shouted, kissing the mouths of the dead, tossing the heads across to friends and branding themselves with Noreelan blood for the first time. Lenora let them celebrate. She knew that by the end of that day they would have reached the tip of The Spine, and from there it was another day's flight across the Bay of Cantrassa to their target.

She listened for her daughter's shade, but there was nothing but wind in her ears.

As she neared Noreela for the first time in centuries, she thought briefly of their initial discovery of Dana'Man, and how the Krotes and Mages had made it their own.

————

TEN DAYS AFTER drifting northward from Noreela, they spied land. It was a vast white island, stretching as far as they could see to the east and west, and the Mages commanded that they should land there. Their ships had no supplies, the Krotes were injured and downtrodden, and a couple more days at sea would likely kill them all. Ice hung from their charred rigging, weighing the vessels down. The stink of death seemed to exude from the timbers. And although Lenora felt strangely reborn since Angel's kiss, she knew that in those desperate days, death was never far away.

They approached a natural inlet and anchored. There was no sign of civilization anywhere: no buildings or boats, and no indication that anyone had ever set foot here before. No wildlife, either, and though that was strange, they were too tired and defeated to let it worry them.

The Krotes had all come from the many diverse races on Noreela, and they knew the legends of the northern seas. Wild lands, dead water, an infinity of lifelessness. Great snow clouds were already oozing over the white mountains inland, promising more heavy falls soon. Ice groaned and creaked around the bay. It nudged against the ships, exerting a painful pressure on the already damaged hulls. Lenora wondered what they would eat, should they decide to stay here. But right then, hope did not stretch that far.

S'Hivez appeared on the deck of one of the Krote ships. He took a rowing boat ashore on his own, climbed a rocky formation sticking out into the bay, made his way to the mainland proper and took out a knife. Even from where their damaged ships were anchored in the bay, most of the Krotes could see the splash of red blood on this virgin land. "You are Dana'Man!" S'Hivez shouted, and the land was named.

Thus ended Lenora's journey from Noreela as a Krote of the Mages, and began her time on Dana'Man as one of their lieutenants. The time of the Cataclysmic War was over, and the beginning of their three-hundred-year exile was beginning. Magic had gone, though sorcerers like the Mages always had something about them. Chemicala, some said, tricks available only to those with the knowledge. But Lenora always believed that they had held on to some of the effects of magic, at least. They had been too wrapped up in it—and it in them—for all effects to vanish in that one instant.

Angel had given her endless life, after all.

———

DRIFTING DOWN TO sea level, spying the faint haze of Noreela on the horizon, Lenora thought only fleetingly of her three hundred years on Dana'Man: finding the old civilizations there; the slaughter and enslavery; the eventual changing of each tribe to live the way of the Krote. That seemed more like ancient history than even their rout from Noreela beforehand, a brief, motionless interval in the long story of the Mages. A story in which she had become a major part.

As she led the first assault on the giant land of Noreela, and a new age began, she heard a shadowy voice at the back of her mind.

As yet she could not make out what it had to say. But there was plenty of time.

———

LUCIEN MALINI LEFT Pavisse on the fastest horse he could steal.

Behind him, the remaining Red Monks spread north and east from the town out across hills, through valleys, scouring forests and ravines, hamlets and farmsteads, searching desperately for the fleeing boy. They knew that if he and his band reached Noreela City they would be lost; they could go to ground there and remain hidden for weeks, and in that time the boy's curse would be working its way out, filling him and spilling eventually to offer itself up again for abuse. Common folk of Noreela would welcome the magic back into their hands, but so would the Mages. And this time—Noreela's armies too weak to fight, its people apathetic—the Mages would have their way. There would be no rout. There would be no repeat of the Cataclysmic War. There would be true cataclysm.

The horse pounded across the foothills, Malini urging it on, plains and woodland to their left and mountains to the right. As they skirted an old swallow hole the horse stumbled and almost spilled Lucien to the ground. He hung on to the animal's mane, gripping with his knees, glancing back at the hole in the land and wondering how many more were waiting beneath the surface. Perhaps they would erupt and conjoin in one final explosive event, swirling the whole of Noreela into a giant whirlpool of earth and flesh, mountains and cities, people and dreams. The land was fading fast—he had traveled far, he had seen it all—and the Monks knew that its eventual demise, or a transmutation into something else entirely, would be the only final outcome. That saddened him, but it pleased him too. It meant that the Mages would be defeated forever. With no land there was no magic, and with no magic . . . the Mages would rot their lives away, unfulfilled, powerless, their evil fragmenting into eternity.

That thinking did not detract from his aims today. The future was a shy place, and it might be far different from how any of them imagined. The Red Monks believed in the final cataclysm, but there was no guarantee, no sure way to confirm their beliefs. It could happen tomorrow, it could happen a thousand years from now. However soon, now that magic was bleeding back into the land they had to fight to keep it from the Mages' hands.

He was riding for the Monastery. The rest of the Order had to be warned that magic had returned. It had gone far beyond those few Monks who had searched through Pavisse, the one that had died in Trengborne without killing the boy. Rafe Baburn was young, naïve and inexperienced, and he should have been killed long before now. Three Monks dead already—each worth a dozen men in strength and tenacity—and still the boy ran, accompanied by the Shantasi and those others that had taken to his cause. Lucien did not mourn the dead Monks, but their failure rankled. This should have been finished already. And he knew that the more time passed and the more powerful the boy became, the more likely it was that the Mages would hear of magic's reemergence.

There would be no recriminations, no blame, no reprimands; the Order was too mechanical for that. The fleeting idea that one of them should have ridden for the Monastery days ago, when they first got wind of the magic in the boy, flashed across Lucien's mind but he pushed it down. The rage had been upon him. There had been no reason to believe that the boy would survive.

So he rode, heading south for the Monastery on Lake Denyah. Night fell and he spurred the horse on, riding by the light of the death moon. Howling things closed in on him and veered away again, smelling his rage and the heat of his hate. Heading away from the boy only kindled his hatred more. The horse stumbled and fell, tipping Lucien onto rocks, but he shrugged off his smashed shoulder and remounted, kicking the horse into a gallop once more. His shattered bones ground together in concert with the horse's snorting. Blood clotted around the bones, easing them apart and stiffening his shoulder into a solid knot of scar. In one small valley he rode through decay, a place where the ground itself had died and was slowly rotting away to the bedrock, giving off a gaseous miasma that caught the moonlight and kept it for itself. Wavering images passed through. Lucien rode through the souls of the land, dispersing them, feeling their coolness, grinning as they tried and failed to freeze his blood. Wraiths called to him in the night but he ignored them, unconcerned at such nebulous entities. His mind was focused on two things: the future—the magic, the return of the curse that had ruined the land.

And reinforcements.

PART TWO
Sunfall

Chapter 19

DEATH BEGAN AS a dust mote in his eye.

Jayke Bigg rubbed at his eyelid, blinking fast, thinking that perhaps the sea breeze had blown grit along the beach and into his face. He looked down at his feet and lifted his eyelid, giving his tears a chance to carry the offending grit away, seeing the broken shells scattered across the sand and wondering if anyone would ever see them again. And the dust in his eye, intruding into his senses like an uninvited ghost, where had that come from? A splinter of stone from a statue to some forgotten god? A shard of bone from an ancient sea creature, long gone and unknown to anyone alive today? Jayke was prone to such musings. Being alone at Land's End made them inevitable.

He sighed, held his hand palm-up before him and stared at it, shifting his vision left to right. There was nothing in his eye. Perhaps it had been an illusion. He looked north again, at the place he was always meant to watch, and the sun shimmered the horizon into haziness.

Jayke resumed his stroll along the beach. He came down here from the cliffs every morning, leaving the old stone house that had been bequeathed him by his parents and theirs before them, enjoying the freedom of the wilds. He felt at peace most in the morning, when the sun rose from the end of the beach and the day's worries and loneliness were still coalescing from the remnants of his dreams. Ring turtles flapped their way back into the sea farther along the beach, their eggs safely buried once more, and Jayke took his time walking that far. He wanted them to be in the sea and away before he dug up one of the nests and took the eggs for breakfast. He knew how they would taste: salty; mysterious; filled with tales of the seas that he could savor, but never know.

Gulls called from above, perhaps afraid that he would scale the cliffs and steal their eggs as well. Cave snakes sang from small holes low down in the cliffs, serenading in the new day before they slithered back into darkness to sleep the sun away. Bubbles the size of his fist blew in the sea-smoothed sand, exhalations of things buried deep.

Jayke paused and looked north again, an unconscious action that he probably performed a thousand times each day. It was as natural as the beating of his heart. This place was a dividing line between worlds, a true wilderness, where the known world of Noreela ended and the unknown, endless North Seas began. It had always been a wild place but, ironically, safe as well. He was here to keep watch for the direst danger of all. Jayke could not recall any real threats for him and his parents in all the years they had lived here. There were natural dangers, true: storms throwing gigantic waves at the cliffs; the extremes of weather through the seasons, crushing them with snow and baking them with sun; an occasional sea tiger, stalking from the waves and sniffing around their home, its tentacles never happy until they entwined around some warm, living meat. But no threats or malign influences.

Jayke reached the place where the turtles had spent the night laying eggs. He glanced to the north again, then bent and burrowed into the disturbed sand. He found five eggs, flaccid leathery sacs that would harden in his oven and taste wondrous with sea salt and lashings of soured sheebok milk. He stood, pocketed the eggs, turned back the way he had come, glanced north—

And there it was again, that speck in the sky that he had thought to be windblown dust. He paused, held his breath, looked slightly left and right . . . and the speck remained in the same place. Just above the horizon, shimmering in the morning heat-haze, a smudge on the clear blue sky.

Oh no.

Birds, perhaps? A flock of gulls?

It couldn't be.

Too far out for gulls. Too steady.

Eyeglass!

Jayke dug his eyeglass from a pocket and opened it, cursing when he realized it had misted up against his sweaty skin. He wiped the lenses carefully on his shirt, never taking his eyes from the blemish in the sky just above the horizon. The fear was coming quickly, as it always did whenever he thought about why he was really here, why his family had lived in this place for generations. He went cold, sweat cooling him further, his heart stuttered, his stomach lurched and he was almost sick.

Dropping to his knees in the sand he brought up the eyeglass and stared to the north.

And then he ran.

No gulls, these. They were too far away to be certain, but they looked like hawks. Dozens of them flying in a loose formation, their massive webbed tentacles stroking the air almost gently, only needing a few swipes per minute to keep their bodies aloft.

Jayke sprinted along the beach, his footprints illustrating his panic. The turtle eggs bounced from his pocket and one of them broke on the sand. It was a bad egg, putrid. If he had eaten it he would have died.

He had read of hawks in one of the many books his family had accumulated. How they were spied only very rarely, how they normally remained way above the clouds, living there, eating, loving, mating, dying, disintegrating on the high breezes that kept them aloft even as they wasted away. He was heading for the path up to his house, and his weapons, and the doves that sat ready to be released with their warning. Because the only time hawks had ever been seen in a group was when they were controlled, harnessed and ridden like horses of the skies. And that was most common during the Cataclysmic War. Back then, the riders had been Krotes, the Mages' warriors.

Jayke only turned to look again when he reached the foot of the steps leading up to the top of the cliff. He had dropped his eyeglass but he did not need it; the threat had closed in all too fast. In doing so the truth had seemingly manifested from his fears. These really were hawks, *huge* hawks, and although they were still miles out he could see the figures seated upright behind the creatures' heads.

He started climbing. His life was over. He had never thought it would come to this—after so long he had come to believe that the

Mages were dead—but now that it was happening he had purpose, meaning, a mission to fulfill before he died. Death was not a frightening prospect for Jayke. He had been here alone for so long, and he saw enough life and death in nature to know that it was an important consequence of existence. Not even the manner of his death worried him unduly; however unpleasant, the death moon would take him to itself and give him to the Black. The only thing that terrified him was failure.

He had spent his whole life here for one purpose: to give Noreela warning should the Mages return this way.

He was halfway up the cliff when he first heard the screams. Perhaps they came from the hawks, he thought. Or maybe the Krotes sitting astride their necks were calling out in glee at the prospect of spilling blood. Either way, Jayke ignored the noise. To turn around now he would have to stop, and that would admit defeat.

If only I'd stayed at the house, not gone for breakfast.

But he had to eat.

If only I could have enjoyed sitting and watching as much as I enjoyed walking!

But he had been here for forty years. He could not punish himself with thoughts of disgrace. Whatever happened now, he had already fulfilled his charge.

Jayke kept climbing, wishing himself higher and closer to the house. There were weapons in there, but first he had to free the doves. There were a hundred birds in all, fit and healthy, trained from birth to fly east and south until their message was delivered into human hands. And that message, tied ready in leather pouches on their legs, was stark and simple: *The Mages are coming.*

That scream again, assaulting his ears and echoing from the cliff face. He could not help glancing back, and he saw that the hawks had spread out just above the water. There were dozens of them—maybe a hundred in all—and Jayke could not help comparing that number with those messenger doves he was desperate to release.

The Krotes started shouting as the hawks approached the beach. There was no meaning to their words, no language other than bloodlust.

Jayke was almost at the top of the cliff. He was exhausted, but fear kept him moving. Thirty paces, that was all, thirty paces to the house, and then he could do his best to give warning to the land. He looked back again in time to see the hawks sweep up from the beach and rise above the cliff, a living wave breaking violently against Noreela's shore.

The flying things were even larger than Jayke had believed. Their hides were speckled black, partly transparent, hideous organs pulsing vaguely inside. They were fat and bloated with gases that aided buoyancy, and their beaks were as big as a man, serrated, yellowed and streaked with the remains of old victims. The downdraft from their movement sent Jayke sprawling to the ground, kicked up dust, blew grit in a whisper against the windows and walls of his house. They rose along the whole length of the cliff, rising on thermals as if blasted straight up from the beach, and most of them immediately headed south, across the island of Land's End and toward Noreela.

Between here and Noreela lay the Bay of Cantrassa, four hundred miles of open ocean. Jayke wondered how fast those things could fly. And whether the doves would fly faster.

A dozen hawks dipped down and came at him, their riders screeching, raising bows and letting fly arrows. One struck Jayke in the shoulder and he spun and fell, cursing, *Not yet not yet not yet.* He found his feet and staggered to the door, pressing through as more arrows struck the walls around him, the door, his leg. He stumbled inside and kicked the door shut with his good leg, unable to turn in the narrow corridor because of the long shafts protruding from his shoulder and knee.

He was dizzied already by blood loss . . . and something else. His throat was swelling, his airway blocking, and he knew that the arrows were tipped with poison.

There was more screeching from outside. The sound of the hawks' venting was like thunder against the house, and one of them landed on the roof, smashing broken tiles down onto Jayke's head. The monstrous creature pecked at his home, and its disregard for his history made him mad.

A hole appeared in his roof, a ragged rent battered and enlarged again and again by the creature's vicious beak. As Jayke leaned against a wall and slid himself along, vision blurring, a Krote peered through the hole.

"I haven't killed for too many moons," the Krote said, her voice surprisingly gentle and calm.

"Fuck you," Jayke muttered, and the Mage warrior laughed as Jayke fell into the back room. His leg was a block of wood, his shoulder stiff and burning with shed blood, and as the poison coursed through his veins it was only rage keeping him moving. Rage, and duty. He *had* to release the doves, to warn the neighboring islands along The Spine if nothing else. He snatched a primed and loaded crossbow from the wall, glancing at the shelves of books he would never read again, and staggered to another door, this one leading into the aviary where the doves were waiting.

They were in tumult. A hawk had landed in the vegetable garden behind the house and it sat there snorting, blood and mucus dripping from its beak. The doves fluttered and fought to back away from the monstrous vision, pecking, crying, and when Jayke appeared in their midst they turned on him.

"No!" he shouted. He hissed to the birds, sounds and words that could communicate concepts and direction, and as the Krote sitting on the hawk started to laugh, the doves immediately settled.

Jayke fell on the handle that flipped open the enclosure. The screens fell away, the Krote raised his bow in a lazy, dismissive gesture and Jayke brought up his crossbow and let fly. The bolt struck home in the Krote's left eye. Mortally wounded, poisoned, half-blinded though he may be, Jayke had lived alone for forty years, hunting rabbit and pheasant with his crossbow. Target practice was something he'd had a lot of time for.

The warrior let out a surprised gasp and tipped sideways in his saddle. The hawk seemed not to notice its rider's sudden death, and it pecked listlessly at the ground as the Krote tumbled from its left flank and hit the dirt.

"First blood," Jayke whispered. He hoped that it was a good omen for Noreela.

He hissed and whistled once again to the birds. They turned to look at him and it was almost as if they knew of his wounds, knew that this time they would not fly home. They cooed, their throats swelled and vibrated, their small leather message pouches so full of hope and desperation. And then, as one mass, they took flight.

Jayke slid down the stone wall, crying out as the arrow in his shoulder was snapped off. It had been morning when he found the turtle's eggs, he was sure, and yet dusk now seemed to be closing in. The sky was growing dark. His vision was fading. And with a hundred doves in the air, it looked as if it were snowing.

The birds parted immediately, some darting south toward the Bay of Cantrassa, others heading east to the neighboring island of Bethwitch, thirty miles distant. The theory had always been that if the doves never made it directly to Noreela, the message would be carried back along The Spine by the communities living there. Now, close to death and near to warriors of the dreaded and despised Mages, Jayke wondered at his people's naïveté. So much more could have been done, surely. So many more precautions.

Hawks swooped down, plunging through the clouds of small white birds and spilling them to the ground. Dozens fluttered and fell, twitching as they hit earth and rock, feathers exploding from smashed wings and burst bodies.

"All of them!" one of the Krotes commanded. It sounded like the gentle-voiced warrior from the roof. "Every single one!" The hawks swooped down and another dozen doves were shattered in mid-air. Some of the Krote riders took pleasure in the target practice, skewering birds with well-placed arrows. One of the hawks seemed to be in a feeding frenzy, following a small flock of doves, snapping at them, showering bloodied white remnants to the ground.

A Krote appeared before the open screens, short, thick sword drawn. The metal caught sunlight, and Jayke was glad for the brief spear of pain the reflection drove into his eye.

"Dove stew tonight," the Krote said.

"Fuck you."

"How erudite." The Krote stepped inside, trying to tread softly. "This place stinks of shit!"

"Fuck you."

"So you said." She leaned forward and slashed Jayke's throat.

"DID YOU CATCH them all?" Lenora asked.

"We think so, sir."

"You *think so?*" She swiped quickly at the corpse's ear and strung it on a chain around her waist. There were others dried and desiccated there, many others, of all shapes, sizes and colors. But this was the first Noreelan ear to ever grace her belt.

"Sir, I'm positive."

"Good. Then we still have surprise on our side. Get ready to move out!" The Krote hurried away and Lenora looked around her. *And here we are,* she thought. *This is where it ended three hundred years ago, and this is where it begins again today.* She stroked the wet ear on her belt, and smiled.

"I'm home," she said. And a long-lost voice echoed her words: *You're home.*

Chapter 20

RAFE BABURN WAS tired. He sat in the cave mouth and watched the witch out in the rain, her arms outstretched as she communed with the skull ravens. The downpour was tremendous, and yet Hope seemed unconcerned. One raven had its beak pressed hard against her temple. They looked like one merged creature.

Rafe's eyelids drooped again, the rainfall soporific, his limbs and shoulders aching, his eyes stinging from exhaustion. Whatever he had done the night before had drained him. He felt hollowed out, distanced from everything—the danger, his parents' deaths, these people around him—and even the voices and whispers had grown quiet.

The Shantasi warrior who had been prepared to die to save Rafe's life—her skin slashed and torn, her ankle shattered, her face a mask of drying, poisoned blood—was slumped farther back in the cave. Kosar the thief sat watching over her, dripping water into her mouth. She moaned in her sleep and sometimes cried out, but the noise of the storm drowned her voice. She was unconscious. The poison was gone from her system. She bled only good blood now. Rafe had cured her.

The touch had not been his own. The surge of something through his arm and hand had risen up from somewhere so deep inside that it was beyond him. There had been a stench as the poison was drawn from her system and scorched by the fresh air, the smell of something rank dying on the breeze, and Rafe had fallen away from the injured Shantasi, vomiting. The witch had caught him and lowered him to the ground, so gently. Like a glass sculpture.

He remembered little since then, other than occasional glimpses of moonlight and the sensation of being carried through the night. There had been whispers around him, amazed muttering, tones of disbelief and faith, anger and relief, pain and epiphany. He had felt as if he was being carried out and away from his old life at last, and transported toward something new and wondrous. Sometime in the night the rain had come, and they had found the cave. Since then it had been quiet.

Rafe supposed that, like him, his companions were trying to come to terms with what had happened.

———

HOPE SHOOK THE last skull raven from her shoulder. It screeched as it flew off, merging quickly with the night, mocking her with one last cry. She cursed, stooping to pick up one of the raven's feathers from the mud. It was smooth and silky. The moonlight caught its perfect edge and it glinted like a knife. The witch put it to her nose and inhaled, but it revealed nothing more.

"Piss and vomit!" she hissed. Perhaps it was the rain, but she could not commune with the ravens. They had taken her invitation willingly enough, sat on her shoulders and outstretched arms, but they were taking, not giving. She had felt the feathery touch of their own senses inside her mind as they pressed themselves to her, their seeking of secrets, but unlike the day before she could not read them. It was not something she had done often, but she knew the methods and the risks. There should have been no reason why it could not work again. *Look for the Red Monks*, she had tried to convey, but they had not listened. They were closed to her now.

Hope trudged back to where the others sat. It was more a hollow than a cave, a natural depression in the hillside sheltered by an overhanging shelf of rock, but it kept them hidden from the storm and prying eyes. The night was dark, the moons peering intermittently from behind low-lying clouds, and they dared not risk lighting a fire.

The Red Monks were likely still searching for them, and they all needed a night's rest to recover from their exertions.

There he is, Hope thought, smiling at Rafe. He sat awake just beneath the overhang, water pouring from the rocks above and splashing down at his feet. *There's my precious boy.* He smiled back weakly, his eyes as fluid and confused as the stormy sky. Hope reached out to touch his head but then walked by, awed, afraid, confused about what the signs meant. From their first meeting she had believed in Rafe, but after last night—after he had touched the Shantasi and drawn out the slayer spider's poison—her belief had expanded into fear. She was a witch, had been one her whole life, but this boy's single touch made a mockery of anything she had achieved. Being a witch in a time without magic consisted mainly of knowing things, shocking people with arcane secrets, frightening them if necessary with the forgotten qualities of nature and paths of the mind, and sometimes fooling them with exquisitely simple deceptions. For her, knowledge was power.

Rafe's demonstration was the opposite, and infinitely more daunting because of that. He was a young boy, confused and shocked, and though he displayed such power he seemed to have no knowledge of it at all. It terrified him.

The boy stared into the night as if searching for answers, and Hope wanted to have him all for herself.

She walked farther back into the cave to where the others were trying to get some sleep. All of them were awake. All but the girl, Alishia, whose strange display had disturbed them all. The fledger sat with her head in his lap, stroking her hair, trying to whisper some life back into her eyes. They were open and staring and so vacant, as if reflecting the darkness from outside rather than showing the hollowness of herself.

"How is she?" Hope asked.

The fledger looked up. "She knew so much. Now she's nothing."

"It scared us all in different ways," she said, thinking of her own ecstatic thrill as she had watched Rafe laying his hands on the Shantasi.

"It didn't frighten me," the fledger said. His comment was loaded, but Hope let it go. *What else has he seen and known?* she wondered.

She turned to Kosar the thief. He was tending A'Meer, using a damp cloth to wash clotted blood from her face, neck and scalp. She had some terrible wounds, but the pain had been drawn away along with the poison, and she had stitched several of her cuts together herself soon after they had entered the cave. Her sleep now was from pure exhaustion.

"I can't talk to them," she said. "The ravens. It was fine yesterday, but now they're unreachable. I can't shake the idea that they're laughing at me even as I try to commune. I feel them rooting around in my head, and I wonder what they see, but they fly away and cry to the rain."

"I wouldn't trust them anyway," Kosar said. "It's unnatural. They might just lead us into a Red Monk's trap."

"Why would they do that?"

"Why wouldn't they?" Kosar dabbed at A'Meer's chin, washing away dried blood to reveal the pale skin beneath.

"There could be dozens of them out there," Hope said, "and they might be anywhere." She sat on one of the saddles they had brought in out of the rain, trying to see through the curtain of dirty water that marked the cave entrance. If only she was the rain, all-seeing and innocent.

"I could see," Trey Barossa said from across the cave. The downpour suddenly seemed to increase in ferocity, and a flash of lightning lit the plains for the briefest instant.

"I've heard about you fledgers," Hope said. "I've met a few, and all of them addicts. All of them lost. They claim second sight, but all they see when they're on their trips are their own deaths coming two steps closer."

"I'm an addict of fledge as much as you are of false magic," Trey said. Alishia stirred and moaned. Hope glanced at the girl and looked away quickly: her eyes were wide-open, staring across at the cave wall as if seeing something too terrible to bear.

"Careful what you say, boy," the witch said. But there was no threat in her voice, not really, and the comment faded away. Circumstances had brought them together, and they had all witnessed something remarkable, something that still echoed in their thoughts. Hope was certain that they had observed the end of the old world and the beginning of the new.

"I can see," Trey said again. "I have fresh fledge. The drug people take topside is old, traveled, stored. It's tainted by exposure to the air. Taking old fledge is like eating rotten meat instead of fresh, and about as good for you. That's why topsiders look down on fledgers; the ones you see up here are slowly poisoning themselves."

"How far could you see?" Kosar asked.

Trey looked uncomfortable at this, so much so that Hope wondered just what he had seen on his last trip. He shrugged. "I'm not sure. And I'm not sure whether I could see something specific, or just anything that's there. If the Monks are still out there I might miss them entirely and see a sheebok in the Widow's Peaks."

"If it's that unreliable, it's likely to mislead as much as help," Hope said.

"It sounds more reliable than the skull ravens," Kosar said. "And the night will be past soon. We're still within shouting distance of Pavisse. The Monks have certainly fled the town to search for us, and we need to set off again. A'Meer will have to be tied in her saddle, and if Trey and Alishia are coming with us—"

"Why should they?" Hope asked.

Kosar raised his eyebrows.

"Why should they?" she repeated. "They know nothing of Rafe."

"I know what I saw last night," Trey said. "And I know what seeing that did to Alishia. I owe her a lot. She saved me . . ."

"You'll put yourself in danger if you come with us," Hope said. "There are Red Monks chasing us, do you know what a Red Monk can do? Do you have any idea what they are?" *And besides*, she thought, *why should we share the boy with you? Why share him with anyone?*

"I've seen worse," the fledge miner said.

Hope scoffed, but Kosar spoke up.

"If he really has second sight with fledge, then he can help us, Hope. And if he's willing to help, I'm more than willing to let him come along. I'm just a damn thief, I don't know what's going on here. We need all the help we can get."

"Help us get caught," Hope muttered.

Kosar stood, gently laying A'Meer's head on a bundle of blankets. He approached Hope, wiping the Shantasi's blood from his hands. "Where would you go?" he asked. "Which way, come daybreak? South, toward Kang Kang? Northwest to Long Marrakash, hoping that the Duke *might* be there, *might* be able to protect us from the Monks?"

"I don't know," Hope admitted. "But now we have *him*! He can protect us."

Rafe looked back at the raised voices. He hugged his blanket closer around him and stared out at the rain once again.

"He's more scared than all of us," Kosar whispered. "We all know what we think we saw last night—"

"Magic!"

"That's what we thought we saw, yes. But even Rafe is scared of that, and everything else happening around him. He may have driven the poison from A'Meer's veins, but I don't think he can help us yet. I think we still need to be helping him. If he has a gift, access to magic, whatever, it's something that's breaking him up. His parents were slaughtered before his eyes. You *know* that, Hope."

"They weren't even his real parents," she said. She grimaced and glanced at the fledger. "Can you do it now?"

"Yes." He reached across to his shoulder bag without letting Alishia slip from his lap. "Care to join me?" he asked.

"I think not." Hope sat down opposite Trey and watched him draw a chunk of fledge from his bag. "I'll just sit and watch."

————

THE NAX WOULD be waiting. He would take fledge, drift out from himself and the cave, search across the hillsides and through the shallow valleys for the Red Monks . . . and he would find the Nax. Touch their minds. Discover the truth: that it was *him* they sought, always him.

But that was craziness, brought on by the terrible few days gone by and the situation he now found himself in: sheltering from rain— which he had never seen before—with people he should have never known. And in his lap, twitching and mumbling incoherently, the stranger who had saved his life. For her more than anything Trey tried to rationalize his fears of the Nax, apply logic instead of terror, and he took his first bite of fledge.

He tasted the staleness of its outer coating. The air had touched it and its decline had begun, but he chewed past this mustiness and found the sweet dry warmth at its heart. The flavor reminded him immediately of home, bringing back sudden memories of his mother's cooking, the ribald laughter of fledge miners as they took a food break, chanting from the cave floor. Lufero with his puppet show, Sonda smiling at him and glancing away again, always glancing away. Trey let the sensations flood in. The sound of the downpour outside the cave changed into the roar of the underground river, coming from and going to nowhere he would ever know. The tang of the rain was the cool tint of spray from the river, so far underground. And the weight of Alishia's head resting on his legs, the warmth of her body across his thighs, was the dream of Sonda, his dream that had never had the chance to come true.

He was doing this to help, but he was also trying to escape. The truths he had seen over the past days were far too awful to bear. Perhaps he was fleeing to where Alishia already dwelled. He hoped that he would find his way back.

As the fledge began to take effect, Trey allowed his mind to wander. It strained at the edges of consciousness at first, still bound to his body as the drug filtered into his veins, a free spirit eager to move on and away. The fledge slowly dissolved the ties that bound him to flesh and bone and blood, and finally he peeled off, glancing back only once as he drifted away.

Alishia seemed to be watching him. Her eyes were wide and terrified, sparkling with minute movement, and her mouth was open in a wet scream she could not utter. He reached out and tried to touch her mind . . . and recoiled.

So tattered, so torn, so abused! Her mind was there, and she knew that he was there too, she knew because insight was all she had left. Her apparatus of consciousness had been slashed and shattered, the psychic bridges that were used to cross from pure spirituality to thought burned by something now absent. Trey pushed and sent comforting thoughts on ahead, trying to calm Alishia wherever she may have hidden away. Her mind was a deep, wide, expansive place, much more so than any he had seen before, and the light of her existence was like a candle in the great night sky; small, spluttering and all but invisible.

He pushed farther and crossed chasms. *She saved me*, he thought. He passed through gulfs that would have driven him mad, had he looked or extended his senses to feel them. *She saved me.*

And then he found Alishia, cowering behind the remnants of her own intellect.

Is it gone? Is it gone? Am I alone? Will it come back?

Alishia, it's me.

Has it gone? It's foul, it smells it hurts, has it gone? Will it come back?

Alishia, Rafe is a good person, he gave out no harm. He has magic in him, real magic!

Not him, it. It. Has it gone? Its hurts so much, it burns where it touched me and kills me, kills parts I never knew I had. Has it gone, Trey? Will it come back? Will it?

Alishia . . .

But he was losing her, she was dispersing and fleeing and hiding again, deeper down than he could ever go. She sounded like a little girl, afraid of the dark and being swallowed by it.

Trey pulled back, reigning in his senses until he was out of her mind and a mere observer again. He saw his own body slumped against the side of the cave, Alishia twitching on his lap, and at least now her eyes were closed.

Perhaps his presence had brought some measure of comfort.

Or maybe now she was dying.

Trey moved away quickly and passed by Rafe, resisting the temptation to reach out. He was terrified of what he would find in a mind such as his. The boy stared into the rain, stretching out his hand now and then to touch the curtain of water dripping down across the cave entrance, testing it, piercing it as if it were a shield between two realities.

Trey moved on, out of the cave and up into the crying sky. He felt an immediate sense of freedom as space grew around him, and as he spun and swooped way above the ground he pushed out his perception, comforted to find that there were no minds nearby. Not human, at least. Skull ravens sat chattering in trees farther up the slope, silenced by his touch. A herd of mountain goats munched wet grass. Nestled against a collapse of boulders far up the hillside, a tumbler quivered and shook in the rain, and Trey steered clear of its multiple captured minds. They were all screaming, and he had no desire to find out why.

He swept back toward Pavisse, passing through small valleys and over low hills, dipping into thickets of trees, finding a few dwellings where families huddled before the fire, hiding from the rain and dark. Some of these minds he touched on briefly, but he found nothing there to interest him. There was little to interest even themselves; they were sad, empty places, bereft of hope, concentrating instead on simple existence. None of them seemed to look farther forward than the next morning, when sheebok would need milking, fields hoeing and planting, ditches clearing, fences repairing . . .

He found the freedom exhilarating, and again he wondered just how far he could project himself like this. Underground there had been miles of solid rock to temper his explorations . . . but he also wondered whether his horizons had been too limited. He had never been tempted to move aboveground to see what it was like, even though perhaps the ability had always been there. As a miner he had often considered journeying topside at some point in his life. But as a fledge taker, he had never been tempted to take full advantage of the opportunities it offered him, other than guilty forays past Sonda's bedroom window. His boundaries had been too insular, he knew that now. It had taken the disaster of the Nax to open his mind.

And then something appeared in the distance, something more powerful and less human. Trey dropped down near the ground, pulling in his exploratory senses and hiding himself as effectively as a raindrop in the storm. It would take some time for the thing to reach him, so he tasted the rain, felt it hitting the ground and splashing back up, loaded with dust. It was a summer storm, warm and welcome, but it carried taints of autumn, smells of dead leaves and bare trees. Things were changing, and even the rain swore to that.

The thing came closer, and Trey did not have to extend himself to know what it was: a Red Monk. He sensed it in the distance, saw it, heard it, felt its horse's hooves shake the ground. It rode slouched in its saddle as if injured, but he thought it was probably trying to track, searching for footprints stamped in mud or hoofprints etched in the loam. Trey sank down into the ground, smothering himself in earth, hiding, feeling a slight tremble around him as the horse passed by not far away. He drew himself in, making his mind less than a point, nothing to see. The Monk did not pause. He had not been sensed.

He waited a few minutes before rising into the open once more. The rain was heavier than ever. He had to return to the cave. It was a good distance away, but the Monk would be there before daybreak.

Trey skirted south to make sure he did not pass too close to the Monk. Its mind had seemed foul, and he had no wish to approach touching it with his own. He skimmed low through a valley, into the lake at its base, shifting past fish and other things that swam in its depths, careful not to touch them. The water was black, and deep down it had begun to freeze. There were shapes struggling against the thickening water. Trey went deeper and sensed more things, large and small, frozen solid.

He surfaced and traveled back through the sky. At least there the rain smothered things that should not be.

———

"NOT FAR," TREY said. "An hour, if it rides fast."

"On our trail?" Kosar asked.

"Perhaps. It was tracking something."

"We have to go."

Trey had stood and wrapped Alishia in blankets, wiping tears from her cheeks. He remembered her voice, that sad voice lost in her own mind: *Has it gone, Trey? Will it come back?*

"I won't let it come back," he whispered, hoping that somewhere she heard his words and hoping they gave comfort.

"What was that?" Hope asked.

Trey glanced at the witch and shook his head, looking away. She frightened him.

Rafe suddenly appeared by his side, standing over him and Alishia. "What's wrong with her?" he asked. "Did you touch her mind?"

"Hardly. It's been driven too deep. She's barely herself anymore." He glared at Rafe, blaming the farm boy and the magic he had wrought. It had terrified Alishia almost to death. This girl who had read so much and seen so little, exposed suddenly to such an event, driven mad . . .

"Then who was she?" a voice said from back in the cave. Trey turned to see A'Meer sitting up, nursing her head with one hand and her elbow with the other.

"I don't know," Trey said, remembering more of his journey, more of what Alishia had been muttering in the deep parts of her mind. "But she's afraid that something is going to come back."

"What could that be?" Kosar said. "I don't know anything of the girl. Is she normal?"

"She's a librarian," Trey said. "This is her first time outside Noreela City."

"Trickery," Hope said. "For some reason only the girl knows, she's feigning this sleep. Has she stolen any of your fledge, miner? Is she guiding the Monks to us, even now?"

"No!" Trey said, fear of the witch fueling his anger. "She's *good*. Something drove her from her own mind, and she's terrified—"

"So why has it gone now?" A'Meer asked. Everyone turned to look at her. "And where? She's only been like this since Rafe . . . since he touched me. We all felt what happened then, we all know what it was, but why would that drive the girl to distraction?"

Nobody could answer. The silence in the cave was loaded.

"Well, it scared the shit out of me," Kosar eventually whispered.

"There was something inside her," Trey said. "I saw the space it left, the scars on her mind. They were *huge*."

"Something left her mind when it saw magic," Hope said, staring at Rafe. "The boy did just what he claimed he couldn't, and something fled Alishia's mind."

"You sound like you blame me," Rafe said.

"I blame you for never believing."

"It's the Mages," A'Meer said.

Heads turned. Nobody spoke, and the rain provided the counterpoint to their disbelief.

"Perhaps they got wind of what was happening, knew somehow that magic was making a return. They have their spies in the land—they have ever since they left—gathering information, feeding back news, trying to ease their eviction with stories of how the land has been failing ever since. Maybe they heard that the Red Monks were on the move. They have access to things most people do not. Hope, they have your arcane knowledge, and much, *much* more."

"But they fled northward, way past The Spine," Kosar said. "It would take a couple of moons to travel that far."

"As I said, Kosar, they have access to things. Trey, did you have to run across the land just now to report the Monk to us? No. Why would the Mages' spies have to?"

"But what . . . ?" Kosar said.

A'Meer sat up slowly, wincing as her bruised and battered body protested. "A shade," she said. "They mastered controlling damaged shades during their reign. Who's to say they don't still have a certain influence?"

"But that's magic," Hope protested. "There *is* no magic!" She glanced at Rafe as she spoke, then looked away again.

"It doesn't have to be magic. I received a message from you, remember?"

"That was a skull raven, that was just . . ."

"Communication," A'Meer finished for her. "We don't have to understand something for it to be possible. Don't ascribe anything you don't understand to magic."

"But what of Alishia?" Trey asked. "What can we do for her?"

"I don't know," A'Meer said, shaking her head. "But we have to assume that the Mages will soon know what the thing in her head saw happen here. And as we all know, they'll want what Rafe has for themselves."

"Well, I don't want it," Rafe shouted. "They can have it, for all I care!"

"What about her?" Trey asked again. They were ignoring him. Dismissing *her*.

"It's precious, Rafe!" Hope said.

"Who are you people?" Trey asked. Alishia trembled, mumbled something incoherent. "How are you going to help—"

"Who are *you*?" Hope asked. "A fledge miner who's obviously never been topside before, and a strange woman who may have betrayed us to the Mages."

"She didn't betray us! It was what was inside her."

"Maybe she's always had it there," Hope said. "She's obviously not the person you thought she was."

"She *helped* me!"

Hope looked down at Alishia where she lay prone on the cave floor. "Let her die."

"You bitch!" Trey felt the drug still lifting him, trying to tear him away from this scene and carry him up and away, into freedom. But he fought that yearning, looked at Alishia, denying the shred of doubt that Hope's words had planted in his mind.

"We don't know who she is," Hope said. "We don't know who sent her, why, when, and what she's going to do next. For that matter, we don't know *him*, either!" She jabbed her finger at Trey and advanced toward him. He stepped back, frightened of the tattoos seemingly squirming on the witch's face, bringing her skin alive.

"We have to leave, and soon," A'Meer said tiredly. "We can talk about this when we're away, but I'm in no state to take on another Monk."

"And who are you?" Hope said, turning on the injured woman. "A Shantasi! And they're about as trustworthy as my own turds! Who's to say you aren't here to steal what Rafe has for your slave-kin?"

"She fought a Red Monk so you could get away!" Kosar shouted.

"And beat it?" Hope threw her hands up. "Nobody beats a Red Monk! They let her win to deceive us. They're probably closing in even now, ready to snuff out the only bit of hope this land has seen for centuries!" She stood at Rafe's side with her back to him, arms spread, as if to ward off any attack from the others in the cave.

"No, Hope," Rafe said. His voice was quiet, but it carried the authority of someone far older than he. "No fighting. No arguing. We don't know one another, but we're here for a reason." He closed his eyes, breathed deeply and sighed, a long, heartrending exhalation.

"You're all here for me. And though I never wished it, there's a part of me that asks that you protect me, as well as you can."

———

RAFE HAD BEEN listening to the arguments: Hope's paranoia, Trey's concern for the fallen girl, Kosar the thief siding with the Shantasi warrior who had given them time to escape and almost died in the process.

I cured her, he thought. *I touched her and drew out the poison from her blood, but through no physical process. The infected blood went nowhere. The poison simply stopped existing. I did that.*

The rain pummeled down outside, and each impact was a whisper in his ears, more knowledge imparted and facts hacked down and burned; new, terrifying truths rising from the ashes. This simple cave, this depression in the land, was turning into a wonderful place in Rafe's understanding. It was as if every crack in the wall, every raindrop, every blade of grass bending under a weight of water knew more than he had ever known. There was a power around him, buzzing to break out. It was terrifying but humbling; the power gave itself tentatively, holding back at every step, pleading with him, *Be careful, be careful.* He was terrified of its potential and awed by its intensity.

Now those people in the cave were looking at him, blinking in surprise at what he had said, each thinking themselves right in some small way. And in one way they *were* all right—magic was breathing again, and it was Rafe who gave it breath. But there was so much more they did not know.

"I'm weak," Rafe said. "I'm eighteen next moon. And I'm a farm boy; I've no fighting experience. I've never *had* a fight other than with boys in the village. I'd have no idea how to defend myself against a Red Monk, intent on killing me for what's started inside me."

"And just what is that?" Kosar asked.

"Magic," Rafe said. "Strong and powerful, but vulnerable as well. It's inside me, gestating, and it relies on me to carry it. It's readying it- and myself for what it will become."

The cave was silent, its inhabitants awed. Even Alishia had stopped mumbling, as if she sensed the import of the moment.

"You cured me," A'Meer said.

"I touched you and the magic bled into me. I just steered it. I think it was . . . an expression of good faith."

"A bribe?" Hope asked.

"A gift," Rafe replied. "It asks a lot, and in turn I ask a lot of you. Requests like that can't exist without some reward."

"So what do we all get?" Hope said. "What does the fledger get? What does the thief receive in payment for his allegiance?"

Rafe shrugged. "I don't know."

"It hasn't told you yet?" Hope asked.

Rafe shrugged once again, saying nothing.

"What do I get?" Hope asked. "I've been waiting all my life, so what do I get?"

There was turmoil in Rafe's mind, brief but violent, and the tang of the rain carried the warm scent of blood for less than a heartbeat. He closed his eyes but saw no less. "Hurt," he said. "If you go against me, you get hurt."

He could never have spoken those words . . . and yet he had. Those in the cave should have laughed at what he said, yet they did not.

He had convinced them. And the voices in his head sighed with contentment, and started to tell him more.

AS THEY LEFT the cave Kosar knew that much had already changed. The rain pelted down and washed old dirt from his body, refreshing him, preparing him for the future. He opened his hands and held them palms-up, and although the wounds on his fingertips still stung, the pain was less than before. The torrent cleansed the dust and grit from his raw flesh, washing his past back into the ground. He hated foolish pride, but for the first time in years he had a purpose.

A'Meer sat on a horse, no longer tied into her saddle. She slumped in pain from her wounds, exhausted from the effects of the poison. But her eyes were bright now when she looked across at him, twinkling with excitement, and Kosar was thrilled that he and A'Meer were together. Somehow, any other situation would have seemed unthinkable. Perhaps this had always been their future.

Maybe they had been steered this way.

Kosar thrust that thought from his mind, stared it at the ground and let his horse trample it into the mud. He had no wish to imagine such a controlling influence over his life.

But A'Meer's eyes said otherwise. Even though it was still dark he could see the way she looked at him, the sense of meaning suddenly exuding from her like a strong smell. He had never considered A'Meer aimless—she was too strong, too intelligent for that—but compared to this moment, she had always been adrift, he realized. Injured as she was, weak and vulnerable, the strength of her new conviction was evident. She had found her true course.

It was a frightening sensation, this sense of belonging. It scared Kosar to the core. And yet he could not deny that it felt good.

As they packed, they had talked about which way they should head. North, eventually, lay the Cantrass Plains, The Spine, Long Marrakash. It was rumored across the land that the Duke was there now, not exactly in hiding but living beneath a cloud of apathy and neglect. His people did not want or need him anymore—Noreela was becoming too fractured, too feudal—but his reign was still recognized by some of those in the north. Kosar suggested that they should make contact with the Duke and beg the protection of his army. Better a thousand fighting men than a witch, a thief, a fledge miner, a dying woman and an injured Shantasi. Hope had agreed, though grudgingly. Rafe had remained silent. He watched them talk about his safety. It was as if he had placed himself in their hands, and now it was their duty to do their best by him.

Also to the north, A'Meer had said, were the Mages. Fled for three centuries, maybe dead, or perhaps weakened or driven mad by exile. Much of their army had gone with them but it would be long-dead by now, skeletons in armor. And yet A'Meer insisted that the Mages would try something. *They were so close to it for so long*, she had said. *They couldn't help but be affected by the twisted magic they wrought. If they're alive, they'll want nothing but revenge.*

They all knew of the Duke's army and what it had become. Remnants lay scattered across the land in the Militia, local police forces that seemed quite efficient in small numbers but which in places such as Pavisse or Noreela City became perpetrators of crime rather than guardians against it. Control was good, but uninhibited power bred greed.

So for now they had agreed to head south. Hundreds of miles due south was Kang Kang, a place Kosar had once traveled close by but which he had no desire to visit again. An unknown place, a land of legend, Kang Kang was the birthplace of tales to scare children and adults alike. Much was said of its mountains and valleys, and if even a half of it was true, it was somewhere to avoid.

But Kosar did not think that Kang Kang was their aim. A'Meer had not commented upon this yet, but he could sense something in her, a new urgency fighting through her pain and tiredness. She had stated her mission to him quite plainly back in Pavisse, and demonstrated it by taking on the Red Monk: she was here to protect Rafe. She would gladly die doing so, but he was sure that she favored an alternative. She wanted to take him home. She wanted to travel to New Shanti.

HOPE WALKED CLOSE to Rafe's horse. Her place was beside him, and she would not leave. She had been the first to find him, see his potential, sense the burgeoning power within, and now she thought of herself as his guardian. He had grown, even in the few days since she had found him curled up in a doorway in Pavisse, but the need to protect him remained. And she intended to be alongside him until the end, whatever the end might bring.

She felt proud of herself and her lineage. For generations her family had been witches, and now here she was, trudging through this filthy night with the source of new magic on a horse beside her. He looked asleep, but Hope guessed he was merely composing his thoughts, staring at his hands where they held his horse's reins, looking inward not outward. Trying to see and understand the strange new landscapes within.

What she would give to be in there with him. What she would do to have just one single look.

She glanced back at the fledge miner and the comatose woman. He was steering the horse, glancing back constantly to make sure she had not slipped sideways in the saddle. It was one of the horses Hope had traded for at the farm, and even in the cool wet night it foamed at the mouth, snorted, straggled behind. It would be dead soon. Perhaps the girl would too.

Hope could find no trust in her heart for someone she did not know. It came from a lifetime of witchcraft. There were those who still feared a witch, but there were many more who knew for sure that she was a sham. Witches of old practiced magic, curving it to their whims and letting it re-form again, molding it like so much clay. Since the Cataclysmic War, a witch was merely a shadow of her ancestors, a pretender, wallowing in past glories or hiding beneath the veneer of legend. To some, frightening in her very madness. To others, pitiful. Hope was a witch and a whore combined, with double the reason to be hated.

Hope had always been a woman on her own—ironic that she had shared her bed with so many men—and now more than ever she felt withdrawn and introverted, longing to hide from the strangers she had been thrown in with. She had never met a fledge miner topside who could be trusted. They always ended up craving their fresh drug, swindling and lying and cheating in the vain hope that they could procure some more without returning underground. They knew so little of the lands they sought to live in, their knowledge confined instead to the caves, the darkness that hid millennia of memories. This knowledge combined with their own peculiar myths—born of the constant darkness, the tremendous pressure of the world surrounding them—to make them unreliable at best, and willfully devious at worst.

And then there was Kosar, a branded thief. He seemed strange. Though not as old as her, he was experienced and well traveled, yet almost naïve in the company of herself and A'Meer. It was as if he shunned the knowledge that he must have been witness to over his years of wandering the lands, excluding it for want of a simpler life. His fingers bled, he tore strips of cloth to cover them and he hadn't once asked whether Hope knew of ways to cure him. There were means—Willmott's Nemesis, administered correctly, would ease his pain and let the wounds heal and close at last—and although Hope had none with her, it would be relatively easy to find. But if he did not ask, she would not offer. She liked him the way he was. Because although thievery was no reason for her to mistrust him, his relationship with the Shantasi was.

Hope's trust was least for this Shantasi woman who knew so much. The witch liked to believe that it was not jealousy, though there was a glimmer of that: Hope had found Rafe, yet it was A'Meer who had fought and almost died for him. And it was the warrior woman who also seemed to know more about the Mages and their ways than any of them. That did not surprise Hope, but deep inside, in the animal part of her brain where reason gave way to instinct, it angered her. It drew her closer than ever to Rafe, and if in her head there was a crude sense of ownership, then so be it.

She knew little of the Shantasi. Some claimed to know them, to have an understanding of their origins and history, but these were almost always proved wrong. Hope had heard many wild rumors, the stuff of storytime, so exaggerated and unbelievable so as to be dismissed without a second thought. Other tales were frightened whispers from men in her bed—traders, farmers, militia and mercenaries—who claimed to have learned the secrets of the Shantasi. One man she remembered well had come close to tears as he related his tale to her, his claim that he had traveled almost as far as New Shanti but then been turned back, hounded out by wraiths and spirits too violent, too *real* to be dead. The chase had supposedly lasted for days, and however fast or slow he had been running, the spirits had always been just behind him, lashing out, not letting him rest for a minute until he entered the Mol'Steria Desert. There the chase had ended, but he had kept on running. He had run so far, he said, that the bones in his toes had begun to crumble, and he lifted his feet to show her.

Hope had smiled benignly, nodded. She knew of potions and suggestions that would imply a sense of pursuit in someone with a weak mind. It was a tale she had heard before.

But then the man had paused, stared at her, seeing her disbelief. He turned onto his stomach and showed her the wounds on his back. They were cauterized slashes, furrows in the skin from shoulders to buttocks, some deep, some barely a shading to the surface. The mark of the Shantasi spirits, he had said. He had remained lying there, and Hope had watched him sleep until daybreak.

A'Meer had too much Shantasi about her for Hope to trust her at all. She had appeared from nowhere, drawn to Rafe and his wakening gift, and without explanation she had sworn to protect him and guide him away from those who craved his destruction. Just because A'Meer and Hope both wanted Rafe protected did not mean that they were on the same side. Indeed, allegiances seemed fickle at best, there being so many aims and desires to be served. Perhaps she wanted the boy for her people. Slaves, many believed them to be, brought to Noreela thousands of years ago. Perhaps magic would serve their purposes of ultimate, long-desired revenge.

So Hope remained close to Rafe and his horse, patting the creature's flank as if to communicate her friendliness. Soon, if things did not go to her liking, she might rely on this creature's speed to help make their escape.

Chapter 21

JOSSUA ELMANTOZ WAS an old man, and he had been waiting for a long, long time. So when the message came that the Nax requested an audience, confusion was his first reaction.

That was quickly replaced by fear.

BEFORE THE CATACLYSMIC War, the Monastery had belonged to the Mages. Now, walking slowly into its hidden depths, through shadows that had never seen daylight and into pits and caverns of permanent night, Jossua felt their influence once more.

He was the only Red Monk alive who had fought in the War. His first contact with the Mages and their armies had been not far from here, at the Battle of Lake Denyah, in the Year of the Black 1913. He had been a young man then, a novice pagan priest, driven by a fervent desire to see the Mages defeated and nature return back to its true state. Young, feisty, but afraid as well. Everyone in Noreela was frightened by then. The Mages had been dabbling in the unnatural manipulation of magic for several years, and news had been coming from their keep on Lake Denyah, more terrifying news each and every day, that their workings had transgressed boundaries never meant to be touched.

Jossua was an academic, studying at his local university in Long Marrakash with a view to making the journey to Noreela City and completing his education there, prior to taking up his priesthood. The dealings of politics had rarely bothered him, their machinations crude and encumbered by emotion compared to the pureness of magic. For it was magic that Jossua had studied. Its powers, its sources, its meaning and use, the philosophy surrounding it, its effects on society and the way the land was run. And especially, its confluence with the land. Because just as air and sunlight were taken for granted, so then was magic. It was as much a part of life as breathing.

The Mages made it go wrong. They abused it. Whatever dark arts they were practicing in their keep were great and terrible, too powerful and awful to be ignored. They turned magic from good to bad; from aiding everyday life, to raising the dead; from keeping the balance, to tipping the natural world onto its side. They sought to control the magic of the land for themselves, and all evidence suggested that they had succeeded. The shock waves were felt right across the land: rivers turned poisonous; volcanoes erupted; earthquakes roared from the depths of Kang Kang, sending things from there fleeing into the wider land. The magic that had once been a part of life quickly became a means of death, and the Duke sent an army to question the Mages' acts.

That had been the start of the Cataclysmic War. Nobody ever discovered what had happened to that first army—there were no survivors to tell the tale, no eyewitnesses to flee Lake Denyah and spread the word—but like a stone thrown into a pond, the first battle and defeat had repercussions throughout Noreela. Magic was twisted even more awry. Great machines turned on their users, plunged into ravines, drowned in lakes or turned turtle and crushed their passengers. Tumblers seemed to sense the imbalance and go mad, slaughtering thousands on the slopes of mountains and in foothills across Noreela. In towns and cities machines went haywire, killing or being killed. The sensitive interactions between humanity and nature were upset. Magic changed almost overnight, and the rot set in.

The reaction of most of the population was one of astonishment and bewilderment. It was as if they had woken one morning to find the sky turned green, or their legs transformed into tree trunks. A law of nature they had lived by for the entirety of recorded history had suddenly been transgressed. Their lives would never be the same again.

Back then, easy communication across Noreela was a fact of life. Machines would carry words and meaning from Long Marrakash to Noreela City in a matter of minutes, delivering it without echo or skewed meaning to the ear of those for whom it was intended. Even after magic changed, this ability persisted; much of the fall was gradual, not sudden, marked by many catastrophic events that caught the imagination. News had traveled fast—the Mages in the west, experimenting, corrupting, powerful, trying to make a part of nature their very own—and the reaction was immediate. A people's army had formed out of the frightened masses, and they had marched on the Mages' keep with the remnants of the Duke's forces.

Jossua had no hesitation in volunteering. His parents and fiancée had traveled to Noreela City with him and cried him away to battle. His fiancée had hugged him and placed something in the palm of his hand, then walked away along the dock. She had not turned to look back, not once. Jossua kept his fist closed until their transport boat started swimming in long, powerful strokes down the river toward Lake Denyah. The sun rose behind them, lighting the boat's wake into flame-tipped ripples. The silver birch trees on either side of the river were aflame as well, holding and reflecting the red dawn, glittering with the fires of life. It could have been metal in his hand—it had felt cold at first, although now the heat of his blood had warmed it—or perhaps it was some other token, of what he did not know. Closing his eyes, Jossua opened his hand over the side of the boat. He was sure he heard a tiny splash as the gift fell into the river.

On the cruise down from San they heard news of defeat after defeat. The Duke's second army had reached the Mages' keep and laid siege, but even their powerful war machines were no match for the Mages' altered powers. They did not want to believe. Jossua's traveling companions were shopkeepers and teachers, farmers and moneylenders, men and women of title, thrilled with the chance of adventure at first, but frightened now, regretting their hasty decision as weapons were placed in their hands. Maybe the tales were distorted in the telling, they said. But several hours before they reached

Lake Denyah, just before dawn of the following day, they could see the glow in the sky as the land burned.

Even now, after so many years to dwell on those events, Jossua could only recall fragments of the weeks following that river cruise. He could remember the beauty of the surroundings as they moved from the river into the inland sea that was Lake Denyah: the hills on either side clothed in purple, pink and red heathers; the sun behind them, its heat warming his neck as if reaching out a pleading hand; the waters themselves, churned by the passing of so many boats of war and yet never upset for long. He could remember the faces of those around him, people he had come to know quickly as fear brought them together. Back then they had seemed determined to win, but upon reflection he knew that their expressions had been of uniform resignation. They could all see the glow of conflict and destruction ahead. Perhaps with the promise of death so close, determination and acceptance were the same animal.

Once they landed and launched into battle, his memory became even more vague. Weeks of his life were all but missing, trampled down into the bloody mud, consumed by the monstrous things the Mages had made and driven at the offending army. A few stark memories had imprinted themselves deep, like dreams still so fresh that he sometimes wondered whether he had survived through that hell only the day before, not three centuries ago.

He remembered his first steps on the shores of Lake Denyah. Jumping from the boat, his feet sank into the mud and he froze there, unable to move. Water lapped at his ankles and people fell all around him, their outlines spiky with arrows as if already scratched from reality. The smell of dead fish was rich in the air, their silvery shapes piled several deep along the beach, gills frozen open as if trying to scream. Farther up the shore, banked against the dawn sun, huge war machines disgorged thousands of arrows and sharpened discs. They were ugly things, not graceful and smooth like machines had once been. Their extremes were distorted with gushing tumors, their metal limbs rusted, stony protrusions cracked as if from a century of frost. But they were dreadfully powerful. The magic powering these hideous machines must have been driven mad, and now it had been offered an outlet to vent that madness.

He heard the hiss of arrows and discs cutting through the air, the thudding as they impacted flesh, the harder thunks as skulls were pierced and spines severed. Ahead of him, one of his friends was pinned to the air by a dozen arrows. When the woman turned slowly and stared at Jossua where he was stuck in the mud, another slew of arrows hit her from behind and tore her apart. He had remembered and forgotten her features a thousand times since then, as if recollection could do the same as a clutch of arrows.

Then there was the sea of wounded gathered in a small valley away from the main fight. There were thousands there, dozens expiring each minute. The Mages' unnatural machines and Krote soldiers used an unidentified poison, and even when the injured could be brought out, they were simply laid down to die. No food, no water, no comfort; that was all spared for those not yet doomed. Jossua made several trips with wounded people on his back. They screamed when they died. Their hands clawed at the air for help that would never come. Over the days that valley became a landscape of frozen, stiffened corpses; no flies or carrion, a still tableau of corrupted flesh and poison still effective in death.

He saw a dead dog. Someone must have brought their pet with them and lost it as soon as the hellish fighting began. It was a mongrel, clean and cared for. There was no sign of injury on its body, and its face was not contorted with the pain of a poisoned death. It hunkered beneath a tree, huddled between exposed roots, cold, stiff. There was a calmness to the scene, an oasis in the storm of battle. He wondered what had killed it. He never found out.

And then a memory of the Mages and a thousand Krotes bursting from their keep. Unnatural light exploded in pockets across the battlefield, spitting fiery balls that consumed flesh and metal alike. Their monstrous war machines shook the blood-soaked battlefield as if it were a blanket laid across the earth, sending the people's army tumbling and leaving them defenseless against the Krotes' tainted swords and spears. A brief roar of victory had gone up at the sight of the Mages leaving their fortress, but it quickly died as the Krotes went about their work. Strange things roamed the battlefield: machines with a screaming bloodlust all their own; shadows that may have been wraiths; fiery balls of magic, bright and yet somehow unclean. And the death dealt that day was as diverse as the lives it took away. The Mages themselves . . . Jossua saw them sat astride flying things that shit fireballs and pissed poison across the besieging hordes . . . He saw them . . .

Much later, he rode a machine into battle. The people had regrouped and magic itself had somehow fought back, offering a final limited burst of pure power and denying the Mages' control one last time. The tide had turned and Jossua was a warrior now, the memory of his former life smothered by weeks of battle and rage. The machine marched on giant flaming legs, graceful and deadly, and he and his squadron harried at the fleeing Mage army's flanks. Men fell beneath his ride's molten feet, their charred corpses sometimes carried along for several miles and providing a cushioned footfall for its rapid sprint. Jossua howled. He felt his face burning with the fury, and even people from his own side moved to let him through. He was a berserker; invincible, unbeatable. When he killed a Krote he drank his or her blood. And he fed well.

His final, abiding memory of that long time of war and death was sitting on the shores of the island in The Spine that would become known as Mages' Bane. His machine lay dead and already rotting behind him, its purpose fulfilled. Magic had withdrawn itself earlier that day, and hundreds had instantly fallen on their swords, sighing as they died. The sense of hopelessness and catastrophe was enormous, and everything suddenly seemed very different. It felt as though any purpose in existence had suddenly gone. A flower he found growing on the beach was rotten, the sun was weak and oily on his skin, a bird drifted down into the sea and did not resurface. The sense of victory and hope he had felt at finally driving the Mages away was brief, because their defeat brought Noreela no victory. All it brought was the sudden absence of magic, and the sense that all good things had come to an end.

Around him, sprouting from the sand like sapling trees and bobbing gently in the waves, were ten thousand torn bodies. Noreelans and Krotes were equalled in death. Here and there were survivors, all of them as silent as he. They stood amongst the monuments of the dead. And in the distance, still visible as a haze on the horizon, the Mages' burning ships showed their tails as they fled Noreela forever.

So long ago. So many moons, and here he was, still alive. Still waiting. His purpose as fresh as ever, his rage as inflammatory as it had been all those years before.

Jossua Elmantoz passed deeper into the Monastery, the former Mages' keep, wondering what he would find when he next viewed daylight.

———

THINGS IN THE basements, one of the younger Monks had said. Forms shifting, shadows moving the wrong way, the smell of turned earth and scorched rock. And then something new.

Jossua was an old man. He barely had the strength to leave his rooms anymore, let alone travel down through the huge Monastery. Too many steps, too many uneven tunnels, known and unknown. And yet, this he could not ignore. A Nax was too dangerous to disregard.

He went on his own. He could have used help, he was not afraid to admit that, but he was the Elder. There were responsibilities to uphold. And the younger Monks had not been able to hide their relief when he instructed them to remain behind.

Prepare, he had said. *Soon you will go out into the land. Your task is at hand. Your lives are about to find meaning.*

He had already passed through the real basements and entered the long, declining tunnel that led deeper into the bedrock. His torch flared brightly, lighting the way and striving to blind him at the same time. The ground was uneven here, and he had to walk slowly to keep from falling. This was harder than negotiating the staircases in the Monastery. At least they had been even, if difficult. Here a ridge of stone could surprise him into a fall, an unseen hollow could twist his ankle and break his old man's bones. If he hurt himself down here, he could not imagine the Monks venturing this deep to find him. His torch would burn down, burying him in darkness. The cold would kill him.

He had never been this deep. He paused and moved the torch around, taking in his surroundings. Water dripped from the tunnel walls, ran from several deep cracks in the stone and gurgled away down the tunnel, contained in ditches formed on either side of the path. Black moss grew around the cracks from which the water issued. Small silver shapes darted across the walls, nibbling at the moss, moving away, encountering one another and touching antennae. The light did not bother them because they were blind. Perhaps they could sting. Jossua left them to their feast.

His limbs were aching and his heart fluttered weakly in his chest, sending spasms of pain into his arms and shoulders. He paused and stood within the circle of light from his torch. Beyond that the darkness was total; it could hide anything. If there were eyes out there watching him, they closed when he looked their way, so as not to reflect the flames.

The walls here were almost totally smooth, but for the cracks where time had shifted them and stresses had forced them open. This was no natural cave, and yet it did not carry the tool marks that would be so evident had it been manually dug. Machines had made this place, Jossua knew. Perhaps those of the Mages—the thought of them walking this corridor, taking up the same space as he, made him feel sick—or perhaps they had been formed many generations ago, for whatever original reason the keep had been built. There were no true records of when or why the place had been constructed, nor by whom, although over the decades the Monks had discovered several distinct layers in the structure. The deeper they went, the older the period of the building's birth, until the basement held its origins in the dim mists of prehistory. A place of worship some said, although to which god or demon they could not say. A retreat, others claimed, a castle and keep wherein safety could be found from outside aggressors. The Mages had thought that to be the case and yet even they, with all their twisted power, had been driven out.

Nobody knew why, how or by whom. Jossua had his suspicions.

Soon, he thought. *I'll see it soon.*

The incline of the tunnel floor suddenly steepened, and Jossua tried to hold on to the wall. Water ran by beside his feet, echoing down into the dark before him. He passed a place where water spewed from the tunnel wall, shoved through by the pressure of Lake Denyah itself, and visions of flooding came to him.

Something moved farther along the tunnel. He felt the breath of displaced air caress him, and with it came a smell. Rich and fresh, the stench of a living thing down in this darkened, dead place.

No animals down here, he thought. *Nothing to eat. Nothing to hunt. That must be the Nax.*

The shadows suddenly closed in. The reach of the torchlight lessened, the deep darkness drew near, and he glanced up at the flame in confusion. It was burning as brightly as ever. Breath caught in his throat as the air around him constricted, threatening to crush him. He thrust the torch forward, defying the night and willing it back, but a section of the dark reached out and closed around the flame.

It squeezed, and the flame changed color . . . yellow . . . white . . . blue. And then it snuffed out into nothing.

Jossua gasped. A memory of the torch remained in his eyes for a few moments, casting a ghost of itself wherever he turned his head. He closed his eyes and the ghost was still there, so he opened them again. The echo faded away. He could hear only his breath, smell the old fear on himself, the mustiness of his great age clashing with the fresh tang of the thing down here with him.

And then something touched his face.

Monk, a voice scoffed. It was androgynous, and the only echo it gave was inside his head.

Jossua could not reply straightaway, such was his shock. That voice had sounded slick and alien, filled with hatred even he could barely fathom. "I'm the Elder," Jossua said. His whisper sounded so loud down here in the dark.

Elder, Monk . . . magic-hater.

"Not hater. Protector."

Protect by destroying. The voice was filled with disdain.

"Better than welcoming it back so that the Mages can take it again."

Truly? We wonder.

A million fears flooded Jossua's mind, but he could speak none of them. He had no idea what the Nax wanted. He blinked at the dark.

Your time is near, Elder.

Jossua did not feel surprised. The Nax was here for a reason, after all, though that reason remained obscure. "Where is it?" he said.

Near the Widow's Peaks. Its taint has awoken us there.

"Did you drive the Mages away from the keep? Was it you?"

No answer.

"Show yourself."

You have no reason to see us.

"Why do you come here?"

We know your reason for being. We have no wish for magic to return.

"Neither do we." Jossua shivered as a waft of cool air broke against his sweaty skin. The Nax was moving along the tunnel. "How does it reveal itself? Where is the magic?"

In a male human. Deeper than his soul. Barely a part of him, but growing.

"How do you know all this?"

No answer. Jossua tried to touch the darkness, but his outstretched hand felt too exposed and he drew it in. The dark was suddenly filled with potential; a drawn breath before a shout, a hanging blade before a cut. He gasped and fell to the ground, tried to curl into a ball. His old bones ached.

We are the Nax, the thing said, and this time its voice came from outside Jossua's mind. It echoed in the rock of the tunnel wall, vibrating the ground beneath him, shook the air, bursting farther along the tunnel in a thunderclap of sound. Jossua cried out but his voice was lost in the cacophony, swallowed by the echo of the Nax's final, violent utterance.

His torch burst alight and Jossua screamed again, able to hear himself this time. The darkness pulled away. He tried to stand, but his legs were weak. From way down the tunnel—deeper than he had been and farther than he would ever go—there came the sound of rock being crushed, pulverized, scorched. Heat blasted back at him, stealing breath from his lungs . . . and then coolness rushed in once more.

Eventually Jossua found the strength to stand. He had nothing to fear; the Nax wanted him alive. And yet he, a man over three centuries old, felt humbled and lessened by this experience. It was as if this brief exchange had held up a mirror to his old foolishness, the belief he had maintained for decades that somehow he was important.

"My time is near," Jossua whispered, and sibilant echoes came back at him from the tunnel walls. They contained humor that had not been evident in his own words.

He turned and began to retrace his steps. *His time was near.* There was much to be done. He had a brief but powerful recollection of standing on the beach on Mages' Bane, staring northward, knowing that even though the battle was over his own long war had only just begun.

As he traveled back along the tunnel, climbing slowly toward the Monastery high above his head, he noticed that water had ceased spewing from rock walls and running past him into the depths. It was as if something had sucked the place dry.

HE HAD LOST track of time. When he found his way back into the Monastery's basements, Jossua was confused that there was no daylight bleeding down from above. He began to panic. *Darkness*, he thought, *there's only darkness.* Maybe they were already too late.

"The dark," he gasped past a tongue swollen by dehydration.

"It's nighttime, Elder Jossua," a voice said, and Jossua felt water dripping onto his tongue. It stung at first, but then the coolness trickled into his throat and he sighed and slumped back to the ground. He was held up, given water, touched softly by hands sworn only to kill.

"How long?" he croaked.

"Elder?"

"How long was I gone?"

"A day," a voice said. "We thought . . ."

Jossua smiled and shook his head. "Oh no, they wouldn't have let me die," he said. "They need us to find and destroy the magic back in the land."

"Magic!"

Jossua glanced at the Monk that had spoken, her face dancing in torchlight. The flames fluttered in a steady breeze coming up from below, and Jossua wondered how much of each waft was the breath of a Nax. "You're surprised, Gathana?" he said. "You're shocked that magic should live again? It's nature, after all—life itself—and life is tenacious." In each Monk's eyes, Jossua could make out two emotions: fear and excitement. Their concern for him had vanished already, but he did not mind. They were not meant to be here forever, listening to him, following his words, looking after him as he grew older and older, less able to dress himself, forgetful, wont to piss the bed on occasion . . .

They were killers.

"Help me up," he said. "And call the Council. You'll all be leaving soon."

————

IN THE KITCHENS meals were left half-cooked, slowly cooling and drying, solidifying in pans that would never be washed. Monks were roused from their beds, donning red cloaks over dirty underclothes. Others were interrupted at half-finished board games. The pieces would forever be at war, victory several moves and an infinity away. In the courtyards and gardens, dogs and wolves remained shackled. They would die on the ends of their chains, starving, fading to bones and then dust. Beyond these gardens lay the vegetable fields, fruit trees and livestock pens. All would be rotten come winter: potatoes in the ground; fruit on the vine; chickens and sheebok melting back into the land. Books were left open, infrequent conversations hung unfinished, a bathtub steamed away to nothing. Quickly, efficiently and with a mounting air of expectation, the Monks converged on the Council chamber at the pinnacle of the Monastery. As the sun rose in the east, its early red light casting a pink glow on the life moon still faint in the sky, the chamber was filled with over three hundred Red Monks. As Fate would have it, one for every year of their wait. They sat in the tiered seating, their presence a bloody red smear across the ancient rock of the citadel.

Jossua Elmantoz was carried up through the portal in the floor of the chamber and onto the central dais. Gathana stood nearby and offered her arm, but Jossua waved her away and stood on his own. He looked around at the assembled Monks, not knowing one from another. He fumbled with his sword, resting his palm on its hilt. His own hood, raised like those of all the men and women watching him, hid the strain on his face. But they would respect that. They all knew the Elder, knew why he was the one to be the nearest they had to a leader. He had fought in the Cataclysmic War, and he had seen the Mages.

"Our time has come," he said.

Nobody spoke. Nobody moved. By then, deep inside, most of them had already guessed.

"Magic is back in the land," Jossua continued. "The Nax have communed with me, and they know where it is, *how* it is. That is all they told me, so I must assume they know no more." He paused for a breath, still exhausted from his day beneath ground. "At present it has a carrier, a male. I don't know his name. He's somewhere in the foothills of the Widow's Peaks.

"We have to assume that the Mages have heard of this recurrence. They have their spies, and if their greed is as strong as ever, they will be coming. An advance army, perhaps, borne by hawks or other flying things, but the bulk of their force will surely travel by sea. Nobody knows how far north they fled, so none can tell how soon they will arrive on Noreela. But their threat is secondary. *Our* time is now. The Mages seek the magic, and without it they are no more than worn-out sorcerers with tricks up their sleeves and false-bottomed boxes. We must find it first. And once found, it has to be destroyed, sent back, purged from the world once more. Humanity was not ready the last time, and since then nothing has improved. It does not belong here."

Jossua pulled back his hood so that he could stare out at the assembled Monks, frankly and honestly. They met his gaze. "Three centuries ago, I stood on the far northern shores of Noreela and watched the Mages flee, and then I felt magic abandon the land. I felt what that abandonment did to Noreela . . . like halting food for a pregnant woman. She withers and dies, and the potential within her withers and dies also. I was covered with the gore of the Mages' Krote warriors, my belly filled with their blood, and even before their burning ships had crested the horizon I swore to myself, *never again*. I was already a changed man. The fury had done that, the hate, and I was a Red Monk in all but name. *Whether it stays away or comes back, they'll never have it again*, I swore. We have had false alarms — there have been signs, hints, and we have killed when we deemed it necessary or appropriate — but this is different. This is real. Whatever their reasons for telling us, the Nax have no need to lie or deceive."

He raised his hand and, with three swipes, divided the assembled throng into three equal parts. "You, head straight to the Widow's Peaks and commence your search. You, upriver to San, guard the waterway and wait for the carrier to cross. You, take the boats across Lake Denyah, then head for the Mol'Steria Desert. Wait there, but look both ways: north, for the carrier of magic; south, for the Shantasi. I suspect they have heard as well, or will soon, and they too will be keen to claim their prize."

He raised his head, drew his sword and set its tip between his shoes. With his palms on the hilt he leaned forward, sighing as he took some of the weight from his feet. "This place has served us well," he said, "but it's time for history to move on. If any of you have any questions . . . your heart is not true."

At that, the three hundred Monks stood and began to file out, quickly and quietly.

"Elder!" someone shouted. "Elder Elmantoz!"

A Monk staggered into the chamber, collapsed to his knees, fell forward onto his face. Jossua hefted his sword and stepped forward, placing its point into the hood of this Monk, lifting slowly to reveal the man beneath.

Flushed red, filled with the rage, the man was breathing blood. His cloak was muddied and torn, his right hand missing two fingers, his face cut and gaping from chin to temple, his shoulder shattered, a sliver of pink bone protruding through a tear in the cloak. "Elder

Elmantoz . . ." he whispered, the strength leaving him. "Magic," he said. "I've seen magic."

"Who are you?" Jossua demanded. The Monks that had left filtered back in, informed of this sudden arrival by Jossua's raised voice. This man was a Monk, yes, but Jossua had never seen him before. That meant that he came from one of the outlying clans. And now here he was, on this very day, talking of magic.

"Lucien Malini," the Monk said. "I have news of magic! A boy, Rafe Baburn, he carries it somehow. The trail ran cold, but we picked it up again, chased hard . . . he had a Shantasi with him, a warrior . . . and a witch, and a thief."

"Where is he now?"

"Fleeing north from Pavisse. Others are in pursuit, I came to warn you, Elder. I came for reinforcements."

"When was this?"

Lucien frowned, tried to stand but fell when his broken shoulder gave out. "Two days?" he said. "Three? My horse died. I ran. I was attacked by bandits, spent time fighting them off, had to—"

"Lead your reinforcements back," Jossua said. "There are a hundred Monks here that will come with you."

Lucien looked up at the Elder Monk, panting.

"That is," Jossua said, "unless you'd like to stay for a few days. A nice hot bath, a meal . . ."

Lucien did not smile, but he stood and drew his sword. The rust of dried blood marked the blade. "Not while this is still hungry," he said.

"Then it will be sated," Jossua said. "Rafe Baburn!" he called. "You seek Rafe Baburn!"

The Monks left, Lucien Malini with them, and soon Jossua was alone. He waited there for a while, climbed the tiered seating so that he could see from the high windows, watched the Monks spread slowly out across the landscape as if the Monastery were bleeding. Then he slid his sword into its scabbard, walked from the chamber and started down long flights of stairs to the ground level.

He sat on a stone fountain to regain his breath. As he examined the ancient, broken Book of Ways taken from the library in Noreela City, a new purpose rose in him, invigorating his muscles, grasping his heart and driving his blood thick and fast, giving him back the bloodred rage he had not felt for far too long. While his Monks would seek out and destroy the new magic, Jossua had charged himself with an even greater purpose.

He would not remain here alone. He wondered whom this place would serve in the future, but wondering was not his cause, speculation had no place in his thoughts. With memories of the Cataclysmic War rushing bloodred through his mind, and the song of ages falling from his withered lips, Jossua Elmantoz left the Monastery and headed south for Kang Kang, seeking the womb of the land.

Chapter 22

ON THE SECOND day of their journey south, dawn rose red. The Monks were probably still pursuing them. The rain had stopped during the night and now the ground had begun to steam. Their clothes were sodden, their horses exhausted and they needed to rest. Kosar found himself turning more unsettled, not less. Rafe was becoming a stranger to them all, and for the first time Kosar had begun to feel a particular, easily defined emotion toward the boy. Fear.

———

THE PREVIOUS EVENING, as they sheltered from the rain on the edge of a small woodland and tried to prepare a meal, A'Meer revealed what Kosar had already guessed: she wanted them to go to New Shanti. She stated her case as plainly and honestly as she could. It was her cause and aim to protect new magic should it arise; it was her duty to return to New Shanti to report its recurrence; and the safest place for all of them would be Hess. It was as far south as they could go without venturing into Kang Kang. They would be protected by Shantasi warriors, and Rafe's magic would have a chance to mature and reveal itself more in its own time. If the Mages returned to Noreela with an army, Hess was the best place for them all.

Hope objected vehemently. *Want it for yourself!* and *Can't trust a Shantasi*, and *Where do we go from there?* It did not descend into an argument—not quite—mainly because A'Meer was still so tired from her injuries. Hope's distrust simmered, but eventually the others discussed the matter and talked her around. Even Hope finally admitted that it was the only place to go. North to the Duke was madness, not only because it would send them against the pursuing Monks, but because the Duke no longer held power. He may well have the dregs of an army, but none of Rafe's protectors had any faith in a failed leader. Directly east was Ventgoria and eventually the Poison Forests; west took them closer to the Monk's Monastery, a place they did not need to be. And any way they went, the Mages could well be on their trail. *We can fight them*, Hope whispered, trying not to let Rafe hear. Sitting on his own at the edge of the forest, he was as distant as he had been all day. *We have magic!*

Fighting is exactly what they want, A'Meer said, and that silenced them all. None of them had seen the Cataclysmic War, but they all knew the stories. They had no wish to see its like in their time. And yet, the storms were gathering. Kosar felt more and more controlled, edged along a preordained path that none of them would have chosen. A descent toward pain and conflict seemed inevitable. Kosar was angry at Fate for entangling him in this, because at last he had begun to feel settled. Trengborne was a nothing village with nothing going for it, but it had started to feel like home.

Now here he was again, wandering the land, heading toward places he had not visited for decades, if at all. And though he was not wise or particularly learned, this journey felt more ill-fated than any he had ever undertaken.

That night, huddled beneath a blanket with A'Meer and enjoying their sharing of warmth, he had told her of his thoughts. She had not answered.

They slept without eating. Trey and Kosar gathered roots, fruits and some edible bark from within the woods, but upon returning to their makeshift camp and starting to prepare the produce, they found it to be rotten. Maggots crawled through the tuskfruit, themselves stinking of decay. The steady shifting of the trees, the soft low groaning of timbers grinding together in the breeze, took on new connotations. In Rafe, new magic slept, but old magic had turned the land sour.

———

"WE'LL BE AT the River San soon," Kosar said. He and A'Meer rode on ahead, sharing a horse now so that Hope could ride next to Rafe. Trey followed on behind, leading the horse with comatose Alishia tied into its saddle. Her mount kept staggering, blood dripping from its nostrils, and yet it plodded on. Kosar had some vague intention to steal another horse when they came to San, but something held him back from planning that far ahead. It was the next hour that mattered the most; if they made it past that, they could plan ahead another hour, and then another. At the end of their journey New Shanti may well be waiting, but they had to move one small step at a time.

"Have you ever been to San?" A'Meer asked.

Kosar nodded. "A long time ago. It was a river-fishing port then. Not much more than a village, but it'll have food we can buy, maybe a horse."

"We need to go around it, not through. Any trace of us in San will give the Red Monks a trail to follow."

Kosar thought about it, knew that she was right.

"And there's the river itself," A'Meer said. "It's wide and slow. We'll need to cross it somewhere. We use a bridge, we'll be seen. We use a ferry, we have to pay our way and the ferryman will see us."

"We could swim it," Kosar suggested.

A'Meer glanced behind them, looked across at Kosar and raised an eyebrow. "I could, even though I'm still weak. You could, even though you're an old man." He protested, and she smiled. "Hope I suspect is stronger than she looks, and Rafe I'm sure could make his way. Trey? Alishia? The horses?"

"We could go upstream. The river's narrower there in the foothills, easier to cross."

"And lose a day. Have you forgotten where this river leads?"

He frowned for a moment, and then shivered as if someone was staring at his back. He turned in his saddle and met Hope's eyes, offered her a smile and faced front again before being disappointed. "Lake Denyah," he said.

"The Monks' Monastery is there." A'Meer rode in silence for a couple of minutes, and Kosar could see her thinking. She frowned and her little nose creased at the bridge. He had kissed her there sometimes, when her face relaxed after sex. He surprised himself at his depth of mourning for older, gentler times.

"We have to assume that word has reached the Monastery," she said. "If they'd known at the Monastery much before now there would have been hundreds of Monks against us in Pavisse, not just a few. But at least one would have ridden south as the others tried to keep on our trail. There's a chance we've thrown them for now, but they saw me and they know where I'm from. They'll know for sure where I'll want to take Rafe."

"The Monastery must be two hundred miles from Pavisse," Kosar said. "There's no way one of them could have made that journey yet."

"They're not people, Kosar. They're obsessed. They're *powerful*. And do you think we'd be traveling this slowly if we didn't have to?"

Kosar glanced back again. Trey and Alishia had fallen behind, their horse struggling under the unconscious woman's weight, snorting, blood misting the air around its nose.

"What are you two plotting?" Hope said, spurring her horse to catch up to them. Kosar wanted to believe that there was a hint of humor in her voice, but her face said otherwise. Her tattoos were sharp and defined, displaying her intense concentration.

"We're plotting how to tumble you from your horse and bury you up to your neck in quicksand," A'Meer said.

Hope stared at the Shantasi, raising her eyebrows. "You and which army?"

Kosar could not help uttering a bark of a laugh. The fact that Hope did not berate him could have been a sign that she was relaxing . . . or perhaps she disregarded him totally. "We're debating how to cross the river," he said. "There are several bridges and a ferry, but we'd rather not be seen."

"Steal a boat."

"It would need to be a big boat for all of us," A'Meer said.

"Steal a ferry."

"And the ferryman?"

Hope shrugged. Kosar did not like the look in her eyes.

"We're no killers," he said quietly. A'Meer and Hope both looked at him, perhaps both doubting their own thoughts. There was an uncomfortable pause, during which Kosar was silently pleading, *Agree with me!*

"That's right," A'Meer said. She did not sound convincing, nor convinced.

"You think the Monks will be coming upriver?"

"Almost certainly."

They rode in silence for a while, the only sound the *clump clump* of horses' hooves on the stony surface. They had been walking across dead ground for an hour now, a place where life had been sucked from the soil. There were no birds, no animals, nothing to eat or be eaten. Here and there, weathered white bones protruded from the hard soil, leathery skin draped across them in defeat. Kosar craved greenery, and he breathed a sigh of relief when they crested a small hill and saw a long, sweeping panorama of grassland and trees heading down to the distant River San.

They paused for a while partway down the hill, giving the horses a chance to drink from a gurgling spring, drinking from their own water bottles. Kosar's throat was parched and scored by the dust of that dead place behind them, and he wondered if things would ever return to normal.

"There's San," he said, pointing into the distance. The village was a thin spread of buildings strung along the riverbank. From this far away it was little more than a smudge on the landscape, but he knew that there were quays in front of each building, small fishing boats tied to them, sprawled nets being repaired or untangled, the stench of fish permanently ingrained in the wood of the place. He had not spent any time there other than to eat and trade for some food, and that had been a long time ago, but he still remembered some of the people he had met. Hard people, their life filled and ruled by the fishing that kept them alive. Sometimes they would spend days traveling down the river, almost as far as Lake Denyah, and return home with nothing more than a few weedy slinks in their holds. Other times—rarer—they would haul in a full catch, and then the village would celebrate for a week. They lived day by day, bartering rather than selling their fish. They had seemed excited when he arrived, and pleased to see him go. Strangers had no place in San; they were just another mouth to feed.

"We need to go around," A'Meer said. "We'll go as far as those hillsides." She shielded her eyes against the sun and pointed east. "We can work our way around behind the hills, down into the valley, find some way to cross the river and then head south."

"Easy," Hope said. "Piece of piss."

"Easy," Kosar agreed. Hope glanced at him and raised one eyebrow. Her tattoos twitched into something that could well have been the beginnings of a smile. "And then the River Cleur to cross," he continued, "Cleur to bypass, then down to Mareton and into the Mol'Steria Desert, providing the Cataclysmic War hasn't changed the landscape beyond all recognition. I've heard of places this far south where the air is frozen into glass." They sat contemplating their journey, the horses splashed in the stream, he nodded. "Piece of piss."

"We should get Trey to do his thing," A'Meer said. "See if the way is clear."

"Every second we sit here brings us closer to being caught," Hope said. "We should move on, chance it. Even if he does look and see the plains between the rivers swarming with Monks, what choices do we have?"

"If that's the case, we could always head east through the Widow's Peaks," Kosar said.

"And meet Ventgoria's steam dragons? No thanks. I'll take my chances with a handful of Red Monks any day."

"How about a hundred?" A'Meer asked. She called Trey over, pointed out their route and nodded as he moved away and sat with his back against a rock. "He'll see what he can see," she said. "And we could all do with a rest. An hour to regain some strength. I'll try to catch some meat, though we'll have to eat it raw."

"No we won't," Hope said. "You catch us something decent and I'll make sure it's cooked before the fledger comes out of his trance. No fire. No smoke to give us away. You haven't tasted spiced sheebok until you've tasted mine."

A'Meer smiled at the witch, clapped Kosar on the shoulder and plucked her bow and quiver from her horse's saddle harness.

As Trey chewed on fledge and Hope sat with Rafe, Kosar stared down at San, the wide river running past the fishing village, and beyond. Way over the horizon lay the Mol'Steria Desert, and two hundred miles south of that was Kang Kang. Beyond that, places that few had ever seen and survived. Once past these rivers and little fishing villages, they truly were entering the wilds.

Air frozen into glass; ground stripped to its bedrock; places where the sky itself erupted into flame. He had heard many tales of how these lands were changing. He had never felt the need to see for himself.

SOMETHING WAS DIFFERENT. The fledge had become stale, perhaps, or maybe he had taken too much in too short a time. He chewed and it was rough, gritty, not smooth and sweet as it broke across his tongue.

For a few seconds Trey panicked. Soon he would have no fledge left at all, and then his final link to his underground life would be gone. He would only have his memories, and those were ruled by his terrible flight from below, his mother's final sacrifice and the fledge-fueled touch of a Nax as it awoke, raging. But then as he chewed he looked around him at the greenery of the landscape, the blue sky peering through the dispersing rain clouds, the glinting strip of the river in the distance, and the fledge found its way into his veins and his mind, ready to move him on.

He closed his eyes and slumped back against the rock. He did not need to sleep to travel with the fledge, but his body's natural re-action was to slip into a gentle slumber. He did not dream—he was still aware of the sounds around him, the breeze stirring the fine hairs on his face and arms, the weight of the mountains in the east—but his mind was buoyed by the drug and given a freedom, released by the first touch of fledge on his heart.

Things were still different. His mind soared but it did not see, not properly. It perceived the outlines of things, mere impressions as if shapes had been pressed into the receptive clay of his awareness. He rose, and as he looked back down he saw the hillside laid out be-low him, but not in detail. He could sense the cool tumble of the stream somewhere to his right, and below him were the blots of his companions like living rocks mired in the ground.

He dipped down again and touched on Alishia's mind, afraid of what he would find. As before, it was vast, and though he could not comprehend the scope of that mind, he could understand its empti-ness. He drifted, passing through places where Alishia should have been. They were cold, and deep. He moved on toward the single light in the darkness, where he had touched on her consciousness back in the cave. As he drew near he heard her muttering. *Yes, yes, there's plenty to see, plenty to know, and yes, yes, I want to.* He edged forward and touched on her mind. *What?* she said, startled. *Who? Has it gone, has it gone for good?*

Whatever harmed you has gone.

Harmed? Killed! It slaughtered me.

Who were you talking to?

Made me empty! Everything I was is in tatters.

Alishia, I'm here to help you. Trey edged himself forward, trying to sense just how much of the girl was left. This could have been madness, or an echo, or even the voice of her wraith, still connected to her dying body through disbelief and an unwillingness to let go.

There's no help to be had, she whispered, and then Trey felt a heavy darkness pressing in from all sides. Alishia did not withdraw; the darkness grew. And it pushed him out.

He was sent away, spinning, rolling through the distorted planes of awareness that the fledge had opened up. He steadied himself and drifted past Kosar, past the witch with her scheming stew of thoughts. The closer he came to Rafe, the clearer the boy's face became, until Trey's mind reached out and touched on something beyond comprehension. So much space in there. So many places to hide.

Reeling, Trey guided his mind across the hillside and down toward the village in the distance. He was glad to be away from Alishia and Rafe—such strangeness hurt him—and he saw the gray-blue of sky and the green smudge of the grasslands, and little else. His mind was soft and blurred. Small rocky outcroppings were lost. Clouds became shadows. Here and there living things passed by beneath him, and he was angry that he could not discern them more clearly.

Solidness suddenly disappeared beneath him and the ground was moving, flowing, carrying a million mixed sensations. The river. Trey followed its course, his knowledge of what was below him hazy at best. He passed by places where the river was interrupted, still blank areas like solid shadows compared to the fluid shades of the running water. He tried a mental blink to clear his vision but it was not sight that was affected, nor his ability to project himself. *Stale fledge,* he thought. *Growing staler.* This might be the last time he journeyed like this.

And then? What would the witch and the others do with him? Would they cast him aside with poor, flailing Alishia, submit them to the mercy of whatever place they happened to be at the time?

Trey dropped down closer to the river, and then sound and taste changed as he plunged in. The water around him was filled with life, so much more than the dead air above, and for a few seconds he reveled in its multitude. Still he could not truly see, touch, query the alien minds around him. But he was there with them, and for a while that was enough.

Then he rose again and moved quickly along the course of the river. He traveled in the wake of centuries, riding the ripples of the river's changes of position over time. It had worn rock here, deposited silt there, shaped the floodplain to its own design, twisting over the space of thousands of years like a giant snake shifting its way from the mountains to the distant sea. Histories lay buried in its silty bed—dipping in, Trey sensed the troubled wraiths of the crew of a sunken barge, already rotted to little more than memories but still haunting the place of their demise—and its banks held more recent stories in their embrace. A buried body here; the prow of a smashed boat there.

He moved on. His vision did not improve, his senses remained vague, but he found that with effort he could still identify what he was seeing and sensing. His own intelligence filled in the gaps.

And then the blood.

The river turned red. The color was a brash blow against the sepia view he had grown used to so quickly. He rose quickly from the bloody waters, trying to look away but fascinated by the wash of red traveling against the flow. He drew in his questing thoughts, afraid of being seen, trapped and pulled down . . . and then the red coalesced into individual parts, and each part was a boat. He drew closer, hiding behind a fold in the plane of reality, and tried to see more clearly.

Each boat was small, topped with a grimy sail, moving across the water like a giant spider, paddles splashing down and hauling them against the flow. They moved fast and the rowers did not tire. They were dressed in red from head to foot.

Trey pulled up and away, fleeing from the river lest he be seen or sensed. These things were powerful, awful and terrifying, but he was sure they could not see as far as him. If they could he would feel them . . . their senses crawling across his mind, engulfing it in their rage.

Mage shit, Trey thought as he shifted quickly back to his own body, *Mage shit, we don't want to meet them.*

"BOATS, FILLED WITH Red Monks," he said. Kosar and A'Meer frowned at him. Rafe sat a small distance away, watching him as he spoke, but saying and revealing nothing. His eyes—haunted and pained when they had first met—seemed to have settled into something stranger.

"How many boats?"

"Four or five," Trey said. "Maybe twenty Monks in each. So *inhuman*. Men and women, but not all there. Like they're stripped away to the bare bone, their souls . . . fractured. Flayed down to the basic. What *are* those things?"

"Things we don't want to meet," A'Meer said. "How far?"

Trey closed his eyes, trying to remember; not sure, but unwilling to reveal his uncertainty. *They need me*, he thought, *and I need them to need me*. "Not that close," he said. "Misted by the distance. It's difficult to judge; I'm not used to casting so far. Before a few days ago, I'd never been more than a couple of miles from home."

"Never mind," Kosar said. "At least—"

"*Think*," A'Meer hissed. "Give us a best guess! We can't leave it to chance. Kosar and I barely fought off just *one* of those red fucks. We meet up with a hundred of them, the first thing I do is fall on my own sword, I swear. We need to know, Trey. We need to know how much time we have."

He blinked at the short warrior woman. Her black hair was tied back from her pale face, her eyes were beautiful. She wore her weapon harnesses and sheaths like a second skin. He was not sure who scared him the most: the Red Monks, or A'Meer.

"Far enough," he said, looking past A'Meer and down at the river in the distance. "We've got time. They're moving quickly, but against the flow of the river. We have the horses."

A'Meer spun away. "We leave now."

"The rabbit you caught," Hope said. "I was about to spice it."

"Do it on the move," A'Meer said.

"Bad," Trey said. "I smell something bad about to happen."

"The river's not what we think," a voice said, and they all turned to Rafe. He had barely spoken since the night before, seemingly content to let them guide the way, steer him forward and take control. "It's much more temperamental than you imagine. It's just as likely that it will bring the Monks to us as we're crossing."

"Your magic tells you this?" Kosar asked.

Rafe looked at the big thief, and for a brief instant Trey saw something flash across the boy's face that made him look very old. Then he looked out across the plains. "It's not *my* magic, Kosar. And no, it doesn't tell me, it shows me." He closed his eyes, but they sprang open again. "Look. It shows us already."

As Trey turned to see what Rafe had seen, he heard Hope gasp: "You're doing that?"

"The land's doing it to itself," Rafe said. "It's all mixed up, it's balance is going awry, has been for decades. Air frozen to glass, Kosar? Sinkholes, Trey? The land is eating itself, and we arrived here at just the wrong time." He shook his head and looked down into his open hands, as if expecting to find himself holding something. "Whatever's in me, it might already be too late."

———

INSIDE, RAFE WAS in turmoil. Like the river across the plains, he was battling against himself, feeling the old Rafe—confused, frightened, wanting nothing more than the peace to mourn his dead parents—trying to ignore the strangeness growing within. He could see it, sense it, taste its power and its need for him to nurture and understand. But he did not *want* it. He willed it away with every breath he took, but like his heartbeat it was always there in the background, whispering to him however hard he tried not to hear.

Such spaces opening up. Such pressure, so precious. And yet this most powerful entity was still much like a baby, needing him, body and mind and soul, to protect it until revelation.

Now it screamed.

———

"WHAT IN THE name of all that's fucking magic?" Hope whispered.

"Maybe," Kosar said. "Maybe." He reached out to touch A'Meer and found her hand outstretched, waiting for his.

Even from far away they could heard the noise. It came in at them across the plains, rolling like thunder, vibrating through the ground, grasses shimmering in waves as if struck by a sudden wind. Downriver from San, three miles distant from them, the river was in revolt. It looked like a liquid eruption, an explosion of water and spray that rose hundreds of steps into the air, fanned out into a mushroom shape and fell, constantly fed from the tumultuous river. Spray was caught in the high breeze: white where the water was fresh, a dirty red where it had plucked clay from the riverbed, spiky green where trees and shrubs had been ripped out and thrown downstream by the upheaval. The river burst its banks and coursed out onto the floodplain, shoving vegetation before it, mud, other things too small to make out.

"What's happening?" Kosar said. Nobody answered because none of them knew.

The river flowing downstream past San continued to meet the watery explosion, feeding it like air feeds fire. Rainbows danced within the eruption's destructive depths, shimmering left and right as the contours of the water mountain changed and shifted. Two rainbows, three, flirting with the water like butterflies. But there was no ceremony here, no one to impress; this was basic, elemental force unleashed, a thrashing power that was whipping out its frenzy on the river surrounding the lowlands.

Downriver, away from the chaos, Kosar noticed that water still seemed to flow along the riverbed. He thought the flow would have lessened, such was the amount being pumped into the air and across the plains, but it seemed full and flush, turbulence transmitted from upstream causing white breakers to batter the shores as far as he could see. Trees downstream started to tilt into the river, their roots exposed and pulled into the mire. But they did not float away. Instead, they bobbed into each other, rising and falling on the disturbed waters but not seeming to move apart from that. Motionless, as if the river was now a lake with no current or flow.

Birds were startled into the air—a flock of geese gobbled their way overhead—and he could see the darting shapes of animals fleeing toward them to seek the high hills. Some were small and he had no concerns about them, but there were a few larger shapes bounding from hedge to bush to copse, instinct still telling them to utilize cover even though their lives may be about to end. *What are they?* Kosar wondered. They looked big. Most were probably cattle kept by the villagers of San, but maybe there were wolves in there, and perhaps a foxlion or two. His hand stole to his sword, but the sheer power of what they were witnessing soon wiped any threat from his mind.

This is the power of nature gone bad, he thought. And then he realized the truth and he knew that he was wrong. This was all-powerful, yes, but it was not nature, not as it should have been. Rivers in nature ran one way only.

"It's turning," he said to no one, but they all heard. "It's flowing the opposite way. It's like the land has tilted and the river's changing direction."

"It hurts," Rafe muttered, and then he screamed: "*It hurts!*"

Kosar turned and saw that the boy had gone to his knees. Hope was there to hold him, talk to him, but there was no comfort to be had.

"It's flooding the plains," A'Meer said.

The tumult in the river had lessened somewhat, but now a wave formed and began its journey back upstream. It growled by the banks, scouring them clear of vegetation, picking up boulders and rolling them along, and the roar was like the land screaming as it was cleaved in two. The wave was way beyond the normal confines of the river now, stretching out across the plains a mile wide and still growing. It rumbled, and the land before it cried as if knowing what was to come.

"San," he said, and he remembered the faces of some of the people he had met. They would be different now, mouths opened in terror and eyes wide, too shocked for tears.

"It won't take long," A'Meer said, as if that could make everything better.

There was a relentless inevitability about the wave. It rolled upstream and over the small village of San. From this far away Kosar could make out little detail of San's destruction, and for that he was glad. A few buildings broke upward, timbers thrusting at the sky, forced up by the deluge. Some of the fishing boats rode the wave for a few seconds before tumbling and being smashed into flotsam, still topping the wave but now in pieces. A couple of the jetties—their posts cast down into the riverbed years before the land had even heard of the Mages—rolled over and over, ripped out and were sent tumbling upstream away from the village.

Of the people from the village of San, he saw nothing.

As if San had been the true target of its upheaval, the wave seemed to spread out and diminish after it passed by. It left little behind. Vague outlines of some of the larger buildings remained, shorn of their roofs and walls collapsed outward. The landscape, the village, the route of the river itself had taken on a uniform graybrown color, silt coughed up from the bed now smothering everything. The water defied its previous confinement, settling into new shapes: lakes and ponds that bubbled and foamed from their unnatural and forceful births.

It took a few minutes for the waters to calm down.

Kosar and the others were silent but for Rafe's quiet crying. He shed no actual tears, Kosar saw, as if not wishing to add to the flood. There was little to say so they simply watched. A large rainbow hung over the scene of devastation, its colors too pure to be welcome. The air was filled with swathes of mist, and the watchers soon found its cool touch coalescing on their skin, bringing with it the smell and taste of the disaster.

Eventually the noise subsided, the mists parted and the river ran upstream.

———

RAFE CRIED ON the outside, and inside the magic still discovering itself howled. Like a sentient thing it mourned the death of its old existence, and though now resurrected it still felt the pain and betrayal at being misused by the Mages so many years ago. It mourned also the ongoing destruction their misuse had eventually caused. Rafe could not shut out the thoughts because he was not party to them; he was an observer—sympathetic, concerned and unequivocally entwined—but still separate from the power raging within. His fingertips prickled with its potential, his toes and other extremities warm and tingling with the force coursing through him. And in its blind rage and raging sorrow, he was not sure what he could see. Anger and hatred, hope and yearning, sorrow and vengefulness, he was not certain where the crying took root, nor what drove that fearsome energy he knew was building somewhere deep inside of him.

Rafe cried from the pain, the sorrow and the fear. But his tears were also for himself because he felt so hopeless.

He had no idea what would happen next.

———

"WELL, NOW IT'S more than a river to cross," A'Meer said quietly.

"We can ride up into the foothills," Kosar said. He turned to look at Rafe, thinking that perhaps the boy could help them. But Rafe barely looked as though he could help himself. "Cross the river at its source."

"Yes," A'Meer said. She was still staring down into the shallow valley, stunned.

"Not its source any longer," Trey said. "What do you think we'll find if we go up into the Widow's Peaks?" He stared at them, his thin face sad.

Kosar barked a bitter laugh. "We're stupid," he said to A'Meer.

He pointed at the river, uprooted trees floating slowly from right to left. "Upriver. We'll find only floods when we get there. How can a river flow the wrong way? For how long?"

"The water will gather in the hills and mountains, and within days or hours it'll come back this way again," Trey said. "Maybe within minutes."

"More than just a river then," Hope said. "It'll be a lake rushing down this way. A *sea*."

"It'll make this look like a splash in a pond." Trey waved his hand to encompass the scene before them, and Kosar knew that he was right. Whatever unnatural cause, however wrong this was, the river could only flow uphill for so long before its tremendous energy would be unleashed once again. And then it would return the way it had come, faster, a million times more deadly.

"But why . . . ?" Trey said, glancing down at Rafe as if expecting an answer.

"This is happening all over," Hope said. "It's the land wearing down and turning bad. Swallow holes, frozen air, flaming skies . . . and rivers running upstream. We're just here at the wrong time. Bad luck. There's plenty of bad luck in Noreela."

"But the magic is back, in him. Isn't it? Isn't that why we're all risking so much to protect him?"

"You're giving magic a character," Hope said. "It's so much more alive than us, so much more *meant to be*, but that doesn't mean it has thought. And why should it? Thinking like us, with our greed and avarice and disregard . . . that's what made the Mages what they are. That's why they did what they did, and magic tore itself from us after the Cataclysmic War. The effects of that are still being felt— we've just seen that—and we can only hope that if it *does* choose to return through Rafe, then it will make everything better again."

"Or much, much worse," Kosar said. The force he had just witnessed was nothing compared to what true magic could accomplish. The stories he had heard, the legends of machines spanning valleys, flying through the air, churning the ground . . .

"The Red Monks!" A'Meer said suddenly. "They may still be on the river, and now its flow is with them. We have to move! Now!"

Confused, shocked, they gathered their gear together, mounted the horses and started off down the hillside. Hope walked beside Rafe once more, and Trey guided the unconscious Alishia on her mount. As they reached the flatlands and the fringes of destruction,

Hope ran from horse to horse, giving the riders a torn shred of the rabbit A'Meer had killed before the river's upheaval. She had used some powder or potion to heat away its rawness, and although still cold, it tasted cooked and spiced.

Kosar chewed on the leg Hope had given him, not really enjoying the taste. There was too much on his mind, and since the idea had suggested itself to him a few minutes before . . . *perhaps the Monks are right* . . . he had been more confused than ever. Here they were racing across Noreela to deliver Rafe to New Shanti, this boy who seemed to have magic awakening within him, using him as a conduit into this world, testing the waters before revealing itself fully. And at the same time it was highly probable that were they still alive, the Mages would have heard about Rafe and perhaps seen what happened when he cured A'Meer. Alishia was evidence of that, the girl whose mind had been torn apart by some psychic invader before the thing fled back whence it had come. The Mages would covet him and this new magic. And if they caught him, snatched him from their grasp or waged war on Noreela to steal him away, magic may well be back in their hands.

And then?

Burning air or rivers running upstream would be the least terrible things. Last time, the Mages had practiced out of greed and lust for power. This time, were they to harness the magic, theirs would be a triumphant return from exile. If their armies were dead and gone to dust, they would make new ones. If their soldiers could not run fast enough, they would build machines. This time, revenge would be their prime motive.

. . . *perhaps the Monks are right* . . .

———

AT THE DIVIDING line between normality—long grasses wavering in the slight breeze, the ground dry and hard beneath them—and the watery transgression of the river's unnatural flood, the horses and travelers paused. Kosar and A'Meer's mounts stamped the ground and snorted, while the weaker horses carrying Rafe and Alishia merely stood with their heads bowed, foaming pinkly at the mouth.

Alishia mumbled something and twitched in the saddle.

Rafe frowned at the ground.

A'Meer headed off first. Her horse splashed its hooves through the first puddle of water, and sidestepped the corpse of a sheebok that had been burst open by some huge impact. Split timber planks were embedded in the mud. In raised areas the grass had been washed flat, most of its subsoil having been washed away, its blades doomed to dry and die in the sun. Other bodies lay scattered around: several chickens' feathers ruffled and coated with mud; a furbat, leathery wings spread as if trying to fly; a girl, braided hair twisted like ropes about her neck. Her eyes stared skyward, filled with its blue reflection, and there were no marks upon her body, no bloody patches on her white dress.

They tried to keep to the high ground. Kosar's horse stumbled once into a deeper puddle, the dip in the ground hidden by the murky water, and he had to twist and hold on tight to prevent being thrown. His mount panicked and struggled to regain its footing, kicking, legs churning the water, and a dead thing bobbed to the surface. It was a fish as big as a man, yellow and bloated. Even the river life had not escaped a violent death.

The sun bore down on the watery destruction and soon a fine mist rose, drifting slowly on the breeze and dancing where air currents were confused. They began to sweat in the balmy atmosphere, but Rafe seemed not to notice. He was looking down at his horse's hooves, watching the dead things they stepped over or around, hiding whatever he felt inside.

They came across a knot of bodies, seven or eight of them tangled together where they had been deposited against a huge rock. Unlike the drowned little girl, these all showed signs of the trauma they had been through. There were men and women, and a couple of corpses that were damaged beyond identification. No carrion picked at their tattered remains; no flies buzzed their opened, washed-out gray wounds. Perhaps it was because they had only just died and the things that fed on dead things had yet to discover them. Or perhaps those things did not wish to feast upon corpses created by nature's upheaval. There would always be plenty of dead things elsewhere.

The mist did not hide the horrific sights, but it made them hazy. In a way that was worse. Truths half hidden were dwelled upon endlessly, their realities filled in with imaginations overwrought by what was around them.

Rafe barely raised his head. If he had magic to cure the ills of the land, he did not show it now.

As they neared the river, higher areas of ground became less and less frequent. The floodwaters were deeper and more expansive, and eventually the landscape changed so that there was more water than land. The horses found it easy wading through the water at first, but Hope and Trey were soon struggling, and eventually they stopped and were hauled up, Hope behind Kosar, Trey behind A'Meer. The four horses continued on their way, the water sometimes touching their bellies.

As they drew closer to what was still, they supposed, the River San, they could make out more of what was left of the village. Its riverside areas had been totally torn away; piers, jetties and fishing sheds all gone, smashed up and spread across the plains along with those unfortunate enough to have been on or in them at the time. Farther inland, there was still little recognizable as part of a village. A stone wall here, a boat there, smashed in half, come to rest against a mound of stones that may have been the remains of a home. There was little evidence floating on the water—the ruins of the village had been washed along the river and distributed inland, floating and bobbing now around their horses' feet, wood and cloth and dead fish and dead people all that was left of San.

"We'll be at the old riverbank soon," Kosar said. He glanced down at where the water washed against the horses' thighs. "It'll be much deeper there. We'll need a boat, a ferry, something to get us across."

"There's nothing left," Hope said behind him.

"There has to be," A'Meer said. Whether she spoke with certainty or desperation was not clear.

"How far away can those Monks be?" Kosar asked. "Trey, they were in boats. Did they have horses?"

Trey, sitting behind A'Meer, frowned and shook his head. "No horses, I don't think," he said. "Just lots of Monks. Small boats, but fast. They were rowing, and sailing as well."

"So if they do reach us before we're across, we'll still have a chance," Kosar said. "We can run faster than them."

"Two of us on each of the good horses?" Hope asked. "And those back there . . . I traded them from farmers who could barely feed themselves, let alone their livestock. I'm surprised they're not dead already. Two minutes galloping and they'll collapse. We should swap . . . Rafe should have one of them, he's the important one."

"We're *all* important," A'Meer said.

"But he's the one we're trying to save," Hope said quietly, tattoos in turmoil.

"Whatever, we can't get much farther than this," A'Meer said. They came to a halt on a mound with its tree-lined head protruding slightly above the water. There was room to dismount and walk to the river's edge, look out across the wide expanse of muddied water at the opposite side, ambiguous in the mist, the true edge of the river indistinguishable from the flooded plain. The waters flowed from right to left, the results of its violent upheaval floating along with it. Trees and bushes, bodies and smashed timber-boarding and a few things still struggling to remain afloat, wings waving, legs kicking. It seemed the animals were stronger in a disaster such as this, because the only people they saw were dead.

"Shit, it's hot," Trey said. He had stripped to his trousers and boots, and Kosar saw the varied scars on his yellow skin, wounds from innumerable accidents belowground. He wondered what Hope looked like beneath her rough dress, whether the tattoos continued out of sight, forming their own secret designs. There was much secrecy about her, however open she claimed to be, and he feared that her shoulder bag held much they had not yet seen.

"Rafe?" Hope said. "Is there anything you can do for us?"

Rafe blinked as if she had spoken an unknown tongue.

"Rafe?"

"I'm only a farm boy," he said. He frowned as he spoke and leaned sideways in the saddle, splaying his fingers and touching this island of grass and trees. "This is good soil."

Hope shook her head, glanced at Kosar, looked across the river once more.

"I could swim it," A'Meer said. "Get over to what's left of San and see if there's a boat there, something left undamaged."

"And then?" Kosar said. "Will you paddle it against the flow for us? Dodge the trees that will hole the boat if they hit you?"

"What else do you suggest?"

"I don't know," he said, shaking his head. "We have to risk it with the horses, I suppose. It may be shallow enough most of the way for them to walk, and then they can swim when they have to. Horses are good swimmers. And—"

"We'll drown," Trey said. "And I can't swim. Not much need of it in the mines."

"He's right," A'Meer said. She kicked a stick, watched it tumble into the waters and drift up toward the Widow's Peaks. "We'll drown." She turned and looked at Rafe, silently asking him the question Hope had just posed.

He had dismounted and was down on his knees, not only running his fingers through the grasses now but digging them in, thrusting his fingers into the wet soil up to the knuckles, kneading it, pushing himself as close to the ground as he could. And he was whining, like a dog about to be whipped or missing its master, punishment or loss, both the sounds of heartache.

"Rafe?" A'Meer asked. He looked up at them. But his eyes were glazed, and in them they saw something much, much more than human.

———

HE SAW MAGIC across the land. The old magic, accepted and revered and honored many generations before the Mages had betrayed it. He saw the good it had done, the ease with which it was incorporated into lives, the benevolent power it exhaled. It demanded no sacrifice, homage or worship, but it honored the respect it engendered, and grew along with the world it served. Its energy was limitless, its boundaries without end. The people of the land translated its efficacy as far as their imagination allowed, and although there was much more—so much more—the magic did not provoke beliefs or understanding that the people were not able to comprehend. They used it to run the machines that turned soil in their fields, when it could have grown the crops themselves. They used it to provide succor to those dying from awful illnesses, when in fact it could have cured those illnesses with a touch. It fed fires when it could have made them, gathered building materials when it could have constructed the buildings themselves, carried messages across the land when it could have passed them at the speed of thought. The people used magic to serve them and entertain them and aid them in the way of life they chose, and even though it could have done so much more it was content with that. It was not a jealous god.

Rafe saw this and recognized the potential he carried, that growing knot of power that seemed so far down that it was deeper than his soul, more a part of him than his own personality, memories and thoughts, and yet totally alien. He fed it his wonder and it fed back a sense of calmness, confidence and security. He thought of where he had come from—rescued from out on the hillside, his parents had told him—and wondered who had left him, what they had known of his origins. He supposed he been destined for this, and though his bloodline was a mystery he did not concern himself with it. It was the here and now that mattered. That, and the love he would always feel for his parents, even though this fledgling magic had indirectly caused their deaths.

And yet beneath all of this, the magic was a child. That such power could labor under such vulnerability was a shock to Rafe. He had not taken time before to consider why it was inside him and nowhere else; he had not wondered at its secrecy; he had assumed that it was a seed, planted and waiting to germinate when the time was right. He had never guessed that it might be hiding.

He, a farm boy of mysterious beginnings, protected by a band of people who all had different reasons and motives, was this new magic's sole protector.

That made him sad. It exposed the true disorder of things, the random and unfeeling dangers of existence, and it was that more than anything that gave Rafe his first truly autonomous touch of magic. And when he fisted his hands around rich soil, he felt a surge of energy pulsing both ways: from him into the ground; and up out of the land, feeding him, trading itself for the small thing he had to do.

Healing A'Meer had been an example for his own benefit. Now, convinced at last, he began to take some control.

———

"THERE'S SOMETHING HAPPENING out there," Trey said. "I can't see . . . the mist . . ."

"Something in the water," Hope said.

Kosar watched Rafe squeeze both hands tightly around clots of mud and drive his fists into the ground. A'Meer glanced across and he nodded down at the boy, not saying a word. The Shantasi's eyes were wide and amazed.

The Monks are not *right*, Kosar thought. *No one has a right to destroy this.*

Out in the river the waters were boiling, sending spouts of spray and steam into the air. The river continued to flow but the disturbance remained in the same place, directly across from the small hillock where they stood watching. A huge tree, snapped by the force of its upheaval, flowed along the river and was nudged aside by the foaming water. The violence in the river began to lessen and something appeared at its center, a solid shape breaking the surface and turning over, like some leviathan touching sunlight for the first time, exposing a moss-encrusted underside as it balanced on end, turned and dropped down into the river with a huge splash.

A boat. It turned in the water, spinning in the current, and then began slipping sideways against the flow. The sound of water breaking against its hull was like a giant voiding a century's worth of flooded lungs.

Kosar looked at the boat, Rafe, A'Meer, back to the boat.

"Witchcraft," Hope muttered. And then she smiled, the tattoos on her face actually forming something beautiful.

As the boat nudged the hillock, Trey and Kosar ran down and grabbed its slimy hull.

"It's been down for a long time," Rafe said. He had dropped the handfuls of dirt and stood now next to the horses, his eyes serene and confident. "There are plenty of others down there—some just added—but this one was the most complete. No mast, no sails of course, no paddles. But it was swamped, not broken. The hull should be sound enough to get us across, at least." He looked suddenly tired, swaying slightly and holding a horse's reins to keep his balance. He glanced back at the ground, seeing something invisible there.

"How did you . . . ?" A'Meer said.

"That's all I can do for now." Rafe let go of the horse and knelt, lay down on his side, closed his eyes.

The four of them stood for a few silent seconds—Kosar and Trey holding the ragged old boat against the river's pull, Hope and A'Meer unmoving, amazed—and then Kosar shook the surprise from his mind.

"Hurry!" he said. "We can't hold this thing for long, and with him asleep . . ."

"Will it take the horses?" Hope asked.

Kosar shrugged. "We can try. The fit ones first, then we'll see if there's room for the other two."

They guided the first two horses over the lip and into the center of the boat, lifted Alishia and Rafe and placed them gently at the stern, then tried to urge the two weaker horses on board. They refused, and no amount of cajoling would convince them otherwise.

"Maybe they're so tired they'd rather just stay here and die," Trey said.

"Maybe they know what they'll face if they come with us," Hope replied. There was nothing else they could do, so they stripped the two horses of their gear, stowed it on deck and shoved off into the river. The horses watched them go.

The current grabbed them instantly, and swept the boat out into the center of the river. Its bow twisted around, streamlining it against the current, and they were soon moving past the remains of San.

They were moving too fast to stand and stare.

"We need to get over to the other side," Kosar said, standing on the bow, legs propped wide. He looked across at where the flood had burst through the banks. Less that a hundred steps would take them to safe ground.

"The river's got us," Trey said. "It's hungry. It'll carry us uphill until the back-surge sets in. The wave coming down will be ten times the one we just saw, twenty, a *hundred*."

"We won't be here when that happens," Kosar said.

"Oh? And how do you—"

"Stop whining and start thinking, that's how," Hope said. A'Meer raised her eyebrows at Kosar and glanced skyward—he was glad to see the humor there, it comforted him and saved him after the dreadful sights of the past hour—and then she started stamping at the deck.

"What the hell are you doing?" Trey shouted. The noise unsettled the two horses and they stamped their hooves in sympathy.

A plank of wood suddenly sprang free of rusted nails, and A'Meer caught it before it fell back. Hefting it in both hands, she walked to port and started rowing. "Paddle," she said.

Kosar, Trey and Hope prised planks from around the gap A'Meer had already created. Within two minutes they had lined up along the port side of the boat and started paddling, turning its nose slowly for shore. The current drove them on but was not strong enough to fight their combined effort, and gradually they came closer to where the old riverbank lay.

They found it with a crunch that almost tore the bottom from the boat. Kosar and Hope went sprawling, while Trey and A'Meer had to clutch at each other to keep their balance. The horses skidded across the wet timbers, snorting in fear, but A'Meer grabbed both sets of reins and talked in a low, calming voice, soothing them. As soon as the boat had grounded firmly A'Meer was over the side, up to her thighs in water and leading the horses out and away from the river. They tried to rear up in panic, but her soothing continued, and she kept eye contact with them as much as she could. They seemed calmed by that. Kosar smiled; he knew how they felt.

The water was trying to tug the boat back into the river—it seemed to be flowing even faster now, as if the waters were keen to force themselves up into the mountains—and Kosar did his best to keep it grounded while Trey and Hope heaved first Rafe and then Alishia out. They held them out of the water and struggled across to where A'Meer waited, and she helped them lift the two unconscious forms up onto the horses. Rafe stirred as they moved him, trying to aid them with weak attempts to pull himself up into the saddle. Alishia was like a corpse, only lighter.

Kosar let go of the boat and stepped back, allowing the river to grab the stern and twist it around the pivot of the grounded bow. Lighter now by six people and two horses, it was snatched from the shore and taken out into the stream. He went to A'Meer and took the reins of a horse from her, patting its nose when it seemed to object to its change of master.

"Let's go," A'Meer said. She was aiming for a spread of higher ground a few hundred steps inland, a place where trees still stood free of the flood and a few small animals milled, frightened and confused. Nobody disagreed with the Shantasi. As if successfully crossing the river had instilled a new sense of urgency, there was no petty arguing about which way to go or how to get there. They all knew that the Red Monks were on the river and heading their way, and now that they were on the other side the need to put distance between themselves and San was great. The Monks would expect them to be coming from the north. Now that they had crossed and could head south, it was just possible that they might fool them and have a clear run to New Shanti.

But Kosar knew just how vain this thought was. He had seen a Red Monk in action, and he knew how persistent they were, how committed. He and the others may well have crossed the flooded river, but there were still three hundred miles of wild terrain between them and Hess, including the Mol'Steria Desert. If the Monks had sent so many of their number upriver, there must be other complements traveling in from a different direction, spreading across the land, searching.

The two horses seemed strong, and they carried the prone forms of Rafe and Alishia with ease. A'Meer was tireless, even after the terrible wounds and infections of the past couple of days; perhaps Rafe's magical touch had done more than cure her. Trey seemed distant, never keen to meet Kosar's eye. Hope stayed as close to Rafe's horse as possible, reaching out now and again to touch him, looking around at the others with barely concealed suspicion. Kosar worried about her. It seemed that she was constantly there, awaiting any dregs of magic that Rafe might throw off, ready to take them into herself. In her eyes, below the suspicion, there lay a deep-rooted madness.

Kosar no longer wondered just how he had come to be mixed up in this. He pushed through the water with the others, sometimes slipping and going beneath the muddy surface, shivering at its coolness, trying not to see the dead things bobbing all around. More and more his eyes strayed to Rafe. More and more he believed that the future of Noreela lay on the back of this stolen horse.

HOPE WALKED ALONGSIDE Rafe, reaching out every now and then to touch him and make sure he was still real. He had long been in her dreams; she was afraid that he would vanish.

So the Shantasi was taking them to her people. Much as Hope hated that idea, she knew it to be the only logical one. The Shantasi were mysterious and powerful, a race apart in Noreela, and if anyone could protect and nurture this new magic, they could.

But once there, the boy would be gone. What would they want with an old witch? They would likely cast her out into the Mol'Steria Desert.

So she walked, her mind in turmoil and her allegiance only to herself. She was terrified of Rafe. She loved Rafe. Perhaps when her mind settled, she could decide her own best course of action.

LATER THAT DAY, when they had cleared the farthest extremes of the flood and were traveling as fast as they could toward the River Cleur, they heard a great roar from back the way they had come. The River San had piled itself into the mountains over the preceding few hours, and now the flooded valleys, lakes and underground reservoirs let go in one powerful surge.

The ground shook. Looking back, they found their view occluded by great gray clouds, but they felt the power of the tidal wave scouring across the land, destroying any trace of their passing. Hopefully wiping out the Red Monks on the river too. Even they would surely not survive such a monstrous release of energy.

"I only hope that sweeps all the way across Lake Denyah," A'Meer said. "Although I suspect the Monks' Monastery is empty now."

Rafe twitched in unconsciousness and whined, and his horse stamped its feet and shook its head, as if hearing something unthinkable in the sound.

———

RAFE WAS AFLOAT in his own mind, unconscious of the outside, barely aware of himself. Fleeting memories came by, images of his parents and his time in Trengborne, and stronger images from the past few days. But behind all these loomed that great dark place, countless and limitless and endless, overshadowing everything with its promise and threat. When the river revolted, this dark place had screamed out, raging at the wrongness of things, and the scream had all but driven Rafe out of his mind. And like a parent giving its child a gift to apologize for some unconscious rage, Rafe had been allowed a bleed of magic to draw the old boat from the silty riverbed, guide it to shore, effect their escape. Even magic was possessed of a survival instinct.

Rafe was a speck in the multitude of existences he imagined. He floated through them like a small fish drifting in an endless, sunless sea, seeing evidence everywhere that the sea itself was alive and exuding power. Each sign was something different: a light; a speck darker than night; a song; a breeze in an autumn forest; a centipede three feet long. Countless images with countless meanings, and each of them whispered to him in a language he was beginning to understand. They babbled like children and hinted at knowledge older than time. There was a pent-up excitement and a wise concern in the voices; excitement at what was coming, concern at what had been. This was magic growing again, simmering and wallowing in its infinite womb, ready to reveal itself when the time was finally right.

But already the threats were great.

The things Rafe passed continued to babble but they issued warnings now, sounds that faded as they drifted to another part of his mind, or he drifted away. Heat behind him, acidic burning before him, and the only place that felt safe was somewhere far away, a land of madness and dangers that Noreelans had all but forgotten.

The voices whispered and cajoled, guiding Rafe, giving him the words to mutter as soon as he came out of his sleep. But his fatigue was great and he slept on, drifting through his own mind and wondering at the greatness it contained.

Chapter 23

ELDRISS MAHAY WAS not having a good time. Yesterday a foxlion had taken three of his sheebok, one after the other. Eldriss had been asleep at the time, huddled under a couple of pelts in a copse of trees. His flock were grazing on the plain, trying to fatten themselves on grass gone weak and pale over the past few years, fading, just as Eldriss had felt himself slowly fading. Age was doing it to him, and apathy as well, a continuing and growing belief that there really was no point to anything. Sleep was a retreat he sought more often than ever. Invariably when he woke up his flock was together, just where they had been when he drifted off, and it would only take an hour to gather them in for the night. Ironically, that would make him feel even more superfluous.

And then he had begun to feel ill. It came suddenly, a thump to his gut and a thud in his head, a swimming of vision and a retreat of his hearing. He had doubled up in pain and fallen to his knees, some of his sheebok glancing up listlessly, and he crawled through the long grass to the shaded shelter of the trees.

He had remained there for some time, and when he came

around he felt like a stranger. The way he reacted to things was different: the heat of the sun on his skin; the shape of the sheebok; the feel of his flaccid tool as he took a piss. Everything had changed, and yet everything remained the same. It was his *perception* that had altered. The grass was still pale green, but it provoked subtly changed emotions. The trees he sheltered beneath were the same size, yet the height made him stretch that much more to view them. And when he thought of his family and friends in Cleur, it was with an interest that he had not felt for a long time.

He had heard the foxlion stalk in and steal the sheebok. The first one taken was almost silent, only the dull muttering of the rest of the flock giving any sign, and with his eyes closed Eldriss had felt something stretch out in his mind to test the animal's pain. The foxlion had returned soon after and chased another sheebok, the flock parting around the pursuit like dead leaves scattered by the hunter's feet, and at the point of capture Eldriss had felt himself lessen, caught and pulled down, as some other consciousness used his senses to observe the kill. By the time the predator took the third of his animals, Eldriss thought he was dead.

Yet he stood and moved and finally walked out from the shelter of the trees to survey the damage. There was little blood, a few scraps of wool and one whole leg, chewed off and left as a defiant sign of the foxlion's intrusion.

Eldriss should have chased it and put a bolt in its skull, but he was barely able to hold his own weight. And yet he stood and was strong.

Something else had him.

Today, with Eldriss still trying to come to terms with these contradicting sensations—greater awareness, numbing concealment—the river had been sucked away. One hour the Cleur flowed full and steady, passing by to the north. The next—and with a sudden rushing sound that had floored birds with its intensity and driven his remaining sheebok running for cover behind rocks and trees—the water had rapidly increased its rate of flow. The banks had started to disintegrate, trees and bushes pulled in, and over the space of a few minutes the violent waters had decreased to a bare trickle.

Eldriss was terrified, but the new, greater part of him was fascinated as well. With new eyes he had viewed the riverbed, already drying in the sun, totally featureless where the rapidly flowing waters had abraded it smooth.

He lingered, but the river did not return.

Back with his sheebok, Eldriss sat beneath the trees and waited. The urge to experience scorched his mind, but his duty ensured that he did not run wild. And not his duty to the sheebok—he barely saw them now, had almost forgotten that they existed—but the obligation he felt to . . . to . . . his god.

His god.

His god would reward him well if he took her news.

So he waited and watched, comfortable in the knowledge that he would know when there was something to tell.

———

THAT SOMETHING ARRIVED at sunset.

Rafe, a voice whispered in his mind, *Rafe Baburn.*

There were four of them walking, two more on horses, both seemingly unconscious or dead. They came toward the copse of trees, and perhaps they had not even seen him yet. He remained still, leaning casually against a trunk, arms crossed.

The woman in the lead was short, small and heavily armed. Her face was pale, even in the pink sunset, and her eyes scanned ahead, worried, constantly looking for danger. Her gaze passed across Eldriss without pause. The shadows of the trees hid him well.

There was a big man walking next to her, leading one of the horses. He looked quite old, but fit and lean. He also seemed tired. His clothes were streaked with dried mud, and he held his free hand slightly from his body as if in pain.

When they were a hundred steps from the trees they paused. The short woman muttered something and then came on alone, one hand resting on the hilt of a short sword.

Eldriss stepped out of the shadows.

Rafe, he heard, but it was echoing inside. *His name is Rafe.*

The woman stopped, surprised, and Eldriss raised a hand in a casual wave. "Hello!" he said. "Beautiful evening!" Two sheebok strolled before him and he patted them as he walked by. They stared up at him, and Eldriss knew that they did not recognize him. They were too stupid to show it.

"Stop there," the woman said, and when he looked up Eldriss saw that she had unshouldered her bow. No arrow notched yet, none drawn from her quiver, but her expression showed that she meant what she said.

He stopped. "No need for nastiness," he said, and deep inside where Eldriss was fighting to surface he was pleased, for a moment, that he had slipped some real feeling into that comment.

"Have you seen Red Monks?" the woman asked.

And the thing that had Eldriss knew straightaway. *Red Monks! They fear the Monks because they are hunted by them, and they are hunted by them because . . .*

"You have Rafe?" he asked.

The woman's eyes opened fractionally, surprise catching and reflecting the sunset.

That was enough for the shade. It pulled away, withdrawing its myriad psychic tendrils with no subtlety, no pretense at caution, and the pain was worse because Eldriss could not scream.

The woman was moving quickly now, squatting down, arm whipping around, her hand holding the bow rising into position.

The shade was free but it thrashed in Eldriss' mind, wrecking, tearing, giving the shepherd only agony for the final second of his life. It ripped away and left the world as the arrow flew, striking the man's right eye and punching a hole through the back of his skull.

Free, alone, stunned by the sudden lack of input, the shade reeled for an instant in an infinity of nothing. But it had been given taste and thought and sensation, and soon the idea of reward ordered its mind. It stopped tumbling and started to flow, passing through and over the world toward where its god waited patiently in the dark.

Rafe, it shouted, *I saw Rafe.*

My good shade, a voice said before an instant of time had passed, *come to me.*

The shade told what it knew and reveled in its god's praise.

———

KOSAR RAN TO A'Meer's side, drawing his sword. The Shantasi had notched another arrow and now she waited, scanning the copse of trees. "I think he was alone," she said.

"You killed him!" Kosar said. "He only said hello."

"He asked if we had Rafe."

Kosar shook his head. A'Meer's impatience was obvious, yet she did not shift her gaze from the trees and the dead man before them.

"How would he know?" she said. "A shade was in him, just as Alishia had one when we first met. The Mages must have sent out thousands, and they're waiting for us."

"But they could be everywhere!"

"They will be. Anywhere and everywhere. Anyone we meet may have one watching for us. Wherever we go, we have to assume the Mages know of our whereabouts."

"What is it?" Trey said, coming up behind them.

Kosar told him, and Hope heard as well.

"So now we have Red Monks chasing us, and the Mages searching for us as well," Hope said. "Well, things could be worse. I have no idea how, but I'm sure they could be."

"One good thing," Trey said, "they aren't after the same thing."

"And that helps us how?" Hope said. "The Monks want to destroy Rafe before the magic can reveal itself. The Mages want to steal the magic away and make it their own. And between the Monks and Mages and Rafe? Us!"

"At least they won't join forces is what I mean," Trey said weakly.

"Well, we can't stay here," Kosar said. "We have to keep moving."

"We need to rest," Hope said. "So the Mages may know exactly where we are . . . it's not as if they'll run down from the Widow's Peaks to take us. They're an eternity away from here, not even in Noreela. We're within a few days of New Shanti, and by the time we get there—"

"By the time we get there Noreela may have changed forever," A'Meer said. She lowered her bow and approached the dead man, nudging him slightly with her foot. She looked up again, sad. "There's no saying where the Mages are," she said. "Perhaps they've already landed their armies on The Spine. They may even be in Noreela themselves. A war might have begun, and there's no way we could know."

"So," said Kosar, "we have to keep moving. There's no time to rest. We owe it to Rafe to travel day and night until we reach New Shanti, then at least there's a chance whatever he has will be given time to emerge."

"Why can't the magic help us?" Trey said. "Fly us there, move us quickly, destroy the Monks or the Mages before they catch us?"

"Magic does not aim itself," Hope said. "What the Mages did last time is testament to that. It's the most powerful force there is, but it's weak in many ways. It makes no allowance for morality. It's in Rafe now, which probably means it wants to present itself to the land again, make itself available to humanity for a second time. But the Mages will do the same again if they catch Rafe: steal it away, twist it to their own means, drive it out once more. And this time they'll be aware of the results of their actions . . . and they'll be ready. Before magic pulls itself away for the second and last time, they'll have everything they want. Power. Control. Revenge."

There was silence for a while, and then Trey spoke up. "You offer a wonderful image."

Hope shrugged, walked back to Rafe's horse and checked on him. "Saying what I think," she said. "This boy here . . . he's the future. Life and prosperity for Noreela, or death and pain. All or nothing. It's the end of an era right now, and we straddle the moment of change."

"So we keep moving," Kosar said again, glancing at A'Meer for support. The Shantasi was still looking down at the dead man.

"He was only a shepherd."

"You had to do it," Kosar said.

"It probably didn't make a difference. I saw his eyes when he died—he went from arrogant to afraid the second I let the arrow fly—and when he died, he was only a shepherd."

"The shade had already left?"

A'Meer looked up at Trey. "We may be doing a lot more killing before we get where we're going," she said, her voice strong and sad.

Kosar offered her an encouraging smile but she turned away, walked past the body and approached the copse of trees. "I'll see if he had anything useful," she said. "Most shepherds carry weapons. We'll need them."

They milled around the body for a few minutes, all of them doing their best to avoid looking. The sun fell below the horizon and the corpse became more shadowed, melding in with the dark ground as if already rotting away. A'Meer found a crossbow and several bolts hidden away between the trees, and a skin of fresh water. No food, no clothing, nothing that indicated that this was any more than a temporary resting place for the dead man.

After dragging the body into the trees they headed off again in the dark. Their way was lit by the shared light of the moons; the life moon fading, the death moon full. Kosar and A'Meer walked together.

"You're quiet," Kosar said.

A'Meer made a sound somewhere between a laugh and a snort. "I just killed an innocent man, Kosar. I'm a Shantasi warrior, not a murderer."

"He wasn't innocent when you killed him. There was some part of him that threatened us. You did what you had to do, that's all."

"That's all?" she said, but her mocking tone was tempered by the dark.

A shower of shooting stars lit up the sky, spearing across the heavens and burning out before they reached the horizon. Trey gasped, Hope muttered some old spell, and Kosar and A'Meer touched hands briefly. Kosar reveled in the contact.

"Once, just before I left Hess, a falling star struck New Shanti and killed thousands," A'Meer said. "Some claimed it was because magic had gone and was no longer protecting the land; the Mystics said it was our ancestors, angry at us for not doing more to reclaim magic."

"They're the souls of the dead," Trey muttered in wonder. "As they go into the Black, so they fall from the sky."

Kosar sighed. "They're just falling stars," he said. "Flames in the heavens that burn out quickly. Nothing lasts forever, and you don't need to find an omen in everything."

"Everything happens for a reason," Hope said. She was looking at Rafe, not up into the sky.

A'Meer seemed not to have heard anyone. "My people will be looking skyward, hundreds of miles from here, wondering what it is they're doing wrong. Our distant ancestors managed to find the truly enlightened path, and they were . . . not as lucky as we are now. They were used and abused, yet they attained spiritual perfection. We've lost that. Almost as if pain and suffering help a soul reach such planes of understanding."

Kosar did not understand. This was A'Meer's moment, not his. The idea that he could help her by listening to her woes comforted him and made him feel special.

"The Guiders will be gathering in the halls at Hess, poring over their old texts and trying to see the significance of the shooting stars tonight, the direction, the number. They'll be agonizing over the inner workings of New Shanti, wondering whether the enlightened path all Shantasi seek has veered from the True, arguing amongst themselves like a flock of birds fighting over a scrap of food." She smiled, and her expression was almost wistful. "Such minor concerns," she said. "Such petty worries when the real fate of things rides on the horse behind us.

"But maybe a few will ascribe those stars to magic. Perhaps one or two of the Guiders will try to ally their appearance with something else, some other sign, and read Truth in them. I wonder what a Guider on fledge could see?"

A'Meer fell quiet, but the silence between them was not comfortable. It was waiting to be broken.

"How long is it since you've been to Hess?" Kosar asked.

"Seventy years," she said. "And now I return with the news my people have been awaiting for so long."

"Can they help us?" Kosar asked. "Will they hide us, protect us? Can they hold off the Red Monks, the Mages?"

A'Meer glanced at him, and in the moonlight her skin was even paler than ever. He did not like the smile on her lips. "You've seen how a Red Monk fights," she said. "Given magic, the Mages will be like tumblers to the Monks' ants. There are thousands more like me in New Shanti, trained to fight specifically to defend magic should it arise. We're a very spiritual people, we were never meant to fight; look at me, my build, how small and weak I look. Perhaps that's why we make such good warriors: we're not made, we make ourselves. And to answer your questions, yes, we can defeat the Red Monks. But the Mages . . . if they catch Rafe before New Shanti can protect and hide him away . . . they'll push us into the sea, just as was done to them at the end of the Cataclysmic War."

"I'm just a thief," Kosar muttered.

"And Rafe's just a farm boy!" A'Meer snapped. "That doesn't mean he shouldn't be special."

"And I am?" Kosar whispered. "Tell me, how am I special? I can barely hold a sword straight because of these fingers, and I have no idea about any of this. The witch knows more than me, and I trust her about as much as I would a Violet Dog."

"You're special to me," A'Meer said.

Kosar was shocked into silence. It was the first true indication she had given since their last night in Pavisse that she had any of her old feelings left for him. She had become a stranger over the past few days, and although there had still been an aura of friendship he had thought her affections lost, shattered by her admission of who she was, killed by the enormity of events surrounding them and steering them on.

They walked on into the night, not knowing what waited ahead of them, nor what followed behind.

———

WHEN MORNING BROKE and cast its cleansing light across the grasslands, Rafe woke up and said that he wanted to go to Kang Kang.

Chapter 24

LENORA LED THE Mages' advance force across the Bay of Cantrassa and approached the mainland of Noreela. They flew low. Their objective was to secure a landing area at Conbarma for the Krote army following on in ships, and as such one of their main aims was to preserve the element of surprise. She knew that there would be a fight once they alighted on Noreelan soil, but it had to be contained, a skirmish rather than a battle. Their landing had to be kept secret for as long as possible.

Lenora had listened for her daughter's shade. There were hints and flushes of presence, but she could not be certain that these were not manufactured in her own mind. *There you are!* the shade said, and *Way away, so far away,* and *See me hear me find me.* But these words made little sense, and Lenora found no comfort in them at all. If anything, they disturbed her more than she could have imagined. If they were the words of her unborn daughter's shade, then there was no warmth or sense of belonging there for her. And if it was not the potential of her dead child's voice, then Lenora was mad. So she listened, doing her best to keep her watchfulness subdued; it was the

Mages' bidding she was here to oversee. Her own aims—her own lust for revenge—had to remain at the back of her mind. For now. But there would come a time . . .

The huge hawks were tired almost to the point of death. They had lost some over the Bay, rescuing the Krote riders whenever possible, and now their force was reduced to around eighty hawks and ninety warriors. The hawks were almost finished, but the Krotes, tired and hungry though they were, perked up at the first sign of land. They knew that there was a fight ahead, and fighting was their life.

Seaweed bobbed on the waves below them, and a few scraps of wood from some wreck, and then their shadows touched a small flock of birds that could have only originated on land. The Krotes called to one another, laughing, singing, making warlike melodies with the metallic impact of sword on knife, stabbing at the failing hawks to add their wounded voices to the song. The horizon concealed land, but they knew it was not far away. After so long in the air these warriors were more than ready to feel firm ground beneath their feet, and enemy flesh around their blades.

They came across a small fleet of fishing boats, and their howls froze the fishermen and women where they stood. Lenora sent five hawks down. The Krotes let loose arrows and poisoned stars, and bodies splashed into the water. A few halfhearted arrows met them on their second approach, but it only took two more passes to ensure that everyone on the boats was dead. Their blood up, the Krotes turned the hawks landward once again. Behind them the fishing boats bobbed with the current, their contents soon to rot in the sun.

Conbarma was a fishing village with a huge natural harbor. It had a massive capacity for ships of all sizes, the docking mole had been built and extended over the last thousand years, and it had long been decided by the Mages that this would be the ideal point for invasion. Mage spies had drawn maps of the land beyond the village; it was relatively level, the buildings low and well spaced out, and the village itself was peopled by fisher folk and a few dozen lethargic militia.

Lenora ordered the hawks in low. The Krotes were not expecting any significant resistance, yet they executed a perfect attack. To fail here would be to leave the Mages' fleet, and their soldiers, open to attack as soon as they touched Noreelan soil.

The great creatures were seen over a mile out. As they drew

nearer, Lenora heard shouts of panic from the village and saw people running through the streets. She veered her hawk away from the initial hail of arrows and bolts, and then she gave the order to return fire. The invaders let loose with their own crossbows and the air was thick with screams of the dying. Several hawks circled back and landed at the harbor, disgorging Krote warriors, who immediately went into battle, screeching in delight as their swords found flesh and bone.

Most of the hawks could barely move from where they had landed, such was their exhaustion, and they became targets of the villagers' fury and terror. One was trapped in a net and hauled into the sea to drown; another had its limbs and tentacles hacked off until it bled to death, whining pitifully for its master to come and save it. But the warrior it had carried into the fray was already streets away, busy with his killing.

Lenora and the remaining hawks flew over the village, circling to disgorge perfectly aimed bolts and arrows before flying on. They passed the outskirts of Conbarma and kept going over the low hills and shallow valleys, until there were no signs of habitation below. They spread out, flying left and right and curving back toward the coast, forming a wide perimeter.

They landed. Solid ground felt good beneath Lenora's feet, and she staggered slightly as she found her land legs. It did not take long. *You feel so strong,* a voice said in her mind, but perhaps she had thought, *I feel so strong.* "Yes," she said, agreeing, whatever the case. "Strong, and ready for a fight." She called to those Krotes to her left and right. "This is just the beginning! Weeks of this to come. Weeks!" They cheered and raised their unsheathed swords. *And then,* Lenora thought, *I can fly on to fight my own battle.*

Your own battle, the shade in her mind echoed. And Lenora decided then that, whether it was her daughter's shade or her own mad voice, she would listen to it until the end.

Lenora and the dismounted Krotes waited in a curve around the village's outskirts, counting the seconds and minutes until they were sure that their comrades would have completed the entrapment. It was peaceful this far inland—no screams or sounds of fighting reached them from the harbor—and Lenora listened to the sounds of nature. Birds sung in a nearby swatch of bushes. Gulls cried overhead, and a moor hawk circled way up high, spying on these new invaders without fear. Her warriors had fallen silent, and she thought perhaps they too were listening to these new, pure sounds. Back on Dana'Man there was little wildlife, and what did exist was unpleasant and often dangerous. The normal noises back there were cracks and groans as the glacier rumbled its timeless way seaward, and the solitary cries of the snow wraiths they had never, ever seen in three hundred years.

Now, on Noreela, it felt as though they were in the real world at last.

At Lenora's call the Krotes checked their weapons and hefted extra arrows, bolts, throwing stars and other killing tools from the saddle bags on their exhausted mounts. The fishing village was hidden by a few low hills and some sparse woodland, but now the signs of battle were beginning to show. A smudge of smoke rose into the sky, and as the battle intensified, so the first sounds of clashing metal and dying screams reached them. The stench of smoke and burning flesh drifted inland, carried by gentle sea breezes to those eager to join in.

"They're playing our tune!" Lenora called. "Let's not disappoint." The Krotes encircling the village commenced their march. The noose began to tighten.

Only a minute later Lenora saw the first of the fleeing villagers. Several men and women on horses came around a curve in the road ahead. Most of them did not see the arrows that killed them, nor the Krote warriors that fired them. One rider rolled into the ditch and stood, drawing his sword and staring wide-eyed at the Krote woman bearing down on him. Lenora acknowledged his bravery, at least.

You feel so real! a voice said in her head, and she smiled and agreed as one of the dead villager's horses ran at her. She stepped aside and sliced the animal's throat. *So real!*

The warriors broke into a run, the smell of blood and battle too much to ignore. The circle would be closing, and villagers fleeing the slaughter of Conbarma ran into the killers out in the countryside. Lenora saw a few fight bravely, willingly taking on the Krotes for the sake of their families, but no fights lasted for long. These were fishing folk, not warriors, and any sword skills they possessed came of a sport or hobby rather than a way of life.

For the Krotes—born, living and dying as warriors—these were the enemy. Their hatred of Noreelans was drummed in from birth. It was easy for them.

Families were put to the sword. Women, children, babies . . .

none could be left alive to provide warning of the attack. Any survivor would flee inland, spreading news and providing advance warning of the invasion to come. And although Lenora knew that the forthcoming invasion would likely go in their favor *whatever* preparations Noreela could muster, the Mages' wishes were that the incursion should be quick and final. After no more than a week of fighting, they wanted Noreela City.

It did not take long for the tightening noose to close around the outskirts of Conbarma. When Lenora saw several of her warriors rushing out of the village in pursuit of fleeing residents, she knew that the fight was almost at an end. They had landed little more than an hour before. Most of the remaining villagers were trapped between those that had landed at the harbor and those moving in from outside, and in a mistaken belief in the idea of mercy, some of them surrendered. The Krotes—bloodied, raving, their pale skins flushed with the excesses of the hour—herded the people into a small vegetable garden and slaughtered them. The screams were of anger as much as pain. Lenora watched, and she felt nothing. After the slaughter she waded into the garden, reveling in the warm wash of blood across her sandaled feet. She drew a knife as long as her forearm, and a woman feigning death screamed as she cut her throat.

My daughter could have screamed like that had she been born, she thought. *She could have fished or hunted, run and fucked. She could have breathed.* She watched the woman's final breath bubble from her slashed throat, and a voice said, *So real!*

She sent a dozen warriors back to bring in the hawks they had left around the village, or to destroy them should they already have died. A dozen more took up station at the village outskirts, watching for anyone who may be in hiding, awaiting a chance to flee. There would be no survivors.

The invaders remaining in Conbarma began a house-to-house search for survivors, killing them instantly when any were found. No amount of pleading, begging or offering did any good; the soldiers had their orders, and the mission was on the verge of complete success. Lenora was delighted, but celebration would come later. Later too, they would be able to take their spoils of war, from villages and towns and eventually Noreela City itself: the wealth of gold and jewels; the power over those that they captured and put into slavery; the drugs rhellim and fledge, able to sculpt their users' minds and guide their desires.

The sounds of killing still echoed through the village.

The final part of the battle was more protracted than she had hoped for, and harder won. The few surviving militia had quickly retreated to the Conbarma moon temple, barricaded themselves inside and prepared for siege. There were maybe a dozen men and women in the building, and although the Krotes were comfortable with the fact that they could not escape and give warning, they wanted the remaining villagers dead. There was work to do, preparations to make for the army's landing, and inconveniences such as this were troublesome. The Krotes attacked, and the besieged militia fought back with the ferocity of those knowing they were doomed.

The temple was a small building with small windows, and this aided those inside. They fired their arrows, and attacking Krotes fell with steel and wood ripping their flesh. Those that could tried to crawl back into cover, but they were shown as much mercy as they had themselves displayed. Krotes took up positions in buildings around the temple, letting their skill as bowmen come to the fore as they put arrows into gaps little wider than their forearms. The exchange continued, and while the Krotes had to send some of their number away to restock their quivers, those inside were being given an unending supply of ammunition. Soon, Krotes began to fall by their own poisoned arrows. The toll inside the temple could not be counted, and yet slowly, inexorably, the rate of fire from within dwindled.

After two hours of this continuous exchange Lenora ordered a change of tactics. They took the battle to the doors of the temple. Six Krotes carried a long boat from the harbor to use as a battering ram, running at the door under covering fire from their comrades. But the building was old and sturdy, dating from centuries before Krotes had last been driven from these shores, and the oak and iron door withheld the assault long enough for the attackers to be shot down or sent away to die with arrows in their flesh.

The besieged cheered and mocked their attackers, their bravado all the more frustrating because of their untenable position. Those inside the temple could never win. And though frustrated, Lenora and her warriors could not help but feel a grudging respect for these last few defenders.

They have their lives, and they revel in them, she thought. *Until the last, they relish existence.* She listened for the voice of her daughter, but the darkness inside her mind was silent. She thought that perhaps she really was mad. She was over three hundred years old, and whatever Angel had given her on the deck of that burning ship as they fled Noreela had been to preserve her for this very moment, this era in time. She was fulfilling the meaning of her life. She hoped she made her baby proud.

Bodies began to pile up. A dozen Krotes had died at the temple, their blood blackening the dust. The village stank of the dead, and half a day after the hawks had drifted in from the sea fresh blood was still being drawn.

Lenora ordered her warriors back, leaving a handful to badger the defenders. The rest set about preparing the village for the main army's arrival. Boats were floated out beyond the harbor, taken a little way along the coast and then scuppered. The mole and harbor were cleared of fishing equipment, and buildings throughout the village were made ready to house as many warriors as could fit inside. Wagons were pulled to the village's extremes and toppled onto their sides, and dozens of quivers of arrows were placed at these defenses, ready in case of an attack from inland. Lenora was sure that not one person had escaped the slaughter—other than those still fighting in the temple—but there was always a chance, and she had to allow for any eventuality.

It was as they gathered the surviving hawks together at the harbor that one of the Krotes suggested how to defeat the temple defenders.

The hawks that could be saved were left with piles of the village dead to eat. Their strength would take days or weeks to return, but the Krotes saw no purpose in killing them yet. Those few that were beyond saving were hauled slowly through the streets to the temple.

Arrows flew. The hawks grumbled and cried out as they were holed a dozen times, two dozen, but being shoved from behind they finally heaved themselves against the walls of the temple, covering the firing holes, dying, far too heavy to be shifted from within.

Stomach gases swelled as they gasped their final breaths. Their hides stretched so thin that they became translucent, ready to burst and let loose the appalling smell that always accompanied a hawk's slow decay. The Krotes withdrew, made flaming arrows and fired them at their dead mounts' bodies from a safe distance.

Most of the small fires went out immediately. Others held on pitifully, and a few spread, crackling their way across the dead creatures'

fatty hides. It did not take long for the first hawk to burst, gushing dancing blue flames across the street. A second explosion followed, a third,
and the flames became voracious.

The fire quickly took hold of the temple. Flaming gases from the
dead hawks vented through the small windows and set the insides
alight. The creatures' fat melted and flowed. There were screams
from the temple, but only a few, and they did not last for long.

The building burned on into dusk. The Krotes tried to extinguish the flames, afraid that the smoke would be seen from a distance, but they were forced back by the heat. The fires had ignited
the hawks' fatty flesh, and the stench of burnt meat permeated the
air across the whole of Conbarma.

That made the warriors hungry. They found wine cellars and
good, fresh seafood in some of the homes, and that night they spent
a few hours celebrating their first victory on the shores of Noreela.

Lenora sat and celebrated with them, but all the while a part of
her mind was farther south, imagining the village of Robenna as she
had last seen it. And as she looked around at the Conbarma dead,
smelled their insides, watched the hungry hawks crunching them
into pulp, she sensed a shade sitting within her. It said nothing, but
it was comfortable. It recognized her.

She knew then that she would see Robenna again. And this
time, it would be on her terms.

———

THE FOLLOWING MORNING, five specks appeared in the sky out
to sea. Lenora ordered a dozen Krotes aloft, while she and the remaining warriors took up defensive positions. The specks grew
slowly, their course unerring, finally resolving into hawks. The
scouts moved out to intercept them, but at the last minute the
Krotes' mounts veered away, spinning seaward, their riders shouting
in dismay, shock and fear. All twelve managed to rein in the frantic
hawks and hobble back toward shore, but by then the five new hawks
were hovering above the harbor, two of them slowly setting down,
tentacles reaching out to make their landing as gentle and graceful
as possible.

Lenora could not bring herself to walk along the harbor wall to
meet them. Her warriors knelt and rested their foreheads on the
ground, muttering words of greeting and reverence.

And the Mages were on Noreela for the first time in three centuries.

"Lieutenant!" the tall one called. "I have need of you!"

Lenora swallowed, smoothed her leather tunic and stepped out onto the harbor wall. She had been in the Mages' presence many times before but never like this, never in combat.

"Mistress," she said, approaching the tall, old woman. She called herself Angel, but few people felt comfortable using that name. It was too personal. "Mistress, what an unexpected pleasure."

"Indeed," Angel said, stretching her bony arms. She looked around at the harbor and the battle-scarred town. "They've done the place up since I was here last," she said quietly. "A few new buildings. Quieter. They must have known we were coming." She looked at Lenora then, her old eyes filled with a knowledge and power that Lenora could not meet for more than a second or two. "What news, Lieutenant?"

"We hold Conbarma, and it's ready to receive the ships." She paused, glanced across at S'Hivez where the old Mage sat slumped forward on his mount. He looked like a mummified corpse, something they would pull out of the glacier on Dana'Man.

"You're talking to me, not him!" Angel said.

"Sorry, Mistress."

Angel stared at her, then smiled. "You of all people need not apologize to me, Lenora. We've been through so many years together—a few good, a few hundred bad—and now it's our time again. Do you feel that?" She drew close, her breath musty and filled with secrets of rage and time. "Can you really sense that, Lenora?"

"Yes," Lenora whispered. And she could. All her memories of the Cataclysmic War and their terrible flight north, refreshed over the past few days, had been instantly wiped away by their first decisive victory. They were back on Noreela . . . and sometime soon, she would go home again. That would be her own personal reward, and not even the Mages need know of that.

"I want you to fly with me, Lieutenant."

Lenora frowned, confused. Angel walked past her and headed along the harbor wall for land, true land, her hand already reaching out to touch the bones of Noreela laid bare for ages. She followed, glancing back at S'Hivez sitting astride his hawk. He showed no inclination to dismount.

"Don't worry about him," Angel said. "He knows we're leaving soon, and he's not one for symbolism. I'm the one who wants to touch this place again."

Lenora followed her mistress, maintaining a respectful distance. They passed one of her men, pressing himself so close to the ground that it seemed he was trying his best to merge with the rock.

"Here we are," Angel said, her voice soft and filled with a timeless grief. "Here we are."

The Mage stepped forward into the first dusty street of Conbarma. She stood there for some time, looking down at her feet then up at the buildings before her, left and right at the shops and taverns that fronted the harbor, back down at her feet. Then she sank slowly to her knees, and from where Lenora watched she was nothing more than a sad old woman, her friends and family dead, kneeling in the dust and wishing to be taken back into it. She picked up a handful of sand and brought it to her face, inhaling, letting some slip between her fingers and drift away on the breeze.

Then Angel suddenly stood, spun around and strode back to Lenora. Any resemblance with that sad old woman had vanished. Here she was, the Mage, Angel, the woman whom in Lenora's eyes had always ruled, the one with power and passion enough to keep going whatever the setbacks. She had built a community far to the north where breath froze on your lips in winter and your piss turned to ice as it left your body. Built an *army*, always certain that her time would come again. And S'Hivez, though he had withered and faded, had gladly watched Angel take control. Lovers once, now they were more like a monstrous mother and son.

"How many times have you dreamed of this, Lenora?" she asked.

"Hundreds, Mistress."

"Is it anything as good as you imagined?"

Lenora smiled. "Better."

"Good. That's because this is a place to live, whereas Dana'Man was a place to die. Do you feel alive? Does the blood on your hands make you feel alive?"

"Yes," she whispered.

"Come with me. The source of magic is far to the south. My shades have seen it, and it's weak and ill protected, and now it has a name. We'll fly there and take it for ourselves. There may even be Red Monks for us to fight! I'll trust my army to land here and do what it was built for."

"You can have full confidence in them," Lenora said.

"I hope so." Angel walked past Lenora and touched her shoulder briefly, squeezing, and she took that as gratitude. "S'Hivez!" Angel called.

Lenora turned in time to see the old Mage sitting up in his saddle.

"S'Hivez, it's time to fly on. This place tastes as good as it ever did, and it'll be ours. But do you want to feel young again? Do you want to feel *better*?"

S'Hivez mumbled and Angel laughed, and her voice sounded like that of a young girl about to slit her own mother's throat. Sweet, poison.

"With us, Lenora, just you!" she shouted. "Tell your Krotes to hold this place for the next week until our army lands."

Lenora turned and ran back to the harbor, heading for where one of her men had landed with his hawk, issuing orders even as she leaped into the saddle and urged the creature aloft.

They're not supposed to be here so soon, she thought, but it was not bitter. The fact they had arrived illustrated that events were moving on apace, and she was glad that her mistress demanded her company. Now that they were back in Noreela, wherever the Mages went was where the action would be. New history being forged.

Lenora was more than happy to be along for the ride.

Chapter 25

"I'VE BEEN THERE," Kosar said. He could not look at any of them, because the memory of Kang Kang was not something to be shared. "At least, I've been *near* there, and that was enough. It's not . . . right."

"And a river that runs uphill is?" Trey asked.

"Kang Kang has *never* been right," Kosar said. "What we saw back at San was a travesty, but one with a very human cause due to what the Mages did. A'Meer, Hope, you must have heard the stories? Those mountains are not meant for humankind, and they should have never been a part of Noreela. They harbor things that should not be and which we can never know. A'Meer? Haven't you heard?"

"Of course I have," she said quietly.

"Hope?" Kosar asked.

The witch shrugged, shook her head. "I've heard a thousand tales, but never from someone I believed had truly been there. Men have always tried to impress me, women to make me jealous or mock me. I've heard more stories than I'd care to recall, but I don't believe any of them. But I do know part of what you say is true, at least: Kang Kang is not of this land."

Rafe sat silently on his horse, the others glancing up at him, down again, trying to make sense. He offered no response to Kosar's argument. He had stated his aim, and it seemed that he had no inclination to discuss it further.

"Rafe, New Shanti is where you'll be safest, I have no doubt of that," Kosar said. "A'Meer has told me a lot about her people, their ways and their aims. They're the opposite of the Red Monks. They'll do anything—*anything*—to keep you alive and safe. A'Meer herself almost died trying to do so, you know that as well as anyone. Imagine ten thousand A'Meers fighting for you."

"A million A'Meers could fight for me," Rafe said, "and I'd be grateful. They could protect me and hide me, but in the end only magic can save itself. That's why I need to go to Kang Kang."

"Is it the magic telling you to go?" Trey asked.

"It doesn't tell me to do anything. It can't. It has no mind, nothing controlling it. Perhaps it leaves hints, offers suggestions, but they're not orders. I don't want to go there any more than you, Kosar, but I simply know it's the safest place for me right now. The *right* place. If there's going to be a war because of me, I'd rather be away from everyone else."

"We should move," A'Meer said. "We can talk about it while we're walking."

Kosar went to touch her arm but she was already turning, heading off ahead to scout the ground. She had her hand resting permanently on her sword hilt, as if certain that they would be battling again before the night was out.

———

RAFE SAT IN the saddle and moved in time with the horse. He had ridden a horse virtually every day back in Trengborne, either going out into the fields to take food to his parents, giving a lift to one of the elderly villagers as they went to and from the market, or simply exploring the hillsides of the wide valley. His mother had often told him that he learned to ride before he started walking. His horse back there had been a dappled Rhoshan, crossbred with a more common Laphal, but still with thoroughbred blood running through its veins, its race memory no doubt giving it dreams of running wild across the Cantrass Plains. He had named her Suki, and he had regarded her as a friend. She was not his and his alone—the poor farmers owned very little, everything was for the use of all—but she was his favorite, and he always believed that she gave a snort of pleasure when he approached, saddled her up and guided her out of the stables. Her Rhoshan blood made her less easy to control, but Rafe had liked that. They had ridden many miles together. He hoped that she was not dead. But it was a vain hope. The stables had been locked, and after the Red Monk visited their village there was no one left to open them.

Thinking of his life in the village comforted Rafe, because it made him feel more like himself. By dwelling on the hard days in the field he found that his own personality came to the fore once again. He rediscovered himself in those memories, pleased to realize that he had been there all along. Driven into hiding, perhaps, by the thing rising in his mind. Shocked into dumbness by its power. It was huge, intimidating, humbling and terrifying, but Rafe was still Rafe. This thing inside him was using him for a ride, just as he had once used Suki. He only hoped that the mutual admiration was the same.

He had lied to Trey, and he did not know why. The magic had not told him to go to Kang Kang, because as yet it did not possess a voice, but it *had* strongly suggested that path to him. In his sleep, in his unconsciousness—and in his mind's eye now if he chose to look in and down toward that deep, dark place—its guidance toward those distant mountains was obvious. Behind them was heat and poison, ahead was danger and conflict, and it was only in the direction of Kang Kang that a successful outcome seemed possible. Just as he had lied to Trey, Rafe had no way of knowing how honest these visions and perceptions were. He did not know this magic. It was as much a stranger to him now as it had been back in Trengborne, as he hid beneath his home and watched the Monk slaughter his parents, heard it whispering to him up out of the grass, the stones, the ground itself. It was greater than it had been, vaster and more complex, and it seemed to expand every second, threatening to burst his mind should he dwell upon it too much. But still it was a mystery. He hoped that he would understand very soon.

He had lied to Trey, and he wished he could lie to himself as well. He wished he could believe that he and his small band of protectors controlled their own destiny, making decisions and planning their own path, instead of letting this mindless, unfathomable power give its own direction, aiding them at moments not of his choosing, turning him into nothing more than a horse to be steered and coerced the way its master desired. He had thought to wake and cure

Alishia, but the magic told him no. He wanted to empower himself ready for a fight with the Monks, but the magic gave him nothing. He was controlled, totally and utterly, and whatever end was destined for him filled him with dread.

That was why he had lied to Trey and the others. He could keep the feeble truth from them, at least.

———

"MONK!" A'MEER HISSED.

Kosar dropped to his knees beside the Shantasi, turned, raised his hand. The others stopped, the two horses snorting and stamping hooves as they sensed sudden fear in the humans.

"Where?"

"There." A'Meer pointed straight ahead at a darker shape in the shadow of a tall tree.

Kosar had to squint, and then he saw the movement, the gliding shadow closing rapidly. "Oh shit," he said.

"Keep to me," A'Meer said. "We attack together, score as many hits as quickly as we can. Damn, I can't see a thing!"

"There's more of them," Kosar said, his heart sinking, his whole body sagging in defeat. He did not want to know what it was like to take a sword between the ribs, yet his mind was reaching ahead, imagining the next ten minutes. "There, look to the left. Two hundred steps away."

"I see them."

"We can't fight them in the dark," Kosar said. "We'd stand a much better chance if we could see them. Damn the clouds for hiding the moons tonight!"

"It can't end like this!" A'Meer said. "It's so *pointless.*"

"You need light?" Hope said. The witch had crawled up between them and now she knelt, shrugged her shoulder bag off and delved inside. "Close your eyes for a second so that you can adapt. Perhaps it'll blind them for a few moments, give us the first strike."

Kosar saw the shadows gliding in across the ground, moving from cover to cover, hoods and cloaks making them all but shapeless . . . but there was no mistaking their intent. He obeyed the witch and closed his eyes.

His eyelids turned red as light burned in from outside. He heard something hissing like a huge snake and could not stop himself from looking. The light blinded him for a moment, and he brought up his free hand to shield his eyes, keeping his sword at the ready. Fire danced in the sky, balls of flame leaping left and right, seemingly bouncing from each other and then ricocheting elsewhere, dodging and lighting the landscape. Kosar gasped, mesmerized for a few seconds by the display, but then Hope clapped his shoulder and whispered in his ear, "It's just chemicala."

A'Meer was standing, facing the shapes that had been stunned into immobility by the sudden illumination. There were six of them, hoods hiding their faces but not their intent. Swords drawn, the Monks readied themselves for the attack. In the sparkling light their cloaks seemed redder, the heathers about their feet a brighter purple. Even the smell of the undergrowth seemed richer. Or perhaps this close to death, Kosar was seeing and sensing with a startling clarity.

A'Meer loosed an arrow into the first Monk, reached back, plucked a new shaft from her quiver, fired, reached, drew, fired. In five heartbeats she had put an arrow into each shape, and they barely moved.

"Passed right through," Kosar said. There was no blood, no sign of any wounds. "The arrows went straight through."

A'Meer paused, then drew and fired again at the first Monk. The arrow struck its face and exited behind its head, hood flapping as its feathered tail flicked it. The shaft struck a rock way behind it, snapping in two.

"So is this bad magic back so soon?" Hope said, aghast.

Trey stood beside them, his disc-sword unsheathed and glinting in the reflected light of Hope's chemicala. "They're not moving," he whispered. The only sound was the hiss and spit of the fireballs.

"Why aren't they attacking?" Kosar said. He remembered the Monk in Trengborne, unhindered by the arrows sprouting from its head and body, driving forward with renewed ferocity each time it was struck.

A'Meer fired three more times at the first Monk, each arrow passing through the shape, none of them leaving any apparent wounds.

"Waiting for us to use all our arrows?" Hope said.

"Are they really there?"

"If not we're all having the same nightmare."

And then the Monks moved.

As one they slowly sank down to the ground, their legs parting and spreading as if melting into the cool soil. They kept their form as they slid down, and Kosar even saw the glint of their eyes as cloaks and hoods were plucked apart at the melting point. Whatever went to make up the Monks shimmered and undulated, flowing out from where the shrinking forms stood and covering the ground around them, glittering like a million eyes in the night.

Hope's lights were fading.

"It can't be," the witch said, disbelief making her sound so young.

"What?" Kosar asked.

The shapes were almost completely gone, the hoods still red, eyes and red faces still there as they sank into the shifting ground. They looked liked six individual puddles, but each one moved a hundred ways at any one time, covering the grasses and stones but never stealing their shape, a coating rather than a covering. Once the Monks had gone, the stuff grew dark, and in the fading light of the floating fireballs they looked like splashes of shadow looking for a home.

"Mimics," Hope said.

As if her utterance had galvanized them, the shapes drifted together, formed one mass and then moved quickly to the right, heading west, disappearing into the night.

Hope's chemicala finally died and plunged them into a greater darkness than before. The four drew back to the horses and stood protectively around them, facing out, waiting for their eyes to adjust.

"What exactly did we just see?" Kosar said. He wanted a response from anyone, but his question was directed at Rafe. "Rafe, what was that?"

"I don't know," the boy said from his horse.

"Mimics," Hope said again.

"They're a legend," A'Meer said, but the uncertainty in her voice was obvious.

"Of course they are!"

"I've never heard of them," Kosar said. "I've traveled, but I've never seen or heard of anything like that."

"Mimics!" Disbelief and delight vied for dominance in Hope's voice. "I've heard of them a few times, even met an old woman who claimed to have seen them once, but I never believed I'd ever see them myself."

"But you *did* believe that they existed?" A'Meer asked.

"I'm a witch," Hope said. "I have a very open mind."

"But why Monks?" Kosar asked.

"A warning." The witch fell silent, perhaps realizing that the mimics' appearance was not really a cause for celebration.

"They showed us six Monks, then they headed west," A'Meer said. "If it's a warning, I wonder how near they are?"

"And why would the mimics warn us?" Rafe asked.

"I think you should know that, boy," Hope muttered. "It seems news of our journey and what we carry is reaching far beyond the human world."

"Whatever and why ever, we should be moving, not standing around talking," Kosar said. "If these things came to warn us, there must be good reason. Unless they're a part of it. What if they're with the Monks?"

"I'm sure they're beyond petty allegiances," Hope said. "They're as far from us as we can imagine. Hive organisms. We probably just saw more mimics than there are people alive in Noreela now. They have their own reason for issuing such a stark warning, and that's the magic that Rafe carries."

"But they could just as easily be leading us to the Monks, not from them."

"I'm sure they could have destroyed us themselves. I've heard stories." Hope said no more, but the silence implied tales too gruesome for the telling.

"Well, let's move," A'Meer said. She took up the two horses' reins and led them forward, walking straight toward where the mimics had manifested just moments before.

They followed. Kosar looked down at his feet, trying to see whether the ground had changed where those things had melted down into a moving carpet of life. Was the heather stripped to the stems or made richer? Was the soil denuded of goodness or enriched? But darkness hid the detail, and his feet were only shadows moving him ever onward.

———

AS THEY WALKED Trey took a finger of fledge. It was very stale now, bitter and sickly, and he felt his mind swaying as it cast itself from his body. He kept walking, kept his eyes open, and he only had to move slightly to touch on Alishia.

Are you there? he thought. *Are you still alive?*

Still here, still alive, but I'm being filled! Her voice was very distant, and it sounded very young.

Alishia! Trey called in his mind.

She shouted back, but it was not any louder.

What's happening? Trey asked. *I'm all alone out here. I miss your company, and you sound strange, lost—*

Lost and found again, Alishia whispered. *Never really lived, but now I'm filled with everything.*

Something came at him then, something huge and dark and not of Alishia at all. It expanded out of the tiny flickering light of her limitless mind, and he retreated before it. There was no real sense of malice in its presence, but there was an intense pressure. He gave in to it. Withdrew. Fell back into his own mind and opened his eyes, and he looked straight at Rafe where he sat astride his horse thirty paces ahead.

He looked, and he wondered just what was going on inside the boy's head.

———

THEY WALKED THROUGH the night, glancing nervously to the west every now and then, expecting to see the shapes of real Monks manifesting from the shadows and rushing them with swords drawn and murder in their eyes. They needed to stop and eat, rest, sleep, but the warning had to be taken seriously. The faster they moved now, the better their chance of escape.

"What do we do if we do come up against Monks?" Kosar whispered to A'Meer.

She did not reply for a long time. He was about to move on when she sighed. "There's not much we can do," she said. "I can fight them as I've been trained, you can join in with whatever passion you feel for our cause, perhaps Hope can poison them again or use chemicala. Trey . . . he's a miner, not a fighter. Perhaps we'll make a dent, and maybe we'll put back the inevitable for a while. But we'll die, Kosar. They're difficult enough to defeat on their own. If we meet them in any great numbers, we'll all die."

"And Rafe?" Kosar asked. "What if Rafe joins in the fight?"

This time A'Meer's silence stretched on, and Kosar did not ask her again.

———

"KANG KANG," RAFE said. "That's the only safe place for me to go, and the only way any of us will survive. Without me, Kosar and A'Meer can make it to Hess much faster."

"I'm not leaving you," A'Meer said.

"I'll look after him," Hope said. *I will*, she thought, *better than you with your swords and arrows. I have much more than that. I have passion. I have a* reason.

A'Meer shook her head. "I'm not leaving him. Not with you, not with anyone." She raised an eyebrow, inviting any challenge to her statement.

At sunup they had climbed a small hill, and now they rested on its summit. From there they could see in every direction. North, back the way they had come, a great mist rose from the land and touched the clouds, linking sky to ground. To the east were rising hills that grew gradually higher until, beyond the horizon, they fell down into the Mol'Steria Desert. South lay scrubland and copses of trees, weak-looking and in need of more than water. In the distance, hazed by heat, the first signs of the town of Mareton was miraged above the ground. And west, where they watched for the approach of the dreaded Monks, grasslands stretched as far as they could see, rolling toward the horizon and offering myriad hiding places.

Hope scanned westward with her spyglass, a present from one of the many men she had entertained. Her indulgence for this particular gift had gone much further than she would ever have liked, but it was worth the cost. For a few transitory moments of degradation she had this tool, something that brought the distance near and could give almost as much advance warning as the fledge miner's drugged visions. Hope no longer trusted Trey's addled mind. Only minutes ago he had returned from another trip, unable to tell them anything they did not know. He had seen the red smear of blood across the land—Monks, he told them, hundreds of Monks swarming over hills and through valleys—but he did not know distance, direction or location. He could not even be sure that it was now he was seeing, and not the past or some clouded future. She had developed a grudging belief in his intentions, but his supposed talents were on the wane. She had seen his eyes when he came back, but he would not meet her gaze.

The others did not see things her way. She left them to their thoughts. She was only a witch and a whore, after all; why would they listen to her?

So she watched, and felt Rafe's gaze on her back. He needed her help to reach Kang Kang, and she would give it, with or without the others. *Without*, she thought. *Really, I'd prefer it without.*

She had heard more stories than she cared to admit about that mysterious mountainous region to the south, and the Blurring that may or may not exist beyond. Kosar had been right in his assessment of Kang Kang's wrongness, but only in part. While his judgment was based on a very subjective fear of Kang Kang and what may dwell there, Hope's knowledge was more deeply rooted in the place itself, a more objective view. She was not only afraid of the place, but also aware that Kang Kang was afraid of itself. In those mountains of madness, fear was a tactile presence, as prevalent as air or grass or rock. It could be lapped up or cast aside, but everyone that made the journey discovered it at some point. That was why few who found Kang Kang ever came back. It was a wild animal, driven mad by its own ferocity and consuming everything.

"If we're here to look after Rafe, surely we should listen to his reasoning," Hope said at last. Her words broke an unsteady silence, one waiting to be ruptured by argument. "He's the carrier of the new magic, he's the one we're prepared to lay down our lives to protect. If he wants to go to Kang Kang, I see no way we can refuse him."

A'Meer, leaning back against a tree with her eyes half closed, waved a hand as if at a worrisome fly. It was a dismissive gesture, and the Shantasi did not even honor Hope with words to accompany it.

"What?" Hope said. "What, Shantasi?"

"Hope." Kosar was standing by the two horses, checking them over, examining their hooves. "Rafe is the carrier, but does that necessarily mean . . . ?" He trailed off, looked down at the ground, back to the horses.

"Mean what?" Hope said.

Rafe raised his head and opened his eyes, staring in interest at the thief.

"Kosar?" A'Meer said.

The thief turned back to them, and Hope was surprised at the determination in his eyes. Whatever he had to say, he believed it totally. "Well . . . does being the carrier mean that he is any more special in himself?"

He glanced at Rafe, then away. The boy returned his glance with resolute interest.

"You told us yourself that it's a thing inside you, Rafe, that you have no control. It's another life living alongside yours, independent, a child sharing your life force and growing separate from you. But like a mother is not the child, so you aren't the magic. Can you really claim to know exactly what it wants?"

All eyes turned to Rafe. *This is where it has a chance to show itself and cast out doubt,* Hope thought. She felt a tingling in her limbs at the idea, a tightening of her scalp, as if a lightning storm was gathering above the hills. *This is where things change.*

"I'm as important as anyone who has knowledge," Rafe said. "Your mind is separate from the rest of you, Kosar. Your shade is still within you, somewhere, a remnant of your potential hiding behind your bones and within your blood. Yet without one, the other will change. Without me the magic will be free, but as vulnerable as a newborn baby. There are things out there that would eat it."

"I didn't mean . . ." Kosar said, looking down at his hands, picking horsehair from the wounds on his fingertips. Then he looked up again. "You never used to talk like this. You're a farm boy, Rafe."

"My eyes are being opened," the boy said. He looked at each of them for a couple of seconds, even the unconscious Alishia propped against Trey's side. "I know you all have doubts," he said. "And so do I. The thing inside me has done a few tricks to try to help us on our way, but it's been a long time. We're blinded to miracles. Sheltered from the truth. But believe me when I say I know what is right." He looked at A'Meer. "Believe me."

"I don't know—" the Shantasi began.

"We're blinded," Hope said. "Blinded by what we can't believe, just like Rafe said. We've all heard of the old magic and what it could do, but do we really believe? You, A'Meer. Can you really *believe*?"

"Of course," the Shantasi said, but they all knew the doubt in her voice. She looked away, out between the trees.

"Not far from here," Rafe said, "there's a place that will make you all believe." He closed his eyes, and suddenly the life seemed to drain from his face, skin growing sallow and lined, flesh sloughing down, as if he aged ten years in ten seconds.

"Rafe!" Hope said. *No!* she thought, darting to the boy, holding his arms, pressing her ear to his mouth. The others were on their feet, gathering around. The witch felt Rafe's breath in her ear, warm on her cheek and neck, and she closed her eyes, wondering what could pass between them should she remain this close. Here, now, inside him, a hand's breadth away . . . but it was not really that close, she realized. Magic was still an infinity away. Even though out of all of them she believed the most, still it was as far away as ever.

"He's asleep," she said quietly, trying to hide her disappointment from the others. Her confusion. Her yearning.

I'll stay with you, Rafe, she thought. *I believe you, and I'll stay with you whether I eventually have what I want . . . or not.*

THEY STAYED ON the hillock just long enough to have a bite to eat and a brief rest. Trey chewed more stale fledge and told them that the land was still smudged red, bleeding eastward, although he did not know how far away that blight lay. He grew quiet when Kosar asked, shook his head and looked at Alishia where she sat slowly fading away. They had all tried to feed the unconscious girl, force water down her throat, but with her mind torn to shreds her body had lost the survival instinct. Food fell from her mouth unchewed, and water drained away down her chin. And there was something else. They could not be certain, but she looked younger than she had before, smaller. Lessened by her experiences, perhaps . . . or maybe something else.

When they set off again, Kosar was consumed by a dreadful sense of foreboding. He looked at them all—Hope, Trey, Alishia, the terrifyingly normal Rafe and A'Meer, the woman he perhaps loved—and they were friends and strangers. For an instant they were characters in a story of his own devising, so close that he could never know anyone better, yet so unreal that their impending loss was a blankness within him. He walked close to A'Meer, brushing her arm with his, trying to see a similar recognition of their fate in her eyes, finding nothing.

Rafe's request and the discussion back on the knoll still lay unresolved. Yet they headed southeast, their route taking them nearer and nearer to New Shanti and A'Meer's intended destination. Rafe sat astride his horse and quietly let himself be led, though now there was a definable tension in the group. Rafe's words seemed to echo back at them from the land: *There's a place that will make you all believe.* Kosar had no idea where or what that place was—none of them did—but they all looked with new eyes now, trying to find hidden truths between blades of grass, epiphanies floating in the sunny air with the dust and pollen. Kosar hoped that they looked with *better* eyes . . . but still he feared that it was greed that drove some of them, guilt others. The purity of their intentions was yet to be proven.

Around midday they paused by a small stream so that the horses could drink. Kosar filled his water canteen upstream from the horses, splashed his face and neck and gasped as the cold water bit through the grime of the road. It had been a long time since he had felt like this. He had worked hard in Trengborne, but it had been a more comfortable life than he had realized at the time. His muscles truly ached, stretched and turned in ways they had long forgotten.

"We're off course," A'Meer said. She was standing in the shade of a large boulder, measuring its shadow with her eye, glancing up at the sun. "We've turned due south."

"I never noticed us changing direction," Kosar said.

"None of us did." A'Meer glanced at Rafe and then walked away, sitting by the stream and drawing her sword. She plucked at her finger and blood smeared the blade. In the sunlight it spread thin and fine.

Nobody said any more about their change of direction, but as they set off again A'Meer led the way, heading away at a noticeable angle from the route they had traveled thus far. Kosar walked with her, but did not ask. Voicing his fear would confirm that control was slowly being taken from them, that their route was being planned and controlled by forces other than their own. That was not something that he wanted to hear.

They dipped into a shallow valley and followed the stream along its base, picking pale fruit and berries from the few errant trees that survived. Kosar sniffed at them. They smelled fine, but he saw a dead rabbit and something larger, longer dead, so he threw the food away. The stream led past small hills and back into the open plains, where to the east they could still spy the foothills of the mountains bordering New Shanti. Ahead of them now lay Mareton, the small town perched on the edge of the Mol'Steria Desert. It was here that they would take on supplies for their final journey across the sands. It was almost two hundred miles to Hess.

"Not far from here," Rafe said suddenly, looking southwest.

"We have to go to Mareton," A'Meer said, "stock up with water and food for the crossing, maybe get some fresh horses."

"Not far from here, just a few miles that way, and something will open your eyes," Rafe said again. "I don't know what, and I don't know how. I only know it to be true. A'Meer . . . a few miles."

A'Meer glanced at all of them, and her eyes never changed

when she looked at Kosar. He felt a brief kick in the stomach from that, confused and sad. "We can't waste any time!" she said. "The Monks could be right behind us. They'll have our trail now, and they won't stop, not even out in the desert. Our only hope is to get out there before them, make a head start across the sands."

The others were silent, waiting for Rafe or A'Meer to say something more.

It was Trey who spoke at last. "I want to see what Rafe means," he said. "If it's something so wonderful, maybe it will help us all."

"And maybe it'll kill us," A'Meer countered. "None of us know anything about what's happening here! I have to take this boy to Hess and let the Mystics figure it out. We go a few miles off track, that's more chance that the Monks will trap and kill us. Perhaps we have the advantage right now—a head start, a few miles maybe—but what happens if we go off on some fool's errand to see some mysterious 'thing'? Remember what those mimics showed us? Monks. Closing in from the west. Trey's seen the same! And you, Rafe . . . after all that, you still want to head that way?" She pointed southwest with her drawn sword, and it whispered at the air.

"He's the reason we're all here," Hope said, "and I'm for following him."

"He's led by something mindless!" A'Meer said. "Soulless."

"But it cares for us all," Rafe said. "It would not lead us into ambush. Most of all, it cares for itself."

A'Meer looked at Kosar, and for the first time since leaving Pavisse there was something of friendship in her eyes, an old knowledge, language without words. But why now, and why here? Because this was when she needed him most.

Kosar felt sick. "I'll go with Rafe," he said. "I believe it's the right thing to do, A'Meer. Just a few miles, to see what's so important. Then we can all finally decide what to do. And if Hess is still the best idea, I'm with you all the way."

A'Meer cursed, shook her head and stormed off southward. She went a few dozen paces and then squatted down, the weapons at her belt scarring the ground. There was no pride, no dented perception of leadership, Kosar knew that. A'Meer simply wanted to do what she thought was right.

She turned around at last, stared back at them, and then *past* them. Her eyes grew wide and her jaw slackened. "Exactly how far is this place?" she hissed.

"I don't know," Rafe said, "but we can make it, and then I think it can get us away."

Kosar turned his back on the Shantasi and looked the way they had come. At the head of the shallow valley they had just emerged from, maybe two miles distant, several red specks were moving slowly down the heathered hillsides.

"Then lead the way!" A'Meer said, standing. "Hope, on the horse with Rafe! Trey, up with Alishia."

"I can't ride fast," the miner protested.

"Learn!"

A'Meer came back to Kosar, panting, and he caught the tang of her sweat in the air. It was a familiar smell and it brought flashbacks, pleasant even in the circumstances.

"You make me hard dressed like that," he muttered, and to his delight A'Meer laughed out loud.

"We never did get to dressing up, did we?" she asked. They stood side by side, staring at doom as it pursued them across the landscape.

"Never really needed to."

"No." She shook her head and leaned in to Kosar, kissing him on his neck. "I love you, you old thief."

He answered with a smile.

"And now," she said, "I suppose we see just how much Rafe knows about what he carries."

Kosar heard the horses moving off behind them, and he and A'Meer turned and followed in their wake.

"How far away, do you think?" he said quietly.

"Maybe two miles. I saw at least a dozen of them in the valley alone. There may be more moving in from the west, heading to cut us off."

"There's no hope against that many, is there?"

A'Meer did not answer for a while, and there was only the horses' hoofbeats and their own footfalls as accompaniment to their desperate flight. "Well," she said at last, "no hope unless Rafe is right. And in that case, who in the Black knows just what we're about to see?"

Who indeed? thought Kosar. *Perhaps no one.*

Or perhaps only the Mages.

————

THEY RAN. THE horses, exhausted though they were, seemed to pick up on their fear, because they put on a burst of speed that took them way ahead of Kosar and A'Meer. A'Meer cursed and struggled to keep up, but Kosar urged her to slow, conserve her energy. They might have a long run ahead.

For a while they moved silently, A'Meer breathing fast but steady beside him, Kosar doing his best to regulate his breath, control his pace, rarely looking farther than the next few steps. He did not know just how long he could do this. It was not something he wanted to dwell on. He glanced up at the two horses, still way ahead even with their doubled cargos. Hope and Rafe were in the lead, their gray dappled horse stepping confidently and calmly, while behind them Trey seemed to be letting his own mount follow the first, hanging on gamely to the reins, bouncing awkwardly, trying to hold Alishia upright between his arms while doing his best not to tumble from the saddle. *He could fall,* Kosar thought, *he and Alishia could fall away and the horse will bolt. What then? Leave them?* It was not an idea he wanted to entertain, but now the thought was there, in the background.

He realized very quickly that A'Meer could use her Pace to leave him behind in the blink of an eye. Yet she stayed back with him. That shamed and pleased him in equal measures.

They followed a rough path through the heather for as long as they could. Evidence of wheel ruts hid beneath new growth, and though that made the going underfoot hazardous it was still easier than running through knee-high bracken. The horses seemed to keep their footing easily, but more than once Kosar stumbled and fell, rolling as well as he could to control the impact. A'Meer stopped to help him up, then ran on without a word. Kosar's first few steps after these tumbles were tentative and slow, ready for the burning pain of a broken ankle.

What then? he thought. *Leave me behind?*

He realized then just how desperate the situation was. He glanced back but the hills they had just left were hidden by a fold in the land, the progress of the Red Monks out of sight. They could be closing quickly, or falling behind. Or perhaps they had not even seen them. But that was a vain hope, and one that they could not allow.

Trey shouted from up ahead. His saddle had slipped sideways and he clung on desperately to the horse's mane, arms pressed around the unconscious girl as the land strove to pull them down. The horse stopped, reared, stamping its feet and flinging its head, doing its best to shake its two passengers free.

Kosar put on a burst of speed but A'Meer reached them first. By the time he caught up she had calmed the horse, tightened the saddle, muttered something to Trey and sent them on their way.

Hope and Rafe had not slowed down.

"What did you tell him?" Kosar asked as he and A'Meer ran together once more.

"I told him if he falls, we'll leave him."

The rough path they had been following faded away into the ground, displaying no final destination, no reason at all for being. Brackens grew up around their knees, sometimes reaching their thighs, and progress on foot was hampered, fronds whipping at their legs and tangling around their ankles.

The horses cantered on, their long legs finding no hindrance.

"Hope is pulling ahead," Kosar said.

"Yes." A'Meer's bare lower legs were already whipped from the plants, long bubbled lines of blood marking where the skin had been scored. She seemed not to notice.

"Perhaps we should call to her to slow down."

"Don't think she would." She cursed as something shifted beneath one of her feet—a rock, a plant, a surprised creature—and went sprawling, outstretched hands fending off the worst of the impact.

Kosar stopped and went to her, holding her beneath the arms to help her up. Her elbows were bloodied and she had a cut above one eyebrow, blood dripping down across her pale skin.

From behind came a cry. Too loud for a human, too mad for an animal, too filled with rage to be anything other than a Monk. Kosar looked back up the gentle slope they had just run down. There was no movement, save the twitching of bracken in the gentle breeze. The sun was behind him, throwing his shadow back the way they had come and he had a brief, crazy image of the Monks catching it, twisting it into their grasp and hauling him down, falling on him with swords drawn . . .

"I see nothing," he said.

"They don't call to each other without reason," A'Meer said. "Come on. Hope and Rafe have gone."

Kosar looked ahead in panic. A few hundred steps away a wood began. He saw Trey's horse swallowed by shadows beneath the trees, and then he and A'Meer were alone in the landscape . . . and yet not. Behind them was the very real presence of the Red Monks, a huge weight bearing down in the sunlight. Unseen as yet, but obvious as a shadow on the sun.

The two ran on, raising their legs high with each step to try to clear the plants and prevent themselves from tripping.

There was another cry closer behind them, this one not muted by any folds in the land, but Kosar did not turn to look.

By the time they reached the woods, he was aware of the silence around them. The singing of birds, the rustle of creatures in the undergrowth, the breath of the breeze whispering its way across the land . . . it was only their sudden silences that made them obvious. The land held its breath as he and A'Meer passed from sunlight to shadow.

The darkness felt no safer.

There may be more moving in from the west, heading to cut us off, A'Meer had said. Perhaps they were here now, Monks hiding between trees and in hollows in the woodland floor, waiting to rise up in ambush as soon as they were all within their bloody red reach.

No cries from ahead, no sound of a fight.

There won't be, Kosar thought. *They'll slaughter Rafe and Hope, Trey and Alishia without a sound. They're not fighters. A'Meer is the only fighter here. Even I carry a sword only by default, not because I have much of an idea of how to use it.*

"It's hopeless," he muttered, and as if in response there came more cries from behind, three or four Monks breaking the silence with their unnatural screams as they pelted downhill toward the woods.

"It's all down to Rafe, now," A'Meer said. "Maybe we should pull back, try to hold them off?"

"What?" The idea terrified Kosar. The thought of entering into battle with the Monks here, between the trees, while the others rode on ahead was awful. Suddenly faced with the prospect of self-sacrifice, he knew just how much he wanted to live. A'Meer may have stated her purpose and aim, but he had never promised to die to save anyone.

They ran between trees, jumping fallen boughs, skirting around rocky outcroppings, forging on almost blindly. To be cautious of what might may lie in wait ahead would only give the Monks time to catch up. They ran headlong into unknown dangers to escape the certain death on their tails.

"Perhaps not," A'Meer said. "Let's see where Rafe is taking us first."

They splashed through a small stream, noticing the disturbed sediment where the horses had recently crossed. Pausing briefly, Kosar heard the sounds of the horses' progress in the distance. He wanted to call out for them to slow down, but fear kept him silent.

There were old paths in here, worn over time until tree roots showed through and nothing grew anymore. Kosar wondered who had passed this way before, recently or in forgotten history, and whether any of them had been as desperately frightened as he was now. They followed one such trail that led deeper into the woods and deeper into shadow. Other tributaries led off, twisting away between trees and behind banks of giant ferns and other, more dense undergrowth. Their destinations remained hidden, never to be known. Kosar had once liked to tread such routes, enjoying the discovery around each bend, relishing new experience. And he had forged his own paths across the land, steered himself to follow many mysteries and tales, and routes such as these had once been his life. Now he wished only for familiarity and safety.

To his left, a narrow path faded away into shrubbery, plants touching across it now but the ground still worn down to the hard mud beneath. Rock was exposed, some of it sharpened by some crushing impact. Whose footfalls could have done that, Kosar wondered? Farther along, the remnants of an old fence had rotted into the ground but a gate stood firm, an intricate iron construct forming a decorative entry into nothing, because only more forest stood behind. It would have looked the same from both directions. *To keep in or keep out?*

The trees grew suddenly denser as they entered an area of the woods given over to pine, and here the horses' trail was easier to follow. A trail of fresh breakages—scars on trunks, snapped twigs and branches scattered across the ground—marked the route Hope and Trey had taken. The forest floor was churned up, fresh disturbances in the pine needles marked by the darker stains of dampness below, and the bewitching shifting as wood ants found themselves exposed to the light. They reminded Kosar of the mimics, so many parts to such a complex creature.

"Here," A'Meer said. "Take this!" She handed him a small wooden ball from her belt. "Don't touch the wire, it'll take your fingers off. Wrap it once around that tree there, knee height, and pull hard. It'll hold fast."

She hurried off at a right angle to their path, turning and twisting between trees, hand trailing behind her as she let out a length of almost invisible wire. Kosar did as she had instructed, passing the wooden ball once around the tree and pulling. The wire attached to it—thin, sharp, deadly—bit into the bark with a soft hiss. The wooden ball looked like a knotted wound in the tree. When the wire had played out A'Meer secured her end and then signaled for them to continue.

"They'll smell our trail," she said as they ran together once more. "The horses' breath, the blood from our scrapes. They'll be running fast. It won't stop them, but it may slow down one or two."

"How many more tricks have you got?" Kosar asked.

"Not many."

Another cry rose up behind them and the tree canopy came to life as birds took flight, fleeing in silent panic as if keen to keep their presence a secret.

"If only we could fly," A'Meer said.

Kosar took the lead. Spiderwebs wrapped themselves across his face and tangled in his hair, and now and then he felt the harder impact as a spider came along for the ride. He wiped them frantically away, remembering the slayer spider that Hope had left in her rooms for the Monks. There was no telling what unknown species this wood might harbor. Trees reached for him too, small branches only becoming apparent as they drew lines of blood into his cheek or clawed for his eyes.

Shadows moved to their left and right. Things following their progress, perhaps. Or maybe tricks of the light.

"I don't know where we are," Kosar said. "I've never traveled these woods. I've been south of here to the borders of Kang Kang, but I never came this way. There's no way of telling how far these woods continue."

"Far enough," A'Meer said. "Long enough for us to have to face the Red Monks in here. The forest is many miles deep—I was here years ago, just after my training was finished and I went out of New Shanti—and there were things here even then. Now . . . more time has passed. The land has changed even more, and old maps no longer hold true. Maybe they're all gone."

"What things?" Kosar asked. "Why didn't you say?"

"I never saw them properly, not even back then. And I can't say they were a danger. But they gave me bad dreams."

As if on cue the two of them stopped running, squatted down, listened to the noises around them. From ahead they could hear the horses crashing onward, not far distant. Behind them, the way they had come, all was quiet; the forest silenced by their own passage, perhaps, or because of what followed.

Something whispered.

"What *is* that?" Kosar said, but A'Meer did not answer. She glanced at him and then looked away, eyes downcast as if ashamed of something terrible and secret. He reached out to touch her, fingers stretched, blood on his fingertips . . . and then he stopped.

They gave me bad dreams, A'Meer had said.

And the whispers made themselves known to Kosar.

Never said sorry, never told Father why I did it, killed his sheebok, cut out its heart to take away to the woods with my friends, never admitted my guilt even though there was blood beneath my fingernails and the stink of death about me, rot in the creases of my skin, pain and guilt in my eyes when I woke up . . . afraid of him, frightened of his big hands and his angry shouts, but there was worse than Father's rage, frightened of my friends, of the things they did in the woods, the things they did with that girl and that sheebok's heart and those knives, those knives . . . frightened but compliant, watching them empty the heart over her breasts and cut her there, the blood mingling, watching from the trees, hard, young and hard . . . and when they came into her and she screamed they didn't hear my own petty cries of pleasure and shame . . . but they knew I watched . . . they always *knew I watched . . .*

"Fuck," Kosar shouted. "Fuck!"

A'Meer held him and whispered in his ear, trying to calm him. "It's all right, don't shout, let it come, accept it and let it come and it'll flow away, it'll hide again. Truth is only what you want to make it. They'll leave you alone soon, Kosar . . ."

Always regretted leaving him behind, that broken boy cowering in the pits of the Poison Forests, waiting to die . . . but his leg was broken, and I'd never really wanted him along anyway, just too afraid to say no, didn't want to hurt his feelings . . . I'd saved his life after all, and he thought he owed me, wanted to repay me for saving him from those tumblers in the Widow's Peaks . . . so he came along and I slipped and he fell too, and I never should have left him . . . said I was going for help, going to find someone to help me pull him out of there, but I knew he'd be dead by nightfall, no way a boy like that could fight off the poisonous things that live there, those birds those bats those spiders . . . left him to die, and not because I was scared and not because

I couldn't have gone back . . . simply because I didn't want him with me anymore . . .

It came again and again, the voice of his sickly conscience, the mad mutterings of guilt, the secret shadows of rejected experience admitting culpability for things he had long ago shut away, driven down, buried deep in denial, clothed in ambiguous memory and turned into tales once heard, not created himself.

. . . should have put it back, never should have taken it . . .

"Kosar, breathe, let it come, they'll lose interest soon."

. . . meant so much but I never told her, and look what happened, look what happened to her!

"Oh Mage shit," A'Meer whispered, tortured by whatever guilty secrets plagued her own mind. Her grip on Kosar never eased.

Forgot again, always forget, never found it in myself to remember just that one special day for my mother, always let it slip away and then fooled myself that look in her eyes was a calm acceptance when I apologized, not disappointment, not sadness . . .

Kosar vomited, the sickness and rot of hidden memories and mistakes flooding his mind and purging his body. A'Meer still held him, groaning and cursing, fighting whatever foul thoughts had been dredged in her own mind. He heaved again and bent double, watching vomit speckle the pine-needle carpet, a big beetle scurrying away with its back coated in his stomach juices. All his bad thoughts crowded in and buzzed him like moths to a flame, some of them battering against his skull and knocking themselves away, others remaining there to fly in again and again, reminding him of all those bad things.

The whispering began to fade away at last. It did not vanish completely—it never would—but reduced in volume until it was a hush in his ears, and then a feeling deeper down, and then nothing, not disappearing, simply becoming too quiet and deep for him to want to hear.

"Why didn't you warn me?" he said, spitting the foul taste from his mouth.

"How could I?"

Kosar looked up at A'Meer and saw that she had been suffering as well, face pale, eyes moist. He wondered what secret shame she had been facing only seconds ago; he did not wish to ask. He turned and looked in the direction the horses had taken. "The others?"

"If the things in these woods get them too, I'm hoping that the horses will go on while they're remembering."

"Bad things. All bad things for you?"

A'Meer nodded, looked away, turned and scanned the woods behind them.

"Why? *Why?*"

"Perhaps it's how they feed," she said. "There are plenty of strange things we know about—skull ravens, tumblers—and some, like the mimics, that are little more than myth. There must be many more that are still hidden to us. Especially since the Cataclysmic War. It's not just the landscape that's suffered since then, changed."

Kosar shook his head to rid himself of those rancid images and guilts. It only served to mix them up some more. "I can't stand this," he said, moaning and holding his head.

"Kosar, they're here!"

A'Meer drew on her bow, let an arrow fly. Something screeched from between the trees, and Kosar saw a red flash behind some shrubs, twisting and wavering in the dappled forest light.

"Come on," A'Meer said. "We have to catch the others!" She ran past him, grabbing his elbow and spinning him so that he was facing the right way. "Now!"

He followed her, imagining that he could leave those foul thoughts of his behind, stewing away into this weird forest floor along with his puddle of vomit.

What manner of things . . . ? he thought. And then the idea came that they would prey on the Monks as well . . . and that, maybe, they would slow them down.

———

HOPE WAS SCREAMING. Not aloud, not through her mouth, because the slew of recollections was drowning any physical response. She was screaming inside.

And still the whispers made themselves known.

I slid the stiletto in too late, waited until he came, and maybe I enjoyed it? Maybe I wanted to feel him flooding into me, wanted to see the rapture in his face before his eyes sprang open at the pain, the realization of what I'd done to him? I could have done it sooner, but he was pounding into me, hard, harder, and then when he grunted I raised my hand and slid the blade into his back, pushed hard, so hard that it cut from his chest and pricked my neck . . . and his eyes opened, and I had killed him, he knew that already, could feel it, the blood bursting inside and stilling his heart, and even as I met his gaze I felt sick with what I had done. Not his fault. He hadn't made me do any-thing. I had invited him in. And in his final exhalation, that last grumbling breath from his slack mouth, there hid none of the truths I believed would be there . . .

"Not me!" Hope hissed. "Not me! I didn't do it, not on pur-pose—not me, it was . . . everyone before me!" *Ancestors,* she thought. *They made me do it. Those real witches who mocked me by passing down their name to my pitiful, fraudulent self.*

Her horse ran on, Rafe held her around the waist, and the open-ing up of the foulest corners of her mind continued.

He was a bad man anyway, he deserved what those things did to him, I could never have unlocked the door and forgiven myself if he escaped . . .

I like it, I like it, I can't help that, I can't help that they're alive when I eat them . . .

He'd have still paid me, still screwed me, even if he had known . . . it wasn't my fault . . . by then nothing would have stopped him, not even the knowledge of what I had . . .

Hope cried through eyes shut tight.

Behind her, Rafe said nothing.

———

HE FELT THE things in the shadows probing him, finding his mind and then scampering away in alarm. They spun away between the trees, dug themselves back down beneath the leaves and needles where they slept for years on end. They were terrified. They had found him, but as those unknown things plunged their tendrils deep into his mind, they discovered something else entirely.

The magic, new and fresh, yet with a history older than they could understand or accept.

Their shock turned to terror when it unveiled itself to them. Its own history—its failings, its shame, its eternal guilt—was laid bare, just for an instant, but long enough to force the creatures away. Per-haps to drive them mad.

Rafe did his best not to see.

———

TREY RODE HARD, Alishia slumped between his arms. *Mother!* he thought, wretched and alone. *Mother! Sonda!* He pulled a handful of the final fledge crumbs from his pocket, and though they were white and stale he swallowed them quickly, whimpering as forgotten deeds were laid out for him to view afresh.

"No!" he shouted, and the gone-off fledge plucked him from his mind and sent him hovering above the pounding horse. He looked down at himself, sitting upright and holding tightly on to Alishia, and he tried to lose himself in the void of her mind. *If I get in there,* he thought, *they won't be able to get at me. They'll never reach the heart of me. If I can get in there . . .*

But inside, touching Alishia and listening to her screams of mental anguish—and then hearing what came next—he began to wish he had stayed put.

I never lived, Alishia whimpered, *never saw, never went out to experience! And here and now I'm dying, that thing as good as killed me, I would have known what was happening if I'd relished life rather than locked myself away, those books, gone to black and no more, only in my head. And they were* only books! *And now—*

Her voice paused, humbled by the sudden, massive presence that arrived in the tattered remnants of her mind. Trey shrank back. Alishia did not even know that he was there. And then she screamed, driving him spinning helplessly through the forest, past the Monks pursuing them, losing himself as the fight went on around them.

Trey's physical body slumped on the horse, the saddle slipping sideways again. His eyes turned up in his head. And then Alishia screamed out loud, a wretched wail that spooked their horse and made the whole forest hold its breath for an instant.

Trey's eyes sprang open. And as the horse twisted and turned between the trees, he began to cry.

———

A'MEER TURNED AGAIN, knelt down as Kosar ran past her, fired an arrow. A Monk screamed as the shaft found its mark. She moved too fast for Kosar to see, pacing from tree to tree, loosing arrows and flitting across the ground like a shadow.

"Run hard!" A'Meer said. "Catch up. I'll try to draw them off."

"No, I—"

"Go!" She glared at him, then leaned forward and pushed him roughly away. "Just go, Kosar. If those mind-things got to Trey and Hope as well, they'll need guiding. I'll catch up with you. Life Moon be with you." She slipped away between the trees, bent over. Her last few words had not sounded convincing.

Head still reeling from the onslaught of hidden memory, Kosar did as A'Meer asked. He watched her for a few seconds more — running from tree to tree, pausing, firing an arrow, making an intentional noise as she stumbled over a protruding root and rolled through a tangle of old twigs and branches — and then he forced himself to turn away, hurrying as fast as he could after the two horses.

Every movement now had the feeling of desperation. A'Meer's departure gave Kosar the impression of a last-ditch attempt to give them more time, though for what none of them knew. Rafe's imaginary destination, perhaps? The place where he could save them? For the first time ever, Kosar realized, they were actually submitting themselves to the safety and protection of this new magic brewing and hiding away inside the farm boy. It had revealed itself to them already, but unbidden, manifesting of its own volition rather than revealing itself at their request. Now they were going where Rafe said it urged him go, and with every step they took they went farther into the unknown.

He heard a scream from behind, high and filled with pain, and as it turned into an animal roar he knew it was a Monk. Another arrow found home, he thought with a smile, and then he frowned as he wondered just how many shafts A'Meer had left. Once she ran out she would resort to her crossbow, and then after that, the sword. By then she would be surrounded. And soon after that, she would be dead.

He followed the trail left by the two horses. He wished their track were not quite so apparent. He would have been able to follow far subtler signs, but as it stood, the Monks could not help but see the route they had taken. The forest carpet was churned up, twigs and branches broken, and here and there Kosar spotted smears of blood on the tips of thin branches, drips on the forest floor. Some of them were already attracting the ants.

He ran hard. He had never felt so exhausted. His heart pounded at his chest, trying to grab his attention. A pain bit into his hip, bending him to the left, but he never let up. To pause now would be to deny the advantage A'Meer had given him by staying behind.

More sounds came from somewhere behind him in the forest: a scream or a shout; something falling heavily, as if from an uppermost branch of the tallest tree; whisperings, urgent yet still secretive; and then the unmistakable sound of battle. Sword on sword. Shouts, grunts, screaming as sharp edges struck home.

Kosar paused, drew his sword and then ran on. A'Meer would not thank him if he returned to try to help. And really, what help could he offer?

From ahead came the sudden sound of a horse rearing up. Someone screamed, though he could not tell whether the voice was male or female. And then the horses were running again, their hooves drumming on harder-packed earth.

Kosar hurried on, ducking beneath branches, skirting around a huge writhing ant mound that had been smashed in two by the fleeing horses. And then he emerged suddenly from the pine forest into a deciduous woodland—the trees more widely spaced, the ground harder, shrubs and tangles of fern growing here and there—and he saw what had startled the horses.

All color had gone. The trees, leaves and trunks, the ground, ferns and shrubs and thorny bushes on the forest floor, the vines hanging from high branches . . . all color leeched away, leaving the whole landscape a uniform, dull gray. Texture and dimension were picked out only by the fall of sunlight, the distinction of shadows. A bird flew from one high branch to another, calling in a weak, croaky voice, and its color was the same.

Kosar gasped, paused, fell to his knees on the forest floor. The leaves there, left over from the previous winter, had taken on this sickly hue. The ants that crawled over and under the leaves were like speckles of ash migrating across the ground. A beetle here, something larger there—a scorpion, perhaps, or some huge insect—all tinted with shades of gray. He closed his eyes, held out his hand and opened them again. His skin was browned, leathery from the sun, his nails black with filth, and the blood that continued to drip from his fingertips was a stark red against this nothingness.

Kosar sighed with relief, stood and ran on. He felt like an invader here, unnatural and alien, whereas it was the place itself that was so wrong. There had been no fire. The leaves still seemed alive, and they even retained a healthy sheen viewed from certain angles, but something had stolen their color. He kicked the leaves at his feet, wondering whether color had been washed away into the ground, but only the compacted dark gray of the dried mud beneath revealed itself.

The trail was harder to follow in here—the trees grew farther apart and there were no broken branches to show the way, no churned ground—but he could hear the horse now, so he followed his ears instead of his eyes.

There were no longer any noises behind him. He was either too far away or the fighting had finished. He could not bear to imagine what that could mean.

At last he saw the horses ahead, swerving around a huge old tree, disappearing again behind foliage. He ran on, the sighting giving him extra strength for this final sprint. It took another hundred steps to catch up, during which the surroundings hardly changed at all: no color; no sound; no hint of pursuit. When he was finally close enough to make himself heard, he stopped and spoke as loudly as he dared.

"Trey!"

Trey's horse skidded and reared slightly, snorting foam from its mouth and nose, and Trey turned in his saddle.

"Kosar! Where's A'Meer?"

"Fighting the Monks," he gasped. "Make Hope stop, just for a moment." Trey nodded and rode on, trying to catch up with Hope and Rafe where they had moved ahead. Kosar looked around at the forest behind him before following at a trot. He found them waiting beside a fallen tree, the horses wide-eyed and snorting with panic and exhaustion. Hope looked pale and startled, her tattoos knotted around her eyes and mouth. Rafe's expression was unreadable.

"The Monks are in the woods," Kosar said. "A'Meer is trying to draw them off. Rafe, where are we going? Is this it?"

"No," he said, shaking his head. "But I don't think it's very far."

"What's wrong with this place?" Hope asked. "What's here?"

"Another bit of the land gone bad," Kosar said, kicking at the gray leaves at his feet. They crackled and spun in the air, shedding gray dust like ash.

"Not that," Hope said. "Back there, in the pines . . . those whispers. Did you . . . ?"

"Yes," Kosar said, catching her eye and then looking away. "A'Meer knew of them."

Trey made a noise—a laugh, a sob—but none of them said any more about what they had seen, felt or remembered.

"We really need to get wherever we're going, Rafe," Kosar said. "I don't know how long A'Meer can fool them or hold them back." They all looked uncomfortable at A'Meer's actions, as if it was already certain that she had sacrificed herself for them.

"Not far," Rafe said again.

"Swap with me," Trey said. He carefully dismounted, letting

Alishia slump forward in the saddle until her head was resting against the horse's mane. "She screamed back there," he said. "They got to her too, even deep down where she is. That's good, isn't it?"

"Maybe," Kosar said. He mounted the horse, put his arms around Alishia and held the reins to either side of her. He glanced down at the miner and smiled. "I'll take care of her," he said. Trey frowned, smiled, plucked his disc-sword from his back and looked to Rafe and Hope for direction.

"That way," Rafe pointed. "The woods stop very soon, and then we'll see where we're heading."

"And where *is* that?" Kosar snapped. He surprised even himself with the anger in his voice. He was becoming furious at being led, steered, pointed left and right as if by a child playing with wooden toy machines, replaying their own versions of the Cataclysmic War. And though he was scared of what Rafe carried, he was angry also at being kept in the dark. "Where are you taking us, Rafe? Ask that thing inside you and—"

Rafe frowned. "A graveyard," he said.

Filled with questions, none of them spoke.

Hope led off, driving the horse slightly slower than before. Panic was still there for all of them, but it was more controlled now, more ordered.

Kosar spurred his horse on, clasping the comatose girl between his arms. There was hardly any weight to her at all. He was surprised that she was not dead. He wondered what was going on inside her head, whether those whispering things had invaded as deep as her dreams, and he hoped that she was well.

Trey ran alongside, his long legs eating up the ground.

Ahead, Rafe rested his head against Hope's back and seemed to sleep.

————

SOMETHING WAS COMING.

Rafe felt smaller, slighter and yet more significant than ever before. His whole body tingled, outside and in, and he felt the thing that lay deeper than his own mind expand to fill his soul, edges ripping and rippling, promising imminent release. He felt on the verge of a mental orgasm, a spewing of knowledge and magic and something new. He was sick and elated, terrified and enchanted; and the knowledge that something was ready to show itself drove his heart into a frenzy.

Still mindless, still needing protection and guidance, the magic inside was ready to emerge.

"It's coming," Rafe whispered, but in the tumult of the chase nobody heard. It did not matter. They would know soon enough. "It's coming."

Chapter 26

THE FLEETING SHAPE emerged from behind a tree ahead of him, the air whispered and an arrow embedded itself in Lucien Malini's neck.

He tried to scream past the wooden shaft, but blood bubbled in his throat and sprayed from his mouth. The agony was intense, its taste raw and satisfying, and as he fell to the forest floor Lucien's rage closed around the pain and drew strength. His rage grew, making the pain a good thing, something he could subsist on even while his blood leaked and eventually clotted, thickened by fury, holding the arrow tight. He stood again, staggered sideways into a tree, screeched as the shaft struck the trunk and twisted in his flesh.

His skin burned, his scalp was tight and on fire, his muscles twitched and knotted with pent energy, and when he began to run his speed was borne of wrath.

Those dreams came again—images of people he had killed, women he had taken, the pathetic, quivering flesh-things that had died in their dozens on the end of his sword—and the whispers deep in his mind were confused, shocked and yet unable to let go. Lucien held them there. The images came faster, but rather than guilt and shame he felt only triumph.

He saw the Shantasi darting from behind a tree and roared his warning to the other Red Monks. The scream split the arrow shaft in his throat and sprayed bloody splinters at the pines. A flash of red to his right, a shimmer of movement to his left, and the Monks closed in.

His sword sang and vibrated with bloodlust. A squirrel jumped from a tree into his path, and Lucien struck out, slashing it in two. Another arrow whistled in, glancing from his cheek and taking a chunk of flesh as it spun away. Lucien laughed.

More memories, more deaths, dredged from the depths of his mind and forgotten merely because there were so many to remember.

There was a scream from ahead, the clash of sword on sword, the flash of sparks flying in the shade beneath the trees. Lucien coughed more blood and splinters and ran to join the fray.

"THE GRAVEYARD," HOPE said. "Oh Mage shit, I never in my life expected to really see this. I never *believed* it."

But Rafe was leaning against her back, asleep or unconscious, and it was for her to make sense of what she saw. The other horse drew near and she heard Kosar gasp. Trey ran up between them, panting, his breath slowing as he looked at what lay before them.

They had left the gray forest several minutes before, and followed a gradual slope up to the crest of a small hill. Now, in a natural bowl in the land before them, lay the graveyard to which Rafe had brought them.

There were no markers here, no headstones or monuments or mausoleums to the hundreds of machines that lay dead in the heather and grass. Their hollowed carcasses almost covered the ground entirely, starting from a hundred steps down the hilltop from where the observers stood, sweeping into the craterlike valley and then climbing the slopes on all sides, here and there actually lying dead on the hills surrounding the hollow. Some looked as if they had been consumed by fire in their last moments, stony protrusions burned black and melted smooth by the heat. Others had died and rotted down slowly, settling into their final resting places as the living tissues that supported them slowly returned to dust. The smallest machine was as large as a man, its spindly iron legs rusted centuries ago into its final stance, and now almost rotted through by the trials of time and climate. Its shell held only air now, where before its workings had merged in metallic and biologic symphony. There were constructs the size of a horse, others even larger, and one, in the low center of the valley, that must have shaken the very ground it once rolled across. It was as large as a dozen farm wagons, its smooth stone shell curved and notched like the carapace of a giant beetle. Its back bore holes at regular intervals, and a few of them were surrounded by the bony stumps of what may once have been legs, or other less obvious limbs.

The land had continued to grow around this place of death and decay. Grasses grew strangely long and lush on the valley floor, fed perhaps by the water that must gather there from the rains. Bushes and small trees had forced their way between and through the dead machines, protruding from gaps in the constructs' bony skeletons and metal cages, pressing through cracks where perhaps there should be none, doing their best to subsume these echoes from the past into this stranger, less happy present. Several large trees had sprouted here since the Cataclysmic War, their roots set deep, their boughs and trunks grown around or through dead things. One trunk had split in two and joined again, trapping within itself the rusting metal limb of a large handling device. It clasped the iron like a wound holds an arrow, and though sickened by the rusting metal its growth still seemed a success.

The shades of old machines—the grays of stone, blackened fire-stained limbs, the dark orange of rusting things—were complemented by the brave greenery of the plants trying to hide them from sight. Giant red poppies speckled the solidified hide of one machine like recent wounds. Yet the dead could never be truly hidden. They were too many, too large, and now a permanent part of the landscape.

"They came here to die," Hope said.

"They're *machines*," Kosar said. "They must have been brought here. It's a rubbish yard, not a graveyard. They're machines, they were brought here . . . they can't have come on their own."

"Why not?" Trey asked. "It was ancient magic that made them, not people. Can we say what they could and couldn't do?"

"They came here to die," Hope said again. "Lost, knowing the Cataclysmic War was its end, magic brought them here to die."

"However they got here," Kosar said, "why has Rafe brought *us* here?"

"Maybe we can hide," Trey said. "That huge one down there, it must have a whole network inside, plenty of places to crawl into and hide."

"He said magic was going to make us believe," Hope said. "There's something else here, not just a hiding place. And the Monks would never give in. It may take them days, but they'd find us."

"He also said that he might take us away," Kosar said.

Hope turned in her saddle and nudged Rafe, almost smiling at how she was treating the carrier of new magic. "Wake up!" she said. "Rafe . . . farm boy . . . wake up!" He was not asleep. His breath was too fast for that, his eyes half-open, his hands clasped tight in his lap, so tight that a dribble of blood ran from his fist.

"We should get below the skyline," Kosar said.

"Down there?" Trey asked.

"It's where Rafe brought us," Hope said. "And as you said, we can hide away in there while we're waiting for . . . whatever."

"But . . ." the miner began.

"It's either down there, or back toward the forest," Kosar said.

Hope glanced past the thief at the gray canopy. Farther back in the forest the gray changed to green, but from here the colorless blight looked huge, stretching as far as she could see from left to right, humps of gray trees retreating back into the woods. "A'Meer must be in there," she muttered, wondering what might be occurring beneath those trees right now.

"She'll find us," Kosar said.

Hope looked at him and saw that he knew his lie.

They urged the horses down toward the graveyard of dead machines. Behind her Rafe mumbled something, but Hope could not make out the words. She nudged back sharply to try to wake him, but he merely held tighter and became looser, head lolling against her back, hands reaching around her waist.

Soon, she thought. *He'll show us soon. Soon we'll know just what it is he has, and it'll be our choice to have faith in it or not.* She looked out over the scattering of dead machines, relics from the last age of magic.

I want it so much, I've always had faith.

AS KOSAR LED his horse past the first skeletal machine, he thought he heard something move. He paused, turned in the saddle, met

Hope's questioning gaze. Perhaps it had been Trey working his way ahead of them, stopping here and there to look into hollowed metallic guts, lift rusted blades, step over something long since sunken into the ground. The miner kept his disc-sword resting over one shoulder ready to swing, though at what Kosar could not guess. The Monks were behind them, fighting A'Meer in the woods. Here, for now, there were only old dead things to keep them company.

The urge to go back and help A'Meer was almost overwhelming. The cold way she had looked at him when she told him to go had been a mask. She had known that she was committing suicide, and that any acknowledgment that this was their final moment together would have changed her mind. She could have said good-bye, but that would have taken a second too long. She could have smiled and given thanks for their good times, but that would have been a breath too far. She had known that within hours or minutes of turning her back on Kosar, she would be no more. That certainty had left no room for sentimentality.

He could help. He could draw one or two of the Monks away from her, perhaps lose them in the woods, hide while they passed him by, double back and do the same again. There were huge old trees in there, trunks hollowed by rot; deep, dark banks of bushes; high ferns. A thousand hiding places, and other areas where he could lay false trails, snapping branches and then working back. Striving together he and A'Meer could confuse the Monks, and in that confusion perhaps find their escape.

It was a crazy idea, and he knew it. If he went back to the woods he would die with A'Meer. She was trained, her early years dedicated to preparing her for this one purpose. He was only a thief. Three minutes against a Red Monk and he would be dead. And knowledge of his death was the last thing he would want to accompany A'Meer into the Black.

"These are all different," Trey said. "Inside and out, they're all different. This one, here . . . I can see right inside, and it has dried veins or bones strung like strings across the spaces." He ran to another machine, chopped at the overgrowing ferns and mosses with his disc-sword, smoothed his hand over its surface. "This one: there's no opening, no way to see inside. Who knows what's in there?" Moving on, chopping again, hauling on a bundle of thorny branches to expose what looked like a giant set of ribs. "This one, we can all see inside. We can all see those fossilized things."

"Organs," Kosar said. "They look like the insides of a living thing, grown hard."

Trey reached in between the stony ribs with his disc-sword, touched one of the hardened things held in place by dozens of solidified stanchions, thick as his thumb. It exploded in a shower of grit and dust, the long rattling sounds indicating that there was much more of this machine buried deep down.

"I still can't believe they came here on their own," Kosar said.

"You've heard of the tumblers' graveyards, haven't you?" Hope asked. "They're scattered around in the mountains, dozens all across Noreela. They're guarded by other tumblers, but there are those that have got through to see for themselves. Thousands of tumblers . . . they go there to die, mummified in the heat, rotting in the rain, petrified in the cold." She looked around at the partially hidden history they were now intruding upon. "Once, we thought that tumblers were only animals."

"They're not?" Trey asked.

"They're not," Kosar said, but he had no wish to continue the discussion. Trey turned away again, exploring, fascinated by this place.

"Is he doing anything?" Kosar asked, halting his horse so that Hope and Rafe could draw level.

The witch half turned in her saddle, reached around and supported Rafe with one arm. "Still asleep," she said. "Or maybe unconscious. And . . . he's hot. Mage shit, he's *burning up!*"

"Let's get him down," Kosar said.

"But—"

"Hope, there's no way we can hide in here. They'll find us. And there's nothing to fight with, if and when they . . . break through." The thought of what "breaking through" meant for A'Meer did not bear dwelling upon.

"And now are you believing? Are you finding enough faith to put your well-being in his hands?"

Kosar shrugged. Rafe's eyes were flickering, red from whatever fever had sprung up. He was nothing special to look at, yet everything was special about him. "It's the last thing left to have faith in," Kosar said.

A scream of agony came from over the hill in the direction of the woods, loud and anguished and rising in pitch.

Kosar shivered, his skin prickling all over, and he turned the horse around, ready to nudge Alishia off and gallop up the slope to the ridge. And what then? Down into the woods, sword drawn, ready to sacrifice himself to the Monks?

"Kosar," Hope said. He looked at her, momentarily furious that she had drawn him back. "Kosar, help me with Rafe! He's burning."

Kosar steadied his horse and slipped from the saddle, easing Alishia down and laying her flat in the low ferns. She moaned slightly, eyes flickering, limbs twitching at the change of position. *Later,* he thought, *I'll tend to you later.*

Rafe was scorching. He grabbed the boy beneath the arms as Hope lowered him down and laid him out next to Alishia. Already the boy's clothes were soaked through with sweat, his face beaded with moisture, and his skin seemed to radiate heat so violently that Kosar actually looked for flames, expecting the boy to ignite at any moment. *And why not?* he thought. *The magic within has to release itself at some point, once he's served his purpose. Why not purge itself through fire?*

"We need to cool him down," Hope said. "Mage shit, I had medicines back home, things that would have helped." She ripped at his clothes, loosing buttons and ties and exposing his chest and stomach, blowing on his slick skin to cool him. He started shivering instantly, so violently that his teeth chattered together.

"Is it happening now?" Kosar wondered aloud.

"Whatever, it had better happen soon. If he brought us here to show us some miracle, we're in dire need of it. Look." She nodded up the slope, Kosar looked, and there stood the first of the Red Monks.

It was a bloody red blot on the landscape, a wound to the skyline, a rent in the perfect world through which a dread wind howled, its mouth wide, hooded head thrown back as it sighted its quarry. There were several arrows and bolts stuck in its body; one through each thigh, a snapped shaft protruding from its face, one pinning its voluminous cloak tightly to its chest. Yet it stood strong and defiant, like a standing stone that has seen ages pass. It was close enough for them to make out its woman's face, and the skin was red. Blood, perhaps. But rage as well. This thing was at its most dangerous. Flushed with the fury of the hunt, enraged by the wounds it already endured.

"A'Meer," Kosar muttered, because he could not avoid thinking of her body ruptured and spilling its precious insides across that forest floor. Perhaps even now her blood was fading to gray, eager to become a part of that wrong place.

The Monk staggered down the slope toward them. It was only two hundred paces away. Its sword was extended, bloody and glinting in the sun. It would be on them soon.

"Come on!" Hope cried. She shook Rafe brutally. "Fuck you, come on! Do it, do whatever it is you brought us here for!"

Trey had returned from his exploring. Instead of hiding himself away, he stood beside Kosar and held his disc-sword in both hands.

"We take it from two angles," Kosar said, walking forward a few paces to take the fight away from Rafe and Alishia. "It's resilient, shrugs off wounds like a splash of water, but it's not that fast. And its swordplay isn't the best."

"Neither is mine," Trey muttered.

"You have that disc-sword," Kosar said. "It has a long reach. As long as you don't let the Monk knock it out of your hands, you can hold the bastard away."

"And you have that apple-picker?" Trey said, nodding at the sword in Kosar's hand.

The blade thrummed, the handle was hot and steady in his grasp. "It's tasted Monk blood before," he said. "It'll do."

"Until the others come from the woods to join their friend," Trey said.

Kosar did not answer.

"Come on!" Hope screamed behind them, slapping Rafe across the face. The unconscious boy's fingers were fisted into the soil, delving into hidden roots and routes, holding him there as if the world was about to up-end.

A'Meer, Kosar thought, *you must have fought hard*. The Monk was close now, and there were several large areas of its cloak that gleamed with fresh blood.

"Not like this," Hope said, her voice changing from challenging to forlorn. "Not like this, it can't all end like this! It's so *pointless*!"

The Monk was twenty heartbeats away.

Something began to growl. Kosar thought it was the Monk, but then he noticed the thing's head turning slightly as it too searched for the source of this noise. It was a high, screeching whine, like two huge swords being ground together.

"What's that?" Trey said.

From behind them, Hope gasped and whispered, "It's happening."

A few paces ahead, from where a flat machine lay all but smothered in a rich purple moss, a long limb slowly extended out across the ground. The movement was accompanied by a metallic growl as hinges, junctions and elbows that had been stiffened by three centuries of inactivity, rain, frost and sun began to move once more. It lifted painfully from the ground, rust the color of dried blood dropping away in a shower to speckle the moss below.

The Red Monk had paused in its advance and stood swaying unsteadily a few paces away from this new, strange, wondrous thing.

"Magic!" Hope called out, laughing viciously. "Magic! Do you like that, you red bastard?"

The Monk hissed at her words, stepped forward and struck out at the long metal appendage. Its sword glanced from the limb, throwing sparks and rust specks into the air, and it staggered back with its arm held tightly to its side. The thing continued to rise, bending in the middle like a human arm preparing to throw. And it seemed to be growing thicker.

"It's changing," Kosar said in disbelief. "Expanding. It's—"

"Magic," Hope said. She turned to Rafe, bent down and put her hand to his face. "He's holding on to the ground as if he's afraid he'll fall off, but at least he's cooled down. No fever. Whatever was building in him has been let loose."

The Monk roared again, and Kosar and Trey raised their weapons in readiness. The rejuvenated metal arm of the dead machine might intimidate the Monk, but it would not hold it off forever. Their fight was still to come.

The arm lashed out. It seemed slow and ponderous, too old to move swiftly, too heavy to shift with any speed. Yet still the machine snatched out at lightning speed. Its metal end—a club more than a hand, a fat knot of rusted metal as big as a man's head—struck the Monk in the chest. An explosion of blood and spittle spattered the metal, and the impact threw the Monk back the way it had come. Its arms waved, its cloak billowing, and when it struck the ground the arm fell across its chest. Kosar felt the vibration through his feet as the heavy metal dented the ground. The Monk gurgled and reached for the sword where it had fallen into the bushes. But it could not shift the weight.

Behind Kosar, Rafe mumbled something, then shouted, and then *screamed*, a cry filled with fury. His fists delved deeper into the ground and his arms shook, lifting his back and shoulders so that he was supported only on his fists and the balls of his feet. His shoulders vibrated with the effort of holding himself up. His eyes had rolled back to show their whites, lips were drawn away from his teeth, muscles standing out in stark relief on his thin neck and forearms. And his fists kept working, opening and closing, fingering downward into the ground to improve that contact.

Something happened to his wrists. *Sparks*, Kosar thought, yet a cool, pale blue, powerful and full of energy but cold as the nothing beyond death and before life; cold as the Black.

Rafe screamed again. The metal arm crushing the Monk sparkled and shimmered with cool light and then lifted up, curling in the air and fixing around the Monk as it tried to rise. The arm was not as solid as it had seemed before, its edges less defined. And as it tightened around the figure, its length rippled.

The Monk struggled, thrashed and battered the thing that was holding it up. It was a demon flailing against the good, an horrendous vision of things unnatural and unwanted. But Rafe's ongoing scream of rage piled more violence onto it, and the flexing metal arm smashed hard into the ground. There was a sound like a fistful of twigs being crushed, amplified a hundred times. This time the Monk did not even scream. The arm lifted it again—the Monk's own arms still waving, but weakly now; legs dangling uselessly—wavered for a few seconds, flipped it over and crashed down again. The Monk's head hit something solid beneath the pretty purple heathers. When the arm lifted once more, its skull was ruptured and leaking.

It bashed the corpse down another three times before dropping it into a growth of high ferns. It almost seemed to Kosar that the reanimated machine wanted to hide the awful sight from these terrified, amazed humans.

The small valley was filled with a few seconds of stunned silence. Rafe was calm again, as if sleeping, and the machine was completely still, as hidden away as it had been only moments before. The whole attack had taken less than a minute.

And then the noises began. Stealthy, secretive, rustling and whispering from the undergrowth, groans and squeals of metal and stone things moving after an age lying still. A bush shimmered here, grass shifted there, ferns waved at the sky and were then still again, a tree on the opposite slope seemed to bend at an impossible angle before springing back, shedding a shower of leaves.

Kosar tore his eyes away from the sight and hurried over to Rafe and Hope. "Is he awake?"

The witch shook her head. "Still unconscious. Calmer now, though." She was staring past Kosar, past Trey. "Did you see? Do you know what that was?"

"A machine," Kosar said.

"A living machine, moving and functioning!"

"They're waking all around us," Kosar said.

Hope looked down at Rafe, stroked his face, wiped sweat from his forehead with the sleeve of her dress. "He's saving us."

"We're not saved yet. And it's not him. I think Rafe is farther from us than ever right now." Kosar looked at Alishia where she lay nearby, struck by the similarity between the two unconscious people.

Hope's eyes sparkled with life, her tattoos stretched her face into the sort of smile Kosar had never seen there before. It was not a pleasant image. She seemed on the verges of madness. "Maybe we *can* get out of this," she said.

"Did you see how that thing *crushed* him?" Trey asked. "It took seconds. If more of those Monks find us here they won't last long! We'll be safe, we'll be saved."

"And what of A'Meer?" Kosar asked, hating the petulance in his voice but sick at the unfairness of it all. Had she sacrificed herself needlessly? "Is this magic so cruel? Does it kill its protectors that easily?"

"She did what she thought was best," Hope said.

"Look!" Trey was pointing up at the ridge between the valley and the forest, where several figures had appeared. The Red Monks stood staring down into the valley, the breeze flapping their cloaks around them, and more were joining them all the time. Some were wounded, but most were not.

"She held them off for a while, at least," Trey said.

"Damn it!"

"Kosar, she held them off. If that first one had come through any earlier maybe it would have reached us before we got here. We could be dead now, and it would have got to Rafe before the magic had a chance to start anything. Now . . . look around! She gave Rafe time. And it's working for all of us."

"We have no idea what's happening here," Kosar said. But he did not take his eyes from the Monks still appearing across the ridgeline above them. His sword throbbed in his hand and his heart beat fast, the need for action and revenge rich in his veins. There were so many of them here now, maybe thirty or more, that the idea of A'Meer still being alive somewhere in the forest was foolish in the extreme.

"So what do we do?" Trey said. "Do we just stay here, let them come?"

"What else *can* we do?" Kosar said.

Hope's grin was still there, that mad grin. "Let them come and try to take the boy. They'll see what it is they're fighting. They'll know the true power of what they hate." She touched Rafe's arm, muttered a few words beneath her breath and waved her other hand over the ground beside her. The smile slipped for a few seconds as whatever she was attempting seemed to fail. But then she looked up again and caught Kosar's eye. "There's plenty of time."

Something rose out of a patch of ferns across the valley, lifting its head from the greenery like a huge snake looking for danger or prey. But this thing had no eyes, no ears, no mouth that Kosar could make out. It was dull black like polished stone. It rose to the height of a man and stayed there, solid, not swaying or shifting in the breeze. The Monks were watching too, some of them pointing, some of them waving their swords at this manifestation of all they hated. A'Meer had been cured and the flooded River San crossed, but here and now the magic was touching and changing the land, establishing itself in the arcane corpses of these old dead machines, moving out of wherever it had been hiding.

And here, facing it in this fledgling state, was the greatest force that existed to ensure its nonreturn. The Red Monks began to howl and screech, voices twisted into something monstrous. They waved their swords and cried out their defiance, anger and hate.

The thing across the valley did not move but was joined by other shifting shapes, several more columns rising around it and shimmering in the fading daylight. The surfaces of these new things seemed to flicker, moving like oil on water, colorless but constantly shifting and confounding to the eye.

"What are they?" Trey asked.

"More machines," Hope said. "Rafe is raising us an army."

"It's not him," Kosar said again. "He's just a conduit. And is it only happening here, for us? And if that's the case, what about when the magic is established back in the land?" He looked down at Rafe's hands where they were still clenched into the ground beneath him. No sparks now, but the power beneath his skin was apparent, the channeling of magic through flesh and bone. "What happens to us then? To Rafe?"

"Why hate it after all that's happened?" Hope asked, her amazement real enough.

Rafe opened his eyes.

Hope gasped and fell back. Kosar caught his breath. Rafe looked directly at Kosar, his smile tight and tired. "It *is* me," he said. "It's happening here so that I can protect us, but that's all. Nothing else. Just . . . protection." He looked at Hope. "So there's no point trying anything like that again, witch." And then his eyes closed, the smile faded and his skin turned pale and began to glisten with fresh sweat.

"He's not that boy anymore!" Hope hissed, her eyes wide and scared.

"He hasn't been just that boy for days," Kosar said. "How can he be?" He knelt next to Rafe and felt his forehead. "He's burning up again. Something's going to happen."

"Those Monks are coming!" Trey said.

Kosar stood and moved forward, putting himself between the Monks and Rafe. "They won't stop," he said. "While there's one of them left that can crawl across a field of blades to get to Rafe, they won't stop." He looked back at Hope and Trey, glanced at Trey's discsword, hefted his own weapon. "Don't believe that this will be easy."

Suddenly spooked, the two horses turned and darted away between the machines, heading for the other side of the valley. They took the saddles, bags and blankets with them. Kosar took one step in pursuit and then stopped, realizing instantly that it was hopeless.

As the sun touched the ridge to the west, and cool shadows rose, forty Red Monks screamed down into the valley. And for the first time in three centuries, magic entered into battle.

———

THE FIRST MONK to die was snatched down into the foliage, pulled quickly out of sight, arms flying up and sword spinning through the air. Its scream was long and loud, but none of its companions spared a glance as they rushed by.

They poured down from the ridge like blood rolling down a

darkening face. The sun still lit the slope and picked them out in glorious color, illuminating also the things that rose to block their path. Weed-encrusted, heather-drowned metal constructs rusted almost to nothing, stone things eroded by time, seemed to turn over lazily, trapping a Monk beneath, crushing down and down until its sword protruded from the loam, hand still clasped around the handle. Some Monks fought what they encountered, and the sound of metal on metal, and metal on stone reverberated through the valley.

Most of the things that rose did so slowly, the creaking and crackling of their first movement for three centuries a counterpoint to the Monks' enraged screeching. The machines appeared tired as they lifted themselves from the ground that had supported them for so long. One seemed to yawn, a great metal carapace opening on a rust-riddled back to reveal thousands of sharp edges. The sun caught the metal teeth, and its touch seemed to be a balm to the recovering machine. Some of the teeth began to shine, as if restored to polished metal; the jaws opened wider, their squeal dying, lubricated by the fading light. And then it fell, gravity guiding its languid way around a rampaging Monk, the giant shell closing, grinding and finally opening to disgorge two twitching halves. It rose again, faster this time, and more teeth shone in magical renewal.

The forty Monks soon found themselves embroiled in battle on the dividing line between light and dark. They drove forward—fighting, dying, learning very quickly that to dodge was much safer than to engage—crossing the line into night and leaving the sunlight behind. Their cloaks darkened immediately, the color of blood grown suddenly old. Their hoods remained raised. As each Monk entered into battle it let out a fierce, jubilant scream, crying rebellion at the sky, slashing its sword against the machine rising to attack, and in their cries all possible outcomes still existed. There was no resigned defeat here, no brave last stand. Only defiance and bitter determination.

Kosar and the others gathered close, shielding Alishia and Rafe in case any Monks broke through. They watched the incredible scenes before them, frustrated at the failing light because it stole away so much detail. But as light faded and night closed in, two things became apparent: the machines were growing in strength; and they were changing.

One metal limb rose and flicked at the air like a giant whip, its lash a loud *crack* that set eardrums vibrating. The next time it came up it seemed thicker, its movement more animated. The crack was just as loud but its tone was deeper, heavier. It thrashed again, catching a Red Monk over the top of the head, sending it spinning across the ground. And this time the limb had grown thick with new, muscled flesh.

Blood misted the air around the limb. Blood that *rose*, drifted *in*, not dropped and sprayed out. New, fresh blood, borne of nowhere natural. It gave the machine renewed life.

It thrashed at the air again and again, the cracks merging into a thunderous roar, tearing the sky as it pursued its victim across the hillside. The machine's base was hidden in the dark heathers and bracken, but its newly enfleshed limb rose high and proud, finding the Monk that had scurried away, pulling back and flipping it forward so quickly that the whiplash ruptured its body. The machine had lifted the Monk so high that his discharged insides were richly lit by the sun for a second before they spewed down into shadow.

"They're *growing*," Kosar said.

"They're coming back to life," Hope said. "And there's more. Don't you see what's happening? Look over there." She pointed up at the ridgeline where the Monks had first appeared. One of them was trapped there, not even allowed to enter the valley, unable to fight its way past a small, thrashing thing that hissed and spat across the ground. Thin silvery limbs spun behind it, throwing up clots of earth and grass. The Monk went one way and the machine followed, lashing at its legs and feet, drawing blood, bringing it down. The Monk's sword flashed out, sparks flew, and the machine fell back, but it left some of its twisting limbs in the Monk's face. The Monk stood, swayed, stepped forward . . . and the thing was there again.

"I don't see," Kosar said. He was confused enough by all of this, without the witch trying to create more complications. Besides, most of his thoughts still lay beyond this valley, down in those grim gray woods.

"That's no fighting machine," Hope said. "These down here, maybe. They have blades and clubs, and other things we've yet to see, I'm sure. But that one up there is a domestic aid, if that. But whatever it is, it's still fighting the Monks. It's back from a long sleep, and it's back for a reason."

"I don't care," Kosar said. He had to raise his voice above the cacophony of battle. He looked around, hefted his sword, ready to use it should any of the Monks come at him.

"You should care," she said. "It's back to protect you."

"No it isn't. It's the boy, always the boy. Not me, not you, not this sleeping librarian we've carried with us halfway across Noreela." Kosar glared at the witch, and though her tattoos seemed to writhe around her mouth and her eyes glimmered with menace, he did not break his gaze. "And not A'Meer, out there in the woods. Magic did nothing to protect her then. It doesn't care."

Hope turned her back on Kosar and returned to her vigil over Rafe.

"Kosar," Trey cried. "They've changed tactics! Look, over there, past that outcropping." He pointed with his disc-sword, indicating a hump of dark green rock protruding from the gentle slope. Beyond there was a blur of battle. A splash of red, a spray of sparks as metal clashed, screams and screeches that could have been animal or machine.

"What?" Kosar said.

"There are five or six Monks there," Trey said. "They leapt down from the rock and took on the machine at its base. But there are others crawling past. See them?"

Kosar squinted, and as he cast his eyes left to right he saw movement along the ground. Slow, careful, methodical. "They're sacrificing themselves," he said.

"Ten die to get one through," Trey said. "Even at those odds, we're finished."

Kosar felt the subtle vibrations within his sword growing by the second. Perhaps it was in tune with the awakening ground, or the battle raging around them. Or maybe it was simply picking up on his own anger. He looked at Trey and offered the miner a grim smile.

Trey, yellowish skin seeming to revel in the dusk, grinned back. "We may yet have a fight on our hands," he said.

"Hope," Kosar said, "some of them may yet get through. Do you have anything that will help us?"

The witch looked up from where she knelt next to Rafe, and for a second her expression was one of pure menace. The thief caught his breath, startled, wondering what he had disturbed. He glanced down at Rafe but the boy was unconscious, fists turned into the ground. A luminescence still fluttered around the joint between human and land.

"Help?" the witch said. "You have magic helping you, what more do you want?"

"It's helping, but they're still getting through," Kosar said. "The machines can't stop all of them. If they kill a hundred and one makes it past, we still probably won't survive. I'm not a warrior, Hope, and neither is Trey. Do you have *anything* that might help?"

The witch looked down at the boy, moved her hand across his body from forehead to the tips of his toes, closed her eyes. When she opened them again that menace had returned, but it faded into a deep, dark sadness.

"I have nothing," she said.

"Maybe the magic *will* help us until the end," Trey said. "It stands to reason. Whatever Rafe is doing to make all this possible would be pointless if one Monk got through and killed us all."

Kosar wished he could share the miner's sudden optimism.

As daylight waned, it seemed that the magic was finding its feet with greater relish. The rusted and rotten bones of dead machines continued to lift themselves from the loam, and within seconds they were clothed in a thin layer of flesh or a liquid covering of molten stone. Fluid flowed in from all around, appearing from nowhere to give the machine back its blood, enclose its old skeleton even as the skeleton itself was solidifying once more. Layer upon layer was built up and around the remains, shifting with new movement, and not always blood and flesh. Wood and stone in one place, water and flexible glass in another, magical new forms of machines arising from the sad remnants of old.

Kosar hefted his sword and kept watch for shadows that should not move. He thought of A'Meer in the forest and tried to imagine her remains, what they would look like, gray forest creatures darting across gray leaves and making away with moist pickings to feed their colorless broods. There had been such pride in A'Meer's life, and there should have been more purpose to her death.

He hated the fact that she was dead, and he hated the reason more. Glancing back at the boy lying on the ground Kosar caught the witch's gaze and held it for a second before glancing away. There was something about her eyes that he had never liked.

"It just better be worth it, that's all," he said. Hope did not reply.

"Oh, what in the Black . . . ?" Trey whispered. "Look. Up there, on the ridge, the sun's still just kissing it. Look!" He pointed with his disc-sword, but Kosar had seen them already.

Monks. Dozens of them, maybe hundreds. Perhaps they had been lagging behind the forward group, running from farther afield in answer to whatever call had brought them here. Now they formed an almost solid red line across the ridge between the valley and the forest, bloodred and ready to pour down and flood the machine graveyard.

"If your magic's still got something up its sleeve, now is the time," Kosar said, directing his comment to Rafe without turning around. Across the valley the sounds of fighting continued, though they were more sporadic now, metal on stone and the cries of Monks being killed by the magic they so despised. Breathing in, Kosar smelled red.

As the wave of enemy began to flow down from the ridge, the first Monk broke through the barrier of reanimated machines and lunged for Kosar and Trey. Steel clashed. And three dark shapes high up caught the setting sun.

———

LUCIEN MALINI WAS bloodied and torn, yet not all of the blood was his own. As he entered the valley, the Shantasi bitch already drying on his sword, he sensed the stink of magic being wrought. It was not something he had smelled before, but the way it pricked at his nostrils, ran in bloody rivulets down the back of his throat, made him sick to the stomach. Yes, this was magic.

When the first machine appeared and engaged him in battle he was not surprised. Its several long, thin arms rose, creaking and whining as they twisted and turned slowly in the air before him, clothing themselves in flesh and blood and more unnatural fluids, and Lucien lashed out with his singing sword. It bit into one limb and chopped it clean through. The amputated appendage spun in the air but it did not fall. It waited. And then, after dodging Lucien's second parry, it reattached itself to the growing machine and struck back.

Wounds opened in Lucien's face, his chest, his stomach and arms. The machine curled itself around every thrust of his sword, and those rare instants when he did make contact caused little damage. As he put a slash into the machine's new flesh, it healed again before his next strike. He aimed at the more stony protuberances, but his sword raised nothing but sparks, seeming only to add more energy to the magical monstrosity.

Lucien raged inside. He had lived, breathed and worked all his life against this ever happening, and now he felt the magic he so hated thrumming through the ground beneath his feet. The air stank of it, the dusk shone with its reemergence, and all across the valley he heard evidence of magic's success: screams, the sound of Monks being cleaved in two, stone and metal hacking through the brave, strong flesh of his brethren. So he raged and fought back, but as each second passed by he felt victory slipping farther away. It was being eaten by these unnatural things, sucked into their new veins and arcane power routes, subsumed beneath the dirty magic that had cast so much damage across the land all those decades ago. They had not arrived here in time. An hour earlier, two, and maybe, *maybe* . . .

Lucien fought long and hard, taking many hits. He meted out strikes too, hacking chunks from the machine, but its suffering seemed only to increase its strength. It had no mind, of that he was sure. It had no soul, no compassion, it had no place in this world. But each wound it bore made it more real.

Still fighting, Lucien sensed a shadow fall across the valley. And looking up, seeing the shapes circling way above the battle, for the first time he truly believed that the Monks would finally lose.

————

LENORA RODE HER hawk hard, diving toward the battle, scenting blood and realizing that this was the most important moment of her life. The creature spat and bubbled beneath her, the sudden rapid descent rupturing its side and sending spurts of blood and fluid into the air. Its tentacles folded in to her command. Its head hunkered down. It had turned itself from a gliding shape into an arrowhead, slicing through the air and moving so fast that splashes of its own torn insides were left behind in bloody red clouds. It screeched and screamed but it was essentially a dumb creature, and it obeyed this command that would take it to its death.

Lenora clung tightly to the hawk's back, knees tucked in and hands twisted several times around the steering harness. She squinted against the buffeting winds. Yet even above this roar she heard the sound of the Mages finally sensing their quarry, the magic they had sought to regain for three hundred years, and which had driven them both completely mad. It was a sound that Lenora, seasoned warrior and soldier in the Mages' army, hoped that she would never hear again.

Angel sat upright on her hawk's back. Air tore around her and clapped behind her back, casting wispy vapor trails in her wake. Her eyes were wide-open. She had seen the object of her desire, and there was no way now that she would lose sight of that again.

To Lenora's left, a few wingspans away, S'Hivez held on to his mount, digging his heels in so hard that they penetrated the creature's side and encouraged its inevitable demise. Blood flew back from the wounds in a fine spray, though Lenora could not tell whether all of it was from the hawk.

Neither Mage carried any weapons. That did not worry Lenora. She had seen them in action before.

Less than a mile beneath them, the battle raged below the setting sun's rays. The glitter of sparks from steel striking steel was visible at this altitude, and even though the air was ripping past at an incredible rate, still the scent of blood found its way up to them. And not only blood—Red Monk blood! A sliver of fear slipped into her mind past the bombardment on her senses, and the fear gave her a thrill. A *real fight*, she thought. A *real enemy*. She was as conscious of the weapons pinned and strapped around her body as she had ever been, ready to employ them instantly upon landing. They were a part of her life and soul, as much a part of her as her own limbs. Extensions of her body rather than mere tools. And soon they would be blooded again.

She could hear the battle now, a whisper of cries and chaos seeping past the roar of air about her ears. She could make out the lay of the land too . . . and what she saw amazed her. She had dreamed so much over the centuries, her ancient memories turning into something that resembled myth in her mind, but she had never truly believed that she would ever see magic in action again. Here, now, directly below her diving hawk, machines were entering into battle. The shimmering blue light of magic cast its sheen across some of their weird constructs, and yet others fought in darkness, their magic contained within. The whole area inside the bowl-shaped valley was a slightly different color from its surroundings: lighter, more animated, more *alive*.

Lenora glanced across at Angel just as the Mage screeched her delight.

Here was their target. Here was magic. And it was mere seconds from their grasp.

TREY HAD FOUGHT fledge blights, vampire bats and cave snakes. Several years ago his cave had battled a plague of the snakes, vicious serpents whose normally pleasing song had been turned shrill and threatening by some weird disease. They had made away with three babies before the men had time to band together and hunt them into the tunnels. Normally creatures such as these would easily elude capture, easing into holes and cracks that could never be penetrated by the fledge miners, however supple evolution had made them. But these creatures had not only grown mad with their illness, but large as well. It gave them a hunger that could not be allayed, and their incessant eating—each other, cave creatures, the babies they had caught—made them large and ungainly. The hunt had been short and brutal. The fat snakes had come apart under the onslaught of the miners' disc-swords, spilling things onto the cave floor that did not bear closer examination.

That had been a killing, not a fight. The snakes had not fought back. And they had not screamed in ear-shattering rage as they came at him.

The Red Monk had been severely lacerated by its encounters with some of the reanimated machines. Its right arm was all but severed, hanging on by threads of gristle and shredded robe. Blood spewed from wounds in its chest and stomach, and Trey knew that this thing should be dead. Its wounds were fatal, surely, and yet it charged like a fledge blight in full ferocity, its voice louder, its rage more obvious, its blooded sword raised high in its left hand. Trey was too stunned to act.

Kosar's sword saved his life. The thief stepped between them and lashed out, stumbled as the Monk fell at his feet, stepped in quickly, stabbed down and jumped back again. It screeched and writhed and Trey, instantly shamed by his inaction, swung his discsword. It caught the Monk beneath the chin and whipped up its head, burying itself in the jawbone and holding fast.

The Monk opened its mouth, but the scream was choked with blood. It turned to look at Trey. The movement forced the jammed disc-sword handle down toward the ground, and though the pain must have been immense the Monk cast its rage-red gaze upon him, marking him in case it had a future.

"Back!" Kosar hissed. He lunged in and stabbed at the floored Monk again, his sword finding and parting flesh.

Trey squatted, twisted and wrenched at the disc-sword handle until the blade screeched free. The Monk howled and thrashed on the ground, its sword lashing out, and Kosar cursed and staggered back, bleeding hand splayed out before him like a wounded spider.

"Kosar?" Trey said.

"I'm all right. Just watch it!"

Trey lunged with his disc-sword again and again, but the Monk's mad thrashing seemed to throw off every parry and thrust. The thing stood and advanced, coming straight for Trey. Its lower jaw was hanging by a few red threads, teeth glistening with blood, and the hissing sound must have been its best attempts at a scream. The miner stood his ground and worked his disc-sword, sending the blade at its tip spinning, catching the last of the daylight on its bloodied rim. The Monk aimed a clumsy strike with its sword, which Trey deflected and countered. Another wound opened through its torn robes. He struck again, aiming high for the Monk's throat and face, but the disc-sword glanced from its bony forehead and took only skin.

Trey looked around, making sure that Hope, Alishia and Rafe were safe, then turned back to see the Monk's sword swinging at his face.

Kosar screamed and deflected the blow, stepping once again between Trey and the demon. He kicked the Monk and sent it sprawling.

Trey stepped forward to slice at the fallen enemy, but Kosar held him back. "No," the thief panted. "No need."

The Monk went to stand but the ground beneath it lifted, an area three steps on edge rising straight up and then folding inward as the wakened machine found its purpose. The Monk was enveloped by green-veined rock, and this strange new machine crushed in and down like a flower in reverse. The Monk's death was quick and horrific. It took only a few seconds for the machine to retreat below-ground once again, leaving little more than a disturbed patch of sod to mark its place.

"Took its time," Trey gasped.

"I suppose they think we should be doing some of the work," Kosar said. He smiled at Trey, then winced and looked at his wounded hand. Blood glistened blackly in the dusky light, though Trey could not tell how bad the wound was. He did not want to ask.

"What's that?" Hope suddenly screamed. "*What's that?*" The fear in the old witch's voice was shocking. Even above the continuing sounds of battle, and the screams of new waves of Monks forging into the valley, her voice held power. Trey had never heard anyone sounding so terrified. His first reaction was to look at Hope, and she was pointing straight up at where the death moon was even now manifesting from the gloom.

Trey saw the shapes high in the sky. They were still within the sun's influence, but it did little to illuminate them. They were shadows against the dark blue background. And they were growing. Trey looked around at the dozens of battling machines—newly enfleshed arms spinning Monks through the air, great metal fists pounding them into the ground, spinning blades rending them in two, a hundred more of the bloody demons dodging between the magical constructs and coming closer, closer—and he wondered why he felt the true threat coming from elsewhere.

"Hawks?" Kosar said.

"Not this low," Hope said. "Not this *low*! They live and die high up out of sight. The pressure's too much for them down here. They're not of the land. Unless . . ."

"Unless what?" Trey demanded.

The witch did not take her eyes from the shapes growing larger above them. "Unless something's steering them."

"The Mages," a voice said. Trey looked down at Rafe where he lay at Hope's feet. "The Mages are here." He slowly hauled his hands from the ground, scraping moist earth from between his fingers, and sat up to face his companions. His face was pale and drawn, as if the arrival of dusk had brought defeat upon him.

Trey hated the expression on the boy's face. It matched the fear he had heard in Hope's voice. "What do we do?" Trey asked.

Rafe did not reply. *Does he know?* Trey wondered. *Can this farm boy really get us out of here?* And he began to wonder.

———

FIRST THERE WAS nothing but pain and shredding, nothing touching the senses but an agony much deeper, searing her wounded soul and burning the exposed endings of her psychic nerves with a cruel conflagration. There was no consciousness of outside, beyond, only of the dark here and now.

I am in pain. I am under siege. And I am not whole.

The thoughts seemed alien, and she tried to pull away from them like an animal from fire. But they were not of a single point, they *were* the point, and they could not be escaped. Her mind quietened and she could accept that, because to think was to hurt. She had no wish to think these things. They made her feel less than she should have been, and although she had no memory of exactly what that was, she knew that she was much reduced.

The voice that had spoken to her in here had faded away, leaving in its place a pause between breaths. She felt the weight of potential.

She drifted, afloat in her own mind, the flotsam and jetsam of her memories bobbing by to offer vague, unimaginable glimpses of a story she could never understand. Every time something came out of the darkness the agonies grew, as if revelation promised only pain. Revelation, and realization. Because hidden behind this blackness she sensed a profound knowledge awaiting rediscovery.

Wisdom and pain, learning and agony. *I know that I must not know.* But even the ability to create that thought hurt her to the core.

And then something was coming.

It was the presence back in her mind, invisible, silent, yet keen as the pain that informed her consciousness. It was huge. Massive in import and effect, terrifying in scope, because it came for her. It *must* have come for her, because there was nothing else here. Yet far from reducing the little she felt, it made her feel more there, more corporeal, and for the first time since she could remember, Alishia knew her name.

There is hope in Kang Kang, the presence portrayed, and Alishia had heard of that place.

Life rises from death, she understood, and she wondered where she factored between the two.

This is for you. She did not know what that meant. She had no inkling. Yet an instant later, Alishia felt whole again. Whole, and possessed of something extra. Something momentous.

She opened her eyes and said farewell to the Black.

"ALISHIA'S AWAKE!" HOPE said.

Rafe nodded. "The magic brought her back." The boy was still sitting on the ground, staring up at the dark shapes bearing down on them. The sounds of fresh battle filled the air as the machines fell upon the new wave of Red Monks.

Hope touched the girl's forehead as she stirred, wondering what was happening inside. She seemed much reduced, as if she had begun to shrink. "Hey!" she said, but the girl did not answer. Her eyes looked through Hope and saw something much more terrifying. "Why did it bring her back?" Hope said to Rafe, but he did not respond.

Hope let go of the girl and pressed her wrinkled hands to the ground, working her fingers below the surface. Kosar and Trey were shouting to each other, looking up at the shapes growing larger in the dusky sky, yet they had not noticed the change in things. Rafe had sat up, moved his hands from the soil where they had been making sparkling contact for the duration of the battle. And yet still the magic worked. Whatever link he had forged was now redundant, because magic was loose again amongst these machines, meting out memories of better times and clothing them in flesh, blood, stone and wood that had been their makeup all those years ago.

Hope pressed her hands in deeper, feeling for the change in herself, *demanding* it. Yet no change came. She whispered an old spell her mother's mother had once used, but it dispersed in the air with her useless breath.

And then Alishia blinked again, slowly and heavily, and she stared at Hope. Her eyes were so full of knowledge that the witch fell back. *She knows!* the witch thought. *She knows what I was doing! How could she know that, unless . . . ?*

Rafe was staring at the sky, as if welcoming the coming attack.

"Rafe," Hope said, pleading, demanding, but though he turned to her his eyes offered nothing.

"They're coming," he said. "Cataclysm falls so soon. It's out of my hands."

There was a pause in the battle then, a moment so brief that Hope thought she might have imagined it between blinks. Swords must have been drawn back, waiting to fall again. Red Monks' breaths were hauled in for the next exhalation of agony. Machine limbs paused between stretches, rusted joints poised to find themselves whole again, denuded metal bones reveling in the softness of new flesh. There was silence, an instant of peace, and when the cacophony began again everything had changed.

The ground around Hope, Alishia, Rafe, Kosar and Trey rumbled and rose, two dozen ribs the thickness of a man's thigh piercing the sky from the ground, curving up and around, and even before the ribs met above and formed a protective cage they had changed from rusted red to silvery gray, catching and reflecting the first gleams of the death moon.

"We're caged in!" Hope hissed.

"They're caged out."

And from above, the promise of death descending.

———

LUCIEN MALINI FLED that valley of death. Almost dead himself, he crawled up to the ridge and down the other side, rolling, leaving bloody marks on the ground behind him. It was lost. It was all lost, all hope, lost to the Mages and those machines awoken here. The land would know magic again and he would see its influence, and that enraged him. Pain was chewing him up now, driving his rage to new levels in failure. He rolled, stood, tripped and rolled again, knowing that all there was left to do was to take whatever petty revenge he could find. He would go to that Shantasi bitch's body and hack it to small shreds, bathe in her blood and use it to replace his own. That image would keep him alive for the next few minutes, at least.

But when he reached the place where she had fallen her body was already being taken apart. He saw the last of it spread and melt away, red turning to gray. And as he fell to his knees and screamed he saw the trees and rocks and ground around him shift, move, melt down into a billion tiny parts. They merged with the disintegrated Shantasi and flowed away to the east.

Perhaps it was simply his vision failing him at the point of death. Or maybe it was something much more important than that; something for him to follow. And that thought alone gave him back a spark of life.

———

THE HAWKS FELL out of the sky. Kosar was amazed that they did not leave a trail of burning air behind them, such was their speed and ferocity. He heard the roar of their movement through the air, and maybe they were growling as well. He could see the shapes sitting astride their gnarled necks, and though Rafe had spoken their names Kosar could not believe what he was seeing.

The Mages? Here, now, already?

For so long they had been the stuff of legend and campfire tales, an evil three centuries old that, though horrendous, had faded slowly away. Time could not extinguish their wrongdoing, but it had smoothed the sharp edges, shedding the intricate details of their crimes and leaving only the wide-scale stories of magic gone bad and war, conflict and death across the length and breadth of Noreela. The results could still be seen and felt, but Kosar had never known a time when the land was untainted. He had seen many strange and horrible sights in his travels, but he had not consciously attributed them to the Mages. They simply *were*.

And now within seconds, the Mages were going to attack.

"What do we do?" he said. "What can we do?"

"They'll never stop," Trey whispered. "They'll smash right through us!"

"They want Rafe alive; they're not here to kill him."

"It doesn't look like that to me," Kosar said.

He could see their faces now, and he was surprised at how human they looked. Fearsome, furious, but human.

Night filled the valley.

The machine caging the five humans began to vibrate, the sensation originating from belowground and shimmering up the tall ribs enclosing them.

When the hawks were only seconds away, slowing down, extending their clawed feet to grasp on to the huge machine, an explosion of light burst from the point where the ribs met and splashed up and out to meet them.

Kosar squinted against the sudden brightness, shielded his eyes and fell to the ground. There were screams from above them, perhaps hawk, perhaps human. When he looked again a few seconds later the sky was clear and the hawks were skimming the ground away from them, shedding specks of light like embers from a disturbed fire. More sparks erupted as their riders slashed and hacked at machine and Monk alike.

"What was that?" Trey hissed.

"The machine protecting us," Rafe said. "It can fight them, but I doubt it'll hold them off forever. It's a distraction. If they can satisfy themselves with fighting the Monks and the other machines in the valley—and they must be raging for blood after so long—then perhaps we can get away."

" 'Perhaps'? Get away how?" Hope was on her feet, staring up at the huge ribs catching the moonlight.

Rafe smiled. "As I said, it's out of my hands."

Kosar and Trey stood beside Alishia and Rafe, still nursing their weapons but more distracted now by the vibrations in the ground beneath their feet, the shimmering of air between the ribs. Something was happening—something invisible and momentous—and the potential filling the air was palpable. Kosar tried to slow his breathing but fear sped it along. *I've just seen the Mages, been within a spear's throw of the demons of the land. And I'm still alive. For now.*

"What was the light?" he said.

"Magic fending off the Mages, that's all that need concern us," Rafe said.

"Magic," Alishia whispered.

"Is it still in you?" Kosar asked Rafe. "Are you still carrying it? Isn't it free now? Isn't this the moment magic comes back to the land?"

Rafe frowned, staring out through the cage at the struggling shadows beyond. "I think this is only happening here," he said. "It's taking a lot of effort."

"So how long does it last?"

"I don't know."

"Long enough for us to get away?" Trey asked. He was kneeling beside Alishia now, touching her face and hands. "Otherwise, what's the point? If magic protects us like this—reanimates the machines, defends us against the Monks . . . the *Mages*! . . . why would it not save us for good?"

"I don't know," Rafe said again. The ground shook once more, a vibration that sent a heavy, rumbling groan up into the air. It mingled with the sounds of battle.

The cage altered in the dark, and when Kosar looked closer he saw that the metallic ribs had turned back to bone.

"We're going to fly," Alishia said.

"What woke you?" Kosar asked. He suddenly did not trust her. He did not trust anyone, not now that A'Meer was likely dead and he was here amongst strangers again. Alishia looked at him and her eyes were both beautiful and terrifying. *For a librarian, she's seen so much*, Kosar thought.

Seeing past the ribs, he could just make out details of the fight. The three dark shapes had seemingly shaken off the effects of the light and were now hovering above different parts of the valley, their riders slipping sideways in their saddles and entering into battle.

Kosar could not tell what they fought—Monk or machine—but he knew that the Mages would find enemies in both. The previously simple battle had now turned into a three-way fight. That suited him fine. Let the Mages and Monks and machines battle it out, so long as they left them alone . . .

Something, Kosar thought. *Something is happening, now, beneath our feet. I can feel it. Like tumblers rolling beneath the ground, as if to change the shape of the land itself.*

"Fly . . ." Alishia said again, dreamy and light.

A roar came in from the distance and a huge shape reared above the horizon, a hawk standing on its tentacles and grappling with something less recognizable. A fiery exhaust burst from the machine and scorched the ground, and the hawk rider lashed out with some unknown weapon, the weapon itself carrying fire, wrapping around the machine's base and bringing it down with an earth-shaking crunch. The hawk screeched again, but this time in triumph.

Monks cried out, crumpled beneath hawk feet, slashed by the riders' blades, crushed by machines.

The land swam in blood.

And then slowly, incredibly, the valley began to fall away.

"What in the name of the Black—?" Kosar hissed.

"It's going," Trey said, looking down. "It's going, it's falling, leaving us behind."

"No," Hope said. "We're flying."

"Flying . . ."

Lights flashed below them and to the side, accompanied by a roar as the ground tore itself apart, freeing the trapped machine. The light flared, lifting them up on a pillar of luminescence. Bursts of a more firelike exhaust streaked across the valley from the machine, enveloping hawks and Mages in writhing flame, sending them spinning away like burning stars. The hawks streamed around the valley, ricocheting from rocky outcroppings and solid machines, dripping fire across the ground and setting the blood-drenched cloaks of Monks aflame. Soon the valley was lit by fire, though the hawks and their riders seemed to shake it off, rising up again.

The battle continued. But now, dazzled by the new fire thrusting them aloft, Kosar and the others were all but blinded to its progress. They saw glimpses of the scattered fires, but the edges of the machine that lifted them up obscured any real view.

Kosar had sat down on the shaken ground. He held on to the

thick grass below him, as if that would anchor him to the spot. He was terrified. Trey glanced at him and Kosar grimaced back, shrugged his shoulders. The strange, it seemed, had just become stranger.

"Where are we going?" Hope asked Rafe. She sounded so matter-of-fact, as if flying was something she did every day.

"Away," Rafe said. He was staring at Alishia, and they both smiled. "Away. Safe. I'm so tired." And he closed his eyes and went back to sleep.

"I wish I could do that," Kosar said.

Hope grinned at him, her tattoos catching the death moon and turning her visage ghastly. "Scared, thief?"

"Aren't you?"

Her smile remained. "Petrified. We're *flying*, for Black's sake!"

The machine seemed to be picking up speed. They felt the bursts and pulses of energy shed from its lower edges, and with each explosion they were pushed higher. Light simmered around the machine's lower edges. And with each gush of motion the machine itself was changing. The ribs had thickened as some dull gray coating grew around them, pulled in from nothing. The spaces between the ribs began to glow with countless points of light. Kosar had once been caught in a storm of fireflies, but this was even brighter. Soon it was bright as daylight within the gray ribs, and then lighter still, so that Kosar had to squeeze his eyes closed. It lasted for only a few heartbeats. When the light faded and he looked again, there was only the vague background illumination left from the pulse down below. And he saw what the light had made. Between each rib, for the height of a tall man, a fleshy skin stretched across. Even now veins formed on its surface and within, flooding it with blood from nowhere, and magic was at work so close, so near, that if he so desired he could have reached out and touched it.

Their sense of velocity increased. Kosar looked around at the others—Hope, wide-eyed; Trey, hanging on to the ground for dear life; Alishia and Rafe, prone, the movements of their limbs perhaps due to the motion of the machine, perhaps not—and he knew that he had to look over the edge. He had never been scared of heights or the unknown, but what terrified him most now was just what he *did* know. He crawled to the skinlike edging between the ribs, knelt up and looked over.

Fires had erupted across the ground. Some of them were small, others seemed to have spread and a few of them still moved. They lit up most of the small valley and the dying things it contained. It was spotted with dead Monks. He could make out the larger machines in the firelight, most of them still now, limbs slumped down, one of them accepting punishment from a group of Monks without defending itself. Their purpose fulfilled, these machines were dead again.

There was no sign of the hawks.

The machine gushed another blast of light, blinding Kosar and sending him reeling back. The roar was immense and accompanied by another burst of speed, thrusting them up and up until, suddenly, the sun found them again. The heat felt good on his skin. To the west the horizon was a smudge of yellow. If they rose forever, perhaps the sun would never set.

No hawks, he thought. *Of course not. They'd have no reason to continue the battle once we were away with Rafe.*

"What do you see?" Hope asked.

Kosar looked over the side again. It was strange looking down into night from a position of daylight. He wondered how high they had come.

"Kosar?" Trey prompted.

"I think the fighting's stopped," he said. "The machines aren't moving anymore. I can't see the hawks."

"They're stalking us," Hope said. "They have to be. It's the boy they want. They'll go back for the Monks later."

"It's Rafe they want," Alishia said, "and they'll get him."

"Go back to sleep!" Hope said.

"Then where are they?" Trey asked. "Why don't they just attack if they want him?"

"I don't know," Hope said.

"You pretend to."

"But I don't! I don't know anything. It's guesswork, all of it. The only one who knows is him and . . . and maybe her!" She pointed an accusatory finger at Rafe and Alishia. "And they're not telling the likes of us."

"So what happens now?" Kosar asked. "Do we just sit and let this thing take us wherever it likes?"

"What choice do we have?" Hope said. "We've never had a choice. We've been dragged along for days, never given any option, no free will. Everything that happens to us is fated. Maybe in an hour we'll all be dead, or free, or somewhere we can't possibly imagine."

"That's helpful," Kosar said, but her words chilled him because they echoed what he had been thinking all along. *No free will.*

The witch stared at him, her tattoos writhing as she grimaced in annoyance. "It's the only help I can give."

"So we sit back," Kosar said. "Enjoy the view." He glanced down over the side again at the wide forests surrounding the burning valley. A'Meer was in there somewhere, dead, already graying into the land. He scanned the darkened treetops, wondered if he was looking right at her.

The machine rose higher and higher, light bursting occasionally from its underside. The air became cold, the sky above them darker, and soon night enveloped them once again. They could not outrace the sun, however powerful the magic that carried them.

They watched and listened for the hawks. *They must still be there,* Kosar thought. *There's no way that single attack from the machine could have finished the Mages, no way. Not after three centuries awaiting their chance to return. There must be more to them than that.* "We should plan," Kosar said quietly. "They'll be coming. We should figure out how to fight them off."

"Don't be so stupid," Hope said.

"And don't be so fucking negative!" Kosar stood on the uneven clump of ground held inside a machine, glowering at the witch where she squatted next to the unconscious boy. "Why did you come along, why did you take it on yourself to protect him? When we first met he was yours and yours alone! Now you're ready to sit back and let the Mages take him without a fight? I don't believe that."

"No, I'm not ready to do that at all," Hope said. "I just admit that we don't have a chance. It's hopeless. How can we fight them? You have a sword, Trey has a disc-sword, I have a few false charms in my pockets that would barely hurt a street urchin, let alone one of *them*!"

"What do you know about them?"

"Enough to know we don't stand a chance."

"You know nothing," Kosar said softly. "You know nothing because no one knows anything. They've been gone for so long that every story about them has been twisted and turned. They could just as easily be sad, pathetic, weak old things that will drop dead at the flick of a knife."

"They got here quickly enough," Trey said. "They have their spies that told them what was happening, and they've flown from wherever it is they fled to claim back what they think is theirs."

Kosar looked between the two of them, shook his head and realized that there was no point in arguing. When none of them knew the truth, what was the purpose of further discussion? They could only discuss supposition.

"But we have to fight," Kosar said, and his words sounded so weak that he sat down and said no more.

"Fight," Alishia said. "Yes, fight."

"What do you know?" Kosar asked her.

Alishia smiled and closed her eyes.

———

TREY CHEWED ON a chunk of fledge—his final thumb of the drug, stale now, bitter-tasting and rank—and he tried to let his mind float out and away.

In Alishia and Rafe he encountered two areas of utter darkness, and he was repelled. There was so much in there and nothing at all, and the sense of threat told him that either could be the case. So much could be things he was not meant to see, ideas that were never supposed to be dreamed; and nothing could only be the Black.

He edged out into space and soared, his flight weakened by the bad fledge, the balance of his mind dangerously uneven. But he was free for a time, and he could see, and if he moved out in concentric circles he may yet be of use to the others. His disc-sword had aided Kosar back there against the Monk, but he felt no sense of victory in meting out death, however repellent the thing he had killed. Rafe was a stranger and what the boy appeared to carry was stranger still, so try as he might Trey could find no real nobility in their cause. He supposed he was fighting for the good, but that was something of which none of them seemed to know. They ran and fought blind. Rafe seemed honest, but did that make what he carried decent as well? Or merely deceitful?

There was no way Trey could know for sure, so he had to follow his instincts. And besides, Alishia was still here, beautiful Alishia, awake now and more mysterious and closed off to him than ever. And she had saved his life.

He sought the hawks and the riders that drove them on.

The space around him was filled with myriad signs of life, all of them small and driven by instinct. Flies, birds, one or two presences larger and more obscure but none of them displayed any purpose in their travels. Basic minds drifted and floated on thermals, some

asleep and others barely awake to the world around them. There was
no real intelligence here, and they retreated from Trey's questing
mind like smoke before wind.

He spun farther out, down toward the ground, sensing the
aching distress of many minds far below. He reached out a tentative
thought and touched on them, recoiling quickly when he found
what they were; Red Monks, dead and dying, their rage dispersing
into the ether. Even as they died they were mourning the failure of
their mission, because many of them died on their backs, looking up.
Up at the dark skies above, up at the memory of the vanished machine that had carried Rafe away. And up toward where the hawks
had flown in pursuit.

Trey drew back quickly to the machine, casting about, looking
behind dark shadows and trying to bridge gaps where things were
obscure to him. Perhaps the fledge had been even staler than he
had thought, or maybe he was losing his ability to use it properly,
his mind polluted by fear or something far more subtle. He hovered for a while at the periphery of his physical self, still aware
of those two huge areas of darkness nearby, knowing who they
were, hating their inscrutability. Rafe he could understand, but
Alishia . . . ?

And then he saw them. The hawks, their riders, storming down
from above where they had been drifting in wait for the machine.
He knew their rage and disgust, their power and rot, and as he
slipped back into his own body just in time to scream he realized
that there had never been any hope.

They were all going to die.

———

TREY SCREAMED, RAFE shouted out in his sleep and something
struck the ribs of the machine.

Kosar was thrown to the ground, landing painfully on his
wounded hand. The thing that had hit them—a hawk—cried out,
shattering the relative quiet. The impact had split two of the ribs and
torn the membrane between them, and blood sprayed black in the
moonlight. The hawk cried out again, still pushing forward, and
Kosar could see the shape standing on its back. Standing, and
preparing to jump across its head into the confines of the machine.

Hope stood and threw something in the same movement. Her
aim was unerringly true. It struck the hawk just above one fist-sized

eye, and something dark and fast spread down across the white of its eyeball, turning it instantly black. The creature screamed, its cry one of pain now rather than rage, and started to thrash itself free of the broken ribs.

The machine squeezed. It seemed to be using its wound to its own advantage, holding the hawk in place, crushing, the raw ends of the snapped ribs piercing the animal's skin and slipping inside.

The shape on its neck was a woman, heavily armed and armored, tall and strong and scarred, no doubt one of the Mages' fighting Krotes. She sat down to avoid being thrown out into the open air, staring through the ribs at the people she had come here to kill.

Kosar stood, drew his sword and smiled. The Krote hissed. The thief felt so empowered by this that he took several steps forward until he was standing within reach of the hawk's trapped head.

"Who the fuck are you?" the Krote said. Her eyes were a shining, pale blue, even in the weak moonlight.

"A friend of anyone you go against," Kosar said, and he lashed out. His sword parted the flesh of the hawk's head and he stepped back as the thing tore itself free and spun back into the night. The Krote watched him as she fell away, and though Kosar knew that this fight had just begun, the brief sense of victory was invigorating.

"Trey!" Kosar called. "We have to protect this breach!"

"Gave the bastard a blinding!" Hope said triumphantly.

"What was that?" Trey asked.

She smiled. "Poison ants."

"Are you crawling with these things?" Kosar asked, partly in disgust but mostly in admiration.

Hope's smile diminished. "That was the last."

There were two more impacts on the machine's construct, one directly above them where the ribs met, the other below, out of sight, down where the ground had torn itself away. Kosar and the others went sprawling again, and the sound of the vicious hawks baying for blood seemed to shut out the moonlight.

Kosar looked up. Silhouetted against the death moon a hawk was standing on the pinnacle of the curved ribs, hacking with its huge beak and crushing them with hooked claws. Blood and flesh spattered down, and then something harder as the ribs were quickly rent asunder. *If only I had A'Meer's bow and arrow*, he thought. The attacker was way too high to reach with a sword, and they could do nothing but watch as it tore into the machine.

But the machine was preparing to fight back. Pale blue light glimmered across several of the ribs. Like electric dust-worms shimmering together, the streaks of light darted across the ribs' surface until they met, several bright spots forming just above ground level, growing larger, brighter . . . and in their glow, Kosar could see the face of the thing staring down at them.

A Mage. It had to be a Mage. He had never before seen such madness, hate and bloodlust.

It opened its mouth and hissed. As if the sound were a signal, the machine launched its counterattack.

Balls of purple light burst up from the glowing ribs and converged on the Mage and hawk. As they flew their shape changed, from unformed fire to things with definite edges, purpose, design. They struck the hawk's feet and chest and erupted into a scrabbling plague of scorpions. Simmering light still played around the lower ribs, and in their glow Kosar saw the scorpion's stingers rising up and down, up and down, puncturing the thick hide of the hawk and pumping it full of venom. More of the creatures crawed quickly up and over the thing's head, saving their venom for the Mage upon its back. And the Mage, wincing and cursing at first as the things struck, but then smiling, finally laughing, plucked them from its skin and clothing and bit off their poisoned barbs with relish.

More light poured out from the machine, the ground shaking with each eruption, and as it impacted the hawk's hide it flowed and manifested into more stinging, biting things. The hawk shuddered and the Mage lashed out, sending bits of shattered bodies raining back down between the ribs.

Kosar brushed scorpion tails from his hair, spider legs from his face, and they melted into the dark. He felt helpless. The sword vibrated in his hand.

The Mage fell from the hawk's body and jammed between two of the ribs. At first Kosar thought it was dead, poisoned by the things magically flung at it by the machine, or perhaps bled dry by the newly formed swarm of bats that harried its head. But then it stretched out its arms and started hacking at the ribs with heavy serrated swords, and Kosar knew that this thing was unstoppable.

It ignored the light exploding across its body, shunned the things biting and tearing and poisoning. It ignored everything but the person lying directly below it: Rafe.

"Trey!" Kosar shouted. "It's coming through! Your disc-sword can reach it, cut it before its free!"

Trey nodded, looked up at the Mage, back at Kosar, fear and doubt in his eyes.

"Trey!"

And then the Mage was through. With a rending of metal on bone it ripped aside the ribs and fell to the ground inside the machine. Small creatures scurried from its body and flittered away into shreds of light and dark. Another purple pulse crashed into it, but the Mage grinned and it simply faded away.

As Kosar ran at the Mage, sword ready before him, Trey lashed out. His disc-sword caught the Mage across the shoulder and split leather and skin. It fell to its knees. Kosar struck with his sword and felt the grinding hold of bone as it entered the Mage's chest. He twisted, leaned his weight on the sword to bury it deeper, and the Mage vented a shrill scream.

"Yes!" Trey shouted. He swung his disc-sword again and took off three of the Mage's fingers. "Yes!"

"No!" Hope cried.

Kosar turned. She had thrown herself across Rafe's body, and at fist the thief could not tell why. But then he saw the black shape thrashing in the disturbed ground, great pawlike hands lifting earth and muck and rock and throwing it aside, and the second Mage quickly emerged into the glow of the machine's defenses.

It laughed. It had the voice of a beautiful, carefree woman, someone who had found the love of her life.

"Kosar!" Trey shouted, and Kosar turned into the first Mage's fist. It had stood and thrust Trey aside, striking out at Kosar at the same time, and its fist cracked his cheekbone and toppled him easily to the ground. He dropped his sword.

"You're not having him!" Hope screeched.

The female Mage snatched up the witch and threw her aside, bent down and scooped up Rafe. It ran at the wound in the machine's side where the first hawk had struck, and as if finally realizing what was happening the machine let out an onslaught of writhing purple light. It slapped into the Mage and Rafe alike, sticking like mud to clothes, forming into blurry insects and birds, lizards and mammals—all of them biting and killing. The Mage screeched but kept on running.

Rafe remained silent.

"No," Kosar said, because he knew that this would not happen. After everything, all they had been through, the power of new magic released to protect them from the Monks, A'Meer's life sacrificed to afford them time, none of this could happen. "No!"

The Mage reached the broken ribs and launched itself out into the dark, open air, Rafe clasped to its chest. More light delved after them from the machine, and dozens of creatures fell, sputtering away into nothing like sparks from a campfire.

"Rafe!" Hope screamed.

Kosar sat up just as the male Mage ran past him. He kicked out but missed its ankles, and it sprinted on. It was waving its hands around its head, batting away a cloud of fluttering things formed of light that were sizzling and sparking across its skin. Screaming, it too jumped from the machine and out into darkness.

Behind Hope's wails and Trey's wretched shouts, Kosar listened for the Mages' falling screams. But he heard nothing. The only sound now was the whimper of their own hopelessness, and the soft, dejected ticking of the heated machine cooling down around them.

———

LENORA RODE AIR currents far below the flying machine. Her hawk was mortally wounded, but she kept it alive with a combination of promises whispered into its ears and pain delivered through her buried sword. The promises were of more pain, not deliverance. The hawk was a creature of instincts, and pain would always be its driver.

Angel's hawk had already tumbled past her, dead, after she had forced it to bury itself in the machine's underbelly. The other hawk was still up there somewhere, though she could no longer see its shape around the machine. It was dark down here, and the coolness of the night air stroked the open wounds on Lenora's body.

It did not take long for Angel to come to her.

Lenora saw the plummeting shape and edged her hawk beneath it, catching Angel and the boy she carried in two of its great webbed tentacles. Seconds later S'Hivez struck the hawk's back just behind Lenora, sending the creature into its final, fatal dive.

But there was no despair, no fear, no sense that doom was upon them. Because Angel held the boy across her lap like a newborn child, stroking his forehead, waiting for his eyes to open and lifting his hair with one long fingernail as if deciding where to cut. When Rafe's eyes did open, Angel drew a knife and sawed off the top of his head. She buried her tongue in the boy's exposed brain.

Mother! a voice said in Lenora's mind, and there was recognition in that shade at last.

And in the Mage's ancient eyes, Lenora saw the knowledge that they had won.

Chapter 27

THEY DRIFTED THROUGH the night. A sliver of the life moon and the glorious death moon shone down on the battered machine, both mocking. Stars speckled the sky and added their luminescence. The machine hummed quietly beneath them, shivering occasionally as if damaged or cold. They headed south. Perhaps there was purpose, but more likely it was simply drifting, an aimlessness brought on by sudden, unexpected, impossible defeat.

The Mages had Rafe. The Mages had magic.

Kosar lay back with his eyes closed, thinking of that first day when the Monk had ridden into their village. Back then he had had no idea of the greater workings of things, and even now he understood so little. Everything they thought they knew was supposition, any decisions they had made based upon uncertain thoughts and Rafe's occasional, mostly unhelpful ideas. Really, he wondered how any of them had ever believed that they stood a chance at all.

A'Meer had been confident and passionate about her cause. Poor, dead A'Meer. Kosar had loved her—he'd always known that really—but it was strange how it took her death to reveal within him the true strength of that love. There was a hole inside, a blackness darker than this night, and it had little to do with Rafe's capture.

"What now?" he said quietly. Neither Trey nor Hope answered him. Alishia had fallen back to sleep, though color had bled back into her cheeks now, and in the darkness she seemed to smile. They had checked her over after the attack. She was growing physically smaller, younger, regressing into some sort of unnatural childhood, though none of them questioned how far this would go. Just more strangeness to live with. And in truth, only Trey really cared.

More time passed, and the machine bore them ever southward. They would reach Kang Kang soon, Kosar knew, but that did not concern him. He had been there before, and it would be no more dangerous than anywhere else now that the Mages had returned.

Myth, legend, stories to tell children by the camp light, old tales carved onto story-walls in the bigger towns and cities . . . and terrifying though the stories were, they were always safely harbored in history, cosseted away, buried as surely as the million that had died in that Cataclysmic War so long ago.

Myths were not supposed to return. Legends were never meant to come back to life.

Hope cried quietly in the night, her tears forming strange shapes on her tattoos, but Kosar felt in no mood to comfort her.

Trey sat next to Alishia, staring down at her but seeing something else entirely. Kosar could sense the pain and loss in the miner's yellowed eyes.

Kosar stood slowly and walked to the edge of the machine, stretching up to look over the membrane between ribs, wondering whether anything had already begun down below.

The land was lost. The Mages had the fledgling magic in their hands, and whatever they did to Rafe to gain control of it—and that didn't bear thinking about, not at all—it surely would not take long. Perhaps down was up already, and black was white, and life could easily swap places with death. With three centuries to plot their return, the Mages must surely know how revenge would be most effectively wrought.

"What now?" Kosar said again.

"Now Noreela ends," Trey said. "Everything that happened no longer matters. I almost envy my family and friends, dead down there from the Nax. At least they died at home. And here I am, a

miner, flying toward my death high above the surface I never should
have seen."

"This can't be it," Kosar said, but he knew the childlike naïveté
of his words. "Hopeless," he muttered.

"There's something about her," Hope said.

Kosar turned and saw the witch standing above Alishia. Her face
was stern, molded by sorrow and anger. "What do you mean?"

"I mean apart from the obvious, the fact that she's a girl instead
of a woman now. However impossible that is, there's something else.
She's not as ill as she was. She's looking better. Less asleep. And for a
while down there . . . just for a while . . . she was awake."

"Meaning what?" Trey asked. He leaned in close across Alishia
as if to protect her from the witch.

Hope stepped back. "We're going somewhere," she said. "Have
neither of you thought of what's happening here? The machine is
still flying. Magic is still guiding us. Thief, you saw the machines in
the valley falling still as soon as we left, their use ended. This flying
machine . . . magic must know that it still has its use."

"I don't care," Trey said. "We couldn't keep the boy from the
Mages, and the four of us will never get him back. That's for certain."

Hope looked at Kosar and smiled, shrugged. The expression did
not sit well on her face and he turned away, perturbed. Was that
hope he had seen there? Greed? Rage? He could not tell. Her tattoos
had hidden her true feelings, as always, and she was as much an
enigma to him now as ever.

"No matter," Hope said. "Time will tell. We'll be in Kang Kang
soon."

Their conversation ended there, and each of them withdrew
into their own thoughts. Kosar sat back against a rib and nursed his
wounded hand and bleeding fingers. He licked the blood from his
fingertips, bearing the brief pain before the soothing sensation overcame them, just for a time. A'Meer had been able to soothe that
pain. Sweet, mysterious A'Meer.

He drifted to sleep reliving images from the past, but time
treated them differently. He fought the Monk in the village instead
of hiding away. He refused to help A'Meer and fled north to the
Cantrass Plains. Rafe drowned crossing the San, their journey ended
by the wretched faults in nature, not by those that had caused those

faults in the first place. And each dream fed into the next with the same sense of incompletion.

———

WHEN KOSAR WOKE up it was still dark. He saw Trey and Hope standing at the far edge of the machine, staring out through the tattered hole in the ribs.

"How long have I been asleep?" he said. "Feels like hours."

"It was," Trey said. "Ten, eleven hours."

"It should be dawn." Kosar looked out through the ribs and saw the dark ridges of Kang Kang to the south, their pinnacles biting at the moonlit sky. Then east, out toward New Shanti, where the sun was not.

"It should be," Hope said, "but it isn't. No sun today, Kosar. There'll be no sun today."

He shook his head, not understanding. Above the eastern horizon there was only a sad smudge, like the memory of life reflected in a pale corpse's eyes. The rest of the sky was the same sickly hue, redolent of the death moon at its brightest. Kosar held up his hand—he could see the shape, but no real color. He could feel the moonlight on his skin, but there was no warmth.

"I don't understand."

"The Mages have made their first move," Hope said. "What are we, any of us, without daylight?"

———

THE MACHINE, BORNE by magic, drifted south, edging closer to the peaks of darkest Kang Kang. While Kosar, Hope and Trey watched for a dawn that would not arrive, Alishia slept behind them.

And she dreamed.

Such dark, fearsome dreams.

ABOUT THE AUTHOR

Tim Lebbon lives in South Wales with his wife and two children. His books include *Face*, *The Nature of Balance*, *Changing of Faces*, *Exorcising Angels* (with Simon Clark), *Dead Man's Hand*, *Pieces of Hate*, *Fears Unnamed*, *White and Other Tales of Ruin*, *Desolation* and *Berserk*. Future publications include *Hellboy: Unnatural Selection* from Simon & Schuster, and more books with Cemetery Dance, Leisure, Night Shade Books and Necessary Evil Press, among others. He has won two British Fantasy Awards, a Bram Stoker Award and a Tombstone Award, and has been a finalist for International Horror Guild and World Fantasy Awards. Several of his novels and novellas are currently under option.

Visit Tim's website at www.timlebbon.net.

Visit the dedicated website for *Dusk* and *Dawn* at www.noreela.com.

Be sure not to miss
the stunning sequel to DUSK

DAWN
by Tim Lebbon

Coming in Spring 2007

Here's a special preview. . . .

DAWN

Coming in Spring 2007

FLYING HIGH ABOVE Noreela, it was easy to believe that the world had ended again.

The evidence of scattered, scared communities lay spread out below: small villages, a few larger towns, all of them lighting fires against the darkness that should not be. Ten thousand faces would be searching for the sun but seeing only this unnatural dusk, and Lenora wondered what they would think were they to see the hawk. Would they know? Would they have any inkling of who or what they were looking at?

Probably not. But soon that would change.

For most of the night Lenora had been trying to hide from the two Mages. She sat motionless and silent, as far back on the hawk's tail as she could go without falling off, two short swords buried deep in the creature's hide to provide precious handholds, and watched her masters with a sense of fear the likes of which she had never felt before. The Mages had changed so much, and they were strangers to her now.

For the past three hundred years Angel and S'Hivez had been bitter, angry and mad, given to lengthy musings on revenge and what it would mean to them. Lenora had served them and listened—their trusted lieutenant—but over time they had become shadows of themselves, bitter old things who showed only occasional flashes of their former brilliance and brutality. Ensconced in their mountain retreat on Dana'Man, they had been fading away, though they had still retained a certain power; things that had once ruled a land could never lose that. And Lenora had still feared them—the mad, sometimes beautiful Angel most of all. But their glories had been fading into the past, and the more time passed, the more her memories of them had been dictated by what they said rather than what she remembered. She had let the Mages' power become a self-serving myth in her own mind, rather than preserving it as a rich memory. Time staled everything.

But now the Mages had made Time their own once more, and they were making fresh memories that Lenora would keep forever.

Angel still clasped the body of the farm boy to her chest, like a mother mourning her dead child. She had sawn off the top of his skull and eaten his brain, sharing it with her old lover S'Hivez, and then together they had opened the boy and sought something more nebulous within his flesh. From that moment, Lenora had felt the raw power surging from them, and they were true Mages for the first time in three hundred years. They had searched, moving bones and organs aside, and somewhere in there they had found what they were looking for.

They had seemed to grow, though their size never changed. They remained silent, contemplative, though everything suddenly seemed to flow through rather than around them. And later, when dawn should have been burning away the night, Angel and S'Hivez had laughed some curse at the sky and painted it dark with their victorious souls.

Angel had been holding the boy's ruptured corpse ever since.

The hawk had died moments after they finished rooting through the boy's insides, and Lenora thought they would fall. The great beast's tentacles were flapping in the wind, its gas sacs deflating with a stench that almost made her pass out. But then S'Hivez had buried his arms in the creature's neck, rooting around inside as he had probed the dead boy's carcass. The fall had ended, the creature had risen again, and from then on the dead hawk bore them northward.

Going away, a voice said. Lenora looked around, squinting against the wind. She had heard that voice intermittently since the fight with the Monks and machines, and she knew what it was: her dead, unborn daughter's shade still craving the unknown comfort of her mother's arms. Lenora buried her face in the hawk's stiffening hide and cried, tears tainted with anger. She lifted her head slightly and looked at them as they were caught on the wind and blown into

Noreela's skies. She hoped they would spread and fall with the next rains, casting her sorrow across plains and valleys, mountains and lakes, where vengeance would be waiting for her. They were a long way from Robenna now—and it was falling farther behind with every heartbeat—but now that she knew she would return, the heat of revenge was growing brighter within her.

The people of Robenna had driven her out, poisoned her and murdered her unborn child. Given time, their descendants would pay.

"Dreaming of death and vengeance, Lenora?"

Lenora looked up and stared straight into Angel's eyes. The Mage had crawled back along the hawk's spine and now sat astride the root of its huge tail, her face a hand's width from Lenora's. Whatever time had done to her, she had now found the power to undo. She was beautiful. The might of new magic flickered behind her eyes, and its potential seemed to light her from within, brightening her skin against the dark skies she and S'Hivez had created.

Lenora tried to speak but found herself lost for words.

"Don't worry," Angel said. She drew closer still, until her blazing eyes were the whole world. "So am I."

"Mistress . . ."

"I frighten you?" Angel raised an eyebrow.

Lenora could only nod.

"That's only right. Fear is good, Lenora. You remember the first time I touched you, casting out your pain and driving away death on that burning ship? You were filled with fear then also, but it was fear of the Black. I saved you from death to serve me, and you've done so well ever since. But you've become casual about your fear, as S'Hivez and I have become blasé about our desires. We've always wanted magic back with us, but maybe discomfort and pain grew to suit us better. Perhaps we became too used to life as outcasts." The Mage looked off past Lenora, back the way they had come. "Do you think that's true, Lenora?"

"No, Mistress. You've always been the Mages, with or without magic."

Angel smiled, and Lenora felt an instant stab of jealousy—she was aware of how she looked with her bald head, scarred body and black teeth—but she cast that aside, shaking her head and silently vowing to serve, for as long as she was alive. And even beyond.

"Lenora," Angel said, "you never have to lie to me. You're almost one of us. You came with us out of Noreela three hundred years ago.

You think the same way about this bastard place, and you want the same thing. So we're *almost* the same . . . except that you don't have this." She reached out and touched Lenora's forehead.

At first, the point of contact burned. And then the sensation changed from heat to one of intense cold, a chill that would freeze air and crack rock, and Lenora's eyes closed to usher in whatever Angel was giving her.

There was one single image: the death of Noreela. Lenora viewed it at the speed of thought—north to south, east to west, passing over mountains and valleys and plains and finding the same stain on the landscape everywhere: destruction. A city lay in ruins, buildings burnt down and blackened, streets strewn with smoking corpses, waterways polluted with rancid flesh. Farms and villages were equally devastated, their inhabitants laid out in lines and fixed to the land by wooden spikes driven through their chests and stomachs. Some still moved, flapping useless limbs at Lenora as she flitted by above them. An army lay dead on a hillside, muddied armour already rusting beneath the blood that had been blasted and crushed from the thousands of corpses. Carrion creatures ate their fill. Horses wandered aimlessly, their riders taken down and killed, the creatures too tame to fend for themselves. A great river was home to a hundred boats, all of them sunk, all of them filled to their watery brims with naked corpses.

And elsewhere, away from the bodies and the signs of a lost war, Noreela itself was suffering greater traumas than ever. A whole mountain range swam in fire, only the highest peaks still visible above the rolling flames. On an endless plain to the south the ground was cracked open, but instead of fire and lava rising up, the land's innards rolled out across the dying grass, giant coils of earth and stone hardening in the twilight and venting scampering things as big as the largest hawk. The air was turning to glass, the ground melting away, water bursting into flame . . . the whole of Noreela was in chaos, and at its center pulsed the sense of magic gone darker than ever before.

"There, at the hub," Angel's voice said, a commentary for the sights Lenora was seeing. "That's us." And Lenora saw. The passing visions slowed, settling toward a huge wound in the land. The wound bled. In the middle of this lake of blood, floating in a boat seemingly made from the bones of countless victims, two shadows stretched and flexed, ambiguous in their shape and yet so obvious in their ecstasy.

With Noreela like a rotting corpse around them, the Mages' wraiths writhed forever in the luxury of vengeance found.

Angel removed her finger from Lenora's head and leaned back, smiling.

"The future?" Lenora said. "Is that what I saw?"

"No one sees the future," Angel said, shrugging. "I showed you what I want of the future: Noreela drowning in the blood of our retribution. And with your help, S'Hivez and I will make it so."

"You know you have my loyalty, Mistress. The boy . . . he gave you the magic?"

"You know he did. Why else have you been cowering back here near the stinking arse of this flying monster?"

Lenora looked down, ashamed and still terrified. "I'm sorry."

"If I were you, I'd be scared too. You have no idea of this power, Lenora! It's like being dipped in molten metal. S'Hivez and I have been communing with shades all across Noreela, and those soulless things shunned by nature are working for us already. They eat the magic and spit it out; it's like food to them. They'll take the smaller places even without our help, because the fear of Noreela will be their ally. And I can see what's happening, here and there, north and south, because the shades tell me! We know that the Monks are dead back in the valley, and the machines are still once more. We know that the Duke's army is weak and formless in Long Marrakash. We know that night is here for Noreela, and it is on our side. I can step from one side of the land to the other simply by closing my eyes."

Lenora nodded, finding herself unable to speak again. The energy came off Angel in waves, like gusts of heat melting through her skin and flesh. She felt the whole of Noreela pivoting on every utterance from her Mistress.

"Our army is yours," Angel said. "When it lands at Conbarma, you will be there to welcome it in, arm it, equip it with the greatest weapons we can make. And then you will take control of Noreela."

"You're leaving?"

Angel nodded, then turned to crawl back along the hawk.

"But where are you going?"

Angel glanced back. "You question me?"

Lenora looked away, shaking her head. "Of course not."

Angel laughed, as if dismissing Lenora's question. But she said no more, and left Lenora wondering what the next few days would bring.

War, for certain. More bloodshed and death than she had ever imagined. But with the Mages apparently intending to leave the Krote army to its own devices, Lenora found doubt stoking her fear.

LENORA SOON LOST track of time. She found the consistent twilight unsettling, as if some angry god had taken a brush to the sky and wiped it from existence. To begin with, when the Mages cursed the dawn away, she had been able to keep pace with the time as it drifted by. But as that day passed and they flew on into the steady night, her mind had become confused. She found herself glancing around to the west, hoping to see the smudge of a bloodred sunset, but there was only twilight in that direction. As the Mages had taken daylight from the world, so too had they removed night, leaving the land perpetually between the two; no sun, no stars. Only the moons remained.

The life moon was a silvery disc, low down to the horizon in the east as if nervous at peering above the edge of the world. The death moon, bright and dusty yellow, rode high in the north. They flew toward it, and it seemed to leak some of its sickly hue across the landscape. There were those who believed that the moons were the remains of ancient gods, cast into the skies by a perpetual hatred and destined to gather as many souls to themselves as they could, in an eternal competition. The life moon was losing, and the death moon was yellow with the swelling of wraiths. Soon, the moon-followers believed, it would burst.

Lenora had no time for such religions. She had her gods, and they rode this dead beast before her. With the Mages here, there was neither room nor need for alternate beliefs. She was lucky, she knew; few people ever got to spend time with their deities of choice.

They flew on, heading northward for Conbarma and the landing site for the Krote army. The Mages let nothing distract them. Noreela lay spread out below them, waiting to be plundered and pillaged just as they had dreamed for three hundred years. Lenora could see larger towns now as they drew further north, splashes of illumination across the shadowed land, and here and there were twisting ribbons of light where people seemed to be heading into the towns from the surrounding countryside. She would have so loved to land down there, take on one of these cowardly groups and show them the true meaning of fear. Since the battle to take Conbarma the whole land had changed, and she craved the feel of her enemy's blood on her skin once again, drying under the faded light which the Mages had summoned with their victory. But the hawk carried them onward, its dead tentacles trailing behind them, gas sacs still gushing at the air to keep them afloat, and Lenora knew that the Mages had a more encompassing revenge in mind.

There would be slaughter, and blood would be spilled. But first they had an army to welcome.

———

IT HAD BEEN dusk when they left the machines' graveyard behind, and when they sighted the Bay of Cantrassa below them, Lenora guessed that it should be dusk again. They had been gone for a full day, and she hoped that her warriors had prepared the harbour for the arrival of the Krote ships. They would be only days away, perhaps even now passing the northernmost reaches of the Spine ready for their crossing of the Bay of Cantrassa. Time was moving on. War was coming.

As S'Hivez guided the hawk down to follow the coastline to Conbarma, Lenora found herself eager to dismount. She craved some time away from her masters. She was tired, her skin was burned by the cold wind, and her mind felt assaulted by the power she had been sitting close to for so long. They had not danced, waved or shouted; they had not revelled in the newfound magic, other than cursing the sky into darkness. Yet they exuded a sickly strength that set Lenora's teeth on edge and sent her tired mind into a spin. They were like holes punched in reality, so distinct and yet so wrong that even she, their servant and lieutenant, could barely endure their presence.

For a while, the voice of her daughter's shade whispered in her mind. Lenora shook her head and Angel glanced back, the Mage's eyes a piercing blue against the dark sky.

"Conbarma," S'Hivez said, the word like glass against skin. He rarely spoke, and Lenora had forgotten his voice.

She edged sideways and looked down at the sea to their right. The Bay of Cantrassa reflected the moons, surging waves rippling across its surface picking up the death moon's yellow and spreading it like a slick of rot. The life moon caught the very tops of the highest waves, as though trying to urge them higher. She leaned left, looked down at the land, and saw the seaport of Conbarma nestled in its own natural bay. She was glad that the fires of battle had been extinguished, though she could still smell the hint of cooked flesh on the breeze.

S'Hivez plunged his hands into the dead hawk's neck and brought it down, curving into a glide that would take them into Conbarma from the sea. They passed just above the waves. The hawk's trailing tentacles skimmed the water, throwing up lines of spray behind them, and by the time they reached the harbour there were several living hawks aloft, their Krote riders armed and ready to repel an attack.

Lenora managed a smile. How their moods would change when they saw what this thing brought in.

S'Hivez landed the hawk on the harbour's edge. He extracted his hands from its dead flesh and flicked them at the air, sending fat and clotted blood to spatter the ground. Lenora wondered whether he saw the symbolism in this, but she guessed not. Angel had always been the one who loved the stories behind action or inaction. S'Hivez simply existed.

The hawk deflated beneath them, spreading across the ground like a hunk of melting fat, and immediately its stink grew worse. Lenora glanced at the boy lying between the Mages. His chest and stomach were open, as was his head, skull tipped back so that she could see the hollowness it contained. She wondered why Angel had brought him this far.

Lenora slipped from the hawk and had trouble finding her feet. Nobody came to help. She looked up, hands on knees, cringing as her legs tingled back to life, and then she realized why. The Krotes were not looking at her.

The Mages were kneeling side by side on the ground. Their hands were pressed to the dusty surface before them. S'Hivez seemed to be chanting, though it could have been the sound of the sea breaking rhythmically against the mole. Light began to dance between their fingers. Dust rose. Stones scurried away from their hands like startled insects.

Dozens of Krotes — those with whom she had flown from Dana'-Man and fought for Conbarma little more than a day before — had gathered around, faces growing pale in the moonlight as they saw who had ridden in on this dead hawk. One or two glanced at Lenora and then away again, back to the Mages, fascination overpowering the fear that must surely be settling about them.

It's good to be scared, Lenora thought. That was what Angel had told her. The Mages had always been a formidable presence, but now . . . now they were something so much more. There was something so dreadfully wrong about the exiled Shantasi and his ex-lover that Lenora found it difficult to look directly at them. It was as though light was repelled from their skin. She thought of the shapes she had seen in the vision, those two twisting wraiths aboard the bone boat on a lake of Noreela's blood, but she shook her head and looked again.

The ground had started to glow beneath the Mages' hands. The surface was stripped, dust and smaller rocks flitting away as if forced by a strong wind. They stung Lenora's lower legs but there was nowhere she could go to avoid the rush. She dared not move. This was something she had to see, and she realized now what the Mages were doing: displaying their power to the Krotes assembled here. They could have landed and talked to their warriors, but a discussion of the magic they again possessed was nothing compared to a demonstration.

Lenora stepped back several paces. Her eyes widened, her heart skipped a few beats, and the many wounds on her exposed skin tingled with something approaching excitement. *This is when we see,* she thought. *This is when they really show us what they can do. Already they've touched the sky. Now it's the turn of the ground.*

The Mages began to rise from their knees to their feet, hands maintaining contact with the ground as though stuck there, and then slowly they straightened their backs, lifting their hands and seemingly bringing part of the ground with them.

Light burned into the dusk, and each of the Mages' hands was lifting a column of fluid stone. The ground vibrated as the Mages' actions upset the balance of the land. Rock growled and crumbled, and strange rainbows were cast in the dust clogging the atmosphere. Angel laughed, and S'Hivez's muttering became louder, the words revealing themselves as something much less complex than a spell. *It's all coming back,* he said, again and again. His voice ground stone together, and then the two Mages turned to face each other and began to work their hands.

Lenora could feel the heat from the molten rock from where she stood, and she saw other Krotes stepping back as their skin stretched and reddened. The Mages began to mold it, twisting their hands here and there, moving their arms through impossible angles, pushing and pulling, prodding with stiffened fingers and picking with long nails, smoothing with palms and nudging with the heels of their hands. And between them something began to take shape. Sharp edges appeared from nowhere; curves hardened; a globe of rock rose up on thin stony stilts. Angel laughed again, and Lenora shivered.

The Mages stepped away from each other, allowing the rock room to move and grow. More flowed from the ground, urged by a simple gesture from S'Hivez, and they molded this around the form already there, thickening the trunk and lengthening limbs. They added more, and more again, and then S'Hivez stepped back and lowered his hands.

He looks tired, Lenora thought. *They have this, they have their twisted magic, but they're not used to using it.* S'Hivez looked at her through the heat haze, and she saw the black pits of his eyes. He scowled. She looked away, her skin crawling, scalp tightening as if the old wound there were about to reopen and spill her treacherous brain to the ground. A thought came, and she could do nothing to hold it back: *He can hear me.* She did not look at the old Shantasi Mystic to see whether this was true.

"Lenora!" Angel called. "A present for you, and it will be ready soon." She threw a punch at the sea and a huge splash rose in the twilight, glowing silver and yellow in the moons' contrasting light. Krotes ducked down as the wave crashed against the harbor wall, tumbling over and rumbling across the ground until it broke around the glowing sculpture.

The stone hissed as its superheated framework was suddenly cooled. There were cracks and explosions, and the sounds that came from the thing were almost those of something alive. And if it did have life, it was in pain.

Lenora could not hold back her own accompanying shout.

As the hissing steam died away, Angel appeared by her side. She leaned close to Lenora, and her breath was as warm as the stone she had just cooled. "It's yours," she said. "Your machine, your ride, and soon I'll give it a life." She turned away from Lenora and surveyed the assembled Krotes. "You'll *all* have one!" she said. "Machines of war for you to do what you've always been ready to do: take Noreela. Soon the ships will be here, and your fellow Krotes will follow you east and south and west. I name every one of you here a captain, and Lenora is now your Mistress. You answer to her, and she will answer to us. And the rewards at the end of this short war will be beyond imagining." She turned back to Lenora and smiled. "I'm giving you my army," she said, "and I ask that you use it well. I know your intentions, Lenora. I know your aims. I know what you hear and what speaks to you, but I ask that you ignore that calling until you have fulfilled your purpose. You're here for me, and because of me."

"Yes, Mistress," Lenora whispered. *Not long to wait*, she thought. And she hoped that the shade of her dead child heard the promise in those words.

"And now . . . life for your war machine." Angel walked back to the fallen hawk with the dead boy on its back. "Oh, S'Hivez," she said, laughing, "even *you* must appreciate the symbolism of this!"

The Mage laid one hand on the hawk and the other on the dead farm boy's arm. Beneath her hands the flesh of both began to shimmer and ripple, and soon the stench of cooking meat once again permeated the air across Conbarma. She moved back slowly, melted flesh sticking to her hands and flowing like thick honey, and then swivelled and thrust her hands at the stone sculpture.

Flesh flowed. Blood misted the air and moved as if blown by a strong wind. Bones cracked and ruptured, spinning through the air and impacting the rock, delving their way inside and crackling again as they fused back together. The flesh of the boy and the hawk melded and filled out the fighting machine, flooding hollows within its rocky construct and then building layer upon layer across its outside. Blood greased its joints. The dead hawk shrank as more of its flesh was scoured away, and the boy's corpse came apart.

Angel lowered her hands and stepped back. Lenora saw that she was panting slightly, her shoulders stooped just a little too much, and she wondered again at how much this new magic was draining the Mages. But then Angel turned and looked at her, and behind her smile Lenora saw a strength she had never witnessed before. Not just physical strength—Angel had always been strong—but strength of purpose. There was no doubt in Angel, and no fear. She was unstoppable.

"Here it is," Angel said. She pointed back at the machine. "And here you are."

Lenora fell to her knees. She clasped her hands to her head and pressed, trying to squeeze out the thing she felt inside, the living, *squirming* thing. She was suddenly intimately aware of the life that had just been created, and even as she felt Angel's calming touch and heard her soothing words, she knew that this was not something that was ever meant to be.

Take care, Angel whispered in her mind, *you're strong, Lenora, and this is feeble and weak—a machine, a tool for you to command and use. It lives like an animal down a hole, not like a proud Krote come to conquer and claim. Its life is less than a hawk's shit, but you and it are linked now by this touch.* And Angel left her mind, leaving that link in place.

Lenora gasped and went to fall forward, but Angel was at her side with a helping hand. The Mage helped her to stand and then leaned in close, whispering once again: "You need to be strong." It was a command, not a request.

Lenora nodded, took a deep breath and opened her eyes. She was looking directly at the machine where it stood motionless and awaiting her touch. "I saw you," she whispered, "and I control you." There was no answer, but she sensed the shade of this thing drawing back in fear.

The machine moved for the first time.

The Krotes gathered across the harbor gasped. *This is the first time they've really seen magic,* Lenora thought. She was the only one here, other than the Mages, who had been alive during the Cataclysmic War. These other Krotes were descendants of those who had fled Noreela three hundred years before, the blood flowing in their veins merged with that of the primitive tribes they had found on Dana'Man and the smaller islands to the east and west of that frozen wasteland. They were fighters, warriors, true to the Mages and faithful in their pledges. But they had only ever heard of magic, never seen it.

Lenora looked around at her captains and saw their fear. She realized that this was a defining moment, not only in her relationship with the Mages, but in the history of the land itself. Everything had changed when the Mages caught the boy, took his magic and stripped his soul, and now that change was about to be expanded to envelop the whole of Noreela. Anything she did now would dictate her own part in that change, and what would follow.

Lenora walked forward, approaching what she perceived to be the front of this new machine. As she drew closer she saw that it had a face. She closed her eyes, still walking, and took a deep breath. When she opened them again, the machine was staring at her.

It had several eyes, placed at various points around its bulbous head. Two of them were watching her. It was too dark to see their color, but she knew that they were not the eyes of a hawk. She lifted her chin and glared back.

The machine lowered itself, stone underside settling on the ground, and Lenora stepped up onto its back.

It had mouths too, and a nose, and other strange protrusions that could have been ears or organs to serve more murky senses. It stank of something more elemental than scorched flesh. It smelled, Lenora realized, of magic.

She sat astride the new machine's back and rested her hands on two bony protuberances either side of its head. *Stand*, she thought, and the machine raised itself on several stone legs. It shook beneath her, the vibrations travelling up her thighs and into her stomach. It gave a strange sexual quality to her fear, and caused her old wounds to ache as if craving the knife, the blade, the arrow once again. *Walk*, she thought, and the machine took its first hesitant steps. They were strong. Its shaking stopped, but she could feel its inner workings throbbing beneath her: no heartbeat, but something that felt like a fire being stoked; no breathing, but gasps as gas was blown out and air sucked in. *Turn*, she thought, and the machine stood at the edge of the harbor, a pace away from tumbling into the water, and turned to face her Krotes.

The Mages watched. Even S'Hivez appeared to be smiling.

Lenora sensed the power at work beneath her. This was not just a thing of stone and flesh and blood, it was also imbued with the Mages' magic, awash with a deadly potential that she had yet to realize. She wondered what it would do when she sent further commands, and the possibilities were thrilling. *Give fire*, she thought, and a ball of flame formed from one of the machine's mouths. She held it there, its roaring echoed by the gasps from the assembled warriors. Then she turned and flung the fire far out over the sea, watching it arc down and then splash into the water. It seemed to burn even as it sank, and for a few seconds the whole harbor's surface glowed from beneath.

My gods, she thought, *what have you created?*

Lenora turned the machine around and stood on its back, two body-heights above the ground and elevated so that she could see right across Conbarma's waterfront. All the surviving Krotes were here now—almost fifty of them—and the Mages, and they were all watching her. She felt the power in that, and smiled.

Angel smiled back.

"There's work to be done!" she cried. "More machines to be built by our Masters. More preparations to make. The sun has fled our Mages' power, scared and cowardly, and the twilight it's left behind will be filled with the death-cries of Noreela. This is your time, Krotes, the time you have lived for from the moment you were born." She paused, looked down at the head of the machine with its mad eyes and slavering mouths. "I once saw the shores of Noreela awash with blood, and that memory has always been bitter, because the blood was my own. Now it's time to stain the land again, but this time with other blood. Noreela will fall, there's no doubt of that. It's the manner of that fall I so look forward to seeing."

More fire, she thought, and the machine formed several balls of fire and sent them hovering above the heads of the Krotes. "Krotes!" she shouted.

The warriors screeched in response. They stared at the machine and raised their hands, and she saw the fire reflected in their eyes. She walked the thing among them, letting them reach out and touch its cool stone and cooler flesh. The fires faded out, but in the twilight they could all see and feel this thing which, when multiplied, would help them win the war.

Lenora smiled at Angel and S'Hivez, and she saw that they were pleased.